QUEST

of the

BROKEN STONE

A WORLD OF ZENTOS STORY

QUEST

of the

BROKEN STONE

By AJ Ashton

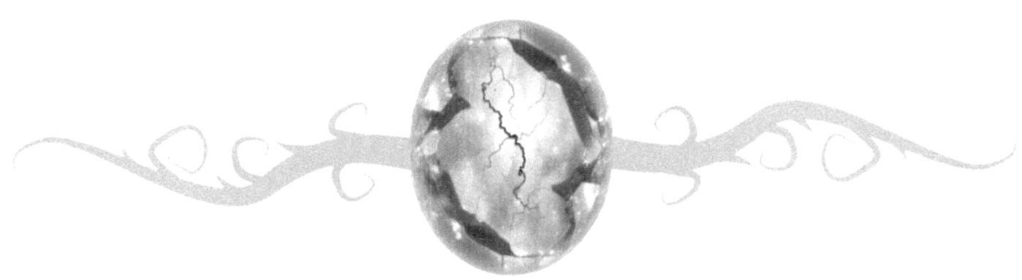

My Awesome Editor: Yvonne Davis, whysewordswork@gmail.com

Formatting and cover design by AJ Formatting

Quest of the Broken Stone
AJ Ashton

ISBN 978-1-916969-02-5

DEDICATION

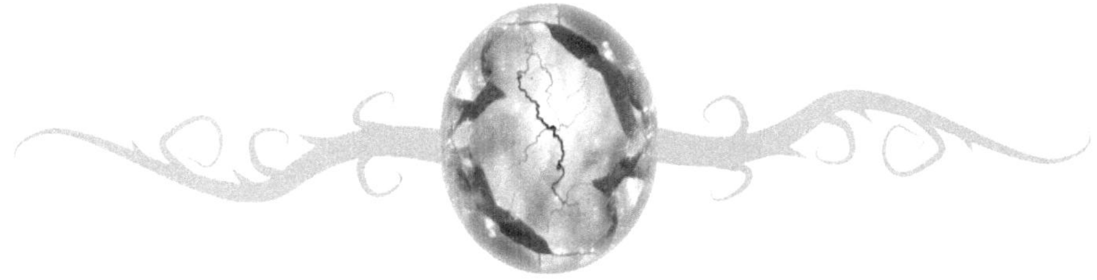

To those who dream. Never stop believing.

WORLD OF ZENTOS BOOKS
IN TIMELINE ORDER

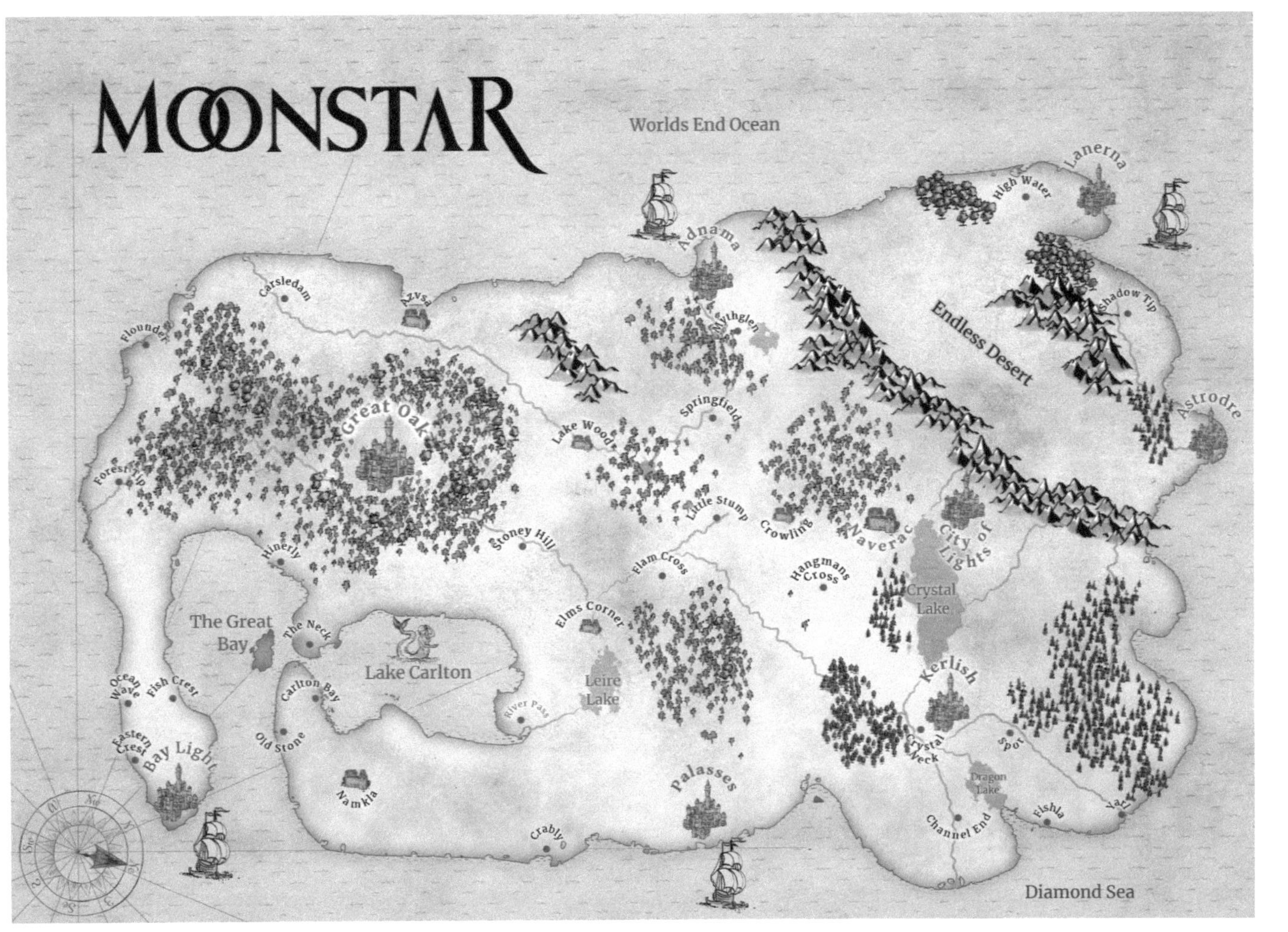

MOONSTAR
Worlds End Ocean
Diamond Sea
Lanerna
High Water
Adnama
Shadow Tip
Endless Desert
Astrodre
Mythglen
Carsledam
Azvsa
Flounder
Great Oak
Lake Woods
Springfield
Crowling
Naverac
City of Lights
Forest Tip
Little Stump
Stoney Hill
Elam Cross
Hangmans Cross
Crystal Lake
Hinerly
Elms Corner
Kerlish
The Great Bay
The Neck
Lake Carlton
Leire Lake
Ocean Wave
Fish Crest
Carlton Bay
Crystal Neck
Spot
Eastern Crest
Bay Light
Old Stone
Dragon Lake
Fishla
Yarl
Namkia
Palasses
Channel End
Crably
vii

ONE

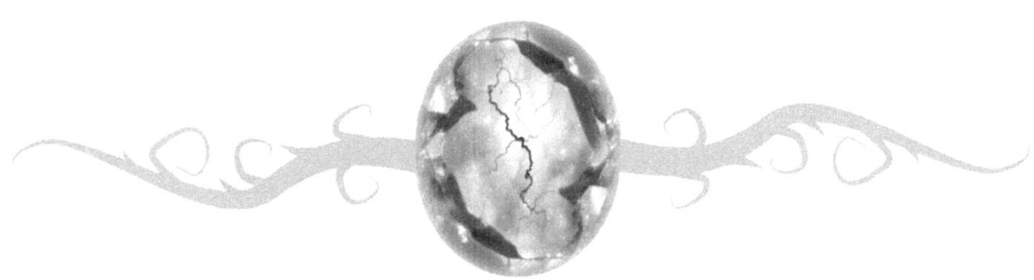

The coffee shop bustled with activity as a queue of customers, stretching almost to the door, waited to be served. Everyone interacted with their phones patiently waiting for their caffeine fixes. Most preferred to have their coffee on the go; others tried to locate a table, but to no avail. The sounds of the coffee machine hissing and grinding were almost drowned out by the buzz of conversations between friends and families taking a rest from an eventful shopping trip.

Evie took a sip of her caramel latte, the only thing she was really enjoying at that moment. The regular meet ups with her mother on Saturday morning were always a mix of emotions. Evie was never sure why she thought their relationship was not good. To be honest, it was the best it had been in years. The older woman had even complimented her black jeans and blue shirt and how her red hair pulled back in a ponytail showed off her features. But there was an underlying issue within her. A self-inflicted pressure that Evie had been experiencing the last few years that made her dread every Saturday. All her parents' friends had become grandparents several times over, and as much as she tried not to, Evie had a pang of guilt when she noticed the envious looks in her parents' eyes. Evie swirled the contents of her oversized cup. The only thing that could remedy it was beyond her capabilities.

Dishes clattered, causing Evie to look up. The coffee shop was busy as always, yet her mother enjoyed coming here and somehow, they always got the same table. Evie was convinced that her mother reserved it to ensure she had the perfect spot to see everything. The older redhead was nattering on and on about some gossip or other, and Evie, as always, just zoned out.

Her mind wandered again, and she started thinking of Moonstar. She had not thought about being there for a while. It had been eighteen years since she had returned from that land.

Why am I thinking about them again after all this time?

"Evelyn Ranger!"

Evie snapped back to the present, focusing on her mother. She hated being called that. As the older woman studied her, Evie noticed how the sun accentuated the copper tones of her mother's greying hair.

"Weren't you listening? I was saying, Margaret's daughter had her second child on Sunday. A little girl."

Evie tried to look interested. "Congratulations to Susan and Thomas."

Her mother regarded her, a shade of disappointment in her green eyes. "I thought by the time you reached your mid-forties you'd be married and have a couple of children of your own."

Evie released a long breath. Each time they met, this conversation would arise, and the ending always hurt. "Mum, you know that's not possible."

"Maybe it was just with Peter?"

She took her mother's manicured hand as she remembered all the doctors' appointments and arguments with Peter. Evie bit her lip. The pressure from him, his family, and hers, had been one factor which had ended the relationship. Peter wanted children, yet she could not have them. "Mum, it wasn't Peter, it was me. You know that."

Her mother exhaled, nodding, recognising the distress in her daughter's eyes. "Sorry, honey, I didn't mean to open old wounds. But I worry about you. At least find someone to spend your life with. There are men out there who don't want children."

Evie knew the older woman meant well, but for some reason, she just did not want to meet anyone and preferred to be on her own. She had loved Peter, but something had been lacking. It was down to the fact that her heart would always belong to one person. Garth. Peter and she had shared a connection, yet every time she gazed into his eyes, they had been Garth's. But that had not been enough.

Her mother observed her closely. "I'm amazed you haven't any men falling at your feet. You only look in your thirties. No idea where those genes came from."

Evie smiled. It was true she appeared significantly more youthful than her age and did not understand why. But she had a rough idea; it had something to do with the magic coursing through her veins. A power she could never use, except in her own home. She sighed inwardly. Since returning from Moonstar she had changed, a lot; she was no longer the Evie from Earth. Because of that, she experienced a void, incapable of realising her full potential.

She had told her parents everything a couple of years after she came back. It had not gone over well. Evie was glad she could wipe the memory before her parents had had her committed. That was the problem. No one would believe her.

Evie exhaled heavily. She had even contemplated going back, but she had no clue where to even start. If she knew how to make portals, she might have found a way. But that was the one thing Slan had never shown her. She remembered trying one drunken night about five years ago and ended up passed out for eight hours with a bloody nose and a migraine for days. Something she decided not to try again.

Her mother continued to talk about Susan's baby, showing the pictures the new parents had posted on social media. The older woman had instantly forgot how much the subject hurt her daughter. Evie nodded, going through the motions. She had realised early on that it was best to just stay quiet and nod. Deep down, her mother wanted the best for her.

When Evie's mother started pointing out men in the queue that could be potential dating partners, she had to suppress rolling her eyes. Evie sipped her latte and glanced at the wall clock. She may need to make up a meeting to leave early. Anything to get out of being tortured. She opened her bag on her lap, pulling out her phone. She texted, 'help', to her friend as discreetly as possible. That was always her ticket out of these situations. Her friend would call in about five minutes pretending there was some emergency and Evie could escape. She turned her gaze towards the older woman, immediately feeling remorse for sending the text. But her mother never knew when to stop. A call from a friend in need was the gentlest way to let her down.

Evie woke and peered over at her clock from under the warmth of the duvet and sighed. 1.00 AM. She yawned, remembering the disaster of coffee with her mother. She scrunched up her face. It had not gone well. Her mind, which loved to torture her, replayed the older woman's word.

Why are you still single? Peter was such a nice man. You should have married him.

Evie rolled onto her back and took a deep breath. It just never would have worked. She had changed so much. And add in the magical abilities that she should never use and could never show. She just could not get her life back on track. That could be more the reason Peter strayed, not solely due to the issue of children. Evie could not blame him; she was a bitch to live with.

Evie stared at the ceiling; she needed to go back to sleep. Then she realised why she had awakened. She had been dreaming of Slan. She had not dreamt about him in years, and had thought of Moonstar for the first time yesterday. It seemed strange. Evie closed her eyes, wondering why she had dreamed of the old sorcerer. She huffed, realising she was wide awake, but still did not want to emerge from the duvet.

She glanced at her bracelet that was fused to her skin. Evie never even noticed it anymore and had cast a minor spell to ensure no one noticed the fact that it was attached to her. Evie's lips curled up slightly. She had got very good at using her powers upon her return. She found most of her use of magic to be hit and miss, but it was still useful. She had even done a few nice things for people when possible. Unfortunately, it had, of course, been in secret, unable to show the world what she could do.

Suddenly, the bracelet glowed. She quickly sat up, just before pain shot through her temples. She cried out. Her room was gone. Slan was before her. It appeared as if they were inside a cave. The musty smell of stagnant water and moist earth invaded her nostrils. She glanced down to see that she was sitting, her t-shirt and shorts doing little to protect her from the cold, damp, rocky ground. Evie looked up at Slan. He appeared dishevelled and on edge.

The sorcerer glared at her with wild eyes. *"Help us, Evie!"*

He lunged towards her to grab her, but she found herself back in her room again. Evie sat there gasping, stunned by what had just happened. She climbed out of bed rubbing her temples. She walked over to the bathroom to get some water, wondering if she was having some type of vision.

Evie went back to her bed, taking a sip of water. She sat down on the edge while rubbing her temples, experiencing her head throbbing. She glanced down at the bracelet; the Stone glinted in the low light from her clock. It reminded her of the dreams she had prior to her first visit to Moonstar; but it felt different.

What is going on? Why was Slan in a cave? Was the Stone trying to tell me something? Was there something wrong on Moonstar? If the Stone is telling me something, what can I do?

Evie climbed back into bed, shuffling under the covers. She needed to get rid of her built-up frustrations and energy. Get her mind to clear. She could go to the dojo in the morning and have a session. That always helped.

TWO

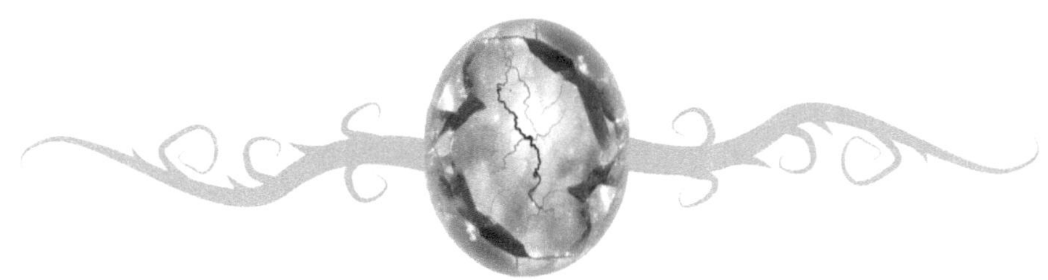

Evie let herself into the dojo, which was not far from her apartment building. Maxwell, the master swordsman, had given her a key a few years back. She knew it was his way of trying to convince her to partner with him, but she did not want to train people in swordsmanship. She just wanted to train alone, or spar with another expert.

She wiped her palms on her leggings before taking a hold of the bokken and striking the training dummy. It did not offer the same tactile experience in her hand as her sword, but it was close enough. She smiled as she repositioned herself, her trainer's soles squeaking on the polished wooden floor, and struck again. Finally, she understood what Ulric had meant about training when he needed to relax. It worked every time.

Evie struck the dummy harder. Changing her grip, she made another move, striking in a different area. As the bokken slammed into the dummy again, a gruff voice called out as someone entered the room. "And what has that dummy done to you?"

Evie paused and turned, grinning at the large man with a very impressive grey beard. Maxwell had arrived early to set up for the Sunday training sessions. His old, tattered Iron Maiden t-shirt and tracksuit bottoms did little to hide his athletic frame.

She answered, "Ha ha. Just needing a bit of exercise."

He raised an eyebrow. "Coffee with your mum?"

Evie snorted. "Well, yes."

"Thought as much." He grabbed a bokken and strolled towards her, twisting the training weapon in the air. "Fancy a session together?"

Evie eyed him. "Don't expect me to let you win."

He laughed. "You allowed me to win?"

She spun the bokken in her left hand and grinned. "Sometimes."

He stood opposite her and took a firm grip of his bokken. "If I win fair and square, will you tell me who trained you?"

Evie could not stop smiling. "As long as you don't hold back."

"When do I hold back?"

Evie shook her head in disappointment. "Every time we spar."

"I do?"

"Yes." She took a fighting stance. "Don't hold back. I can take it."

Maxwell regarded her as he stood ready, with his feet slightly apart. "Okay, I won't hold back."

Evie eyed him. "Good."

She swung her bokken, and the big guy had to parry at the sudden move. Soon, the two were fighting each other, the larger man pulling his strikes. Evie rotated round, her bokken slapping against his shoulder as she snapped, "I told you *not* to hold back."

He towered over her. "But I'll have the advantage."

Evie swung again, her bokken only tapped him with what could have been a killing blow. "Really?"

Maxwell grinned. "I thought I was the master swordsman here."

She laughed and swung again. Maxwell parried her move. She stated the obvious, "You keep underestimating me."

He swung at her again and asked, "Who the hell trained you, Evie?"

She gave him a sly smile. "Someone you wouldn't know."

Maxwell swung again, and Evie blocked him. "Come on, Evie. I know most who specialise in swordsmanship."

Evie grinned. "Honestly, you wouldn't know them."

He went at her again, and again Evie parried his move. She proceeded to swing again when pain shot across her temple and Evie heard Slan's desperate voice. *"Evie, we need you."*

Evie sucked air in through her teeth as the pain subsided, but Maxwell's bokken hit her knuckles.

He grinned. "Ha! Got one!"

Evie shook her hand and then winced as her temples throbbed. She eyed him and Maxwell cursed, "You *let* me win."

Evie smiled. She had not, but she was not about to explain that someone trying to contact her from another world had distracted her. Evie shrugged it off. It was just a lack of sleep. Or it could be something else entirely.

She went to make a move again, when she heard Slan's voice calling her name. Something was not right. She let out a long exhale. It could not be Slan.

She parried Maxwell but she could not focus. Her mind returned to the sorcerer, wondering what was happening. Pain shot through her head again and she dropped the bokken gasping.

Maxwell froze, looking on with concern. "You okay, Evie?"

She sucked air between her teeth as the discomfort lessened. "Sorry, migraine. Think I best call it a day."

Maxwell frowned. "Alright. Do you want me to walk back with you?"

Evie shook her head as she put the bokken back on the rack with the others. "No, but thanks. I'll be fine."

He eyed her. "You sure? Marybeth has trouble seeing when she gets them."

"I'll be fine."

"Well, take it easy for the rest of the day. It'll ease."

Evie signalled her appreciation silently. "Let Marybeth know I'm looking forward to next weekend."

"I will. It makes me feel like a fifth wheel, but she does like to have a good chin wag with you."

Evie chuckled. Maxwell and Marybeth were a lovely couple and never judged her. They were also childless, and somehow Evie knew that was why she had bonded so easily with Maxwell's wife. As she strode from the dojo, Evie stated, "You best go easy on those noobs today."

Maxwell's response had amusement in his tone. "When do I not?"

She looked back at him and eyed him. The older man laughed and turned his attention back to setting up his dojo for class.

Evie woke up early and groaned. She had a big meeting first thing, and Peter would be there. She sat up and rubbed her face. It should not be as awkward as the meetings right after their split. Even though he had left and returned to New York, the new firm he was with represented the same client. Whenever she saw those familiar eyes and heard that voice, sadness would always wash over her.

Evie climbed from her bed and strolled to the kitchen, yawning. She picked out a mug and flicked on the kettle. As she waited for it to boil, she put away the pots she had washed the night before, trying not to stress about the meeting she had in a few hours.

A sudden pain shot through her temples, and she cried out. The wine glass she was holding dropped into the sink, and shattered.

Evie was in the cave again. She was able to sense the moist rock beneath her exposed feet.

Slan shouted, *"Prepare Evie! I think I can get you here."*

Evie staggered backwards in her kitchen once more. She felt sick. The second vision was even more painful, but it was different. She sensed the magic coursing through her and wondered if Slan was trying to create a portal. If he was, she could not stand there dazed. Her instincts were telling her to move. Evie ran back to the bedroom. She grabbed the black jeans and blue shirt she wore on Saturday, pulling them on quickly. She needed boots. Evie looked around, snatching up her socks before remembering they were by the front door.

Evie ran and got them, coming back to her bedroom. She sat on the side of her bed, pulling them on. If Slan could get her back to Moonstar, she would ensure she was ready.

With her shin-high brown boots and clothes on, she stood in the middle of the bedroom waiting, her shoulders tense. She drew a long breath while pulling her hair into a ponytail. After a few more minutes of standing still and nothing happened, she felt stupid.

Why am I just standing here like an idiot?

She sank onto the bed, expressing her frustration. That was another reason Peter had left. She was always waiting, wanting to go back, but it never happened. He thought she was crazy, yet there she was at five in the morning dressed, and waiting for a dimensional portal. She laughed, almost hysterically, thinking she was such a fool. She cursed and stood up, unbuttoning her shirt.

The room became icy cold. She paused, feeling static in the air. It had a sense of familiarity. Then a portal opened right beneath her. Evie gasped, as she dropped into the hole.

THREE

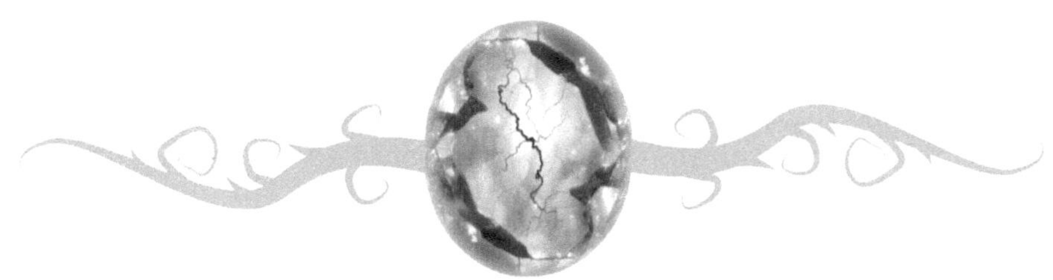

Evie landed with a thump into a pile of dry leaves. She laughed, sitting up. She could not believe what had just happened. She fell back in the leaves and grinned, taking a deep breath of the sweetness of unpolluted air. Looking up at the night sky, seeing the familiar stars between the bare branches. Tears of joy rolled over her lashes as she laid there briefly, taking in the sensation that she was home. She sat up, wiping her eyes and looked around. It was Moonstar.

As she got to her feet, Evie brushed herself down. She was back in Flamvile Woods; it had to be. Evie took a deep breath, her lungs filling with the smell of the woods all around her. Memories of her previous arrival resurfaced. It had been so cold and wet then. And wearing a strappy designer dress had not helped matters. As she took in her surroundings, she realised that she also did not seem to have any sickness like the first time. Her stomach churned a little, but otherwise, she seemed unaffected. It must be her magic helping her. She placed her hand on her lower back, her skin warming slightly as she magically stopped the dull ache on the part where she had landed. Evie gazed at the trees, placing her hand on the closest one and sensing the roughness of the bark beneath her fingertips. She never expected it to happen again. Her cheeks were aching from all her grinning. She turned her attention back to the night sky and let out a joyful whoop.

"I'm back!"

Despite her joy at being back, she pondered why she had returned. She glanced around, orienting herself, removing some stray leaves from her shirt. Evie closed her eyes for a second. Her fingertips tingled as the magic flowed through her and a wisp of pale blue light pulsated in her palm as it swirled and grew into an orb. She let it drift up just above her head to light the way.

There was rustling in the trees and Evie peered towards the noise, trying to see what was lurking in the depths of the woods. She kept still as wisps of blue energy flowed up from her fingertips to the sphere overhead to make the light grow brighter. Amongst the branches, two yellow eyes glared back. Evie instinctively reached for her sword, even after all these years, and cursed. While she inhaled deeply, she observed the creature that stayed at the edge of the light illuminating from the globe. It kept a safe distance, its instincts telling it to be cautious around her. Her fingers tingled as electricity built in her hand and tiny sparks flickered into the air. The creature watched her momentarily, sniffed the air, and then scampered off. Evie remained alert, watching the trees, but the creature had gone. The power in her fingertips dissipated.

Evie needed to get to safety and remembered the Traveller's Rest Inn was to the east. She scrutinised the trees, unable to see any lights. She glanced at the globe now floating above her. At least it would illuminate her way. Evie walked through the forest. It was cold, and she rubbed her arms to warm herself up, but glad that it was dry. At least she was wearing boots and a bit more clothes and hopefully would avoid getting hyperthermia. Evie took a quick glance behind her, towards the path she had taken, but the creature seemed to be long gone.

She wondered what the welcome would be like when she got to Brak's inn. It would be good to see some familiar faces again.

How long had passed here? About six or seven years? I can't be sure; time moves slower here than Earth. But that doesn't matter, it's just great to see Moonstar again and to catch up with old friends.

Evie's mind wandered to Ulric. She smiled, wondering what the formidable Sword would have got up to. Somehow, she felt he would have left a few broken hearts in his wake.

When she emerged from the trees, reaching the major route, her thoughts of Ulric and her old friends paused. Across the dry dirt track was a derelict building. Evie looked up and down the deserted, moonlit road, frowning.

This was the right route, but what had happened to Brak's inn?

Evie walked over the uneven, tree lined road to the ruins, making the globe of light slightly larger so she could study what remained of the building.

What happened here?

Some of the external walls were still intact to roof level, but most had fallen over. The internal walls seemed to have a little more structure, but the roof and second floor were gone, apart from a few fire damaged support beams. There was the odd window frame, still somewhat intact. The main door was a charred mess and the door frame was half gone. The remains seemed old, it probably happened many years ago.

Evie spotted something partly hidden near the remains of the entrance. She strode over, pulling it free. It was the inn's sign. The words *Travellers Rest* were barely visible. Evie glanced back at the derelict walls, hoping Brak and his family were okay.

Placing the sign back down where she had found it, Evie gingerly stepped over the threshold; the door frame crumbled when she grabbed what remained. By examining the walls that were still divided into sections, she could piece together their original configuration and realised that she was positioned in the remaining portion of the primary bar area. She stepped around the charred detritus of chairs and tables. Her eyes focused on the enormous fireplace; the only thing still intact against the far wall. Evie remembered the first time she had been there and sitting in front of the raging fire trying to get warm, her designer dress torn to shreds.

Evie strolled towards the fireplace when excruciating pain ripped through her mid-section, making her double over. Her vision blurred, she placed her hands on her knees, taking a deep breath. Moments later, pain burned through her wrist. That was not a delayed effect from coming through the portal. It really seemed as if someone had plunged a knife into her, then . . . Her attention shifted to her wrist as she flexed her fingers. To obtain the bracelet, they amputated her hand. After a few breaths, she straightened back up.

Something had happened here which had involved me. But what?

She took her time observing the ruins. Her stomach was filled with apprehension. Her skin prickled as she sensed the chill of death all around her. *What had happened to Brak, Sari and Von?* Tears welled in her eyes, her hand clasped over her mouth to suppress a sob at the thought of such a kind family losing their lives.

Evie paused when she heard movement at the back of the inn, where there was still a bit of shelter. She turned towards the sound, making the ball of light move in that direction. Her fingers tingled as she readied to make a plasma ball. "Who's there?"

A crooked figure emerged from the shadows and abruptly stopped, as if shocked to see her. Evie tensed, she could not make out who it was.

Would the stranger know who was to blame for what occurred in this place and what happened to me?

A familiar voice gasped, "By the Gods, it worked." The figure stepped forward, pulling back his hood.

Evie smiled, recognising the old man's features, the power in her fingertips dissipating. "Slan!" She rushed over to him and gave him a big bear hug.

He chuckled as they parted. "It's good to see you too, Evie."

She studied him with affection for a few moments, noting that he seemed several years older than she remembered. Then glanced around. "What happened?"

The old sorcerer let out a tired breath, looking weary. "We need to get somewhere safe."

Slan seemed skittish, his eyes flicking over her shoulder like he was wary of being seen. Something terrible had happened, and she knew it was wise to follow his lead. She walked with the old sorcerer out of the ruins and back into the woods, in the opposite direction from where she had come. Evie pressed, "Slan, tell me what happened."

"Not here Evie. When we are safe."

Evie gazed at his back as he led the way. She had never seen Slan look so old and frail, and the fear in his eyes concerned her. Evie wondered what had happened after she had left. She glanced back towards the remains of the inn, which were lost amongst the trees. What puzzled her most was the reason behind experiencing her own death.

They walked deep into the woods, Slan kept looking around, making sure they were not being followed. Then he stopped by a large bramble. He moved his hand across the overgrowth in a sweeping motion, and it parted to reveal a concealed cave entrance. Evie could not help but question why Slan was on edge. She chewed her lip, fearing the worst.

Silently crouching, she trailed behind Slan as they stepped into the small cave. Upon entering, she heard the brambles move and glanced back to find the entrance concealed again. Turning, she continued through a short tunnel that sloped downwards. She then entered a sizable cavern, lit by four small torches that were attached to the rocky walls. There was a smouldering fire in the centre, a makeshift bed, some chests off to one side, and books scattered about. It seemed Slan had been inhabiting the place for a considerable period of time.

Why would he be here and not at his tower? Evie regarded him with concern as he gestured to her to sit by the fire. As she sat, she asked, "Slan, you're worrying me. What happened?"

Slan sighed, looking exhausted. He poked the fire with a stick while making a little flame develop on his hand. He blew the small flame from his hand into the embers, making the fire come to life once more. "This isn't the Moonstar that you would remember."

He then studied her with his ancient blue eyes. Evie warmed her hands by the flames. Her eyes on his, concern furrowing on her brow. "What do you mean? Bazertari was dead."

Slan swallowed and said, "Aye, and there was peace." He shot a quick look in her direction. His facial expression altered with a sudden shift, his lips drawing downwards in sadness. "But a warlock changed it all."

"Warlock?"

"Aye, the one I believed helped Bazertari's followers and sent you those dreams."

Evie felt sick. She dreaded hearing what Slan had to tell her. "W—what did he do? Is Ulric—"

"Nay, he lives."

"Then what happened?"

Slan gazed upon the flames of the fire and mumbled, "All changed. So much has changed."

Evie peered over the fire, seeing Slan looking even more drawn. "Slan . . . at the inn . . . I felt something. It felt like my—"

"Death?"

"Yes. But that's not possible. I came here and saved this land." She inquired, her voice firm, "Slan, what aren't you telling me?"

He rubbed his temples, muttering to himself. "I can't tell her all of it, not yet."

She stood and moved to sit by him. "Slan, you're not making any sense. Tell me what happened."

The sorcerer directed his gaze back up at her. He seemed surprised to see her, then took her hand in his. "I thought I couldn't do it, but you are *really* here."

"Yes, I'm here, Slan. Why are you living in a cave?"

He surveyed his surroundings, only just becoming aware of his location. "My tower is nay longer safe." He paused, shaking his head. "Nay where is safe anymore."

Evie scrutinised Slan's features. He appeared extremely pale and thin. "Slan, when did you last sleep? Or eat?"

He observed her and glanced at her hand, still patting his. "I had to get you here. Had to find a way."

"Why Slan?" asked Evie, "tell me, *what happened.*"

He turned his eyes away from her, shaking his head. "The warlock found a time crystal. He changed so much."

Evie's gut twisted. "So, all of this?"

His blue eyes looked back at her, the dark rings beneath them giving him an appearance of being nearly at death's door. "An alternative Moonstar."

Evie glared at him for a moment and snapped, "What?"

"It's all changed."

Evie pulled her hand free of his, her fists clenching. They were in an alternative timeline. Everything she had gone through. All the sacrifices. Her chest tightened as the realisation dawned on her. "So *everything* I did. Garth's d— death. Was for *nothing!*"

Slan flinched at her tone and muttered, "All gone, everyone gone."

Inhaling deeply, Evie fixed her gaze on the old man. She needed to keep calm; Slan was barely holding on. *How long has he been hiding?* Evie frowned. She needed answers. Evie reached out and took his hand again, smiling gently at him, trying to keep her frustrations under control. "How do you know that happened?" She paused and added, "How do I know?"

Slan focused back on her features. He took a slow breath, steading himself, trying to focus. "I am unsure how I can remember, it's either deliberate for punishment or by chance. As for yourself, being in your own realm, you would be unaffected by the spell."

Evie leaned forward, sensing discomfort in her stomach. "So, *what* did he do?

Slan breathed out deeply. "The warlock used it to go back, and changed one significant moment."

"*What* did he change?"

Slan muttered, his gaze distant again. In trying to tell her what had happened, he was losing himself in the memories. "The Guild members are all gone."

The foreboding that Evie experienced in the pit of her stomach intensified and the recollection of the dream she had on her initial night in Palasses rushed back. Her grandmother's spirit informed her that the Stone needed her to understand that only she could recite the spell within the bracelet. Evie had tried to convince her grandmother's spirit that Slan could use the Stone instead, but she had been wrong. Landor had placed a spell to defeat the evil warlock into the Stone and sent it to earth before he died in the process of imprisoning Bazertari. The kind sorcerer Landor had chosen her and her alone to be the one to use the Stone. If she had asked to go home, the Guild would face Bazertari and lose. The image she saw of all those slaughtered bodies in the square, the blood drenching the cobblestones, still haunted her to this day.

Would it be the same outcome if I died? Did that mean Garth was dead? Tortured to death, like in that dream? Had the warlock known where I would appear and killed me?

She asked, "What happened to the Guild members?"

Slan had a sullen expression. "Morag and Garth killed them."

Evie frowned, had she just misheard him? "W—what?"

The sorcerer redirected his attention towards her and glanced upwards. "He became dark, was manipulated."

"Who?" asked Evie, dreading what name he was going to state.

"Garth."

Evie's breath caught in her throat. "Garth's alive?"

Slan clasped her hand, and his features appeared serious. "I'm sorry Evie; but he's not the man you knew."

She took a shaky breath, trying to take in what she was hearing. Her mind wanted to know everything that had happened. Her heart ached to see Garth again. She was finding it hard to believe, but the look in Slan's eyes made her falter. She needed to think. Evie gazed at the old man. She could not push him too hard, she had to be selective about her questions. Whatever happened had scared him deeply. She needed to keep it simple.

Evie chewed her lip. She had to focus on what she needed to know, the rest could be learned later. "So why have you brought me here? Do I need to find the time crystal and change things back?"

He shook his head. "Bazertari has ruled this land through fear for over nine winters now. The warlock and the crystal vanished early on in our fight against Bazertari, when he first took power."

She leant forward. "Who fought him?"

Slan grew distant again. "All gone."

Evie paused, remembering not to push him. "So, what can *we* do?"

"Use the Stone."

She glanced downwards at the fused bracelet. "But I cast the spell when I killed Bazertari. The Stone still holds power, but not the spell."

"*That* one, aye. But the one *here,* in *this* Moonstar, still holds the spell."

"It's still here?" Evie gazed at him, with a sense of hope.

"Aye, when they killed this version of you, they took the bracelet and they hid it at Great Oak, in a vault."

Evie glanced down at her wrist. "That explains the pain."

"Pain?"

"Yes, when I was by the fireplace at the inn. I experienced the sensation of being stabbed, followed by the feeling that my hand was chopped off."

Slan shook his head, looking disgusted. Evie asked, noticing the sorcerer seemed to be coherent again. "Why didn't Bazertari destroy the bracelet?"

"He can't. Remember when he tried to do that with you?"

She replied, "Yes, but I thought that it was some combination of my magic."

"Nay, even with you dead, the Stone still cannot be destroyed. But with nay one to wield it, Bazertari just keeps it locked away. Therefore, I brought you here, as *you* can wield it."

Evie breathed out deeply, releasing Slan's hand to warm hers against the small fire, her fingertips sensing the chill in the air. "So I have to face him again?" She paused, wondering, "But can two Stones coexist?"

Slan glanced at her and shrugged. "That I do not know, but it is a risk we have to take."

She asked, "So I need to head to Great Oak?"

Slan replied, "Nay, not there! Evil has made it a dark place."

Evie saw he was going distant again. "Slan, I need you to focus. You brought me here to use the Stone, remember?"

"Aye, so you can wield it."

"To wield it, I will *need* to go to Great Oak."

He gave a slight shake of his head, seeming to focus again. He rubbed his temples. "I'm sorry. In my exhaustion, my mind, it wonders."

Evie clasped his hand again and smiled. "It's okay, just take your time; tell me what I need to know."

The old man looked up at her. "First you need to find any Guild member that may be still alive. You cannot do this alone."

"But where do I look?"

"Ulric will know."

Evie's features brightened. "Where is he?"

Slan leant forward. "You must understand this, Evie. Everyone here except me does not know you. With this land being under the threat of Bazertari; spirits are broken, all hope is lost. Ulric is not the same man you remember."

She acknowledged slowly, absorbing it all. "So where do I find him?"

"Last I heard, he was in Palasses." Slan paused. "I must warn you; it will be Garth who will shock you the most. Try not to come across him. The one you knew is gone. They have manipulated this Garth for over seventeen years and corrupted him to the core. If you face him, you must understand, you will *have to* kill him."

She observed the sorcerer, her shoulder muscles tightening. Evie hoped she would not have to face Garth. If she did, she was not sure she could kill the man she had loved, heart and soul. She had to remember that it was not her Garth. He died in her arms, saving her.

Evie sighed, "If I remember right, Palasses is about six days' ride from here?"

"Aye." Slan regarded her. "You are better attired this time. Remember this; strangers aren't welcome here these days, so keep yourself covered. People leave hooded figures be, fearing they may work for Bazertari, and this will be to your advantage."

She nodded. Slan rose and moved towards one chest. He pulled out some clothes. "These will suffice."

Evie took the bundle and changed what she needed, putting on the black jerkin and adding a belt. Then she put the rest in the saddlebag Slan gave to her. He then passed her a couple of daggers and a few throwing knives. She put one dagger into each boot; the others fastened to her belt.

He paused, gazing into the chest, then slowly he passed her a sword. Evie recognised the scabbard. "This is mine."

Slan said, "Aye . . . well, it was meant for the Evie of this Moonstar. Of course, here it has never been used."

Evie noted the hint of sadness in his voice. Taking the scabbard, she pulled the sword free, the leather covered hilt felt familiar in her hand. Evie gazed at the blade, admiring the workmanship. She smiled sadly, remembering Garth had known the swordsmith who had made it. While examining the blade, she furrowed her brow, observing new engravings down the centre.

Slan stated, "Those are runes."

"Runes?"

The sorcerer acknowledged with a nod. "Aye. I have imbued fire and ash into your sword. They may very well be needed in this world."

Evie regarded them. "How do I . . .?"

Slan smiled and pointed to each symbol. "This is fire, and this is ash. When you wish to use them, visualise the symbol and mummer what they are."

Evie held the blade and did as he instructed. As she murmured the fire rune, it glowed. In the cave's chill, it was clear to see the sudden heat radiate from the polished blade.

Slan continued, "This will help against most demons. But with vampires, use the ash rune."

Evie held the sword in her hand, all but forgotten. "Demons? Vampires? Slan, will I have to face those on my way to the city?"

He shrugged. "It's wise to be on your guard." He locked his eyes on her and added, "But I think you'll be safe."

As she took a shaky breath, she sheathed the sword and strapped it to her back. The weight felt familiar there, even after so long. "But how will I know what to use for what?"

"Your magic will give you a sense of what you are up against. Remember, use fire for most creatures."

"I know Ulric mentioned those creatures when I was here before, but we never saw any."

Slan explained, "Aye, the creatures have always been here, but with Bazertari in control, you will cross more. Some are desperate as their homes and places of safety are now gone."

Evie listened, realising that the land she once cherished had become a wicked place. She donned the black cloak with a large hood to keep her features covered.

Slan regarded her. "A horse is waiting near the inn for you. It has everything you will need. Remember, this isn't the Moonstar you know. Don't trust anyone. Try to keep exchanges to a minimum, as they will know you are not from here by your accent." He leant into the chest again and pulled out a heavy pouch. "Here, you'll have enough coin to last you for some time. If you need more supplies, you can purchase them."

Evie smiled, taking the pouch and placing it in her jerkin pocket. "I'll be careful. I'll find Ulric, and get him to help me find any others." She paused. "Then do we go straight to Great Oak or back to you?"

Slan sighed, "If you feel ready, go straight there, but if you need respite, come back here. I must be careful, as I know Bazertari would have sensed the portal bringing you here." He focused on her green eyes. "Remember, with pulling you here, I have been able to activate a link between us. If I am in great need or you are, both of us will know."

Evie gave a confirming gesture, studying the sorcerer, wondering if she needed to ask anything else. Evie had so many questions, but she opted to wait until she found Ulric.

She gave him a big hug and said, "I'm thrilled to see you again. Even in these circumstances."

"And I you. Now be safe."

After leaving Slan and the cave, Evie returned to the inn. As Slan had stated, a brown mare was waiting for her, with sleeping blankets and provisions. As she got closer to it, she experienced the static buzz of a magical shield. She patted the mare's neck and observed the dark road, noticing the horse snorting and appearing unsettled, its breaths billowing in clouds before it. The creature she had seen earlier might have been close by.

"Easy girl."

She fastened her bag and sword to the saddle. Evie mounted the horse, eying the trees with caution, the woods were silent. If the creature had spooked the mare, it was not here now. Evie glanced around to orient herself and guided the horse away from the ruins.

"Come on, girl, let's head north and leave this forest behind, shall we?"

The horse snorted in response and seemed eager to make its way along the road, away from the woods. It had been a while since she had ridden in the saddle, but it felt familiar and good to be in one again. Evie exhaled deeply, absorbing everything Slan had told her. She was saddened that such a wonderful land was in so much darkness. She directed her eyes ahead, making an effort to push aside memories of the first time she travelled to Palasses.

Evie wondered what Ulric would look like, and about everyone she had known. *What would their lives be like now? Why was this Garth such a dark person? What had the warlock changed?* Slan mentioned that someone had manipulated Garth for seventeen years. That was years before her arrival. *Had the warlock gone back further in time? Was it a significant event in Garth's life that had caused this Moonstar to change and not my death? Were Corun and Iesha still at the farm? Or are they also in hiding like Slan is? Or were they...* She shook her head. *No, I don't want to know.* Evie drew in a long breath. There were so many questions she needed answers to.

She re-directed her focus, she knew she needed to avoid contact with anyone on the main roads. She glanced up at the clear night sky. At least she could cover a respectful distance by riding through the first night. She remembered there not being any inns on the way to the city, so she would be sleeping rough. Evie would make sure she moved off the primary route when she made camp. She thought about spells and wished she asked Slan about portals. Evie did not believe there was too much of a time constraint, just that they needed to deal with Bazeratri.

She nibbled on her lip, trying not to dwell on the fact that she would be alone for the next six days. She sensed a surge of happiness at the thought of seeing Ulric again, even in such a dark circumstance.

FOUR

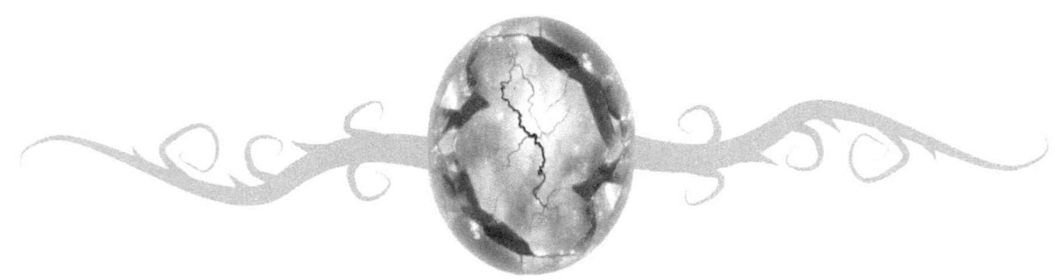

Bazertari descended into the palace dungeons. He walked past the iron barred cells, ignoring the few that were still occupied, and continued along the damp corridor, reaching the stone steps that led down to his personal dungeon. At the bottom of the steps, he could see the carved-out entrance to the deepest cells in the low torch light. As he walked closer, soft moans reached his ears, echoing through the dark and damp corridors beyond. He sucked in a breath, following the crooked form of the jailor and gagged at the foul stench of the man as it invaded his nostrils. He grimaced and breathed through his mouth. Part of him wanted to strike the man dead, for violating his senses in such a disgusting way.

For almost a decade, the crooked man had faithfully served Bazertari, looking after the prisoners held captive in the sinister dungeon that Bazertari had meticulously created beneath the palace and its cellars. Despite the evil that permeated the depths of the dungeon, the jailor had endured the torment of such a haunting environment. Only his human form bore the scars of the evil that had consumed him, leaving him with a twisted and bent appearance.

They entered the tunnel to the dark dungeon, the evil magic hummed in the surrounding air, which made Bazertari's fingers sting slightly at the familiar dark presence. After fifty days in its enchanted depths, the evil would have devoured the human souls. Only the most primitive instincts remained. All that were strong enough physically at the end of that time were transferred to a room in the depths of his black tower in the Demon Forest. There, Bazertari used his dark arts to then make them his slaves. The warlock smirked. Bazertari ensured that many of the Guild members Garth had captured were placed in the dark dungeon to become his personal guard. The irony was that they had sworn to kill him in their human life, and now they obeyed his every command; even killing their fellow Guild members.

The jailor slowed and stopped at one of the dungeon cells. The crooked man peered up at the warlock through thin, lank hair, his dark beady eyes full of hopefulness. "This one, sire."

Bazertari stepped closer, trying not to smell the jailor's foul breath. He peered in through the door's slot, spotting something huddled in the corner. "How long has she been down here?"

"'Bout fifty days."

The warlock ordered, "Open the door. I need to see that she has potential."

The crooked man agreed, choosing a key from the bunch in his hand. "As ya wish."

The metal door opened and Bazertari ducked his tall, lean frame into the cell. He glanced back. "What was she?"

"A Sword, sire. Seems the Guild had contracted her to cause issues with our supplies to the men in the north."

The warlock turned back to the huddled figure. "Let's see what the darkness has done to you."

As he stepped closer, a soft growl vibrated from the prisoner's throat. The jailor muttered, "Careful, sire."

Bazertari glanced at him, raising a dark eyebrow. As he turned back, the prisoner pounced like a feral beast. The warlock stood still, his hand snapped up, and the prisoner stopped dead in the air, like hitting a solid wall. Bazertari tilted his head to one side as he observed the emaciated woman covered in rags. She hung in the air, wrapped in the invisible grip of his magic. Her grubby hands, with long claw-like nails, desperately tried to slash him. He pursed his lips as he stared at her black, wild eyes. It appeared as though in her human form she had possessed beauty, but the darkness had taken it all, leaving a deformed husk. She growled louder, still trying to get to him. Bazertari smiled and catapulted the woman across the room, her writhing body hitting the wall with a dull thud.

He stepped out of the cell, smoothed and straightened his elegantly made deep green robe as the jailor locked the door behind him. "Bring her to my chamber at my tower in a few days. She is ripe to become one of my guards."

The man tilted his head and asked, "Do ya want to see the beast while ya here? It has spawned again."

The warlock cast his eyes further down the corridor, into the darkest depths. "Aye. Will some be ready to be transferred?"

"Aye. I can have them ready, sire. Then I'll put the potion in ya men's food in a few days. Then, as they sleep, the worms can crawl in undetected."

Bazertari smiled. "Excellent. I am already having issues with Morag. I want to ensure my men, especially my general, knows their place if they ever step out of line."

The jailor chuckled as they walked further into the dungeon. As Bazertari got closer to the den where the beast dwelled, the darkness of evil made the air thick and acrid. The warlock stopped and allowed the jailor to open the thick metal door.

As he entered, he turned to the crooked man. "In two days, ensure we harvest the larvae."

"Aye, sire."

Bazertari entered the cave. His fingers zinged as a ball of flickering green light grew from his hand then floated up into the air. The darkness of the cavern slinked away from the green glow of the globe. There was movement in front of him and he smiled as the light illuminated the immense Devil Worm. The creatures normally only grew to the size of a hunting dog, but the one he imprisoned was the size of a horse. It was a bloated, slimy mass, too gorged to move. Its mouth, that could easily take a man's arm, gaped open and saliva dripped from its small sharp teeth as it growled at the warlock. Scattered around the black flesh of the beast were rotting corpses of animals and humans.

Bazertari smirked. "My queen."

The creature's head moved towards him, and it wheezed. "You cannot hold me here forever, Bazertari. A day will come when you weaken, and I will devour you."

The warlock chuckled. "Ah, but it is your own greed that keeps you prisoner."

The beast tried to slither toward him, but the weight of its own body was its chains. "You will pay for using my children!"

The warlock glared at the creature, his face grimacing in disgust. "Your larvae ensures my men do my bidding. I do not use them. I give them purpose."

The creature growled, its rolls of flesh rippled as it tried to reach him. The warlock continued to smirk, knowing the creature was so engorged it could never move. Bazertari had trapped and nurtured it through magic, making it a queen so he could harvest the worms. She could not leave the cave because of the spells he had placed around it, but becoming too large to move had been to his advantage. It also ensured her larvae were strong and malleable, which was what he wanted.

All the men that served him had at least one parasite inside them. At any given moment, he could take control of the larva, and the body it infected. Of course, over time, the human body would learn to repel the foreign matter. Hence why the warlock held the creature captive, so that he would have an endless supply. But what interested him more was to infect a magic user with the parasite. Then there could be even more possibilities of what he could make them do. Bazertari wondered if he could infect the old fool, Slan, with one. It was something to consider.

Bazertari cast a brief glance at the creature as he departed and then redirected his focus to the jailor, who was locking the door behind him. "You have done well. Make sure you harvest the larvae."

The dungeon keeper bowed and gave him a toothless grin. "Thank ya, master."

Bazertari strolled back up through the dungeons. As he entered the corridor to the palace once more, he paused. His fingers prickled, his body sensing the use of a powerful spell.

He swore, "*Slan!*"

He hurried, sensing the presence of a massive portal being opened. *What was that fool sorcerer up to?* He paused mid step, sensing something scratching at the back of his mind. *This is new.* He felt another presence that was similar, yet not. He shook his head and snapped orders to the palace guard near the royal chamber entrance. "Bring me Garth, *now!*"

The guard in his black and red uniform made a brief affirmative gesture and quickly strode down the corridor. Bazertari entered the imposing great hall. His old nemesis still held memories of all the changes made by the time crystal as punishment. The warlock wondered if the old fool would still be causing issues if he had not remembered what had been. Perhaps it would be in his best interest to ensure Slan ingested one of the larvae. Then the fool would stop being a problem. Bazertari gazed up at the tapestry that covered the entire wall to the left of his throne. He was growing bored with Slan's antics. It was time for Garth to have Slan brought before him. Then he could engage in a new experiment and end his troubles, both at once.

FIVE

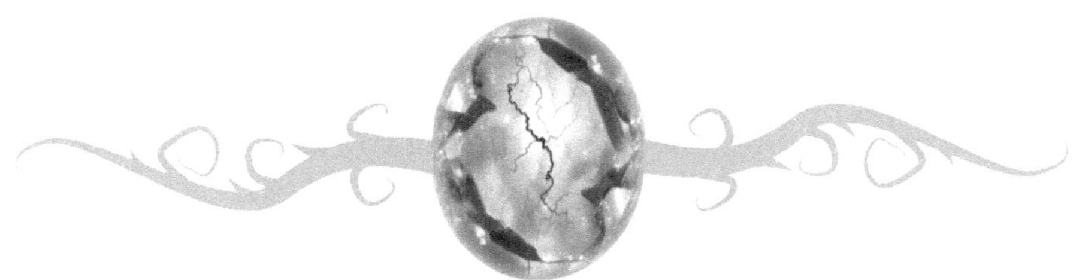

Garth strolled up the wide corridor to the great hall, as his eyes roamed over the macabre paintings that adorned the dark-golden walls. He hated the paintings ever since Bazertari had them commissioned. With an irritated breath, he looked ahead towards the guards on duty. The warlock had ordered one of Garth's own men to find him down in the mess hall where he had been enjoying a drink with Krif, his second in command. Garth had kept his features neutral; it was not wise to let it be known how much Bazertari annoyed him lately. Garth was biding his time, waiting for the right moment to move on. Until then, he would have to tow the line.

He slowed his pace and looked back at the paintings, making sure his heartbeat was steady before entering the throne room. The last thing he needed was the warlock sensing his aggravation. Then Morag stepped out from a side corridor. She moved towards him and gazed at him with dark, sultry eyes. The Sword looked at her with annoyance, attempting to walk around her. The older woman, in a figure-hugging red dress, mirrored his moves, keeping him from progressing. He directed his gaze towards the two helmeted guards, who observed silently as they stood on either side of the ornate oak doors to the great hall. He knew that neither would move from their posts. Garth's jaw set firm in irritation as he focused back on the dark-haired woman. The Sword's fingers twitched, he stuffed them into the pockets of his black leather trousers to keep him from grabbing her neck. Within moments, his booted foot tapped with impatience. His athletic frame loomed over Morag, but his intimidating presence did not seem to affect her.

Garth glared at Morag while inhaling through his nose. She had once been his lover and wondered what he used to see in her. It had taken a while, but he had learnt what a cruel, power hungry bitch she was. Garth smirked, knowing how much it vexed her that he was Bazertari's general and not her. Garth and his men had had to clean up so many of her mistakes and, of late, they were getting worse.

Morag stood gazing up at his handsome features, his short hair accentuating his jawline. She purred, trying to use her seductive nature. Her eyes lingering on the jagged scar down his left cheek. "Why won't Bazertari see me?" She glanced back at the guards. "Those beasts won't let me in!"

Garth responded in a flat, bored tone, "You know why, Morag. Yet again, your incompetence let a Guild member escape. If you'd been more vigilant in Dalimar, that member would be in the dark dungeon now. Go clean up the mess you've made."

She glared at him. "It wasn't *my* fault."

Garth sneered, "Really? You have lost your edge, Morag, and everyone knows it. If I were you, I'd keep scarce for a while. Bazertari isn't happy!"

She spun on her heel, heading back the way she had come. Garth watched her go for a few seconds, then turned and headed towards the great hall. He acknowledged the guards with a subtle movement of his head, prompting one of them to open the large door for him to pass through.

Garth entered the spacious room, his booted footsteps echoing across the grey marble floor. He eyed the warlock's helmeted personal guard that were positioned around the room next to the impressive marble columns that matched the floor. They all wore the same palace uniform, which was black trousers and a tunic. Positioned in the centre of their torso was the warlock's coat of arms of a red skull. The only difference was these guards' helmets had visors to hide their hideous appearance.

Early afternoon sunlight seeped into the open area from the windows near the ceiling, making the polished silver metal shine. A tapestry depicting Bazertari's battle against the sorcerer Landor centuries ago covered the wall to Garth's left. It had taken over a year to make and several men to carry it into the immense room to hang.

The Sword took in the image of Bazertari striking the much older sorcerer down. It was his last great achievement before he was imprisoned for centuries. Garth remembered the books he had read as a teenager about the Guardians of the Stone and how Bazertari was the enemy. He had then become the Guardian, ready to fulfil his mission of destroying the warlock should he escape his imprisonment. That was until he saw what the Guild was really like, when they had let his parents be murdered. Garth smirked. Now the Guild was gone, and he was the warlock's most trusted ally.

Garth turned his attention to Bazertari, who was on his onyx throne with a red-headed lass squirming on his lap. Garth raised an eyebrow. He had warned the girls in the palace to not be alone with the warlock after he had heard that Bazertari liked to play with his conquests. His eyes focused on the purple mark developing near the young girl's eye. Garth's shoulders raised slightly, his muscles tensed. From what he had learnt, Bazertari used his magical abilities to do things to the girls. Some had even gone missing. The rumours of experiments on prisoners in the dark dungeon was something that he could turn a blind eye to, even if it made his skin crawl. But he could not when it was with the palace occupants. Garth had bedded several girls over the years as a means to an end, but he disagreed with Bazertari's unusual tendencies.

Garth bowed his head and said coolly, knowing it was prudent to hide his distaste from his master, "My Lord."

Bazertari glanced upwards, his well-groomed black beard highlighting his pale, slender features. He pushed the redhead from his lap, discarding her like a piece of rubbish.

"Ahhh Garth," his voice was deep and cruel.

Garth eyed the redhead as she left. He focused his attention towards the warlock. He must ensure the girls remain in pairs for the foreseeable future. After years of service, working with Bazertari had become a partnership of convenience for Garth, and, at least in his position, he could help the innocents from his master's evil clutches.

The Sword said, ensuring his distaste for the evil man was not apparent, "You sent for me, my Lord."

The tall, dark-haired warlock slowly stood, his deep green robe and cloak obscuring his frame. "I did. It seems that hermit, Slan, is up to something."

Garth scowled, the one member of the Guild he had not been able to kill and the one he blamed most for his parents' deaths. "What is that fool up to now?"

Bazertari stated as he strolled down from the dais, "That's what I pay *you* for."

Garth smiled without emotion, then tensed when there was shouting from outside the great hall, and Garth picked up Morag's shrill voice. The warlock turned his attention to the entrance, a flick of his hand resulting in the doors swinging open. Both could see the dark-haired woman trying to push past the guards. Garth let out a frustrated breath and quickly shifted his attention to Bazertari. "I had ordered her to leave."

The warlock sneered, "Leave now, Morag. You bore me."

She glared at the two men; the guards keeping a firm hold of her on the threshold. "You *need* me Bazertari!"

The warlock turned his back to her and flicked his hand towards the doors, making them close again. Her cries of protest became muffled.

Bazertari turned to Garth. "I want *her* dealt with."

Garth replied, "Of course, my Lord. And with Slan?"

Bazertari crossed his arms. "Seems he's been dealing with magic again and this time, something big. I experienced the sensation of a portal being opened."

"To where?"

Bazertari glared at him. "That's what I want you to find out."

"Should I kill him?"

The warlock paused for a moment. "Nay. I have other plans for him. But if needs be, you can hurt him badly."

Garth acknowledged with a nod. It would not be the first sorcerer he had badly wounded for Bazertari, and of course, he had killed far more. He briefly wondered what plans Bazertari had for Slan. It would just be far easier to kill him.

The old fool irritated Garth and he would feel better with him gone. But Bazertari had his reasons, and it was best not to go against them. "Where should I start?"

The warlock pursed his lips. "It seemed to originate near Flamvile Woods."

Garth's features expressed contempt; he had not been to that dung hole in years. "If I find anything, shall I see where it leads me?"

"Aye, and kill anyone in your way."

Garth responded, "With pleasure."

The Sword turned and left. First, he needed his most trusted men to deal with Morag. Then he could concentrate on what Slan was up to. He strode to the back of the palace where the barracks were. His men would still be relaxing in the mess hall with a few ales.

As he descended the stone steps to the mess hall that was down in the basement below the armoury, harsh arguments and conversations bombarded his senses. It was a rowdy place full of men and women loyal to Garth. As he strode along between the two rows of tables cluttered with food and tankards of ale, Garth wondered where Morag's men stayed. All knew not to venture down to the basement, it was his turf. Several of his soldiers paused and showed their respect by gesturing with their heads as he passed. He glanced at two muscular men arm wrestling, their colleagues yelling insults as coins passed between them. Garth smirked. He let them have their freedom down in the basement: gamble, fight, whores and ale, but when it was time to work, they followed orders without question.

Garth made a low whistle and a group of six, four men and two women, stopped what they were doing and left their tables, following Garth through the mess hall. One reluctantly left the whore he had been merrily kissing and had to rush to catch up. All strolled through a large archway at the far end of the long room to a quieter section where meetings could take place. They stood to attention and waited in the open area near a long oak table, where Garth stood watching them in the dim torch light. He knew every one of them would obey his command without question and would even lay down their lives for him. Despite their loyalty, he still needed to ensure they feared him to keep them in check.

One man near the front with a clouded eye and a scar that started at the top of his bald head and went down across his face said, "What do ya need, boss?"

Garth smiled at the man who was bulkier and taller than himself. Krif was his second in command, and most trusted soldier. They had done a lot of nasty things over the years, and Krif would do everything he was ordered to do. Even a brutal injury from an axe had not stopped him from finishing the job Garth had sent him on.

Garth sighed, regarding the group. "Morag."

One woman sneered. "What's that bitch fecked up now?"

The group laughed, even Garth sniggered. "Well, the list goes on. Seems Bazertari has had enough, and she needs to have an *accident*."

The group showed agreement. The other woman who would have been a true beauty if it was not for the scar across her cheek and chin, making her thin lips on the right side permanently turned down. "So not just a lovers' tiff."

Two of the group sniggered; the rest looked at her, fear in their eyes. Garth sneered. All knew that he and Morag had once been lovers, but it was a subject not to be spoken of. "Watch your mouth, Landera. Any more talk like that and you can have a few nights down in the dark dungeon."

The woman stiffened. "Sir, I . . ."

Garth glared at her, then the rest, his tone clipped, "Just do your job. If you fail; a week in solitary!"

All quickly diverted their gaze, understanding what that signified. Solitary for most was a sealed cell, except for Garth's elite, it meant the same but in the dark dungeon. All in the palace feared the cells that were set deeper than the castle's original dungeon, and the rumours were rife about the strange creatures that roamed freely down there.

Garth glared at the group, knowing his men had heard the whispers of all he had sent down there. As well as what became of the royal family, who he had imprisoned down there early on when Bazertari had taken control. Even Garth was curious if the king or queen were now one of Bazertari's personal guards or one of the creatures roaming freely in perpetual torment. He knew very well that his men did not want to even spend an hour down in that hellhole. All his men were loyal, but he liked to make sure they knew who was boss.

Krif asked, "What about her men?"

Garth stated, "Kill any that won't be loyal to me. I want to know where all her men are, so follow her. Find her base of operations and then deal with them, and her, how you see fit."

Krif and the others indicated agreement. Garth glared at them when no one moved. "Well, fecking, get on with it. Bazertari assigned me a job, so Krif, you're in charge."

The man gave a slight affirmative gesture, and the group departed. Their booted feet echoed through the much quieter mess hall as the others watched, curious as to the mission Garth's elite team had been sent off on.

Garth walked back through the mess hall barking orders to any soldier still there, making them scurry off to attend their duties. He headed to the stables. Bazertari had enchanted his grey stallion so it would take him half the time of any other horse to get to Flamvile Woods in the north. As he rode away from Great Oak, Garth wondered what Slan was up to. The only person he knew that could have been a threat to Bazertari was dead. From what the warlock had told him, it was the Stone in the bracelet that could kill him. It was secured in the palace and, with no one to wield it, useless.

So, what was Slan doing by making a portal?

Garth sighed. Whatever the sorcerer was up to, it would not work. Bazertari was too powerful for anyone to overthrow him. Garth would see what he could find and follow any leads, but already knew it would come to nothing. Just like every other attempt Slan had tried. The Sword recalled the sorcerer's failed attempt to bring someone through a portal years ago. He was just an old fool, holding on to a hope that was well and truly lost.

SIX

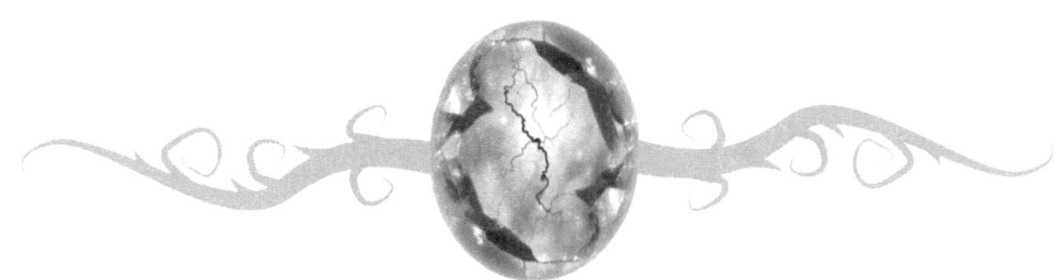

Evie sat near the back of the Deaf Bard Inn, observing the customers from the shadow of her hood. Her fingers traced the handle of her mug of ale as she searched the sea of faces looking for Ulric. Evie winced when the flamboyantly dressed bard in the corner could not reach the desired note of the song he was trying to sing. Most of the customers cheered, then continued singing along or chatting with their companions.

Evie stared at the bottom of her beaker, her eyes were captivated by the rich, amber liquid. Ulric had to be close, unless the spell had not worked and she was wrong. The thought of having to face Bazertari alone made her stomach knot with nerves. It had been difficult to find any of the other Guild members during her previous time on Moonstar, as Garth and Ulric had been unaware of any outside of Palasses. In the present timeline, the members had scattered during Bazertari's assault, it could be nigh impossible to find even one.

Evie chewed her lip, her mind pondering over several possibilities, as her body felt the lack of sleep from the last few days. She thought back to her ride from Flamvile Woods and it made her realise the land was not a safe place, especially alone.

The first four days had been uneventful. Evie had recognised a few places on the route from travelling with Garth and Ulric, which had given her mixed memories. It seemed unusual to be travelling alone, and it occurred to her that she had always been accompanied by Garth, Ulric, or both.

Being alone, it was fortunate the route to Palasses had been quiet, and she had passed no one. It was on the fourth day when she came across one lone traveller, a tradesman, heading south-east. He acknowledged her with a silent greeting as he passed on his small horse and cart, but did not pause. As the light faded, Evie left the road and made camp on the edge of a grove of trees.

Evie unsaddled her horse and tied the mare to one tree, letting it graze. She brushed it down and gave the horse an apple as an extra treat. Evie then set up a small fire and sat on her sleeping blanket, eating bread and cheese from her food pack. Evie examined the small group of trees. She had heard wolves the night before, but the area was almost silent. She was not sure if that was a good or bad thing.

Once she had eaten and was ready to settle down for the night, Evie concentrated and, as she had done every other night, put up a protective shield. The dome of invisible energy shimmered slightly as it enveloped her camp and her horse. The first time Evie had set one up, it had taken her a few attempts before it was stable and had not unsettled the mare. Having perfected the spell, the shield settled in place with ease. If nothing else, it provided her with the perception of being secure.

Her mind wandered to Ulric, as the campfire beside her kept the chill of the night air at bay. Evie thought about where the Sword could be in the city. It would not be easy if he were in hiding, and Slan had not given her any ideas about where to look. Evie mulled over her past conversations with the two Swords last time she had been in Moonstar, wondering if there was any place they would visit often. She pursed her lips. Ulric could be at an inn or tavern that he used to go to with Garth. She let out a deep breath. The only way to track down Ulric would be with magic. Evie closed her eyes. What she really needed was sleep. Once she reached the city, she would figure out a plan to find him.

In the very early hours Evie woke to the sounds of her horse becoming unsettled. She glanced around. The fire was just a small, smouldering pile, and with no moon, Evie could just barely make out her horse in the starlight. Her gaze took in the shimmer of the protective shield around her and the animal, which meant it was still in place. Turning back to the mare, Evie saw it was pulling against its tether and stomping its hooves. She got to her feet and went to the mare, whispering in the young horse's ear to soothe it. A soft, blue magical mist floated from her hand, calming the horse further. She glanced around, curious about what had unsettled the animal. Evie then heard a movement in the grove of trees. With her attention fixed on them, she made an effort to look through the branches, but she could not discern anything.

Evie closed her eyes for a moment. Her fingers tingled and conjured a small, glowing globe. As it grew brighter, Evie froze on the spot. Between the trees was a werewolf. It was close to seven feet tall and had a humanoid, muscular build that was covered in thick brown fur with a wolf-like head. It was bending over something. As the orb grew even brighter, Evie could see the remains of a deer. The werewolf paused, then turned its head and fixed its gaze on her. The towering beast stayed where it was, watching her. Its deep brown eyes glistening in the magical light of the globe. Evie held her breath, glancing at her sword that laid by her blanket. The werewolf sniffed the air, taking in her scent, sneered, then turned back to its prey and continued to devour it.

Evie slowly dimmed the light of the sphere and crept over to her blanket, her eyes never leaving the area where the werewolf was eating. From its size, it could end her in an instant; yet it seemed more interested in its kill than her. She frowned, opposed to what she had read in her world, these werewolves did not need a full moon to change. She reached her blanket and sat down, all the while watching the creature, barely able to distinguish its enormous form in the trees.

After what seemed hours, it finished its meal, glanced at her one more time, and then ran off to the west, away from her and the primary route. She guessed that because she had not threatened it, it had left her alone. Or it could be that it had sensed the magical shield. She observed the trees, apprehensive if anything else was hiding within them, but all was silent. Evie's intuition urged her to pack up and continue her journey as she watched the first rays of dawn break through the horizon.

Evie had been travelling for over half a day, the sun high in the sky. As she glanced ahead on the open route, she squinted her eyes and noticed that there was a group of travellers up ahead. They seemed to be inspecting something off the major route, and she wondered what they had found. As she rode towards them, Evie realised the beings were not human, but something else. Their heads, which were dominated by formidable jaws filled with razor-sharp teeth, overshadowed their small, misshapen bodies. As she drew closer, she observed their long, spindly limbs with razor-like claws tearing their victims apart.

She slowed her horse as the breeze changed direction and the thick, foul smell of death invaded her nostrils. Evie tried not to gag, the smell was so overwhelming. Her horse snorted nervously as it picked up the scent. She closed her eyes, imagining the mare not being startled by what was round them. A pale blue mist drifted from her fingertips. The tendrils of it slipped into the mare's nostrils and it relaxed. As she watched the macabre scene, she murmured a second spell, creating an invisible shield against the creatures as they quietly passed by.

The shimmering shield covered Evie and her mare, blocking their scent and obscuring their position. She regarded the small feral creatures, vaguely remembering the images she had seen once in a book at Corun's and Iesha's farm. From what she could tell, the creatures appeared to be like ghouls. The small, crooked monsters would search for the remains of the dead and tear the flesh from them to consume the bones. As she focused on the group, she saw that their prey was four bodies and three horses. Evie placed her hand over her mouth in shock, trying not to make a sound. She needed to get past the area as swiftly as she could, while the ghouls concentrated their attention on the corpses, devouring the bones beneath the rotten flesh.

Evie glanced around as she continued forward, and briefly wondered about who or what was responsible for the deaths of those individuals. Once far enough away, Evie heeled the sides of her horse, making it run as quickly as possible. She kept glancing back until she was at a safe distance. It seemed the route, once a safe passage, had become dangerous under Bazertari's reign. She directed her eyes ahead, filled with a sense of tension about what else she would come across.

Evie continued along the primary route, her shoulders slumped with exhaustion. As she reached the brow of the hill, Evie could see Palasses in the distance. It did not look like the affluent city that she had visited all those years before. The walls appeared damaged and unkempt, no banners adorned the watchtowers, and the gates showed signs of increased fortification. As she rode closer, the guards who stood at the gates behaved more like petty thugs than a disciplined army. The crowds queued up outside the city, waiting in fear.

Evie yawned as she rode towards the main gates. Two nights before, after hearing the ghastly cries of ghouls, Evie, filled with fear, had ridden away on her horse as quickly as she could. The only reason they would be out was if there were more bodies. When she tried to sleep after that, even with magic traps and a shield, she had found most of the time she would lie awake listening.

Upon reaching the city, Evie could only hope she would not run into any trouble at the gates. She just wanted to get into the city and have a decent night's sleep in relative safety. Despite the fact that she was entering a bustling city that appeared to be controlled by a criminal gang, it still provided a sense of security compared to being alone on the road.

Carefully keeping her hood in place, she rode towards the gates at a slow pace. Her eyes focused on the rough-looking guards. They stopped almost everyone, asking them about their business. Evie did not want them to stop her. They would know from her accent that she was a stranger and that would cause issues. She observed the trader's wagon in front of her. She directed her horse beside the carriage, keeping it at a steady pace. It was very overloaded and unstable. If she timed it right, she could use it to make a scene. Then the guards would be too busy with the trader, she hoped, to notice her.

As Evie got closer, she pulled her hood further over her features, keeping her head down, shielding herself behind the wobbling wall of supplies. As she had hoped, the guard stopped the trader and started asking questions. The old man quickly grew annoyed with being delayed, while Evie kept her eyes on the other guards. Two were on her side of the carriage and if something did not happen, they would question her. She needed a distraction straight away. Evie brought her gaze forward and, with a flick of her wrist, sent a small bolt of plasma to the back of the unstable wagon. The axle snapped and the back wheels buckled under the weight. The contents poured onto the road, rolling into horses that became skittish, and people ran towards the supplies to take advantage. The old trader shouted in distress and the guards on Evie's side moved towards the mayhem. People were grabbing what they could and fights broke out.

With everyone focused on the chaos, Evie took her chance. She egged her horse forward and quickly passed through the gates, filled with apprehension in case someone suddenly stopped her. Evie did not relax until she was further into the city and lost in the crowds. She took a quick look back to see the trader had jumped from his carriage and more were fighting over the ill-gotten gains. None of the guards were looking her way or had even noticed she had slipped by.

Evie relaxed a little and carried on. She had not gone far when she came upon the non-human quarter of the city. After narrowly escaping encounters with ghouls and a werewolf, she was determined to avoid any more creatures. She turned her horse and rode along one of the major streets, feeling saddened by the unappealing appearance of what was once such a wonderful city. Some of the side alleys and back streets seemed to thrive where there was more criminal activity. She breathed in deeply and focused; she needed to find Ulric.

The city was a maze of streets and alleys, with several inns and taverns. She had been there only a few times and, in every case, Garth or Ulric had led the way. She had never taken much notice. She cursed, wishing she had paid more attention to the street names and routes, and struggled to figure out where to even begin.

Should I locate an inn for the night and then search tomorrow? Can I even remember the name of an inn that I had been to before?

She turned her gaze upwards to the cloudy mid-afternoon sky, sighing, knowing she would more likely get hopelessly lost. She knew it would be for the best to look for Ulric, but when it grew late, she would find a decent inn for the night and continue her search in the morning.

After careful deliberation, she cast a minor spell which did not require a potion or an extra magical object. She just used her own magical abilities through the bracelet. She thought of Ulric and wanting to find him, then the bracelet glowed for a moment. Evie hoped it would be enough to help her track the Sword down. If she had done the spell correctly, when she rode near his location, the Stone would pulsate. The closer she got to him, the vibration would intensify.

Aware of the potential risks, Evie decided to remain on the main roads instead of venturing onto the side streets and alleyways. She rode around the city, using the spell to track Ulric down. She ventured into an impressive market that was still full of activity. When the road split into two, she took the one to her right that was lined with shops and several armourers and blacksmiths; hearing metal being shaped into weapons. Evie glanced at the shops, wondering if one of those armourers had been where Garth had bought her first dagger. She exhaled sharply and focused on the task.

Evie had not gone far when she entered another, smaller square. She paused, taking in the inn before her. Despite its worn condition, she could still make out the words 'White Ox' on the sign above it. Memories of her first arrival at Palasses came flooding back, leaving her with a wistful smile. She observed the square itself, there were no window boxes brimming with flowers and the area appeared worn at the edges. Evie swallowed nervously as her eyes focused on the dry fountain in the centre of the square. Then a flash of the dream she had when she first arrived in the city all those years before. The square lacked the numerous dead bodies, but resembled the dream that had shown her the deprived splendour of Palasses. Along with the account from Slan, it seemed the bracelet was correct about what would happen if there was no traveller.

Evie quickly dragged her hand across her eyes as tears slipped over her lashes. While taking a shaky breath, she redirected her focus to the whitewashed inn. She needed to maintain focus and not get overwhelmed with everything before her. It did not help that her body ached, and yearned for a good meal and bed.

Taking stock of the inn again, it would be a good place to stay and rest, and she knew the rooms were reasonable. She then wondered if Cron still owned it. Evie raised her eyes to the cloudy sky and directed her horse out of the square. There were still a few hours yet, if she had not found Ulric by evening, she would ride back and book a room for the night.

She carried on riding through the maze of streets and saw a tavern ahead. It was impressive, taking up two buildings; the sign revealing the name The Lone Dragon. Evie glanced at her bracelet, but it was dark and silent. With a sigh, she carried on down the road and circled back towards the major market again. Once there, she took the other road to the left; keeping her horse at a steady pace as she focused on her surroundings.

Evie observed what appeared to be an inn further down the road she was on, and the Stone pulsed softly. As she ventured closer, the glimmer faded. Evie stopped her horse and backtracked, the vibration becoming strong again. She peered down a side road, it opened out into a small square with what appeared to be another inn. She turned her horse and took the road. As she ventured closer, her bracelet started to get warm. It glowed and pulsated, hidden from view under her cloak. She knew she had found the right location when the pulsation intensified, becoming an almost constant buzz. The inn, The Deaf Bard, which must be where Ulric was, took up one side of the square and, from the noise coming from within, it was busy. She fastened her horse to the hitching post and cancelled the spell. With her saddle bags and sword in hand, Evie pondered the name as she ventured in.

A ruckus of cheering pulled Evie's thoughts back as the bard broke into another tuneless song. She focused on the inn again, peering at all the faces. Ulric had to be somewhere within. Her bracelet vibrated so much, it had to be right. It was hard to tell where he was with all the customers about. Perhaps, instead of returning to the White Ox, she should stay at The Deaf Bard and search again in the morning. After thanking the barmaid for her second ale, Evie took a small sip and glanced around again. She could not see him anywhere and wondered if the spell would work at all if she tried again. Then a person stood up across from her and Evie froze.

With an unobstructed view, Evie spotted Ulric at a table near the back. His appearance seemed older than she recalled and mentally calculated that he must have been in his early fifties, at least. Even though he was wearing an ill-fitting black shirt, he still had a warrior's build. His hair was long, down to his shoulders, and had grey streaks. It was a greasy, straggly mess, just like his thick, matted beard. As her eyes met his, she released a sigh. The Ulric she had known had always taken pride in his appearance. As she peered at him, she realised he was in a full drunken stupor. His face, that she could hardly see from the curtain of hair, was flushed from all the alcohol. He had the appearance of one of those unfortunate alcoholics that were frequently found in the corner of any drinking establishment. He drunkenly checked the jugs on his table, finding some ale in one.

She thought about wandering over. No one was giving him a second glance, but she wondered if she should wait till the inn quietened down a little, in case he did not enjoy having company. She did not want to make a scene and draw too much attention. Especially with a couple of rowdy groups already present.

After some time, she witnessed a group of intoxicated lads stand up to depart, and one of them glanced at Ulric and momentarily paused. He regarded the old Sword for a few moments, then walked over to his table. Evie watched, wondering if a bar fight was about to break out. The lad said something and laughed, his friends joining in. Ulric glanced upward, shrugged, and returned to his ale. The lad pointed and laughed again, then left. Ulric did nothing. It seemed he was a quiet drunk, and Evie decided it was time to stroll over.

Standing, she strapped her sword to her back under her cloak. Then grabbed her saddle bags and ale. She made her way around the tables towards him, trying not to make it too obvious where she was heading. She did not want to spook him. He was not the Ulric she knew, but she could not complete the quest on her own, even with a drunkard, it would still help.

As she reached the table, Ulric had grabbed the barmaid's arm and asked for more ale. The girl shook her head, stating, "Ya've had enough today, old man."

He looked up at her and slurred, "Hey, less of the old."

The barmaid walked away. As she passed Evie, she whispered, "Hope ya don't have business with Ulric. He's too drunk to even stand today."

Evie watched her go, then turned to the old Sword as he tried to get even a single drop of ale from the empty jugs on his table. She sighed and put her ale down on the worn wooden surface. Evie dropped her saddle bags on the floor, then spun her chair round so she could sit opposite him, without removing her sword.

She could smell the stale ale from where she sat. It was evident that he had neglected bathing for months. He took his time to gaze upwards, his blue eyes unfocused and face flushed.

Ulric blurted, "I don't talk to strangers."

Nervously, Evie chewed on her lip as she regarded him, saddened to see such a fine Sword so broken. She slid her ale over to him and said softly, "You can have mine. All I ask is for you to listen."

His eyes focused on the full mug, and he licked his cracked lips. He briefly glanced towards her, straining to make out her features hidden by the cloak hood. His hand hovered over the mug momentarily, then snatched it towards him, taking a sip. "I'm listenin'."

Evie leant forward and said, "This is going to be hard to believe, but I know you, Ulric. I know you well."

He paused, the mug hovering near his lips, he smiled in disbelief and then continued drinking. Evie glanced around the inn. It had quietened down a lot, but she had to risk it; she pulled her hood back enough so he could see her face. Ulric choked on his ale as his cobalt blue eyes focused on her features, and smiled drunkenly. "Myyyy greeeen eyed girl."

Evie's spirits lifted. *Does he remember me?* "Do you—"

"La—Lara, what ya doin' here?"

Evie's hopes fell. Her heart ached that her dear friend had no recollection of her at all.

She expressed her frustration audibly and said, "I'm not that green-eyed girl, but we know each other."

He snorted and then continued drinking, some of his hair plopping into the ale. Evie expressed her disappointment, wishing she had not given him the drink. He was so drunk she would get nothing out of him. She pulled her hood back to cover her features and got to her feet, walking over to the barmaid. Ulric raised his eyes, snorted, and resumed drinking the ale.

Evie walked back to the table, just as Ulric drained the ale she had given him. She firmed her hold on the bucket of cold water she obtained from behind the bar, and threw it over him. The old Sword jumped to his feet, staggered back two steps, and swore his head off. He stumbled towards his sword that was leaning against the wall, missing the hilt with his attempt.

Evie snapped, "Ulric! Sober up!"

Ulric glanced upward and stumbled backwards, ultimately tumbling into the table and chairs behind him. He pushed his wet, grey hair off his face, then pulled his hand down over his beard, squeezing the water from it.

He glared at Evie. "What the feck!"

She snarled, "I need you *sober,* Ulric!"

His attention shifted beyond her to the barmaid, who was laughing. He turned his attention back to Evie and sneered, "I don't know who the *feck* you are, but you can *feck off!*"

Evie narrowed her eyes at him, her voice rising in anger, "Where's the Sword I knew?" She looked at him in disgust. "Instead, I'm looking at a sorry ass drunk!"

Ulric staggered towards her, clenching his fist. "Anyone who talks to me like that gets a fist in their face!"

He ran at her, but Evie dodged. Ulric fell onto the table behind her toppling chairs. He staggered back to his feet and made a swing at her, which she easily evaded. Frustrated, Evie punched him square in the face. He staggered back, stunned. Evie then spun around and kicked him in the mid-section. He tumbled backward, landing in a heap. Evie shook her hand, the knuckles burning in pain. She looked down at him. Dazed, with blood pouring from his nose, Ulric struggled to get back up. Evie had not expected to hit him so hard.

She turned to the barmaid and asked, "Do you have a back room? I need to talk to him in private."

The girl made a confirming motion with her head, displaying some astonishment that someone half Ulric's size had managed to take him down. "Aye, I'll get me pa to help ya get him in there."

Evie acknowledged, taking her saddle bag and Ulric's sword, which remained untouched against the wall.

SEVEN

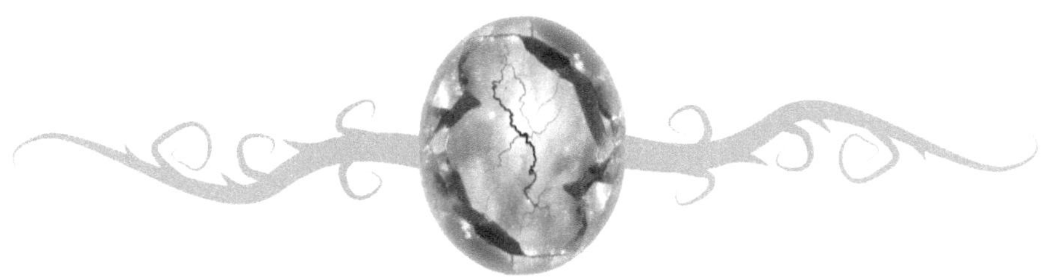

Despite his repeated attempts to break free and intimidate the large innkeeper, Ulric was unable to succeed, and the man dragged him to the back room, where he forced him to sit at the table. Ulric was uncomfortable in the wooden chair. The cold water soaked through his hair and shirt, still trickling down his back and into his trousers, causing him to fidget. Ulric used the cloth the barmaid gave him to dry his face and wipe the blood from his upper lip. He then checked his nose carefully. It throbbed, but it was not broken.

Ulric narrowed his eyes as he watched the hooded woman come in with her belongings and his sword after the innkeeper unceremoniously pushed him into a chair. Ulric watched as she thanked the innkeeper; the rotund man tried to hide his amused smile, and nodded to the stranger before he left. Ulric glanced back at the woman, who closed the door behind her. For her size, she hit like a bull. The Sword had not expected to have been downed so quickly.

His eyes followed the woman as she placed his sword against the wall beside her saddle bags and his cloak. With shame filled eyes, he focused on the hilt of his sword; he had not had a chance to even pull the weapon free. As he turned his gaze back, he observed the bulge of her own sword concealed beneath her black cloak. From her stance, Ulric knew there were daggers close to her grasp, too. She had the air of a seasoned Sword and wondered who had hired her to find him.

Ulric's head was throbbing, the pain of the punch swept across his forehead. He should not have let the girl get the better of him. But his mind soon wandered back to getting another nice tankard of ale. He glared at the woman again, wiping blood from his nose as it trickled towards his lips. Ulric watched her, his hand curling into a fist. The element of surprise would not work on him twice. If she tried anything again, he would be ready, and his sword was not too far from his grasp.

Secure in the privacy of the room, the woman pulled down her hood, revealing her delicate, red-headed features. She then removed her sword from her back, revealing a decorative scabbard, and then sat opposite him as he continued to glare. The redhead gazed back, disappointment in her green eyes.

Ulric eyed her pale features, still trying to place her. At first, when he had seen those green eyes, he mistook her for Lara; he had not seen her for almost twenty winters. His heart always ached when he thought of her. The woman in front of him had her presence and eye colour, but that was where the similarities ended. What confused him was that she was sure that he knew her, but he had never seen her before in his life, unless it had been some drunken encounter.

His shoulders still tense, he asked firmly, "So, how do we know each other?" He glanced at her hand that had turned red from the earlier impact. "I would know that right hook anywhere."

The redhead regarded him, her hands laid on the table on top of each other, looking relaxed. "I'm Evie and we fought side by side to save this land."

He wiped his nose again, inspected the cloth to see the bleeding had stopped and tossed it on the table. He then looked back at her and snorted. "I think I would remember that."

Evie leant forward, studying him with affection. Her hand slid across the table to touch his still clenched fist, but he pulled it back. He saw her pause for a moment, hurt on her slender features. She then whispered, "What happened to you, Ulric?"

He snapped, his body unable to relax. He could see his sword from the corner of his eye. If he was quick, he could reach it. "What do you care?"

She said, "I care because we're friends."

He exhaled, the statement making him realise he had no friends left. Ulric felt forlorn; he did not want to remember. Ulric observed her with suspicion. "I think I would remember if we were."

"Trust me, we know each other. We were very close."

Ulric glanced away from her eyes. He was sobering up. He did not want to sober up. "Well, I failed all my friends, so I don't think we are. Anyway, there was only one that I regarded as close."

"Garth."

His eyes snapped up at her, his features full of shock. "What?"

Evie smiled, her hand still on the table close to his. "Like I said, we're close friends and fought side by side." She let out a sigh and gestured with her head towards the door. "But Moonstar wasn't like that."

Ulric studied her, shaking his head. *What is this woman talking about? Did someone drop her as a babe?* He rubbed his temples, experiencing the sensation of his mouth being filled with dry sawdust. He needed a drink. "Sorry, lass, but I think you have mistaken me for someone else. As I don't know you."

Evie agreed, with a deflated expression. "I know."

She darted her hand forward and took his in hers. He kept his eyes fixed on her without pulling away. *Why does her touch seem familiar? Did we have an encounter one drunken night?* He sighed, which was his usual state lately, and he could have slept with her without recollection. He swallowed. *She isn't carrying, is she?* The last thing he needed was to find out he had seeded a child. He shook his head. *No, it doesn't feel like she's here because of that.*

Evie regarded Ulric, seeing the confusion on his flushed features. She could tell he was trying desperately to place her. "What I am about to tell you is the truth."

Ulric pulled his hand free as he leant back in his chair and eyed her. "So?"

She combed her fingers through her shoulder length hair, trying to figure out the best way to tell Ulric since he did not remember her. She needed to prove that they were once close and the land had changed drastically. Evie focused on his flushed features, noting the tension in his shoulders. Evie had not missed the few times he had glanced at his sword. She would have to tread carefully. She had punched him; her hand was throbbing because of it, and she would not blame him if he put up a fight if the opportunity arose. It was best to keep to the facts. "So, I know about the Guild and the prophecy."

His brow furrowed; his fists clenched. She took a slow breath, noting she hit a nerve. Evie dragged back her sleeve to show him the bracelet. "This is the Stone that killed Bazertari about nine years ago. Eighteen years in my world."

Ulric's eyes widened as they focused on the bracelet, sobering quickly. He leant forward with his attention fully on her wrist. "But that's . . ."

"Not possible?" He shifted his focus to her and nodded. Evie added, "It was in the Moonstar I travelled to. It was you, me and Garth fighting side by side." She paused, knowing she had to tell him everything. "Garth gave his life to protect me, but you and I killed Bazertari."

Ulric fixed his gaze on her for a few moments, then burst out laughing. He then stopped and glared at her. "Who *fecking* put you up to this?"

Evie slowly exhaled; he did not believe her. *How can I convince him?* She bit her lip. *Could it be possible to reveal it to him, somehow? Could I show him my memories?* It was something she had not tried before. She had removed memories from her parents to make them forget she had told them about Moonstar when it had not gone over well. *So could I also do the opposite?* It was worth a try.

Evie leant forward, capturing his hand in hers, cradling it. She tried to focus on her power, willing a connection to Ulric's mind. Her skin tingled as she felt her magic working. "This may feel a little strange, but I need you to know I am telling you the truth."

Ulric frowned, glancing between her features and her hand that glowed. He attempted to pull away from her, but Evie gripped him harder.

He sneered, "What are you going to do?"

She responded, keeping her grip firm, "Just relax."

Evie closed her eyes, keeping her hand with the bracelet on his. By allowing the magic to flow through her into Ulric, she enabled him to see all her memories of Moonstar. Evie sensed a jolt of electricity when their minds connected. She saw a flash of Ulric taking the ale from her earlier. Evie took a deep breath, as his memories flooded into her mind and she experienced all his pain. Evie tried to stop his memories, not wanting to invade his privacy. But it stalled hers from flowing to him. She chewed her lip and focused, trying to ensure he could view her memories without her being overwhelmed by his. She felt her pain again as Garth's death flowed into Ulric's mind, but she needed him to see everything. Evie could not hold back, she had to make him believe.

After a few minutes, Evie pulled her hand away, tears rolling down her cheeks. She focused on Ulric, his features pale, tears welling in his eyes as he processed everything Evie had shown him. Evie sat silently, waiting for the Sword as she tried to process his memories that had flowed into her. While taking a deep breath, she attempted to not be engulfed by the grief that seemed to drown him. It would take a few days for Ulric to understand everything, but she hoped it would be enough to convince him.

He fixed his eyes on her for a good few minutes, not moving or saying anything. Evie wondered if he would believe the memories she had shown him. She stated, "It may take a while to process it all, but that happened on the Moonstar I knew."

He focused on her features. "I—"

Ulric stopped, shook his head and rose, then walked around the table to her. Silently, he pulled her out of the chair and gave her a big bear hug, sobbing on her shoulder. Evie melted at his touch and started crying, too. They stayed like that for a while. Evie relished Ulric's embrace, sensing his body trembling as he wept. When they parted, the well-muscled Sword gazed down at her and wiped the stray tears from her cheek.

He regarded her silently, taking in her features. "It seems like a trick. But I *feel* those images."

Evie raised her eyes to look at him and explained, "They are my memories. You will experience the emotions I went through. But I didn't know how else to get you to understand."

Ulric focused on her eyes for a few moments. He said, "So how come everything is so fecked up?"

Evie sighed as she gestured at him to retake his seat and then sat opposite. "From what Slan has told me, a warlock loyal to Bazertari used a time crystal. I think he picked the moment Garth was with Morag and just nudged things enough to change this Moonstar."

Ulric stiffened in his seat. "That day has haunted me for years, wondering if I hadn't been delayed and had arrived there a day earlier."

Evie leant over, grabbing his hand gently. "I know."

He glanced downwards at her hand holding his and pulled it away. "So, why are you here now?"

Evie leant back. "Slan thinks I can destroy Bazertari."

Ulric eyed her bracelet. "But didn't you say you killed Bazertari, so you would have cast the spell?"

"Yes, on *this* Stone," nodded Evie. "The one in this Moonstar hasn't been used."

Ulric raised an eyebrow. "You mean he didn't destroy it?"

She responded, "No, because no one can, not even Bazertari. So, he's locked it away. If I can get to it, I can cast the spell from that one. I don't think I'll have the help I had from Landor like last time, but I still remember the spell. To be honest, I've had eighteen years of getting used to my powers. Compared to what I could do in Moonstar before, and what I can do now, I know I'm more powerful and in control."

She fell silent, studying Ulric. She felt more ready to confront Bazertari again.

Ulric acknowledged silently as he considered all that she had told him. After a moment, he exhaled deeply. "So, you need my help?"

Evie replied, "And if possible, anyone else we can find. Given that Bazertari has been ruling for about nine years, I believe his army will be bigger than what I—I mean, *we* faced before."

Ulric rubbed his temples, his brow furrowing, evidence of a headache forming. "I don't know if we can find anyone else. Almost everyone in the Guild and their allies were wiped out, causing those who remained to flee into hiding." He paused, pursuing his lips, then gave her a big grin, showing the gap between his front teeth. "But it will honour me to stand by your side." He raised an eyebrow. "Even hungover."

Evie's lips curled upwards, glad to have Ulric by her side once more. "Slan thought you may know where some of the Guild are."

He scratched his bearded chin, thinking for a moment. "Well, I heard Irric was somewhere north of here. Far north."

Evie leant forward; she did not recognise the name but there were many members she had never met. "Do you think you could find Irric?"

Ulric shrugged. "It may be worth a try." He focused his attention on her. "When it comes down to it, there's a large possibility it'll just be you and me. From your memories, that's how we faced the warlock before."

"From what I gather, Bazertari has an army now."

"True, with Garth as his general. We only need to cause one distraction." And he beamed at her, a smile showing the gap in his teeth again.

She studied him, wondering. "Have you ever seen Garth over the years?"

Ulric leant forward, holding her hand in his, Evie felt the calluses from his years of using a sword. "Aye, but listen, Evie, he's not the Garth from your Moonstar. This one is evil to the core."

She nodded slowly, her voice soft, "Slan told me the same."

Ulric sighed, "I haven't seen him in years. The young man I knew has gone. He's the enemy now." He paused, letting go of her hand and leant back, bitterness in his voice, "If I cross paths with him again, I will kill him where he stands for what he has done."

Evie responded, reflecting on the emotions she experienced from Ulric when she shared her memories and understood his sincerity, "I know. Let's hope we never have to see him."

The old Sword gave her a wistful smile, then took a deep breath, rubbing his temples. "I need to sleep this off. Talk to Rauk. He'll give you a room for the night. Then in the morn, we'll head north." He paused and added. "But *after* dawn."

Evie chuckled. Ulric was pale and she knew he was suffering. The two stood and Evie gave him a big hug. "It's so good to see you again, old friend." She gazed at him as they parted. "I know this isn't the Moonstar I knew, but I have missed this place. It feels like I'm back home."

With each passing moment, Ulric's condition deteriorated, and would be more so by the morning. He gave her a gentle kiss on the cheek. "As we ride north, you can tell me about your time back in your world."

She smiled and agreed, observing his dishevelled look as he took hold of his sword and cloak. "Ulric, can you do me a favour?"

The Sword eyed her as he opened the back room door. "What?"

Evie replied heavily as she pulled up her hood to hide her features. "Get a bath."

He frowned, sniffed his clothes and wrinkled his nose a little, then chuckled. "Aye, I will, lass."

They left the back room, Ulric pulling on his cloak and headed out of the inn. Evie walked up to the middle-aged innkeeper and asked for a room. The man gave her a key, stating it was one of his best. She focused her eyes on him, curious if he said that for every room. Evie did not really care, she just wanted to sleep in a bed for once.

Evie slumped down on the bed, the exhaustion she felt when entering the city hitting her fully. She directed her attention towards her red knuckles. Evie had not expected to hit Ulric so hard, but she had been frustrated with him. She concentrated on the sore hand; it glowed a little and when it faded; the redness had gone, and her hand stopped aching. If Ulric still felt rough in the morning, she would use a little magic on him. It was the least she could do.

She regarded the room while pulling off her cloak. It was very similar to the room she had when she stayed in Palasses all those years ago. It brought back fond memories and made her think about Garth. As she exhaled slowly, she had a flash of one of Ulric's memories. When Evie connected to his mind, she had not expected that to happen, nor to feel all of his guilt. She wondered if that was the reason why he drank so much. He said he had not crossed paths with Garth for several years, but she had seen a glimpse of the young Sword. Cold cruel eyes and a jagged scar down his left cheek.

She laid back on the bed. Despite her body being exhausted and achy, she remained too alert to fall asleep; for the first time in days, her mind wandered to her home and Peter. Being back on Moonstar, she understood why life felt so hollow when she had returned. Moonstar was her home, not Earth, and part of her realised it always had been. She had never fit in that world, even before her first visit to Moonstar. That could have been the reason why the Stone blended with her so seamlessly. *My place is here, not there.* Evie gazed at the ceiling and sighed; it was not quite the Moonstar she remembered, but it was her home, and she was glad to be finally back.

EIGHT

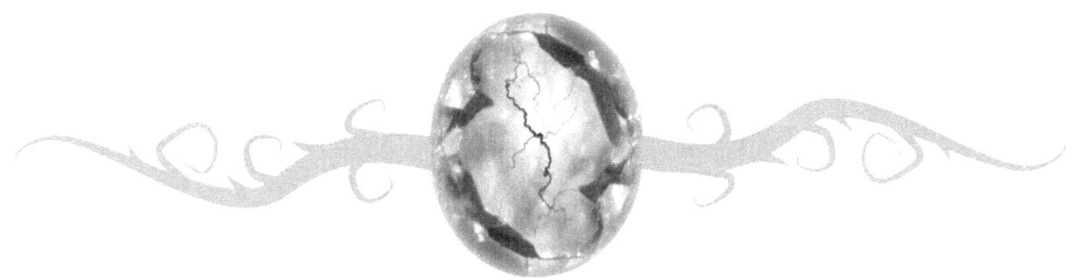

Ulric pulled up the hood of his cloak to cover his features as he left the inn and stepped out onto the almost deserted street. His breath billowed out before him as he sensed the nip in the night air. It would not be much longer until the winter established a firm grip, not the most ideal time to leave the city. Ulric strode towards the first side street as he checked the pouch in his jerkin pocket; not that heavy. He had saved some money from odd jobs and hoped that the coins he had in his flat above Iesha's would suffice. He would need to purchase a horse as it had been an expense he did not need while in the city. He briefly looked up at the clear sky. If the weather was taking a turn for the worse, they would also need furs.

As Ulric strode into the side street, a gust of icy wind blew around him, causing him to pull his cloak further around his bulky frame. He had heard that Ronric, one of Elmera's men, was in the city. Ulric had not expected the corrupt businesswoman to send some of her thugs down from Kerlish. If the rumours were true, he preferred not to risk bumping into anyone. Ulric had hoped Elmera would forget the coin, but the elf had a long memory. It seemed the beating Ulric had taken many years ago had not been enough, and the elf was after what she was due. With Evie's arrival, that was the worst possible scenario.

Ulric continued down the narrow side street with only the moonlight guiding him. His mind was racing, taking in all that Evie had shared with him. *Could there have been a Moonstar like the one she showed me?* Ulric let out a weary breath, massaging his temples.

Everything was a jumbled mess. He needed to sober up, get his head together. Ulric had gone along with what she had said while in the inn. After the punch to his face, it was prudent to tread more carefully. With the chilly air clearing his head, he pondered whether it was wise to face Bazertari or if it would be better to get Evie out of the city and into hiding.

It would not take long for Garth to figure out that the traveller had arrived and what she set to do. Then there would be death squads out on the streets searching for her, and anyone who helped her. He shut his eyes for a moment. Ulric's shoulder muscles knotted, the memory of his hands aching as he had held his sword so tightly, sneaking round these very streets trying to get Guild members and their families to safety. He stilled as his memories became more vivid, the metallic taste of blood almost gagging him. Despite all his effort, there were still many deaths. He inhaled deeply, attempting to suppress the image of the blood and dirt smeared faces.

Ulric cursed Slan. *What was that fool thinking?* He had put Evie in danger, and now she would constantly be on the run. He pressed his lips together, contemplating if he could get her off Moonstar altogether.

Would there be any captain willing to do this after all these years? Or will it be simpler to get Slan to send her back? Despite everything it took to bring her here, would the sorcerer even consider it?

Ulric rubbed his tired features. His nose ached and his head throbbed even more from the hangover that was developing. Part of him wanted another drink, but he needed to focus. Unfortunately, in sobering up, he would also have to remember. He sighed. He had been avoiding having to think about all that had happened for years. Ulric understood that at some stage, he would have to confront the entirety of it. He wondered if helping Evie escape would keep him preoccupied.

He turned a corner and swore, his way blocked. Two large men glared at him. One grinned. "On your way somewhere, Ulric?"

The Sword regarded them from under his hood. His headache was becoming relentless. He groaned, "Look, Ronric. I'll have Elmera's money in the next few days."

The large man smirked. "Well, time's up."

Ulric exhaled heavily. "I'm fecking hungover lads. Let's not do this now."

The two blokes laughed. Ronric's companion taunted, "You're a drunken has-been, Ulric. You think you can fight us, *old man?*"

Ulric clenched his fist in annoyance, even if his knees and shoulders would agree with that statement. Inhaling deeply, he pulled his sword free from under his cloak. The cold soak at the inn and the walk had cleared his head a little. He was not at his full fighting potential, but he still believed he could out skill the ruffians.

"One way to find out," he challenged.

The two pulled their swords free, the sing of steel echoed down the deserted street. Ulric eyed them. They were too cocky for their own good. Ulric paused as he touched his temples, holding the sword in one hand.

Ronric's companion ran at him. Ulric's sluggish reflexes were still fast enough to deflect the blow. Unlike his unprepared state at the inn with Evie, he was now more than ready to counter the parries directed at him. The older man turned to the younger and swung his sword again, slicing across his stomach. The young man dropped to the ground, cradling his bloody mid-section. Ulric turned to Ronric and shot him an angry stare. "I have a *fecking* headache, Ronric, and I am not in the mood to do this now. I will pay Elmare back."

Ronric smirked. "Ya had ya chance, Ulric."

The old Sword exhaled and, in one swift move, slammed the pommel of his sword into Ronric's face who went down like a rag doll. Ulric sheathed his sword. It was a pleasant sensation to win after so long. Maybe it would not be so bad if he got sober.

Ulric sneered at the one cradling his mid-section, "I'd think twice before you cross me again, lad!"

The younger man turned his eyes towards him, grimacing in pain. "Feck you!"

Ulric smirked. The young man would recover in a week. He had not cut that deep. As he applied pressure to his temples again, Ulric carried on through the city. Once he got Evie to safety, he would visit Elmare and pay his debt.

Ulric strolled down the side alley, to the back entrance of Iesha's small shop, and quietly entered. He needed sleep and to mull over everything Evie had told him. He paused in the dark, narrow corridor near the back stairs when he saw candlelight from a side room. Iesha was still up. The lass was always working too hard. Ulric had to remind her on multiple occasions to rest. If she carried on tailoring into the early hours, her eyesight would soon fail her.

He sighed, wondering where he would be if it had not been for Iesha. *Probably, my corpse would have rotted away in the very alley behind her tailor shop. How did I reach such a low point?* It seemed like another life. He sighed. *Had it truly improved since?* Evie's memories were making him think of the past too much.

For years Ulric had always been one step ahead of Garth's men. Until that dreaded night. Upon hearing that the group led by Garth was seen heading towards Flamvile Woods, he immediately rode south as fast as possible. Ulric clenched his fists. His nostrils flared as he smelt the stench of burning flesh. The flames were intense, despite the cold and wet night. Ulric cursed, his chest tight, reliving it. That dreadful night had been the tipping point when he began losing himself to drink. All hope for the Guild finally gone.

As the years passed, he began to drink more, to the point of being in a drunken stupor, just to stop seeing all the deaths; and the mistakes that could have prevented all of it. He gazed at the wooden door that was ajar. Ulric still found it difficult to fathom that in that alley, passed out in his own puke, his clothes soiled and torn, Iesha had seen it in her heart to help him. How she had dragged him into her home he still, to this day, had no clue.

Ulric pulled off his cloak and scabbard. He gazed at the sword, studying the decorative, worn scabbard in the candlelight. Ulric had sold it for ale, but Iesha had found it. He had asked how she recognised it as his. The slender brunette told how she had seen him years before at an inn telling stories of his adventures, a time before the evil. Ulric's lips curled up. He must have made one big impression on her. It had taken him months to pay her back. She did not want him to, but Ulric had insisted, and he had been glad in the end that she had found his sword. Having it had given him some purpose; but the lure of the ale and the opportunity to forget was stronger.

Ulric placed his cloak on the bannister and leaned his sword against the wall before entering Iesha's sewing room. The small, cluttered room was brightened by candles of various sizes and shapes scattered all around. To one side, on a long, thin table were several bundles of material in various colours. In the centre, sitting at a large oak table covered with pieces of cloth in various shapes, Iesha was sewing an elaborate design on a shirt. Oblivious to her surroundings, the woman remained focused on her work as the large Sword entered unnoticed.

Ulric gazed at Iesha's back, pondering why she had never settled down, even in her late thirties. Even though their relationship was platonic, Ulric could not miss that Iesha was a beauty. Despite having countless offers of companionship, Iesha had opted to live, and manage the make and repair tailor shop, on her own. Perhaps she just never discovered her perfect match. Ulric exhaled deeply. There were so many like that in Moonstar. They seemed displaced, like fate had fecked up. As Ulric stepped closer, making a sound, Iesha turned and smiled at him with tired eyes. Ulric swallowed putting things together, remembering Evie's memories and suddenly knew. In changing Garth's destiny, it made a significant impact, and affected more lives than Ulric had expected.

Iesha observed him, her brown hair tied back in a long plat. Her brow furrowed and asked, "Are you alright?"

Ulric nodded, experiencing his heartache for her and what she could have had. If Corun had not been made guardian, and gone missing while on the run, their lives would have been so different.

His voice faltered, "I'm going to be leaving in the morn."

Iesha appeared sullen, putting down her sewing and getting to her feet. She rubbed her back absentmindedly, it ached from sitting in the same position for too long.

"If you don't have the money to pay me, you can stay for free. I've told you that."

Ulric disagreed and smiled. He wanted to hug her and tell her of the life she could have had. He inhaled deeply; it was better that she did not know.

He said, "I have to find an old friend."

She responded, "You are welcome back here when you return. I like your company."

Ulric's lips turned up slightly, a hint of sadness showed through as he peered down at his feet. "Even when too drunk to make it up the stairs?"

Iesha gazed at him, resting her hand on his arm. "This land is a cruel place. We all have our ways to deal with it, Ulric."

He agreed, regarding her tired features, thinking of Evie's memories and seeing Iesha laughing with joy. His chest ached and drew in a long, deep breath to gain control of his emotions, hurting for the woman he regarded so dearly.

Ulric asked, "I was wondering if you could help me with something."

"What?"

"Prepare a bath."

She carefully watched him and sighed, "Finally!"

He frowned. "What?"

Iesha replied, her voice full of amusement, "I care for you, Ulric, but you smell like an alehouse."

He sniffed his clothes again. "Why didn't you say?"

She shrugged. "You were hurting Ulric. I didn't have the heart to."

He smiled, thinking it might be a good idea to help Evie make Moonstar a more positive place. Then kind souls like Iesha could have more in their lives. He just wished that Corun had been alive to have met Iesha. As Ulric knew, his old friend would have fallen for her kind soul in an instant.

NINE

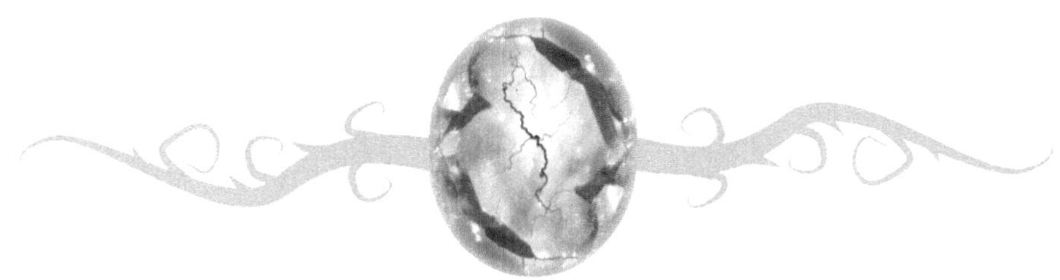

Garth's gaze was locked on the fireplace, recollecting he had been in front of it when he had killed her. He scrutinised the ruined inn with disgust as he kicked a rock across the floor. It scattered to the far corner, disappearing down a hole and making a small rodent run off to find safety.

That night had gone perfectly to plan. The group had waited in the inn hidden beneath their hoods, watching. Garth had hoped Corun would have showed; his replacement when he had 'disgraced' the Guild. However, the majority of Guild members had fled prior to the arrival of the traveller. He sucked in a deep breath, looking at the charred fireplace, which pulled at his memories.

Garth felt the handle of his dagger against his calloused palm. The inn was busy, but as he scrutinised the faces from beneath his hood, he recognised two or three of the Guild. Where had they all been hiding these last few years? He passed his gaze across the room a final time, his men were strategically placed around the inn. Was the traveller coming tonight with the storm? The warlock had never let them down before, and with the Guild present, something was expected to happen.

As the inn door flew open, a young girl stumbled inside. The emerald dress she wore seemed better suited for a bed chamber than a winter's night. It clung tightly to her slender, shivering body, and she seemed very disoriented. Garth took a strong grip on his dagger, dragging it free. From her accent, as she asked Brak some questions about her whereabouts, she was not from these parts. The warlock was right. That had to be the traveller. Garth turned his eyes towards Krif, who was seated near the innkeeper. With a quick nod, his men moved.

The inn erupted into chaos. The few Guild members present tried to fight, but most were caught off guard and their blood soon stained the floor. Garth had one target; the traveller. He could not let her activate the stone. Garth weaved through the fighting, killing any that got in his way. He saw Krif; his second had grabbed Brak as the innkeeper tried to defend the traveller. Brak had even shouted for her to run, but the girl stood there in shock. Garth grabbed her firmly. The traveller looked at him; her face full of fear, not that of an evil sorceress.

Her green eyes gazed at him as tears flowed over her lashes. Garth placed his dagger to her throat and snarled, "You're ours now."

Brak insisted as he pulled against Krif, "She's nay one. Let her go!"

Garth turned towards the innkeeper and growled, "Shall we check?" Garth turned to his second. "Search him for the talisman."

Brak tried to stop the larger man, but Krif head-butted him, the innkeeper's nose broke and blood poured down his face. He then stilled as another of Garth's men pulled a woman and a teenage boy from the back. Garth saw the look on the innkeeper's face and knew they had to be his family. Krif snatched a black stone from Brak's pocket and threw it over to Garth.

Still clasping the girl, her skin cold against his touch, Garth snatched the stone in mid-air and turned to her. "Shall we see if you're the one we seek?"

She pushed and pulled against him, her face pale. "Who the fuck are you?"

Garth huffed. She was putting up a fight. He gestured with his head to one of his men, who loomed over her and forcefully seized her arms. She sneered at him and tried to break free, but his man was too strong. Garth glanced at the bracelet. It matched the warlock's description, but he had to be sure. As he *held onto her hand, he split open her palm with the blade of his dagger. As her hand unclenched in response to the stinging pain, he set the black stone on the exposed flesh. As soon as the girl's blood touched it, the stone glowed. Garth beamed and focused his attention on her. "So you're the chosen one."*

She cast her eyes down at the stone, then back at him. "What the fuck!?"

Garth ignored her, throwing the talisman into the fire. He then tightly grasped the bracelet and pulled. The girl screamed in agony as the bracelet did not come free. Garth pulled harder, but the bracelet would not move. The man holding the girl offered, "Maybe we take her back? Let the warlock get it?"

Garth observed the redhead, her eyes brimming with tears.

She murmured, "I just want to go home. Let me go."

He turned towards Brak, who tried to pull free of Krif's grip, then his wife cried out as one of her captors placed a dagger against their son's neck. Garth redirected his attention to the traveller. The warlock had practised some dark arts over the years, using Guild members as his experiments.

Should I take her back to the warlock? What would he do with her? Would he keep her to have his way with her? What horrible experiments would Bazertari do to her?

The girl pleaded, pulling against his grip. "Please let me go."

He released a heavy exhale. "That I can't do."

She sobbed, "Please!"

Garth glanced at the bracelet, then directed his gaze towards her features. He had killed many over the years in the warlock's name, but he did not agree with the experimentations. All they needed was the bracelet. He cursed, gripping firmly onto his dagger, as he pushed it into her midsection. Her expression filled with astonishment as he drove the blade deeper. If he cut right, she would not suffer.

Brak cried out in anguish. The Guild's last hope was bleeding out as she dropped to the floor. Garth ordered, "Yanric, your axe."

The dwarf stepped forward, passing Garth his short axe. Garth took it, and in one swift motion, chopped off the dead girl's hand. He bent down, snatching up the bracelet.

He turned to see Brak trying to break free. The innkeeper yelled, "YOU FECKING BASTARD!"

Garth headed for the door. "Nay witnesses."

Krif responded by slicing Brak's throat, claiming the gold coin he held as a souvenir.

Taking a long breath, Garth pulled himself out of his memories and gazed round at the remains. Even though it had been cold and wet that night, the inn had burned with vigour.

Just a few months later, they finally found Corun. The Sword had been bent on revenge with the news that the traveller was dead; he had killed all of Bazertari's followers that he could find. In his rage, Corun had not been as careful, and they trapped him in Kerlish. Garth did not kill the Sword, Bazertari gave strict orders not to; it seemed the warlock had plans. And because Garth had killed the traveller, it had been in his best interest not to do the same with Corun.

Garth looked around and was surprised to find no bones left in sight. Someone must have taken and buried them. He stared at the fireplace again and realised even back then, he had lost count of how many of the Guild and their sympathisers they had killed. Any they found but did not kill, mainly the higher-ranking ones, had ended up at the black tower. There was nothing left of them after that. *Nothing human, anyway.* He wondered if Corun had become one of the creatures that guarded Bazertari. It would be ironic if he had.

Garth released a heavy sigh. Even then, he had to clean up after Morag. So many had slipped through her fingers, including Corun, until he had found them. Then again, she would not be a thorn in his side for much longer.

His mind wandered back to Slan. Bazertari found it amusing that the old sorcerer would have to witness everyone being slaughtered and not have any allies left. Garth still thought it would be better to have Slan killed, then he would not have to be trekking round the land to find out what the fool had been up to. Yet Bazertari seemed to have some plan for the sorcerer. Garth was still curious as to why he was not in the dark dungeon with everyone else.

Garth turned towards Flamvile Woods. He had gone there first and found tracks coming from the woods to the ruins. From the ones he had found that the recent rain had not washed away, they were only a few days old. He looked back at the inn, wondering who they had met here. *Was it Slan? Had they come through the portal that Bazertari sensed?* Unless he found that old sorcerer, he would not know.

He surveyed the main road by glancing in both directions. There were several tracks, most just passing by. One set started from the inn itself, heading northeast. Made sense for the stranger to head to Palasses, it was the closest city. From the rumours, Ulric had last been seen there. *Were they searching for him?* He snorted; they would not get much from him. Ulric was just a drunkard these days. Garth inhaled deeply and strode towards his grey stallion. He would get nothing more from the ashes.

Garth mounted his horse and paused, glancing across at the trees behind the inn. He had a strong certainty that he was being watched. He called, "Are you hiding, old man?"

The cool breeze rustled through the trees, but there was no other movement.

A familiar voice murmured in the air, "Bazertari's days are numbered. Time to pick a side."

Garth stiffened, peering into the trees, seeing no one. He glanced over his shoulder at the inn, a shiver going down his spine. The place gave him the creeps. His mind wandered back to the voice. 'Pick a side', the voice had said. He snorted again, he knew which side he was on. His.

Garth egged his horse northward. He would get some answers in Palasses, and probably get round to dealing with that drunkard while he was at it. Garth would check with his spies in the city to see if there were any strangers about. The stranger would have a head start, but he would soon catch them. Then Garth would make them talk, find out why Slan had gone to all the trouble of opening a portal. Like every other thing Slan tried to do, it would lead to nothing. *When will the sorcerer see Bazertari's invincibility and the advantage of joining the warlock? You just have to move on before your usefulness wears out.* That was Garth's plan. Until then, he had a job to do, and he would ensure that he dealt with it.

TEN

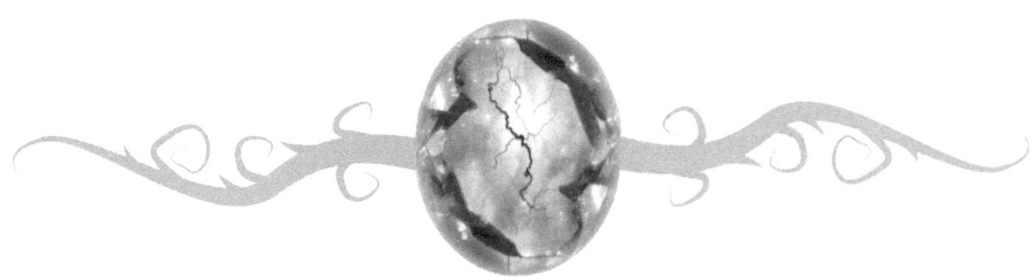

Evie wiggled under the covers and huffed. She punched the pillow and laid back down, staring at the wall. Turning, she grabbed the pillow and flung it across the room, then grabbed the cooler one next to her. She shifted her shoulders and tried again. A flash of unfocused eyes staring at herself passing over a tankard of ale. Evie rolled on to her side, endeavouring to free her mind, but it focused on the memories from Ulric again. She was still seeing the horror and brutality the warlock and his men had inflicted on Moonstar and the Guild.

Evie sat up, running her fingers through her dishevelled hair, and released a deep breath. It was no good. Her gaze flicked across to the window, staring at the moonlight seeping through the thin curtains. Another flash, this one clear, a sword blade cutting through flesh. Evie twitched, and applied pressure to her temples as she let out a yawn, then rotated her tense shoulders. Evie decided meditation could help calm her racing thoughts. It had been effective for her work-related stress. She inhaled deeply, her eyes shut. Another jumbled, alcohol infused mess flashed through her mind. Evie squared her shoulders, trying to keep focused on her exercise. If only she could clear her mind just enough to get some rest.

Evie covered her mouth to stifle the sob escaping when she saw Iesha in the jumbled memories. Even though alone in such dark times, the brunette had still been warm and kind. After she opened her eyes, Evie wiped at the tears that were running down her cheeks. Part of her was desperate to see her friend again. But knowing all that her close friend had lost, Evie was reluctant to even talk to her. She closed her eyes, more tears cascading down her cheeks. It would be for the best if she never met her. Let Iesha live her life as she had been.

Evie fixated her gaze on the ceiling, slumping back onto the pillow. Her body was sore from exhaustion, but her mind would not rest. Then she thought of Peter, of him comforting her after she woke from the nightmares she used to have when she first returned. Evie rolled over and buried her head in the pillow and screamed. She hated that when she could not sleep, her mind would dredge up the past and dwell on things she could not change. Yet, more events with Peter mingled with Ulric's memories. Evie rolled back over, staring at the ceiling. Seemed she would get no sleep tonight.

Just after dawn, Evie came down feeling refreshed, even with the lack of sleep. With her belongings in hand, she found Ulric already sitting in the empty inn, appearing pale, and pouring what seemed to be water into his tankard. She smiled as she walked over, regarding him. His hair was scrapped off his face and bunched in a knot at his neck, exposing the white scar across his eyebrow. He was also clean shaven and wearing fresh clothes. It seemed he may have taken her suggestion the night before about having a bath.

Sitting opposite him, the Sword regarded her, his eyes closed slightly, probably from a headache he was attempting to overcome. With a smile on her face, she caught his gaze, picking up a scent of herbs like the ones Iesha used to use in her baths at the farm. Evie remembered how effective they had been when she had been training, and knew they would help with Ulric's hangover.

The barmaid arrived with waffles and Evie greeted her with a pleasant good morning. As she put down the plate, the barmaid gestured a welcome and then left the two alone. Evie scrutinised Ulric, about to ask why he had not ordered any breakfast. Then she remembered he would not be able to eat, maybe for a while. The memory of the celebrations at Iesha's and Corun's farm after defeating Bazertari came flooding back.

The next day both Ulric and Corun had been so hungover and of course Ulric had been unable to eat a thing. When the sweet aroma of the waffles invaded her nostrils, Evie quickly tucked in, suddenly realising how hungry she was, as she had had nothing to eat since she had arrived.

Ulric observed Evie as he drank a large gulp of water, his hand shook a little. The aroma of Evie's waffles heightened his sense of queasiness. It was strange having water, when for years his breakfast had been a mug of ale and nothing else. He exhaled slowly, hoping it would soothe his stomach.

He said, attempting to keep his head as still as possible with the pounding headache, "I've arranged a food pack. Do you have any winter furs?"

"No, just what I'm wearing," responded Evie. "Slan gave me a few spare clothes, bed roll, blankets, flint and stone, and some kindling. As well as a water bottle and food supplies."

Ulric made a gentle gesture of agreement. "Well, eat up, then we'll walk over to the market before we leave the city." He gazed at Evie for a moment, her hood hiding her features. "Keep that hood up, also don't say my name while in the city . . . erm, there are few I'm trying to *avoid*. So, it's not safe."

Evie scoffed, "I'm capable of looking after myself."

Ulric smiled, his features pale and clammy. "Aye, my nose knows."

Evie cast her eyes downward, consumed by a sense of guilt. "Sorry. How's your head?"

"Throbbing," he muttered, experiencing his stomach churn again. "It'll take a few days to fully recover and . . . sober up. I've been drinking ale for a long time, in excess."

She arched an eyebrow, glancing at her bracelet. "I could help."

Ulric's eyes darted around the room, shifting in his seat, and leant forward. "Don't Evie. Using magic is *forbidden*."

She studied him. "Oh . . . Why?"

Ulric sighed, downing the rest of his water and said, "I have a lot to tell you, lass, but not here where there are ears." He glanced over her shoulder at the barmaid and innkeeper. "Wait till outside the city."

Evie responded, "Understood."

Ulric smiled. "Now eat up. We have quite a journey ahead of us."

Once Evie had finished, they left the inn, both making sure their hoods covered their features well. Evie followed Ulric through the streets to the bustling market square near to the heart of the city. She wondered how far they would go north, as she had only been as far as Adnama years ago, and not in winter. If they were needing furs, it was going to be a hard ride.

When they found the right stall, they inspected the merchandise which were made up of several pelts with lush fur collars. Evie stayed quiet as Ulric asked for two winter furs, one for him and one for her. The market owner directed their gaze towards Ulric after placing the thick cloaks before them. "That'll be twenty."

Ulric grabbed the well-worn money pouch from inside his cloak. The Sword paused as his attention shifted to several of the copper coins in his large, calloused hand. Evie saw it was not enough. She watched as he quickly rummaged in his cloak pockets. His brow furrowed in confusion. Then a quick flash of relief when he patted his jerkin. Then he checked his pockets again.

Evie wondered what he had in his jerkin that was not coin for the furs. *Was it for the purpose of getting us away from the city?* It was pure luck that she had entered with the help of a distraction. *Will we have the same issue getting out?* If they needed to bribe guards, she hoped she would have at least enough coin if Ulric did not.

The market stall owner glared at them and pushed. "Well?"

Evie placed a hand on Ulric's arm and then pulled out her purse and poured some silver coins into her hand, counting out the right amount. The market stall owner took it and thanked her. As Ulric took the furs, he gazed at Evie sheepishly. "Sorry, lass. I thought I had checked and had enough."

She smiled at him softly and they walked away from the stall. "It doesn't matter." She observed the market with a curious gaze. "Do we need anything else while we are here? My treat."

Ulric glanced around, his hand subconsciously rubbing his stomach. "That herb stall. I should get some peppermint or ginger root."

Evie gave a silent agreement, and they made their way towards the stall. They explored the offerings of the other vendors and found a few more things. Ulric chewed on some peppermint leaves as they strolled away from the market and down the busy street towards the inn.

He gazed at Evie. "Thank you again for paying for some of the items we needed. I was sure I had enough coin."

Evie smiled in his direction, observing his features. "It's alright. Slan gave me enough for both of us."

"Still, I should have checked."

Evie squeezed his hand. "Ulric. It's alright."

He acknowledged and glanced at the inn as they walked towards it. "I'll go get the food pack." He pointed towards a black horse waiting outside the inn, with a well-worn saddle. "That's my horse."

"Mine's in the stable. I'll meet you here."

Evie watched Ulric venture inside and she then walked down the side street to the stable behind the inn. Most of the stalls were empty, a young lad was cleaning them out. Evie proceeded to the stall with her horse after giving him a quick nod of greeting. As she saddled the mare, she thought of Ulric. He seemed somewhat doubtful of himself. The brash man she knew was almost a shadow. Her mind wandered to his memories again as she placed the saddle bags in position. After enduring so much, she feared that she had lost the man she knew and cared for forever.

After leading the horse back to the entrance of the inn, she discovered Ulric already mounted on his horse and prepared to leave. She mounted her own, and they rode through Palasses towards the north gate. As they got closer, Ulric stated, "We need to take a smaller exit. The guards on the main gate stop any that leave as well as enter."

Evie responded, "Alright."

He added, while inhaling deeply, "I have a way to ensure the guards turn a blind eye. But if the guard I know isn't on duty, then we may need coin."

"Don't worry." Evie smiled. "As I told you, I have plenty." She eyed him. "What do you have if the guard you know is there?"

Ulric grinned, patting his side where Evie had seen him check earlier. She could understand the relief on his features when he was reassured that it was still there. "He has a weakness for runes. And I have one that I think will give us passage."

Evie observed the path ahead as they rode down the side street. Ahead was a small iron gate with two men standing guard. She cast a quick glance in Ulric's direction. "Is one the man you seek?"

Ulric looked ahead, the only evidence from the movement of his hood. He responded, his voice low, "Aye. Best stay silent, lass. Let me do the talking."

Evie kept her eyes ahead with the expectation that Ulric's plan would work.

Upon nearing the side gate, Ulric dismounted, nodding at Evie to do the same. Whispering to Evie, he passed her the reins to his horse, "Stay behind me." Then he moved towards the gate.

She gave a small gesture of agreement and gripped the reins of both horses while she watched.

Ulric pushed his hood back a little and said to the scarred man before him, "Good day Beck."

The man eyed Ulric, glancing past him at Evie. "Don't see you venturing from the city these days. Ya usually cradling a tankard of ale."

Ulric chuckled. "I have business to attend to."

"Ya mean Elmar's thugs found ya? I heard ya gave them a fair fight."

So, that was who Ulric was avoiding. Evie suddenly realised. She then noticed Ulric's hand twitched, and she tightened her grip on the horses' reins. If his bribe was not enough, they would need to take swift action.

Ulric responded, "Well, I still have the skill, even if my shoulders protested."

Beck burst out laughing. "Aye, we ain't as young as we once were." He glanced at his companion. "Take a patrol. I've got this."

The younger guard complied with a slight movement of the head. He eyed Ulric with suspicion, then strolled off down the street. Evie shifted her attention back to Ulric as Beck said, "So, ya gonna make it worth my while to let ya out?"

Ulric pulled the rune from his pocket. "I think this may pay for our exit from this fine city."

Beck raised a dark eyebrow, eyeing the rune in Ulric's hand. "Is that—?"

"Aye, devil fire rune."

Beck turned his eyes towards him. "How'd ya get it?"

Ulric tapped his nose. He glanced back at Evie, who silently watched, trying to remain relaxed. Ulric asked, "Well, is it enough?"

Beck grinned. "Oh aye, for both of ya. Seems me memory is a little hazy as to if ya left or not."

Ulric glanced down the road. "What of your friend?"

Beck looked in the same direction. "Oh, him? He'll keep quiet if he knows what's good for 'im."

Ulric passed over the rune. Beck opened the gate and Uric signalled for Evie to go through. The Sword followed, looking back at Beck. "If I find any more runes, I know who to give them to."

The scarred man chuckled. "Aye. And don't worry, I never saw ya."

ELEVEN

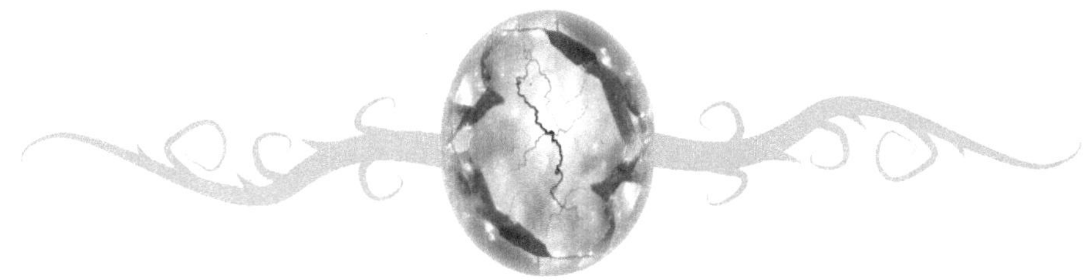

They both rode together along the major route towards the north. They passed some traders with heavy supply carts heading south, but there were few heading north like themselves. Once distanced from the city, the road was deserted, except for the two of them.

Evie asked, "So why do I have to be careful using magic?"

With a brief glance at her, Ulric guided his horse to avoid a large rock in the road. "Once Bazertari got power, magic users would go missing. News soon spread that he had his men round up all that they could find."

"Why?"

Ulric peered into the distance. "I asked the same question to the ones I came across over the years." He turned his gaze to her. "It seemed the warlock gave them a choice; work with him or die."

Evie swallowed. "Oh. Did some take his deal?"

"Aye. But many perished. Those who could, ran. Since then, anyone using magic has remained hidden."

Evie suddenly wondered if Bazertari had sensed her using her power since arriving and hoped nothing came of it. She casually glanced at Ulric, deciding not to mention her concern, as he already appeared worried.

"I see. I better be careful then."

"Aye, you need to be, lass. Nay one knew why he took the magic users. So I could only think he did it to gain more power over the land."

"Yes, it would give him an advantage. Maybe a spy network?"

"Aye, you could be right, lass, since they couldn't stop him."

"The only thing that can defeat Bazertari is the spell."

"And that's with Bazertari."

Evie inclined her head and stated, "Hopefully, after we find the others, we can go and get it."

Ulric gave a short, bitter laugh. "Not a simple task." He waved his arm around the space ahead of them. "Look at this place, Evie. It's full of evil and darkness. Great Oak is at the heart of it."

She studied him, keeping her horse in check at a slow pace. "I understand, but I *must* go there. With or without you, Ulric. I am not going to let Bazertari keep this land in such fear when I know I can *defeat* him."

Ulric regarded her, a shadow of fear in his eyes, his features still pale and clammy. "This is *not* the Moonstar that you know. It's evil to the *core*. I think Slan has brought you here on a fool's errand."

Evie focused her attention on him after pulling up on her reins to bring her horse to a halt. "Where's your fighting spirit, Ulric? Last night, you didn't seem to have any doubts."

He snapped, his hands shaking as he clung to the reins, "*Last night I was fecking drunk!*" He stared angrily at her. "It's because of me that the Guild is gone! Why innocents are dead!"

Evie could see the tears rolling down his cheeks. With him no longer dulled by drink, he was overwhelmed by fear and probably guilt. She leant over, grabbing his arm gently. "None of this is *your* fault."

Ulric sneered, pulling his arm away, "It *fecking is!* You showed me your memories and what could have been. If I had been there when I was supposed to be, *NONE* of this would have happened!!"

Evie barked, "I know what that *fucking* warlock did! He made sure *you* were delayed in getting to Garth. He made sure *Morag* knew what to say to him. It was never *your* fault. It was that *bastard!*"

Ulric fixed his eyes on her, then drew in a deep breath, shaking his head. He wasn't looking well. "Nay, it's mine. *All of it."*

Evie studied his distraught features. She stated, her voice softer, "No, it isn't."

Ulric turned his eyes away from her. He mumbled, "Nay, I should have been stronger. I could have . . . stopped him that night." He sadly shook his head, a sob escaping from his lips. He faced Evie again, more tears rolling down his cheeks. "I could have . . . " He trailed off, shaking his head.

Evie wondered what he meant. It seemed to be about more than the day Garth met Morag. Even though she felt guilty doing so, Evie knew she had to access Ulric's memories. It was the only way to understand what he meant. However, some memories became tangled and, with such an abundance of sorrow, Evie sensed the likelihood of becoming engulfed by them. Ulric was adamant he could have done something. A path he could have taken but did not. She was missing something.

Evie leant over, taking his arm, making him look at her. "Those memories I shared, you saw how well we worked together, even with Garth's death," her voice faltered. "And we still stood strong. Ulric, I can't do this on my own. I *need* you." She paused, glancing away from his blue eyes. "But if you can't do this, then I will have no alternative but to face Bazertari alone."

He wiped his eyes and clasped her hand gently. "Nay, lass. I can't—I can't let you do that." He inhaled with an unsteady breath. "I will be here for you. It's just that after years of evil and fear across the land, it . . . it takes its toll."

Evie smiled softly. "I understand, but we *can* do this."

He gazed at her intensely, his features full of trepidation and doubt. "I don't know, lass."

"We can." Evie gently rested her hand on her chest, near her heart. "I feel it here. We are strong together, Ulric. We defeated Bazertari once and we can *again.*"

He took a momentary glance at her, his features stern. He pulled his hand from hers and started riding, deep in thought. Evie gazed at his broad back hidden beneath his grey cloak and slowly followed, as they continued to head north.

What if the old Sword could not get past his doubt? Her teeth sank into her lip, her throat growing tight. The stubbornness in Ulric's features scared her. This Sword was a stranger to her, he was not the one who would jump at the chance of adventure. *Would I be able to convince him to help? Will I have to face the warlock alone? Could Slan help me?* The way Slan was when she first arrived, his mental state was worse than Ulric's. Even though Garth was alive in this Moonstar, he was the enemy. Her stomach churned as the realisation sunk in. If Ulric could not help her, she would be alone in her quest.

They had been riding for a while when Ulric slowed, looking unwell. Evie rode past him, but then paused when he stopped his horse. She looked back, and asked, "Are you alright?"

He began to say something, then paled and hastily dismounted from his horse, retching on the side of the road.

Evie slowly climbed down from her horse. "Do you need to stop for a while?"

Ulric gave a confirming gesture, as he bent over, his palms resting on his knees, then threw up again. She sighed, knowing he must be suffering after drinking to excess for so long. She walked the horses off the main road and found a clearing in the shrubland. Ulric followed, cradling his tender stomach. When he reached her, she passed him the water bottle.

He took a large gulp, rinsing his mouth out, spitting the water on the grass. Then had some to drink as he gradually lowered himself to the ground. "I just need a moment." He glanced at her, his features looking less placid, but he was sweating a lot. He said, "Sorry, lass, about my outburst but . . ."

Evie sat on the grass opposite him and smiled softly. "Don't. I understand how all of this has taken its toll on you, and everyone else. But together, we can free this land. Make Moonstar peaceful again."

Ulric took another sip of water. "I just don't know. The odds aren't in our favour."

Evie focused her gaze on him. "But they *are*, Ulric. Bazertari thinks he's unstoppable. But I can stop him. If I can get hold of that bracelet, then I believe I can kill him."

He locked his eyes onto her. "I love your spirit, lass."

"It's more stubbornness, to be honest."

He chuckled and asked, "So, while I wait to stop feeling dizzy, can you tell me about your world?"

With a quick look, Evie observed him as he took some more peppermint leaves to chew on. Then realised she had never had the conversion with this Ulric. She smiled and sat opposite him. "Well, where to begin?"

Ulric took a few deep breaths, cradling his stomach. "Wherever you want, lass. I'm not moving for a while."

She smiled softly and told him about her world.

They reached an inn after a day's slow ride and got a couple of rooms for the night. The inn was quiet, and they took a table towards the rear to chat and for Evie to enjoy a meal, as Ulric's stomach was still in no condition to eat. From talking as they rode; Ulric seemed to have fewer doubts about the task ahead. Evie was also beginning to see the Ulric she was fond of and cherished once more.

As they sat in the inn, she asked, "So, can I ask you something?"

He observed her while he drank water, his hands still trembling. "What do you want to know?"

She shot him an inquisitive glance. "Did you still meet that green-eyed Sword for hire? When I showed you my face, you said, 'my green-eyed girl' and then her name. So, I'm thinking you did?"

Ulric chuckled. "Ahhh. I haven't thought of Lara in years." He studied her. "And aye, in my drunken haze, I thought you were her for a moment. Your eyes are just like hers, but different hair." He glanced down at his drink, clenching his fist, when he saw his hand shaking. His eyes lifted, and he smiled softly. "I met Lara before Garth had taken the post as Guardian. She was a fine woman. I often wondered where she would have got to."

Evie regarded him with affection. "Do you think she was here in Moonstar?"

He shrugged. "If she was, she would have put up a good fight. Lara was a formidable Sword, with experience well beyond her years. If she had been here in Moonstar, she would have been a valuable asset to the Guild."

"So you think she didn't come?"

Ulric pressed his mouth together. "Nay, she didn't. When we were together, I had asked if she wanted to come back with me, but she didn't want to be tied down." He paused, his gaze fixed on the tankard of water in his relaxed hand. "I felt she had had a loss that cut deep, but she would never say. We were both young, so when we parted, I travelled a bit and then came back to Moonstar. Not long after that, Garth won his place as guardian."

Evie smiled, focusing on his eyes, gently touching his hand with affection. "I think we all have at least one loss that cuts deep."

Ulric turned his hand to hold hers. "Aye." He sighed, still looking very ill and exhausted. "We should get some sleep; we have a long way to go yet."

Evie gave a silent agreement, entranced by his piercing blue eyes for a moment. She squeezed his hand and finished her drink. "Shall we meet down here at dawn?"

Ulric gave a slow, affirmative gesture. "Aye. Hopefully, I'll feel a little better."

Evie smiled as they both got to their feet, and walked to their rooms.

Evie sat on her bed studying the Rosh pendant that hung around her neck, the small brass medallion held gently between her fingers. Her mind wandered to the days travelling with Garth. Those were good times. She smiled softly, remembering when they had met Ulric on the road. That had been an eventful evening. She released the pendant and let out a breath. Evie leant back and wiggled her toes, glad to be out of her boots.

Ulric had been such a loud, talkative character then. He was quieter now, but even though it turned sad, it was nice to get him talking about his adventurous past. She attempted to get him to reminisce, as it seemed to bring back the familiar Ulric she treasured.

Evie thought about the Sword called Lara. *Had she been in Moonstar without Ulric's knowledge or had she stayed in Barberium, where Ulric had first encountered her years ago? If she were here, would she even be alive? How many more of the Guild were still out there? Or, like Ulric feared, were most gone?*

Evie stood, pulling off her black trousers, then climbed onto the soft bed, in just her cream shirt, her limbs relaxing in delight. She gazed at the ceiling. Maybe there were not a lot of the Guild left and it could end up just being her and Ulric facing Bazertari. They had done so in the past, and Evie had confidence they could do it again. She bit her lip. Even if it was just her and Ulric, she would try her best to free this land.

TWELEVE

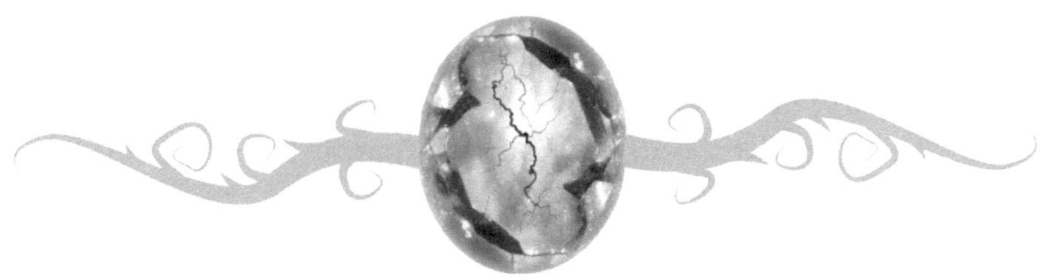

Garth pulled back on the reins, observing tracks that veered towards a cluster of trees on his left. The Sword's breath swirled before him; the mid-afternoon sun provided little relief from the chilly air. Garth twisted in his saddle as he peered from beneath the cover of his dark cloak hood, scrutinising the area. It was not wise to leave the major route; it was a known werewolf patch.

Garth pursed his lips as his gaze returned to the tracks. *Could these belong to the person Slan had teleported?* It was a powerful portal for Bazertari to have sensed it. *So, they aren't from Moonstar. Who had he brought through? A sorcerer? A Sword?* Whoever they were, they would soon realise the mistake Slan had made.

Intrigued, Garth dismounted beside the road, and followed the tracks to the remains of a small campfire. Garth crouched, scrutinising the blackened remnants. The camp was a few days old. His hazel eyes concentrated on the grassy ground; there did not seem to be any evidence of a struggle. Garth had heard how any that stopped round these parts did not live to see another day, or became the one creature they feared.

His eyes narrowed as he examined the ground beyond the charred residue, taking note of a faint circular imprint around the camp area, and smirked. It was a sorcerer that Slan had brought through. He moved and crouched again, examining the pale line with his fingertips. He could always spot the use of a magical shield, which less skilled trackers would have missed. Many of the magic users that he had tracked over the years had used something similar, hoping to be shielded from harm or prying eyes. Perhaps that was why the werewolves refrained from harming the traveller.

Garth stood, focusing on the trees and then at the sky; the light was fading fast. He released a lengthy breath and strolled back to his horse as it became unsettled. It would not be long before the werewolves came out, and he wanted to be as far from the woods as he could. He mounted his horse, and carried on along the major route. He eventually found himself surrounded by the vast expanse of the open moorlands, with darkness creeping in.

Garth sat on his sleeping blanket and chewed a chunk of dry meat, his campfire cracking in the silence of the evening air. He stared at the mountains in the distance, pulling his cloak tighter round him against the chill. Even though he hated Palasses and Flamvile Woods, he did like the open land. He remembered seeing those mountains as he grew up, and how his father used to tell him tales of adventure. He sighed deeply; it had taken years to get over his parents' murder. The Guild used them as bait to draw out Bazertari's followers, then used his family's own guard against them. Even though he had dealt with many members of the Guild after that dreadful day, he still felt he had not been able to avenge his parents fully.

He tightened his lips, wondering if anything came of the farm. He had not been there since their deaths and had no intention of ever doing so. The Guild had occupied it for a time, but with all of them gone, it was probably just falling to ruin. He took a sip of water, contemplating if he should go have a look. He quickly decided it was best to leave it be. He did not have time to reminisce.

Garth leant back on his saddle and admired the stars. It was peaceful away from the cities. He did not have anyone after his attention, not even Bazertari, with his incessant needs. That was what annoyed Garth the most. He was the warlock's general, not his servant. Once he discovered and dealt with whatever Slan was up to, he may reconsider his position. Krif was good as his second, he could be promoted to General of Great Oak. Then Garth could move on. He could see about that position up north. The warlock had informed him that when the time was right, he could have his own outpost, rule a city of his own. Garth smiled softly. He liked that idea.

He used his nail to prise some meat free from between his teeth, directing his focus to the subject at hand. Whoever Slan had teleported would reach Palasses in the next day or two. When he reached the city, he would make Ulric give him the information he needs. Perhaps convince him to explain why he had lied about his parents' deaths.

The old Sword would kill him without a second thought if he could, but Garth wanted to spare Ulric from the torture of the dark dungeon. They had been friends once, and even though they had been enemies for years, Garth could not let Ulric be transformed into one of Bazertari's personal guards. Once Ulric was dead, Garth would then find the stranger and put an end to Slan's plan.

Garth reached Palasses after a couple of days and rode through the busy city to the inn he always used. Cron was about the only innkeeper he could trust. Also, the old man was nosey, so the innkeeper would soon know what was going on in the city. The Sword stopped outside The White Ox and dismounted. The inn sounded rowdy within. As he walked in through the entrance, he was met with the enticing scent of food, the cosy warmth of a blazing fire, and the lively conversations of the customers. It was only mid-afternoon, but the inn was always busy. A handful of people glanced upwards upon his arrival, while others swiftly lowered their heads or exited. It seemed Garth's reputation preceded him.

The Sword approached the main counter and acknowledged Cron with a subtle gesture. The large man's grey hair had receded with the passage of time and his aged features appeared tired. On seeing Garth, he grinned. "Good day, Garth. Your room is always ready."

He leaned on the counter and glanced round as Cron poured his ale. He turned back, taking a big gulp from his drink and inquired, "Where's that drunkard, Ulric, these days?"

"Oh 'im. He's been seen at The Deaf Bard. He always drinks himself into a stupor most nights." Cron lent forward. "Also heard he owes Elmare coin, and she's sent Ronric to collect."

Garth gave a silent agreement, his eyes lingering on a blonde barmaid as she weaved past him with an order. He responded, "Well, Ronric is a fool if he thinks he'll get Elmare's coin back from that drunk." He took another gulp of his ale. "Any news of strangers?"

Cron smirked. "We get many 'ere, Garth."

The Sword pierced him with his gaze, and Cron paled. He said, his voice cold, "I'm not in a fecking mood for your wise cracks, Cron."

The innkeeper swallowed. "Well, there was one. Two days back. They kept their face hidden. Wondered round the city on horseback for a while, like they were lookin' for someone. Heard from Meara that they ended up at The Deaf Bard. Spoke with Ulric for a time in a back room."

Garth raised his dark eyebrow, the sorcerer had found Ulric. He downed his ale and snarled, "I want my horse brushed and fed. I'm off to The Deaf Bard." He went to leave, then turned back to Cron. "I may need to leave in a hurry, so make sure my horse is at the ready."

The innkeeper agreed and barked orders to his stable boy in the back.

Garth walked across the city, taking the side street to The Deaf Bard inn. He always found the name amusing. Their bard was tone deaf, but somehow, he was popular. Garth had been there twice and could have slit the middle-aged man's throat for the noise he made. He let out a breath of relief when he could not hear any caterwauling coming from the inn as he reached it.

The Sword strode in, his eyes scanned the room for the barmaid. She always seemed to gaze at him with doe-like eyes whenever he approached her. If he turned on the charm, he knew she would willingly share all her secrets.

As predicted, the young girl fluttered towards him, giving him a huge grin. "May I 'elp ya, sir?"

He stared intensely at her, her blue dress hugging her curvy figure perfectly, and strode toward the bar counter. "A tankard of your fine ale and some information."

Eagerly nodding, she trailed behind him, heading to the counter. While her father, the innkeeper, dealt with other patrons, she poured Garth a tankard of ale. He gazed at the girl, dazzling her with a grin, ignoring the nervous glances from the customers at the counter.

She placed down a full tankard before him and asked, "What do ya need to know, sir?"

He drank a bit of the ale, and his nose wrinkled. Not the best he had tasted. He shifted his gaze to the young woman, his eyes drawn to her ample bosom. "I heard Ulric likes to drink here."

She replied, licking her lips and gazing at him seductively, "Aye, he does. But he's left the city."

Garth glared at the barmaid with annoyance while placing the tankard back on the counter. "So, he's gone."

The young girl grew nervous as Garth's features suddenly changed from welcoming, to hard, cold stone for a moment. "Aye, yester morn. With a lass."

He arched an eyebrow; it seemed the conversation was not a loss. "A woman?"

"Aye, didn't see her face, though. She kept it hidden." The barmaid giggled. "She could take care of herself though. She were armed, and floored Ulric when they seemed to have a bit of a disagreement. Then me pa helped drag him into the back room where they talked for a while."

Garth leant forward, tracing his fingers across her arm and asked, "About what?"

The girl blushed slightly. "Not sure."

He regarded her, flirting more. "Oh, you must have heard something?"

"Nay, the lass wanted it to be private."

He rested his hand on her arm and smiled. "Anything else?"

"Well, Ulric left in a hurry. Whatever they talked about, he seemed preoccupied when he left."

"Can you tell me more about the girl?" Garth started making gentle circular motions on the girl's arm, noticing the goose bumps raise up on her tanned skin.

The girl gazed at him, her breathing became irregular. "Well, she ain't from these parts."

Garth's eyebrows raised with intrigue, focusing on her hazel eyes. "Really?"

"Aye, pa said he had never heard the accent before. I must agree when I came upon her in the morn having breakfast with Ulric. Though he wasn't eating, think he had a hangover."

Garth regarded the young girl and pursed his lips. "So, they met again?"

"Oh, aye. Ulric was even clean. 'Aven't seen him clean in a while. They spoke in hushed voices. But he'd ordered a food pack from me pa."

Garth wondered what they had spoken about the night before to get Ulric out of his stupor. "So, they intended to leave the city?

"Aye."

"Do you know which way they headed?"

"North, I think. I heard Ulric mention furs. Think they went over to the market to get 'em. Then they came back 'ere for the food pack and went."

Garth inhaled deeply, pulling his hand from the girl's arm and clenched his fist. It could not be good if Ulric had gone with the woman. *Is he planning to take her into hiding? Or potentially even off Moonstar?* He glanced at the amber liquid in his tankard, his taste buds refusing to have to endure anymore. He turned on his heel and left the inn.

Lost in thought as he strode back across the city, he wondered if they were going to try to find other Guild members. Garth knew some of them still lurked about in hiding. He hastened back to the White Ox. He needed to get moving; they were not that far ahead, and he could easily catch up to them. Then he would get some answers.

THIRTEEN

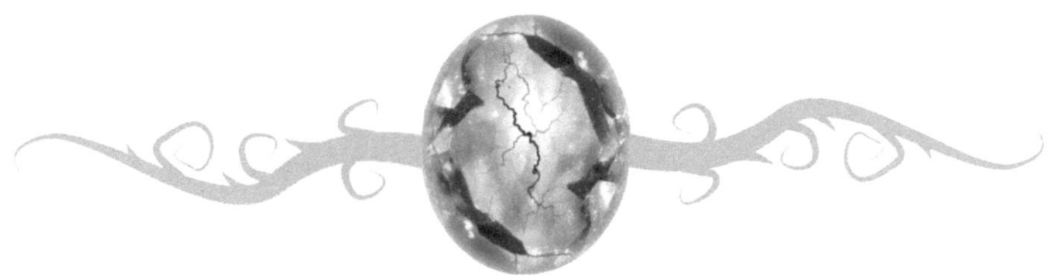

Ulric and Evie continued at dawn from the inn, having had a good night's rest. They had not gone far when Ulric's horse threw a shoe. The Sword cursed and yelled that the blacksmith had ripped him off. Evie watched the spectacle of him pacing by the horse, and learned several profanities she had never heard before.

Still mounted on her own mare, she said, once she could get a word in, "Have you calmed down yet?"

Ulric inhaled and snapped her a look. "I have a good mind to . . ."

Evie sighed, "There's nothing you can do, Ulric. To go back wouldn't be wise."

He stopped pacing and observed the horse's front hoof with the thrown shoe. He then gazed up the road and rubbed his chin. He said, "If I remember right, there's a hamlet close to here."

"There's a blacksmith there?"

"Aye." He turned to her. "And a tavern."

She frowned, "Ulric, I—"

He cut her off, "Nay lass. My ale days are over. I'm thinking about yourself. Then you don't have to wait out in this cold."

She smiled, looking at the frost covered trees. It had turned bitter overnight and somewhere warm to wait sounded inviting. "Alright then. Lead the way."

Evie dismounted, and they walked up the primary route, then took a side track to the hamlet.

As Ulric had promised, it was not far and it had a small tavern. There were a few cottages, and the blacksmith was just to the north behind the dwellings. When they stopped outside the tavern, Ulric stated he would not be long. Evie watched him continue up the track and past the cottages, then tied her horse up and ventured in.

The tavern was small and cosy, a raging fire kept the afternoon chill at bay. There were just a few people present, and each one observed Evie with suspicion until she found a seat at the rear. Catching the barmaid's eye, the young girl walked over and took Evie's order.

Evie sampled the mulled wine. The little she had drank had taken the chill from her bones after the ride and walk. She gazed down at the red liquid, a hint of cinnamon invading her nostrils. Her mind focused on Ulric. She was still getting used to this version of the Sword that she had once known well. She had never thought she would ever see him so scared; but then again, everyone seemed broken. No wonder he had lost himself to drink over the past few years. Last night and today, he seemed to be a little back to his old self, even if still hungover. With the task ahead, she hoped he would still be the formidable Sword she needed.

Someone sat down opposite her at the table, breaking her thoughts. Evie glanced up smiling, expecting Ulric. Her smile dropped as she took in a sharp breath. Her eyes welled, fixated on the hazel ones before her, but they were not the ones she knew and loved.

Evie realised she was shaking and quickly moved her head downwards, hiding her shocked expression of seeing Garth sitting before her, breathing. Keeping her eyes under the shade of her hood, she continued to gaze at him. He was so young, only in his early thirties. Her eyes were drawn to the jagged scar across his left cheek, and she pondered about its origin. It was strange to see him with his dark hair cut short and no braid of his Guild status that he had worn with pride.

Evie tried to calm her breathing as Garth peered back at her, trying to see her features as she kept her head at a downward angle. He sneered. "People who hide their faces are not to be trusted."

Evie shrugged, her voice failing her. His deep, dulcet tones, made her heart flutter in recognition. She felt sick, she knew she would have faced him eventually, but had hoped she would have been more prepared. As she glanced up at the Sword, she finally grasped the true meaning behind Slan and Ulric's words. This was not *her* Garth.

He snapped, looking impatient, "Are you dumb?"

She breathed in slowly to compose herself, and murmured, "No."

He leant forward, striving to see her facial features, but Evie kept her head slightly angled down, leaning back in her seat. "Just want to drink my wine in peace."

Garth smiled as if about to leave, then with lightning speed, reached out and yanked her hood back, exposing her head. Evie gasped, not expecting such a move, and glared at him, trying to hide her emotional state.

Garth leered at her. "Well, well. I can see why you're trying to stay hidden." He glanced around the almost empty inn. He added, as his eyes rolled slowly down her body. "A woman alone."

Her eyes locked on him, biting back the tears welling in her eyes, when the man she had loved so dearly held no recollection of her in his eyes. *Not the Garth I knew.* She repeated in her head.

Garth continued to regard her, and Evie was unnerved by his icy stare. She stood up, but Garth leapt to his feet and jumped into the aisle, blocking her way. His athletic frame towered over her. His voice came out menacing, "Oh nay, nay. Not yet, pretty. I want to chat a little longer."

He stood over her and waited. Evie remained frozen and gazed across at the occupants of the inn. Everyone appeared frightened and averted their gaze, unwilling to be involved.

Garth smiled, glancing to where her eyes were lingering. "Nay one is going to help you. You're all mine." His voice hardened. "Now *sit!*"

Evie did as he ordered, her fists clenched. She would play along for the time being, but if he tried anything, she would defend herself. Once she was seated, Garth adjusted his chair to block her view of the room and sat back down opposite her. His chosen position also blocked the gap between him and the next table. He moved the chair next to her with his outstretched foot, and rested his right leg on it, blocking her from the aisle. For her to leave, she would have to move his leg and push past him or jump over the table. He had ensured she was trapped, his captive.

Garth smiled. "Good girl." He regarded her. "I don't recognise your accent, so I suspect you're not from around here."

She responded coldly, sensing unease as he leered at her. "From overseas."

He tightened his lips. "Few *come* to Moonstar these days."

Evie smiled coldly. She went to have a small sample of her wine but noticed her hand shaking. Clenching her fist, she pulled her hand back onto her lap. Garth had seen the movement and reacted with scepticism.

He shifted his attention back to her green eyes. "So, what brings you to our fine land?"

"The sights."

Garth chuckled. "Wit and beauty." He leant forward, his eyes glancing towards her chest, and the gap in her shirt, where the amulet of Rosh hung. He concentrated his eyes on it for a few moments before looking back at her eyes. "What business do you have here?"

Her gaze fell upon his distrustful, cold, hard features. *What happened to the man I loved?*

"Just travelling."

He quirked an eyebrow, glancing back at her pendant. "A follower of Rosh, I see."

Evie took hold of the goblet placed before her and took a slow sip, hoping the wine would steady her nerves, and shrugged.

Garth eyed the sword propped up against the wall behind her. "If you are a Sword for hire, you must have registered your services in Palasses."

"Why, so you can keep track of me?"

Garth smirked. "As a protector of this land, I like to make sure nay one will cause any trouble."

She turned her attention to him. "Why would you presume I would cause trouble?"

Evie detected Garth's left leg lightly touching hers. He leant further forward as his hand brushed her knee. He breathed, "From the look of that sword and your stance, I think you need to make sure you're fighting on the right side."

Evie pressed her teeth into her lower lip. To have Garth touching her again made her body respond with pure delight. But when she focused on his cold eyes, her stomach tightened in fear. That was not the touch of a gentle lover and knew she had to get herself out of that situation. *But could I really kill him?* Evie tried to keep her voice calm. "I am on the right side."

She saw movement behind Garth, which broke her thoughts, but she did not move or look at Ulric, who had joined them. Instead, she kept her eyes on Garth's, avoiding alerting him. The cruel Sword stiffened when a dagger jabbed in between his shoulder blades. The touch of his hand on her knee lifted.

Ulric growled, "She's not interested."

Garth smiled and slowly turned his head towards the larger man, trying not to move too much because of the dagger. "Well, if it isn't the *old* man. Thought you'd be passed out in a puddle of vomit, in some shack of a tavern."

Ulric responded coldly, keeping the dagger firmly in Garth's back as he pulled out the stool next to him, "I sobered up."

Garth winced as Ulric pushed the dagger harder between his shoulder blades as the larger man sat.

Evie hastened, knowing what Ulric was about to do, "Ulric, *no*. I want to talk to him."

Garth swiftly glanced between the two, eventually fixing his gaze on Evie. "So, you're the one Slan brought over."

Ulric snarled, "She is."

Garth frowned, ignoring the large man and studying Evie. He asked, "*Who* are you?"

There was only one choice to make. Evie slowly exposed her bracelet, letting Garth have a good look at it. "Look familiar?"

He studied it, confusion on his face. He looked back up, glaring at her. After a few moments, realisation filled his eyes. "But I *killed* you."

Evie stared at him. It felt as though she had been struck by a truck. Her heart stuck in her throat; her chest tight. She wanted to throw up. The man who had loved her so much was her killer. She glanced at Ulric; his features had paled, but more in shock that she had not known the full truth.

Ulric growled, "I should kill you for what you *did*."

Evie clenched her fists. She had to stay focused, otherwise, Ulric may kill Garth where he sat. She leant forward, quickly stating, "*No*. I want Garth to *know*."

He directed his attention towards her, the point of the dagger still at Garth's back. "Evie, he's not the Garth, *you* know."

Garth smirked, glancing between the two. Adjusting his position slightly as Ulric's pressure on the dagger lessened. "The old fool thinks he's found a way." He directed his gaze towards Evie and regarded her with disdain. "So, you're an alternative traveller."

Evie responded, "Yes, one that destroyed Bazertari."

Garth laughed. "Nay one can defeat him. I'll kill you like I did the other one. Slice your stomach open and let all your guts fall out."

Leaning forward, Evie focused on him. She sensed the bile attempting to rise up her throat, but she had to maintain control. The reality of what Slan and Ulric had warned her about sank in. She needed to stay strong. "On the Moonstar I went to, I defeated Bazertari with you and Ulric by my side."

Garth darted his eyes between the two of them, his face hard. "Impossible. I would *never* work for the Guild. They're murderers and deserve everything I did to them."

On her Moonstar, Garth had fought the grief over his parents' deaths and won, but here, with Morag's influence at the right time, he seemed overwhelmed by it and had lost. She had to convince him. Evie stole a quick glance at Ulric and chewed her lip. She had shared her memories with him, and it had worked. If nothing else, it might make him question what he knew, and maybe disorient him for a while so they could get away. It was a risk she had to take.

She turned to Ulric. "Hold his arm."

Ulric grabbed Garth's arm and slammed it onto the table and clamped his large hand over Garth's lean forearm, keeping it firmly against the wooden surface. Garth attempted to break free, but Ulric pressed his dagger deeper into his back, the tip of the blade slicing into his flesh. Garth winced and glared at Ulric when the older man snarled, "This is gonna *feck* you up."

Evie laid her hand on top of Garth's rough, tanned one. The bracelet resting gently on the back of his fingers. Her skin prickled at their touch like it would with the Garth she knew. When his gaze met hers, she observed him briefly hesitate. She briefly wondered if he experienced it as well.

The bracelet glowed and, as she did with Ulric, she shared all her memories of her time on Moonstar. She gasped as his hatred and fear surged into her like a tidal wave. Her cheeks grew wet with the flow of tears. Her gaze locked on his hazel eyes, witnessing the shock and disbelief as he saw her memories, and the tears welled in his own eyes. Ulric let go of the young Sword's arm and pulled the dagger away, as Garth sat frozen to the spot, lost in Evie's spell as she shared it all.

Once done, Evie let go of his hand. Briefly, Evie was overwhelmed by what she had seen from Garth. Her tear-filled eyes focused on him as he sat there, frozen. Then Garth jumped to his feet, staggering back, his expression slack, his eyes unfocused. He appeared disoriented, uncertain of his whereabouts. He glared at Evie. "Not possible." Then turned and ran from the tavern.

Ulric went to follow, but Evie, wiping her eyes, said in a rough whisper, "No, let him go. He won't bother us for a while."

He turned his attention towards her. "Are you sure?"

She nodded, experiencing a surge of anger washing over her as she wrestled to control the emotions that had originated from Garth.

Ulric slowly sat opposite her. "Was that wise?"

Evie shrugged, trying to look unfazed by what had just happened, in what she had seen of Garth's memories. "No, but I had to try something." She looked at Ulric. "He may be evil, but I couldn't kill him."

Ulric sighed, looking across the tavern at the doorway where Garth had fled. "Well, I could."

She picked up the goblet of wine, her mouth suddenly dry, her hand shaking, and took a sip.

Ulric saw her hand and gently touched it. "Evie?"

She glanced in his direction and offered a gentle smile. "I'll be okay. When I share memories, it goes both ways."

Ulric studied her with concern. "You seemed alright after you did it with me."

Evie shrugged. "I saw your memories, but somehow Garth's were more . . . intense."

He asked, concern in his features, "Do you need to rest?"

She took a big gulp of the wine. "No, just a drink."

Evie glanced at Ulric while attempting to remain composed. She felt sick, her mind shell shocked. The connection with Garth had been so intense, and she wondered why.

Was it because of our connection from before? That had been a strong connection that almost seemed fated. With that, would the connection in sharing memories be stronger? Or had he been so tortured and fuelled by anger for so long it made his emotions so much more heightened?

She breathed in deeply, still trying to regain some control, and not succumb to the unsettling sensation that overwhelmed her core. She sensed her whole body shaking, the rush of emotions from Garth almost overpowering her. His anger over years of torment had hit her hard. She gulped down more of the wine, glancing at Ulric. Evie did not want to alarm him. Even though he was not saying anything, she could see the concern in his eyes.

Garth ran from the inn, mounted his horse, and galloped away from the hamlet as quickly as possible. Everything became a blur around him as the stallion galloped at a phenomenal speed. He gave his head a quick shake, trying to clear it. It was just a witch's trick. They were trying to make sure he could not follow them. He focused on his hand holding the reins, the one she had touched; his skin had prickled like a faded memory. He glanced back toward the hamlet. The tavern had already faded away in the distance. She was more than just an alternative traveller; he had suspected that she would be a sorceress, but not such a powerful one.

More memories flooded his head. Garth closed his eyes, trying to clear them. He released his grip on the reins and grabbed his temples, trying to stop all the emotions that were overpowering him. He screamed in agony as a sharp object pierced his mid-section, then he hunched over and fell from his horse, tumbling over the ground. For a moment, he laid there, gasping, staring at the sky. He had experienced his own death!

Garth sat up on the side of the road, his horse already disappeared into the distance, and sobbed, sensing Evie's grief following his death. He wiped his eyes angrily.

What's wrong with me? I am Bazertari's general, feared throughout the land!

Garth turned to glare back at the road, then looked to where his horse had gone. He should go back there and kill them both. He cursed as more memories flooded to the surface. Garth needed to know what they were planning. *If she was the traveller, they would try to get the bracelet at Great Oak, but why were they heading north?*

Garth looked ahead, and sobbed again as more grief overwhelmed him. He hit the side of his head with the heel of his palm and staggered to his feet. Garth moved his head and glanced in the direction he had travelled. He needed to follow them. Find out what their next move was. Garth strode up the road; he needed his stallion back first. He had covered too much distance to reach the tavern before they left. Garth made a sharp whistle, certain the horse would hear it, as it was not enchanted for nothing. He inhaled deeply in an effort to suppress more memories, and glared up the road. He would follow them, they may expose more Guild members. Then he would kill them all.

FOURTEEN

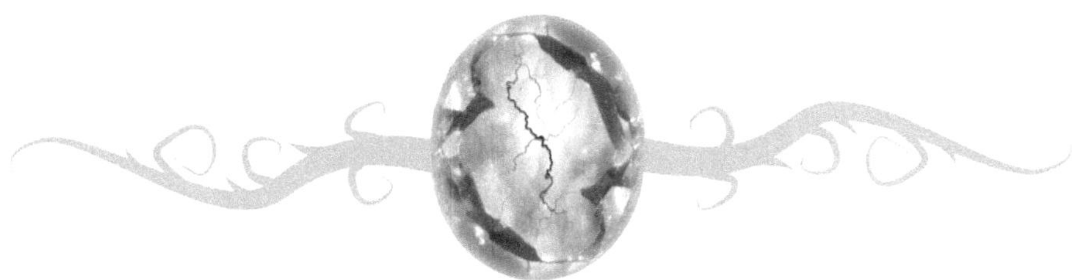

In the tavern, Ulric watched intently as Evie sipped from a second goblet of wine, her cheeks regaining their colour. He concentrated on her hand as she put down the goblet, noting the slight tremor in the fingers. When she had broken the connection with Garth, Ulric had never seen her look so pale. Whatever she had seen from Grath's memories had affected her more than she was telling him.

Ulric sensed the tightness in his shoulders, his body twitched. When Garth confessed to murdering the traveller, Ulric was taken aback by the shock on Evie's face. It seemed Slan had chosen to keep information that everyone already knew to himself. His eyes travelled to the entrance, wanting to leave the tavern, find Garth, and strike him down. Evie had advised him to let it be, which contradicted his better judgement. The Sword inhaled through his nose. It had not been ideal facing Garth so soon, and it made him think more about trying to get Evie off this god forsaken continent. Since the conversation shortly after leaving Palasses, Ulric had not raised his misgivings over her plan to face Bazertari. Garth knew of her now, and the young Sword would soon want her dead. Travelling to Great Oak would be far more dangerous.

Ulric regarded Evie. She was a tough girl, and it seemed she had learnt some time ago that she would have to rely on herself. Ulric would not say anything, but vowed to Rosh that he would make sure she would always be safe. Even if that meant giving her false hope in her quest and then smuggling her on a ship, away from Moonstar.

Ulric raised an eyebrow and observed Evie intently as she stared into her goblet of wine, lost in her own thoughts. He said, breaking the silence between them, "You know he'll follow us."

Evie's head moved in a slow, affirmative motion, her gaze still locked onto the wine. She then took another sip, almost draining it. Wiping her lips with the back of her hand, she held Ulric's gaze and asked, "How did he find us so fast?"

Ulric laced his fingers together on the table, trying to loosen the tension in his shoulders. "As Bazertari's general, he has an enchanted horse. So, he can travel vast distances in less than half the time. Someone would have informed him I left the city with a stranger, and he chased after us."

She sighed, "Well, I'm hoping those memories will confuse him for a while. But I suspect he's an excellent tracker."

"Aye," snorted Ulric. "I trained him. That would be how he found us."

Evie studied Ulric, the light-headedness and sickness she had felt in the pit of her stomach fading. She glanced down at the empty goblet, her mind becoming hazy from the alcohol. She was still getting flashes from Grath's memories, but was gaining a firm hold in controlling them.

Taking a deep breath, she directed her gaze back up at the Sword. "You won't like this, but I'm going to use magic to cover our tracks. We need to find this other Guild member and then return to Great Oak."

Ulric sighed, "Alright, but we leave now, while he's unable to process what you've done to him." He pressed his lips together, thinking for a moment, then added, "This will add five days to our journey, but I think it wise to head across the country, away from Kerlish and then take the ferry crossing at Channel Neck. From there, we can double back."

Evie agreed. "Okay, that makes sense. And with no tracks to follow, it'll delay him, hopefully."

Ulric eyed her. "You know you just fecked this Garth up and have fuelled his anger."

She shook her head as she stood. "No. I think it'll give him doubts. I felt his pain, Ulric. I think this will make him question if he's on the right side."

The Sword watched her intently as they departed from the tavern. "I hope you're right, lass."

The two mounted their horses and Evie cast a spell, ensuring their horses left no trail. They cantered away from the main road and set off across the country.

Evie pulled on her horse's reins, looking out through the blizzard conditions. The river ahead of them was a churning mass of freezing water. She turned towards Ulric as he halted beside her. "Is this the ferry crossing?"

He responded, his face hidden under his hood, "Aye." He dismounted, landing on the ground almost silently in the ankle-deep snow, then added, "The ferryman will be at a tavern in the town keeping warm. I'll ring the bell, but we'll have to wait for him."

Evie gave a silent agreement, keeping her eyes on Ulric as he rang the large bell by the dockside. His large frame looked enormous with the furs round his broad shoulders. She dismounted, pulling her furs further round her. Even with them over her thick black cloak, she was still shivering from the bitter cold of the early evening. She tucked her gloved hands further under her cloak, her fingertips feeling like icicles from holding the reins. The biting nature of the weather was still seeping through to her joints.

Ulric's large cloak engulfed her, and he said, "Here, share my body warmth for a while. Once at Channel Neck, we can get hot food and a warm bed."

Evie snuggled up to him under his cloak and responded, "And a hot bath."

Ulric cast a brief glance at her. "That can be arranged."

She smiled, experiencing the heat of his body, reminiscent of a furnace. His powerful arm round her shoulders made her feel safe, reminding her of her first night out under the stars with Garth all those years ago.

The sound of a bell rang out, echoing through the blizzard towards them.

"That's the ferryman," announced Ulric.

Evie sighed, exposed to the harsh weather once more, when Ulric strode toward his horse. She grabbed her horse's reins and stepped closer to the water's edge.

A few moments later, a flatbed ferry docked that was large enough to hold a horse and cart, as well as three more horses and their dismounted riders. Both ends gave access to the open decks with a low barrier on the longer sides to give the passengers and cargo some security from falling overboard. Along the centre spanning the length of the ferry was a thick chain that was part of a simple pulley system. The chain disappeared into the water at each end and was secured somewhere deep below the water's surface.

All the two could see of the tall ferryman standing in the centre of the ferry next to the chain, was a bundle of a cloak and furs. He peered out from beneath his dark hood, his breath billowing before him, signs of an impressive beard poking out. "This is not a day to travel, my friends."

Ulric nodded and shook the man's hand as the two boarded. Ulric responded, "Nay, think my fingers are icicles, along with other things."

The ferryman gave a quick laugh. "Nay, usually that shrinks to nothing."

The two men's laughter at the crude joke soon ceased when the horses became skittish as the ferry rocked and butted against the dock from the force of the water. Ulric patted the neck of his, whispering to it, Evie doing the same with hers.

Ulric said, once the horses were settled aboard, "We're looking forward to hot food and fine ale."

The large man chuckled as he grabbed the pulley again, and the ferry made its way across the river once more. "Aye, the inn isn't too busy and the fires are raging."

Ulric patted the man on his back as the ferry rocked from the river's current. "That'll be a welcome sight."

FIFTEEN

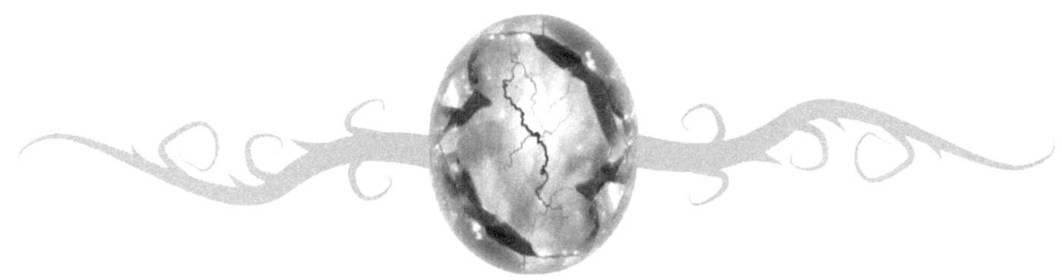

As they moved away from the ferry, they strolled alongside their horses through the small town towards the inn. Ulric chatted a little with the ferryman as he walked back with them. The steep, winding streets were quiet, from the lateness of the day and the bitter winter weather. Evie trudged along by Ulric's side, listening to the ferryman when he told Ulric an amusing story of a trader's cart and a spirited horse that was afraid of water. She gazed ahead, seeing windows lit by candlelight glowing in the softly falling snow since the blizzard had eased. Evie was overwhelmed with exhaustion and could only think about finding a comfortable bed to sleep in.

Evie smiled with relief when she saw the inn, aptly named The Ferry Man, ahead. Ulric said a farewell to the ferryman as he entered the inn to get warm. Ulric followed Evie as they took their horses to the stables at the back. Once the horses were unsaddled and settled, the two took their belongings and swords. They ventured into the warm, inviting inn where two enormous fireplaces were raging, keeping the freezing weather at bay. Evie chose a table by a fireplace at one end of the room, while Ulric headed to the counter to order rooms, food, ale and water.

Evie stood with her back to the fire, welcoming the warmth to her chilled bones. She took off her furs as she watched Ulric chatting to the innkeeper. She stared at him. The Ulric she remembered from her last visit seemed to have returned, and she found comfort in seeing the man she had cared for almost back to his old self. She thought about his cloak around her at the ferry port and she smiled softly. She had not thought she would have savoured his embrace so much. On the Moonstar from before, she had become very close with that Ulric during those last few days. It seemed like such a long time ago, but she still remembered Ulric's kiss on that final night. She sighed, chewing her lip. This was a different Ulric, and Evie knew it was sensible to focus on the task at hand and not the what-ifs.

Once she was warm enough, she took a seat at the table as Ulric approached, carrying his saddle bag and two tankards. He smiled as he placed the tankards down on the table, and removed his furs and cloak. Then he went and stood by the fire, warming his chilled hands. He gave a brief glance at Evie as she took a sip of the ale he had placed before her. "I have ordered stew for us both. Also, rooms and asked for a bath to be prepared in yours."

Evie turned towards him as he returned to the table and sat opposite her. She smiled. "Thank you. Don't you need a bath too, to help get warm?"

Ulric chuckled as he tasted his water. "Nay lass. I'll be fine."

The barmaid came over with two steaming bowls of stew, spoons and the keys to their rooms. She stated, as she put the bowls and spoons down, "The bath will be ready by the time you've eaten. I've asked me pa to set up the bath in the Bowline room. The other room, the Reef Knot, is next door."

Ulric beamed a big grin at the girl, making her blush. "Thank you, lass."

She inclined her head and quickly left. Evie laughed a little; even in his fifties, Ulric seemed to have a way with the ladies.

He briefly glanced in her direction and asked, "What?"

"You made that poor girl blush."

"All I said was thank you."

Evie eyed him. "You have no idea the power of that smile of yours, Ulric."

He arched his brow and chuckled, then beamed a smile at Evie. She rested her hand on her chest, faking a swoon. "Oh, Ulric."

He erupted into laughter, his entire chest vibrating. Her eyes locked onto him, smiling, glad after such a hard ride they could relax enough to joke. The Sword stared at her momentarily, still chuckling. Their eyes locked, Evie again remembered the intimate moments they had shared before she had to return. It had been bad timing, but deep down Evie had always wondered. She quickly pulled her eyes away, the aroma of the stew making her stomach rumble. As soon as their gazes broke, Ulric also shifted his concentration to the stew.

The two ate in silence until Ulric glanced up, and stated, "It isn't far to Kerlish from here. I know who I can ask about Irric, and they can be trusted."

His eyes met hers as she lifted her gaze towards him, her body no longer experiencing coldness from the ride.

Evie asked, "Do you think he will help?"

"Aye. It's been a few years since I've seen him. If he is the Sword I remember, I believe he will."

She smiled. "I hope so." She hesitated and stared at him. "Do you think we can find any others?"

Uric shrugged, scraping his bowl clean, then said, "That, I don't know, lass. So many had scattered and now, after such a long time, I don't know if I can find them. Irric may know, but nay one in the Guild knew all the members or where they were located. Then, when everyone scattered, information was lost. Slan helped till he had to go into hiding. By then, with all the chaos, it was everyone for themselves."

Evie nodded. "I understand. So, it may just be the three of us."

"Aye, but if I can't convince Irric, then it may end up being just the two of us." He paused, eyeing her. "But after crossing paths with Garth, I still think that I should find you a ship and get you off the continent."

Evie sighed, her brow frowning, "No Ulric. I can't leave Moonstar when I am the sole person capable of stopping this."

He inhaled deeply. "But how will you do that when ya dead?"

"It won't come to that."

Ulric moved his head from side to side. "Nay lass. You haven't seen what I have. Garth and his men, they were relentless. The death squads that Bazertari sent out . . ."

Evie swallowed. "Death squads?"

"Aye, they slaughtered most of the Guild. Garth himself, killed the key members."

She leant forward, grabbing his clenched fist. "Like I said, it won't come to that."

Ulric inhaled deeply and shook his head. "Lass, you're foolish to think that. I think, regardless if we see Irric or not, I should get you on a ship and out of here."

Evie stared angrily at him. "*No, Ulric!* I will not do that."

Ulric made an irritated sigh, "Lass, it won't work."

"Listen Ulric, I can take care of myself. Whatever they throw at us."

His eyes narrowed, his voice full of scepticism, "Enough to kill Garth?"

"I—"

He snorted. "Thought not! Evie, you saw him at that inn. I saw the look in your eyes. You know he is nay longer the man you knew."

She glanced away from him, pulling her hand away. "I know, but I don't think I could kill him." She raised her eyes towards him. "We can save this land *and* help him understand his mistakes."

Ulric grasped her hand again and looked at her. "I've been trying to save this land for years, Evie. There was a time when I also had hope for Garth. You must understand, when something has nay hope, then you need to let it go."

Evie said, her face full of optimism, "But you didn't have me. I *know* I can wield that spell. I *know* I can destroy Bazertari."

Ulric sighed, "But at what cost?"

She smiled softly. "We *must* try. Even though I'm scared to death of having to face that warlock, I will do it. I'm more powerful now than I was last time, Ulric." She squeezed his hand. "Like I've been telling you, I'm capable of looking after myself."

He fixated on her eyes, losing himself in their depths. "Aye, but even a powerful sorceress like yourself still needs someone to look out for them."

Evie grinned. "That's what I have you for."

They gazed at each other. Ulric let out a sigh and showed agreement with a slow movement of his head. "Alright, we'll talk to Irric. But promise me, if the odds are stacked too high, you let me get you away from here."

Evie took a profound breath and turned her attention to him. "I promise."

He patted her hand, looking at her for a few moments. Evie could sense his lack of conviction. She hoped that when he saw Irric, he would see it her way.

Ulric then glanced at her half full bowl of stew. "Eat up, lass. Get that bath and an early night."

She smiled and carried on eating her food while Ulric leant back and surveyed the inn. She directed her eyes towards him, as his gaze was elsewhere. *What if he is still adamant about getting me off Moonstar? What would I do then?* Evie looked at her stew. She did not like the idea, but knew if she could not convince him, then she would have to do it alone. Sneak out in the dead of night, if she had to, and get as much distance from him as she could. She could not help but look back at him as he savoured a sip of his water. He would follow her; Evie was sure of that, and by then, he would be obligated to help.

Once she had finished her meal, Evie bid Ulric a good night and headed to her room. She had to contemplate what the Sword had told her about the ship and Garth. Also, she needed to have a plan in place if Ulric decided not to help. When she entered the room, and saw the steaming water of the bath, she pushed all her concerns to the side and quickly undressed and climbed in. Her aching limbs tingled in delight.

The fire and hot stew already warmed her, but the bath was still welcoming. Sitting in the bath relaxed, she finally had the time to process her conversation with Ulric and the memories from Garth. She sighed deeply, deciding to focus on the memories first. She examined them more closely than she had dared during the previous days. Tears streamed down her cheeks as she experienced Garth's pain and anger.

While they rode, Evie had tried to understand why Ulric's memories had not had such an effect on her. She had sensed his pain and fear, but in contrast to Garth's, they were not as intense. The only thing that made sense was Garth's, and hers, destined connection. Perhaps, despite love not blossoming between them, the connection remained strong. That had to be why the experience had been so overwhelming. She tried not to focus too much on it all, but still saw a flash of her face, tear ridden and full of fear. Then his dagger cut into her mid-section again, causing agony to shoot through hers. Tears rolled down her face when she felt his cold detachment as he severed her hand and took the bracelet from her dead body. She paused, wondering why Slan never told her. *Would I have done anything different had I been told?*

She wondered how Garth was processing the memories. *Would they make him think differently?* There was so much hatred in his soul, she could only hope it changed something. She sighed, worrying what she would do if they crossed paths again and there was no choice but to kill him. Ulric had asked her earlier if she could do it, and she knew she lacked the ability to strike a killing blow, but Ulric would do so without a moment's hesitation.

She shut her eyes, attempting to stifle the sobs she sensed in the pit of her stomach. She needed to give her full attention to the task at hand and use Garth's memories to their advantage.

Maybe that would convince Ulric to face Bazertari. If not, would I be willing to run, like Ulric hopes I will? She nervously nibbled on her lower lip. *Then why would Slan bring me here if, like Ulric believes, there is no hope? Is Slan hoping, like I am, that the Ulric I had known will return and want to ride to Great Oak and deal with the evil man?*

Evie took a deep breath and submerged herself under the water, wanting her mind to stop racing. Then Evie climbed out of the bath and dried herself off. She had a few minutes' respite while submerged, her mind had stopped for just a few moments.

Putting her shirt back on, she knew she had to finish sorting Garth's memories. She shuffled under the covers of the bed, getting comfortable. Then she concentrated on them and began delving through them carefully. If Bazertari trusted him as a general, then Garth would know where the bracelet was kept. If she found the exact location, maybe she could convince Ulric. She smiled softly, finally seeing where the bracelet was located at Great Oak. It was in a room cluttered with other trophies the warlock had taken over the years. Not in a vault, as Slan had believed.

She lifted her eyes to the ceiling, struggling to regain control of her emotions. Evie just needed to stop experiencing all of Garth's anger and pain. It was overwhelming, but intertwined within that was something else. There was also a distaste for Bazertari. His conflicting feelings towards the warlock indicated Garth had not completely been lost. Perhaps, over time they could convince him to return to their side.

It would take Garth some time to comprehend all of it, and Evie hoped it would give him some doubts. She just did not know if it would end up positive or negative for her and Ulric. She had taken a gamble and hoped it paid off. She worriedly gnawed on her lip, thinking of Ulric again. He was so frustrated at her when she told him not to go after Garth, and she knew how much Ulric despised his once close friend. Evie just hoped that it would not cloud his judgement if they were going to head toward Great Oak. The fact that Garth was pursuing them, meant that they would come across him again. If so, then she may have to decide on the one thing she was dreading.

SIXTEEN

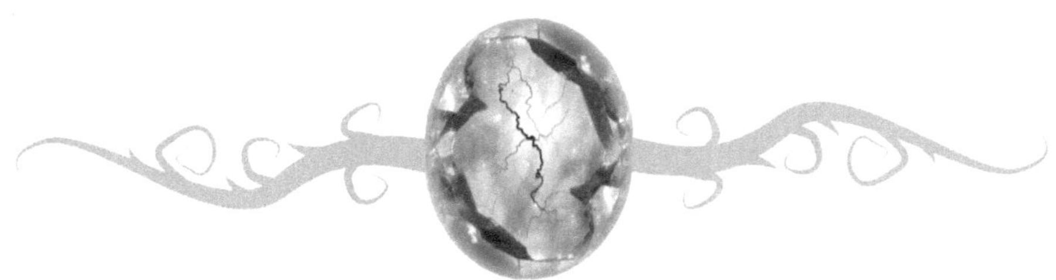

Garth cursed; he had lost them. He glanced over his shoulder towards the main road, his breath swirling in the freezing night air. If he had got his head cleared sooner, and if his stallion had not been reluctant to heed his call, he could have followed them. Whatever that sorceress had done, it had taken Garth a while to get focused again. By the time he returned to the tavern, both were gone.

He stood up, brushing his black trousers down and cursed again. The barmaid at The Deaf Bard only knew they were heading north. Then, at the hamlet later that evening, the locals just said northwest. His instincts told him they had changed course to go across the country to lose him, and they had succeeded. He knew the route they would take; it was one he had used before and it would end up at the crossing at Channel Neck. He looked up at the billowing clouds; the weather was on the turn, and it was not worth the risk in trying to follow them.

Garth was convinced that their destination was Kerlish. There had been rumours a few years ago of Guild activity in the city, and surmised that Ulric must still have contacts there. Garth would see what his informants knew in the city and get them to keep their eyes open.

He calmly approached his horse and mounted it. His mind wandered again to the memories that Evie had shown him. He took a deep breath; he needed to concentrate. One thing was for sure, when he found them, he would kill Ulric, but Evie was going to answer some of his questions. If she resisted, he had a way to loosen her tongue. If nothing else, he would persuade her to undo what she had done to him. Garth had another flash of Evie gazing at him as they both laughed. He inhaled deeply, understanding what Ulric meant now about fecking him up.

He tightened his lips as he pondered if he should take Evie back to Bazertari, but he did not want the warlock to know what she had done. He was determined that Bazertari would not find out they had compromised him. If he did, then Garth would end up imprisoned in the dark dungeon and turned into something else. He would never let that happen. It would be very easy to ensure this Evie did not make it either. All Bazertari needed to know was the knowledge that there was no threat to his rule. The details of who Evie was would not matter, especially if she was dead. He had killed one traveller, killing another would not be hard, and even though brutal, it was a far better outcome than what Bazertari would do to her.

Garth turned his horse back towards the major route and headed north. He gazed upwards at the dark night sky. At least he would arrive at Kerlish in a few days on his enchanted horse. He egged his horse into a gallop, and soon the surrounding scenery became a blur.

Garth reached the walled city of Kerlish by late morning after just a couple of days. Despite the bitter weather and snowfall, traders and travellers still crowded the road to the main gate. A group of rough and ready men stood on guard and kept the high red brick walls well fortified.

Garth gave a quick nod to them as he rode through the gates; the men watching all who entered with suspicious eyes. The city was rough, with several skirmishes a day, and not a place to wander about at night. That meant there was always a firm presence of the guards in the city, yet, most of the time they were the ones making the trouble. Garth did not mind. The men served a purpose. They were his eyes and ears and paid careful attention to the rival gangs in the city.

Nokon, the alpha, was in charge of the men. Garth did not trust demons, but the werewolves could hide in plain sight and be able to track almost anyone. Garth also liked to keep Nokon on his toes, making him understand that his power could easily be taken away. And to a werewolf alpha, that was a bigger threat than anything else.

Garth rode through the city, heading straight for Nokon's home. He had arrived ahead of Ulric and Evie, giving him time to prepare and make sure that Nokon's pack were alert. They had spies within most of the rival gangs, and if they did not, they watched those patches closely. When Ulric and Evie arrived, Garth would know quick enough.

As he arrived at a tall building with white columns, he approached the large oak door and pushed it open. The werewolves would not like him just barging in, but they could not do anything about it. He strolled along the main corridor between walls covered with different swords. They had been up on display for years and he wondered if they belonged to the alpha or the previous tenants.

He walked into the alpha's study. The dark-haired man gave him a fierce look. "Just stroll in, why don't ya!"

Garth smirked at him without emotion and took the seat opposite of where Nokon sat. "I need your men, Nokon."

Nokon glared at him, then slowly agreed. Garth smiled. The alpha hated him, but also knew it was smart not to refuse him. Garth glanced around the room. He needed a drink and noticed a bottle of alcohol. Getting up, he walked over and poured himself one. He noticed the look of disdain on Nokon's face again, but the alpha said nothing.

Garth took a hefty sip and turned back to the large man. "I need your men to keep an eye open for a couple of people. They'll know of one. Ulric. He's travelling with a red-headed woman." He paused, looking around the room at all the books. He was curious as to why the werewolves had so many books. Putting his drink down, he pulled a large, brown one from the bookcase near him, *The Book of Laycain*. He flicked through the pages and put it back. As he topped up his goblet, he continued, "The redhead interests me. Your men are not to go near them. Just find out where they are staying and if they meet with anyone."

Nokon asked, "When do you expect them?"

"Within the next day, maybe two. I'll be staying at The Bull."

Nokon gave a silent agreement. Garth downed the rest of his drink, placed the empty goblet on the desk, and strolled out. One of Nokon's pack walked towards him, looking at Garth with disdain, just like Nokon had. He gave a quick nod and continued past the younger man. Garth snorted. He did not care what they thought of him. They did what they were told or died. As he exited the building, he mounted his stallion and headed back towards the main square. He would get something to eat and drink at The Bull. The innkeeper was loyal to Bazertari and always made sure Garth had the best room and service.

Ulric and Evie reached the city of Kerlish in a day. It was a tough ride, the snow did not let up, and the wind was icy cold and unforgiving. The furs covering their frozen bodies did little against the bitterness of the weather. Both focused on the fact they would soon experience the cosiness of a pleasant room and hot food. When they reached the main gates, Ulric discreetly glanced at her and signalled for Evie to keep her hood covering her face. With the snow falling steadily, just shy of being a blizzard, most of the guards were trying to keep out of the stiff wind. Some warmed their hands on the brazier by the side of the gates, but there were still a couple that kept a firm eye on all that entered. Ulric regarded the people in front of them waiting for entry and found a group of Swords just ahead. They needed to get in without being stopped. The guards were not as vigilant as those at Palasses, but it was still wise to ensure they went by unnoticed. Ulric did not think the guards would recognise him, but did not want to take the risk. If Garth had arrived first, he would have circulated both of their descriptions.

He stole a glance at Evie and touched her arm. She turned her attention towards him as he whispered, "Stay close to me and them. But not too close, we need to slip past when the opportunity arises."

Ulric saw the movement of Evie's hood as she indicated agreement, and manoeuvred her horse closer to his. They then fell in behind the group of hooded Swords. As they got closer to the gates, Ulric tensed, observing the group in front of them.

As he had hoped, the Swords started chatting and moaning about the cold. The guards recognised some of the men and the conversation became more involved. With the guards distracted, Ulric signalled to Evie. They slowly rode by, keeping their heads down, and slipped into the city without being stopped.

With a quick glance back at the group, Ulric half wondered if it had been too easy. *Has Garth told them to let us in with nay harm?* It would not surprise him if Garth was interested in discovering where they were heading. He looked ahead. All they had to do was get to The Raven inn. Once there, they would be safe. If he was right, they would not encounter any obstructions, but someone might keep an eye on them. He decided it would be wise to go the long way to that side of the city. Once close to the Raven, it would not matter what Garth did. Dran had too many of his own men in that area for spies to infiltrate the streets, let alone the inn.

SEVENTEEN

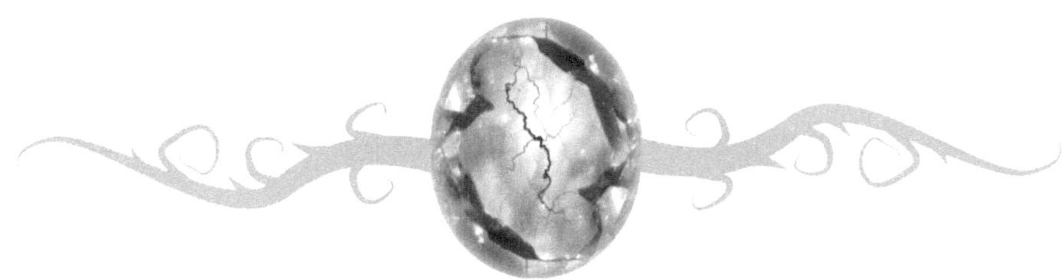

On their way to the city of Kerlish, Ulric informed Evie that shortly after Bazertari assumed control, criminal gangs quickly seized power and governed Kerlish for their own purposes. It was a major port and under the gangs' control, they also had control of some of the more profitable cargo routes. Ulric added that the rivalry between the many gangs had been to the Guild's advantage. By utilising the aid of one gang, who also owned several ships, it had been possible to smuggle the members to faraway places.

As they travelled through the city gates, Ulric leaned towards her and cautioned in a hushed tone, "Stay alert, lass. There are some unsavoury characters that may see you as a profitable asset to acquire."

Evie snapped her gaze to him and whispered, "What? Am I in danger?"

Ulric shook his head, looking ahead. "Just stay close and you'll be alright."

As they rode up the main street, Evie watched everyone as they passed. Her shoulders tensed as she wondered if it was such an advisable choice to go there at all.

Evie trailed behind Ulric, keeping as close as she could as they navigated the busy, narrow streets, which were rapidly becoming deserted as the residents sought shelter from the freezing cold. After taking several side streets, they reached an inn called The Raven. The gang Ulric had been talking about was located there, and Ulric hoped he could contact Irric through them. Stopping outside, they allowed the stable boy to tend to the horses, and the two entered the large inn with their saddlebags and weapons. The Raven was not busy, but it was obvious that the occupants were criminals. When the two entered, all stopped talking and turned their attention to them. The muscles in Evie's back tensed instantly, sensing it was a trap.

She grabbed Ulric's arm, reluctant to go any further and asked, "Is this wise?"

He stole a glance at her under the shadow of his hood. "Just stay close. You're safe."

Evie gave a confirming gesture, observing the occupants through the cover of her hood. All eyes glared at them with suspicion. Evie noted a few near the door had their hands ready on the hilt of their blades. Evie sensed her magic flowing to her fingertips, ready to protect herself and Ulric if necessary. She knew it was advisable to use her weapons, but whenever she sensed danger, her magic always seemed to flow more fiercely.

When Ulric reached the bar, he signalled to the innkeeper. Evie stood close behind him, attempting to avoid appearing too obvious about how nervous she was.

A large burly man with a brown leather patch covering one eye and a jagged scar on his face walked over. His face pinched with sour suspicion. "I think ya have the wrong inn, my friend."

Ulric leant forward and admonished, "That's not what you say to an old acquaintance." He pulled his hood back slightly so the man could see his features. Ulric added, "Unless you nay longer want to do business for the Guild?"

The innkeeper suddenly smiled, his whole demeanour changing. "Welcome, my friends."

Immediately after that announcement, Evie watched with amazement how all the occupants turned back to their own business, and conversations flowed once more. As the innkeeper passed two large mugs of ale, she redirected her attention to Ulric.

The muscular Sword stated, "We'd like two rooms and hot food." He pushed one tankard of ale back. "Water for me."

The innkeeper lifted an eyebrow. "Of course." He placed a mug of water on the counter. The innkeeper regarded them both. "Can ya share, as I only have one room left."

Ulric turned round to Evie and asked, "What do you think, lass?"

She turned her gaze to him and shrugged. "Is this the safest place to stay?"

"Aye, lass. It isn't safe elsewhere."

Evie responded. "Alright." She eyed him. "Just don't get any ideas."

Ulric faced the innkeeper again, chuckling. "Aye. We can share."

The innkeeper passed over the key and said, "It's nippy out there. Take the table over there. Me girl will bring ya stew and dumplins."

Both signalled their agreement and Evie followed Ulric over to the table next to the large, open fire. The heat from the bright flames kept the chill at bay. She surveyed the inn, no one was giving them a second glance.

Once seated, Ulric sipped his water and directed his gaze towards Evie as he pushed his hood down. "You can lower your hood in here. We can trust them, but outside these walls, keep your hood up. A city like this, the enemy has eyes everywhere." His gaze was directed towards her features as she pulled her hood down and added, "Are you sure you're alright with sharing the room?"

She suppressed a smile. "It's alright. At least having travelled with you for a while, I know you don't snore."

He said, "Aye, that's true. And neither do you."

Evie took a sharp breath in shock. "You cheeky bastard!" Ulric laughed. She drank a bit of her ale and remarked, "Just so you know. I'm having the bed."

Ulric stopped laughing and grinned. "I wouldn't want it any other way, lass."

"So where do we find Irric?"

His eyes were fixed on her and replied, "Near to here. We'll go in the morn. It's been a tiring few days, so let's get some rest."

Evie nodded as the barmaid brought the food over, then lowered her head, taking in the stew's aroma and hearty dumplings. It was satisfying to experience the warmth of a fire and a hearty meal. They ate without speaking until Ulric left her to speak with the innkeeper who signalled for his attention. She watched him as he spoke to the one-eyed man quietly. Evie then slowly looked around the inn. Ulric claimed it was safe at The Raven, but the look of the men and women present did not inspire a feeling of security. Ulric had told her, 'needs must in these hard times,' and to help the Guild members get to safety, they had to deal with some unsavoury characters. For the Guild's sake, the criminals had kept their word over the years, so she understood why Ulric said they would be safe. Evie briefly worried about the other gangs and their turf wars. It would be smart to maintain a low-key presence.

Her gaze swept across the inn as she wondered what Kerlish would have been like if time had not been changed. Evie paused as she returned to the present. What fools she and Slan had been. It was not just Bazertari they needed to face now, but the other warlock, too, Bazertari's apprentice. Evie had planned the endgame solely on facing Bazertari. Perhaps locating the apprentice to revert time would be the easiest solution. Evie focused on Garth's memories, in hope that he would know something. She froze, seeing an image; Bazertari had killed the other warlock. She frowned. The warlock had been Bazertari's ally for years. Bazertari must have felt threatened by him. It would have taken an immense amount of power to change time like the apprentice had. Evie smirked, that was probably more the reason than anything else. Bazertari did not want any competition.

If the time crystal was the key, perhaps she and Slan could use it to return everything to how it was meant to be. A sigh escaped Evie as another memory showed her that Bazertari had destroyed the crystal too. She tightened her lips. Bazertari had made sure there was no way to change anything back.

Evie finished her food. Ulric returned to the table and sat opposite her, tucking into his. She glanced at him; she decided not to tell him about the time crystal. There was nothing they could do anyway. She glanced over in the direction of the innkeeper as he attended to a customer.

"Is everything alright?"

"Aye. Seems the rival gang has had some of their men nosing about."

Evie studied him. "Should we be concerned?"

Ulric replied, "Nay." He briefly glanced at her finished plate and passed her the key. "Best get an early night. You look exhausted. I have told the innkeeper to set you a hot bath. I'll stay down here for a while to give you some privacy."

Evie was not about to argue. With the key in hand, she gestured a farewell and proceeded to search for the room. All her joints ached and just wanted a hot bath and then sleep. Shortly after she entered the room, the barmaid and a couple of the kitchen workers arrived with hot water jugs. Once the bath was prepared, and the fire in the small hearth lit, they quietly left. Evie locked the door, making a mental note to unlock it before getting into bed so Ulric could enter. Her eyes fixed on the bath as she stripped, her limbs already anticipating the warm, relaxing sensation. She climbed into the herb filled water, her body releasing its tension. She leaned back and shut her eyes.

Her mind wandered to Bazertari and the differences on this Moonstar. Since she arrived here, she had not been having the nightmares that she had when she was here before. She pondered on whether it was because of the unfamiliar land or if her magical powers had something to do with it. Whatever the reason, she was glad Bazertari was not trying to invade her mind. That was hopefully to their advantage. She paused, suddenly realising that the person responsible for her nightmares had not been Bazertari at all. If Bazertari had killed the warlock who assisted him, and he was responsible for the nightmares, then it would make sense why she had had none.

Ulric had mentioned that Bazertari could sense magic, the reason the older Sword did not want her to use it, and there was no denying the fact her magic was much stronger now. If Bazertari could tell magic was being used, he must have sensed when Slan conjured the portal. There had been no attack for her using her powers, but then again, they were not as powerful compared to a portal being made. Or Slan could have shielded her somehow. That could be the reason why Garth was tracking them. Bazertari had sensed the portal and sent his best man to find out what had happened. Garth knew who she was and she worried that he had told the warlock. If he had, Bazertari would soon be tracking her, she would need to be extremely cautious using her abilities.

Evie sighed, her mind unable to relax. She thought of Irric, hoping Ulric could convince him to join them and that three would be enough. In her previous encounter with Bazertari, he had followers, but by Evie's observation, he did not seem to have them now. Again she wondered if that had more to do with the other warlock that used to help Bazertari. Based on what Evie could remember, the warlock who had invaded her dreams had been as evil as Bazertari. Perhaps he had travelled to change the future and that was why Bazertari had no followers. But since Bazertari had made sure there was no threat of a traveller, there was no need for any followers.

Evie rubbed her face. Time travel; hell, in the films she used to watch, it seemed complicated, and it had actually happened to her. She plunged herself under the water, trying to stop herself from overthinking. She needed to relax. Evie rose from under the water, sweeping her wet hair to the side, and sighed. It did no good, her mind was still racing. If they were to confront Bazertari, then it would be his army they would have to face first. Evie sighed again, and focused on the ceiling, her body warm and relaxed. She needed to probe Garth's memories once more, but every time she did, she experienced his pain. She felt guilty for invading his private thoughts, but the information she needed was in there. Evie bit her lip; she had to know.

Climbing from the bath, Evie dried herself off and pulled on her shirt. She unlocked the door and then reclined on the bed and concentrated. Evie searched Garth's memories, trying not to let herself linger on any too long. She found his memories of the palace. The guards' numbers at Great Oak were less than she had expected. Bazertari's overconfidence could be his downfall. She just hoped Garth did not increase the guard when he realised they were heading there. But somehow, deep down, she sensed he would not.

Evie sat up when she heard a soft knock on the door. She was glad of some company to take her mind off things. It opened slowly. Ulric peered in and asked, "Are you decent?"

She smiled and adjusted her shirt to cover herself. "Yes." As he entered, he took a brief look at the bath and Evie added. "Waters still warm if you want to make use of it."

He gazed over at her, then at the bath. "I am tempted."

Evie smirked. "Promise I won't look."

Ulric chuckled, setting his things down near the bath and turned his gaze towards her. He slid his hand into the water, checking that it was still warm. He began unbuttoning his jerkin and said, "I'd get some sleep, lass. It's been a long few days."

She pulled the covers back, getting under them and asked, "Where will you sleep?"

Ulric glanced round. No chair for him to rest in, he glanced back at the bed. "Well . . ."

Evie smiled. "You're welcome to share the bed with me."

He replied, "I'll sleep atop the blankets."

She moved over to allow the large Sword some room to share the double bed. She turned on her side, watching the Sword, and asked as he pulled off his jerkin. "So, how long have you worked with this gang?"

Ulric sat on the side of the bed as he took off his boots. "On and off for about eight winters."

She stared at the back of his head as he undid his shirt. Pulling it off, he exposed his muscular back and Evie saw raised, pinkish lines across it. She frowned. They had the resemblance of scars caused by a whip.

"What happened? Those scars—"

He briefly looked at her as he laid back on top of the covers and responded, "Oh those? I forget they're there these days."

Evie leant on her elbow, regarding him as he switched positions to face her. "What happened?"

Ulric directed his attention to her eyes. "Long story, lass."

She fought back a yawn. "Was this from helping the Guild?"

He leant his head on his hand and sighed. "Let's just say, it's best not to borrow coin off the wrong sort of people."

Evie was finding it strange how much this was the Uric she knew, but also so different. "I'm sorry."

He sighed, "Don't be, lass. It was my fault." He looked away from her eyes and added, "I hit a couple of low points throughout the years, ones I don't want to repeat."

She touched his arm gently and murmured. "I think we have all had those over the years."

He took her delicate hand in his and squeezed it gently. "Get some rest, lass."

Evie turned on her back, closing her eyes. If Ulric did not want to talk about it, she would not pry. She stifled another yawn and murmured, "Night Ulric."

She felt him lay back, and he whispered, "Night, lass."

Ulric glanced over at Evie as she turned onto her side, away from him. He took a gradual, deep breath, thinking about the scars on his back. It had been a foolish idea, but when Elmare suggested he could fight for drinks, it seemed a good one. He made the mistake of being overconfident and thinking it would not matter if he won a fixed fight, so he bet on himself. That had not gone down well with Elmare, and she had her men knock him out before he knew what was going to happen. Ulric filled his lungs with air as he focused on the cracks in the ceiling. He still had no recollection of how he had dragged himself back to The Raven. However, had he not done so, he would have perished in the alley where the gang abandoned him. He owed Dran his life, something he could never repay. Dran had never held it over him, and Ulric respected the man for that. Perhaps that was why he knew Irric would be secure under Dran's protection.

Ulric briefly observed Evie. She had to be fast asleep by now. He slid from the bed and stripped then climbed into the lukewarm bath. He gasped in pleasure, not realising how much he needed it. He glanced over as Evie muttered, "I knew you'd take the bath."

He chuckled. "Go to sleep, lass."

She scooted under covers and fell silent. Ulric glanced towards her and grinned softly. He still thought taking a ship away from Moonstar was the best option, but since being with Evie, he was starting to believe that there may be some success in facing the evil warlock. Ulric shut his eyes, relishing the bath. He would know more when he saw Irric tomorrow, that is if he could convince Dran to part with him.

EIGHTEEN

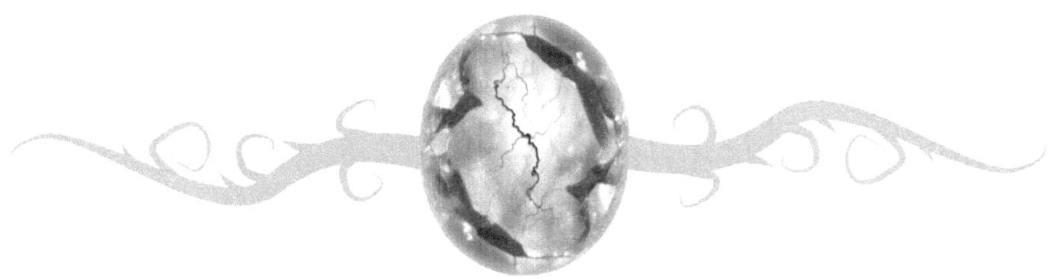

Garth felt the weight of a slender arm across his chest, warm breath against his neck. He inhaled deeply, the scent of roses filling his nostrils, and opened his eyes. When his eyes focused on the young woman lying beside him, he did not see the barmaid he charmed into his bed, but Evie. Her red hair draped across her delicate features. He had no desire to move; with her beside him it was just too perfect. Gently he brushed the hair from her face, his lips curling up slightly. It had been years since Garth experienced contentment.

Her eyes fluttered open and breathed, "Good morn."

Evie's hand slid down his torso, towards his groin, fingers curling around his cock. "Would ya like some more, my lord?

Garth snapped awake; the image of Evie replaced by a brunette barmaid. He cursed as his body betrayed him and pushed her from him, almost kicking her off the bed. "Out!"

The girl scrambled off the bed and gathered her things, then hastily left, sobbing. Garth sat up, leaning his back against the wall, scowling towards the door as it slammed shut. He tapped the back of his head rhythmically on the wall, trying not to let the memories take hold. Ulric was correct, it had fecked him up. It had been days, and they were still as strong. He pressed his palms against his temples as more images flashed in his head. *Why won't they stop?*

Garth heard the creak of a floorboard and turned to see that someone had pushed a note through the gap at the bottom of the door. He reluctantly climbed from the warmth of the bed, strolled naked over to it, and snatched the note from the floor. He unfolded it and quickly read Cron's scrawled writing. It seemed two hooded strangers had entered the city in the early evening and were staying at The Raven. Garth crunched the note up in his fist and threw it across the room as he cursed. That was Dran's territory. If Nokon's men wandered round there, they would raise suspicion. The last thing Garth wanted was to start a turf war. He had enough just dealing with Evie and Ulric. Dran was rumoured to have aided the Guild before. *Did he have contacts for Ulric? Were they going to get Evie out of Moonstar?* Garth pressed his lips together. *If they got her on a ship, what then?* There would be no way to get her to reverse what she had done. He shook his head. Evie would not leave Moonstar. His instincts told him that she would try to face Bazertari. If she was indeed the traveller, then she would not abandon her path. From her shared memories, he had also a sense of her personality and it was a stubborn one at that. She would not give up that easily. That meant only one thing; their next move would be to head for Great Oak. Which meant there had to be a Guild member in Kerlish who could help them. One right under Nokon's nose. That werewolf was completely useless.

Garth glanced across at the window, taking in the city's view. There was not much more he could do. He needed to get back. Despite the city of Great Oak being heavily fortified, Garth had an interest in ensuring his men were prepared.

He pressed his fingers against his temples; he needed to think clearly and thought about the witch at the capital. She may be able to clear the memories from his head. She was the only one he could trust with something like that. Garth smiled. That was the plan: return to the capital, prepare his men and get that witch to fix what Evie had fecked up in his head. He hated Kerlish anyway, and would sooner return to Great Oak. He paused, but he would have to make sure Bazertari did not know about the memories. The very last thing he needed was the warlock to think he had been compromised. There had been a few things he had kept from Bazertari over the years. Frankly, the warlock only cared about his whores and that there was not too much trouble in Great Oak.

Garth grabbed his clothes, getting dressed. These days, Bazertari seemed a little complacent. Yes, he monitored magic users close to the capital, and Slan, but if there was some big turf war outside of Great Oak, he just did not care. Garth had the sensation of being the one who was running the country more than the warlock. He was not really bothered by that; he enjoyed the freedom of being able to do as he pleased. And when the warlock decided he was no longer needed, Garth had too many allies to go down quietly.

Ulric woke up at dawn, aware of an arm draped over him. Evie was snuggled against his back. He smiled warmly, daring not to move. He had not woken with a woman next to him in years, and the emotion was something he thought he would never miss. Closing his eyes, he experienced his body betraying him as he sensed her warm breath on the back of his neck. Slowly and carefully, he lifted her arm and slid from the bed, trying not to wake her. As he glanced back, Evie rolled over, still fast asleep. Ulric stared longingly at her, his body longing to feel her skin against him once more. But he had to stop thinking that way. He needed to help Evie, not bed her.

Grabbing his shirt, he fastened it as he gazed across at her again. Wetting his lips, he craved the feeling of hers against his. Then he had a brief flashback of one of her memories. Seemed Evie had experienced something for Ulric in her world but . . . He shook his head. *No. This is not that Moonstar and I'm not that Ulric.* He inhaled to regain control of himself and cleared his mind. He tugged on his trousers, then boots, he would leave her to sleep and talk to Dran.

When Ulric came down, the inn was empty. The innkeeper was already behind the bar, cleaning it and readying for his first customers of the day.

Ulric asked, "Good morn Dran. Where's Irric at these days? Is he still your swordsmith?"

The innkeeper replied, "Aye, he forges my men's weapons and makes repairs in exchange for a safe place to live. We make sure he gets nay trouble. Honestly, I don't even think Nokon knows he's here."

"Unusual for Lycans. They usually pick up everything."

Dran gave a confirming gesture. "Aye, but think he's getting complacent, not sure if it's on purpose. You know he hates Garth with a passion."

Ulric snorted. "That's mainly down to the fact Garth calls them werewolves."

"Lycans hate that."

"Aye." Ulric paused, studying him. "I'm hoping you'll be willing to part with your swordsmith for a while."

Dran raised a suspicious eyebrow. "I was wondering why ya was here." He leant forward. "Depends. What's in it for me? And who's the redhead?"

Ulric replied, surprised the gang leader had not asked last night, "We'll compensate you. As for the woman, that's a need to know."

Dran's eyes narrowed, his shoulders tensing. "If ya turn up here about to take my best swordsmith, I believe it's necessary for me to know."

Ulric raised his hands in a calming gesture; Dran had a reputation for sudden mood swings. The Sword wanted to avoid the meeting becoming bitter unexpectedly. Ulric said, his voice calm, "Alright. When she comes down, we'll have a private chat."

Dran responded, "That we *will*, Ulric. We have an understanding, and even though we are happy to help Slan, and what's left of the Guild, that can change." He paused. "Even if I like to piss Nokon off."

Ulric regarded the gang leader. "Don't worry. I owe you too much, so we won't want to break our deal with you. And like I said, when Evie's here, we'll talk. Then you'll understand."

When Evie came down to the common room of the inn, she found Ulric talking to the innkeeper. She was surprised the Sword had left the room without waking her. She strolled over and said good morning to the two.

Ulric regarded her. "We need to have a meeting with Dran here before we can go to see Irric."

She pressed her lips together sensing a bit of tension between the two and wondered what the problem could be. "Understood."

Dran walked out from behind the counter and strolled towards a back room. "We can talk in here."

Evie followed Ulric, hoping there would not be a situation that would interfere with their mission.

Once in the back room, the large man observed the two, his arms crossed. "Well?"

Ulric turned to Evie. "This is Dran, the leader."

She glanced at him, understanding why everyone had relaxed last night once he welcomed them. "So, what's wrong?"

Ulric responded, "He's a little reluctant to just hand over his best swordsmith." Evie looked at Ulric and frowned. He added. "Irric."

She gazed up at the one-eyed innkeeper. "So, you want to know why?"

Dran replied, "Aye. And who are you exactly as you ain't lovers." Dran eyed Ulric, who shuffled his feet awkwardly, as he added, "I haven't seen Ulric in years. Now here he is, sober, and acting like the Sword he once was. I think you're the reason."

Evie glanced between the two, noticing Ulric's uncomfortable reaction when Dran mentioned lovers. She then focused on Dran and asked, "So, what do you know about the existence of the Guild?"

Dran glanced at Ulric. "All of it."

She regarded him. "So you know why Moonstar is the way it is."

He snapped, "I don't need a history lesson, girl."

Ulric raised his hand in a calming gesture, moving slightly to protect Evie, and responded, "Let her speak."

Dran pursed his lips, focusing on Evie, and waited. She continued and pushed up her sleeve to show the bracelet. "I'm the traveller."

Dran burst out laughing. "Nay ya not, that Garth killed her. Everyone knows that."

Casting a brief glance at Ulric, Evie observed his mild awkwardness. *He had known too.* She returned her attention to Dran. "Yes, I know. But I'm not from *this* Moonstar."

Dran slapped his thigh and laughed. "So, the fecking old man did it."

Both Ulric and Evie frowned, studying him. Dran explained, "Slan came this way some years back. We had a little too much ale, and he went on and on that he thought he may have found a way to use an alternative portal. He'd found some rare crystal that would help him."

Evie studied him. "So, he has been planning this for years?"

Dran agreed. "Aye, he tried twice here, but all failed. Seems he finally got one to work."

Ulric sighed. "The old fool. I'm amazed Bazertari didn't send out Garth to kill him."

Dran shook his head. "He sent that harpy, Morag, but my men smuggled Slan out."

Evie sank into a nearby chair, realising she could have been brought back sooner. Dran observed her. "So why do ya need my swordsmith?"

She looked up at him and said, "I'm going to kill Bazertari."

Dran arched an eyebrow and asked, "How?"

Ulric responded, "The Stone that's here, Evie will wield it."

Dran tightened his mouth. "But with Bazertari gone, it could be bad for business."

With an intense stare, Evie stood up again. "*Really?*"

He shrugged. "These lawless lands have been in our favour."

Ulric glanced at Evie, then said, "What if we made a deal? Nothing will change overnight; it will take years to get Moonstar back to what it once was."

Evie added, "With Bazertari gone, anyone loyal to him will be weakened. You could then take over."

Dran grinned, pointing at Evie. "I like this girl."

Ulric sighed, "Alright Dran. We'll make a deal. But if you cross the line—"

Dran held up his hand in a defensive manner. "I want this city to prosper and get those Lycans in check."

Ulric put out his hand. "Then let us shake on it."

Dran spat on his palm and took Ulric's firmly. Evie observed the two.

"So, are we able to talk to Irric?"

"Aye, one of me men will go with ya." Dran paused, studying them. "For security."

Ulric agreed with some hesitation. Evie could tell he was not happy about it, but compromises needed to be made.

They left the inn, with one of Dran's men in tow, both having their hoods up to ensure they were not spotted. They did not have to go far. The swordsmith's location was only down a couple of side streets. When they reached it, the work bench outside was empty, but the door to the shop was open and they could see movement inside.

Ulric briefly glanced in Evie's direction. "Let me do all the talking."

She gave a silent gesture of approval. Dran's man stayed outside on watch, and the two walked into the shop. Ulric pushed back his hood and walked towards the lean man at the back working on a scabbard. Evie glanced round at the weapons displayed on the walls. The counter to the side had several daggers on display. From the weapons on show, Evie could see why Dran kept Irric here. He was a very skilled weapons maker.

As Ulric strode to the back, the swordsmith stated, not looking around, "I'll be with you in a moment."

Ulric responded, "What about for an old friend?"

Irric stopped what he was doing and turned. He was in his early forties, had a muscular physique reminiscent of a Sword, with a shaved head and rugged facial features. Irric smiled at seeing Ulric and came over to greet him. He said, his northern accent thick, "It's been years, Ulric. You're looking well."

Ulric gazed down at the shorter warrior and smiled. "You look well yourself."

Irric glanced past him at Evie and raised a blond eyebrow. She smiled and stepped forward. "I'm Evie."

He gestured a greeting to her and refocused on Ulric when the Sword stated, "We need your help on a quest."

Irric regarded the two, his blue eyes sharp and asked, "For what?"

Evie stated, "To kill Bazertari."

Irric laughed. "Impossible," he said as he eyed Ulric. "Are ya drunk?"

Ulric shook his head. "Fully sober. What Evie states is the truth."

Evie pulled back her sleeve. "Here's my proof."

Irric leant forward, studying the bracelet. He looked at Evie, and then Ulric. "Looks like the bracelet in the books, but it's fused to you."

Evie explained, "That happened when Bazertari tried to remove the bracelet from my wrist." She paused, then added, "Then, with Ulric's help, I destroyed him."

Irric gazed at her. "You *destroyed* Bazertari?"

Evie nodded.

Ulric stated, "In the Moonstar that Evie went to, that land was unfamiliar, but she didn't just destroy him. Garth was the Guardian, and the three of us fought alongside each other. The Guild was whole and protecting the land."

Irric observed her, disbelief evident in his blue eyes. "That seems impossible."

Evie surveyed the room full of weapons. "This Moonstar seems impossible to me."

Irric gazed upward at Ulric. "I don't know, my friend. This seems to be an impossible task and what the Guild has gone through . . ."

Ulric said, "Aye, I know, and I had my doubts too. But the more I got to know Evie, the more I feel we may stand a chance. But if you believe that it's impossible, I understand, and we'll come up with a new plan."

Irric slowly indicated agreement and sighed, "I trust your instincts, Ulric. If you feel there is a chance, then I'll stand by you." He glanced between the two. "So, what's the plan?"

Evie responded, "Go to Great Oak, take the bracelet, and use the spell within to destroy Bazertari."

Irric shrugged. "I see. That seems easy. Except for the army Bazertari has and not knowing where the bracelet is kept."

Evie smiled and confessed, "I know exactly where it is. It was in Garth's memories."

He frowned. "His memories?"

Evie acknowledged with a nod.

Ulric stated, "Aye, Evie shared her memories with him. In the process, she saw his." Ulric grinned. "It fecked him up."

Irric chuckled. "Now, that I would have loved to have seen." He regarded the two. "So, when we reach Great Oak, how do we get in?"

Evie smiled. "There's a secret tunnel. It will give us access. I would then need you both to make a distraction while I find the bracelet. Then I'll face Bazertari."

Ulric fixed his eyes on her. "You'll need protection."

"I'm a lot more powerful than I was when I faced him before."

"Even so, I would be happier to be by your side."

She smiled softly at Ulric. "Then we'll make a slight change to the plan, but understand this; we can plan what to do, but once there, we might need to improvise."

Irric responded, "I agree. We have a basic plan, then see the situation and how many guards." He observed both of them. "What about Garth?"

Ulric forewarned, "He is aware of Evie, and he will have worked out what we plan. If he gets in the way, I will kill him."

Evie gave him a concerned look.

Ulric briefly studied her. "I followed your lead and we let him go, but I will kill him if I face him again."

She made a slow, affirmative gesture with her head. She worried if she could stand by and let Ulric kill Garth. Evie could not think that far ahead yet. She needed to make it to Great Oak and then see what they were up against. Perhaps there was a chance they could sway Garth into helping them. She casually glanced at Ulric. He would not like that idea.

Irric observed them closely and asked, "What did Dran say?"

Ulric answered, "He wasn't happy to lose his swordsmith, but we have made an arrangement which will work to his advantage."

Irric smirked, then asked, "So, when do we leave?"

"At dawn," stated Ulric.

The younger warrior nodded. "I'll meet you at The Raven."

They both agreed silently and departed, making their way back to the inn with Dran's man, who had been patiently waiting outside. As they walked, Ulric stated, "It will take us about sixteen days to reach Great Oak. Most of it will be cross-country. Garth could already be there. If so, he will have warned Bazertari and will have the army on alert."

Evie exhaled. "That's not very reassuring, yet it's what I'm expecting. But studying Garth's memories, I don't think the numbers are as high as we think."

Ulric studied her and asked, "Are you sure?"

Evie responded, "From his memories, there are a maximum of thirty at Great Oak, fifteen on the palace grounds, fifteen patrolling the city. It seems Bazertari doesn't expect any trouble, and the men in the palace are mainly Garth's."

Ulric smiled. "That gives us a clue, but we still need to be careful, in case he's pulled more back."

Evie agreed, "And we will. Bazertari has his personal guard, if what I have interpreted from Garth's memories is correct. It will still be a hard task, but I'm hoping the tunnel will get us into the palace undetected." She studied him from under her hood. "But we might have to separate once in there."

Ulric nodded. "Aye, I know. From what you showed me, you are an accomplished swordswoman and sorceress, so I know you can take care of yourself, but you are our only hope, Evie."

She smiled. "It will work, I know it."

Ulric eyed her. "It has to."

Irric finished the scabbard he was working on, his mind on what Ulric and Evie had told him. Irric found it too hard to believe there was a Moonstar where they had killed the evil warlock. He breathed in as a slender hand curled around his waist. He smiled warmly and said as soft lips caressed his ear. "I was just about to finish."

His female companion murmured, "Was that Ulric I heard?"

He turned his eyes towards the slender brunette who was in her late thirties and kissed her gently. "Aye, he's asked for my help."

She raised an eyebrow and responded, "So, when do you leave?"

He averted his gaze from her hazel eyes. "In the morn."

"Oh."

He held her soft hand in his and smiled. "But if what he plans works, we could have a better life."

She stared at him intently, asking, "Really? Could we stop having to live under Dran's rules?"

He swallowed and imagined Bazertari was gone. *Could I get my life back?* Being Dran's swordsmith had kept them safe, but at a cost. They could not leave or travel. Everything had to be approved by Dran, and if it was not in his best interest, then the answer was always no. But to keep his lover safe, Irric had agreed to the restrictions. She wanted a family, and he had put her off for far too long. If he helped Ulric, maybe they would have the freedom to do as they wished and raise children in a land free of evil. It was a risk he was willing to take.

He enveloped her slender waist with his arms and smiled softly. "Aye, I think we can. I don't know how long I will be gone for. But I promise you, I will return and take you away from all this."

She tenderly brushed her lips against his and smiled. "Good. I want us to get that farm and do what we want, not what Dran needs."

Irric hugged her, wiggling her body against his. "Aye. We will." He glanced in her direction, arching an eyebrow. "And have my wicked way with you every night."

She giggled, gazing at him, raising a mischievous eyebrow. "What's stopping you now?"

He grinned and bent slightly, putting his arm under her knees and carried her up the stairs, their lips never parting.

NINETEEN

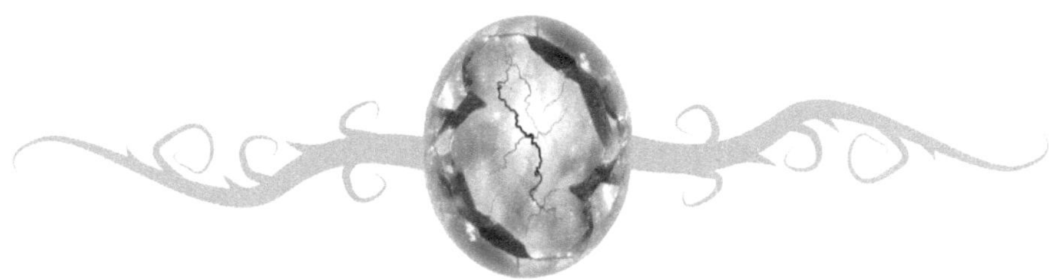

Garth reached the southern capital of Great Oak after ten days. The weather was notably warmer than in the north. As he rode south, he mulled over the events with Ulric and Evie. He knew that if he told Bazertari everything, he would be in the dark dungeon before the day was out. The very last thing he wanted was to become one of those things guarding the warlock. Garth had found over the years that his superior did not have to be aware of everything that occurred under his rule.

As soon as Garth had returned, Bazertari summoned him to his study. Two large windows overlooked the palace's private gardens below. The late afternoon sun streamed into the room, the shadows that fell across Bazertari's features gave him a more chiselled look. The Sword stood before the evil man, his clothes still covered in dust from the ride. Garth had maintained a consistent rhythm to his heartbeat as he informed the warlock of the abridged version of the events since arriving at Flamvile Woods. The Sword remained impassive, hoping he had given his leader no indication of lying.

The warlock regarded Garth from where he sat behind his impressive desk. "So, they plan to get the bracelet?"

Garth responded with a slight upward movement of his head. "Aye."

Bazertari strummed his fingers on the desk surface. "They will fail."

Garth directed his attention to the wall behind the warlock. Similar to a couple of the other walls in the room, it was lined with bookshelves filled with strange items like animal skulls and coloured crystals of various sizes. He shifted his focus back to the warlock as he slowly stood and walked from behind his desk over to a cabinet that had a few bottles of alcohol in various colours on top of it.

The warlock turned his gaze back at Garth and asked, "Drink?"

Garth acknowledged with a nod. The warlock poured two drinks of a dark-coloured liquid, passing one to Garth when he came to stand near him.

The warlock continued. "This woman is of nay threat to us. Slan has found a sorceress, that is all. And none can wield the spell within the Stone but the traveller, and you dealt with her."

Garth took a big gulp of his drink. If he had disclosed everything to the warlock, then Bazertari would have immediately confined him in the dark dungeon. The young Sword gazed at his drink, wondering if any of his human self would be left. He turned his concentration back to the matter at hand. Garth had given Bazertari enough facts for him to know there was a threat. It was not necessary for him to find out that there was another traveller out there. He was confident that even if Evie used her powers, she would still be no match for the warlock. Of course, things would be different if she got to the stone, and Garth would not let that happen. He had killed the first, and would soon do the same to the next.

He said, "I will double the watch and guard the vault," and took another big sip of the dark alcohol.

Bazertari pursed his lips. "Nay don't guard it. That would give them the idea that it holds something important. They will never penetrate the palace, anyway." He paused. "But if you wish, place guards in another area, find a room that could be used as a trap. Then we will have them."

Garth asked, "How about the west study?"

Bazertari said with approval, "Perfect. I will place a magic trap there." He finished his drink. "Ensure your men force them that way *if* they get that far."

Garth confirmed, "I will, but I plan to eliminate them before they even reach the palace. I have lookouts at the city gates, so we will know of their arrival."

Bazertari gave a gesture of agreement, patting Garth on his back. "That is why you are my general."

Garth smiled, downing the remains of his drink. This was not the first time he had lied to the warlock, but until he had the issue of the memories dealt with, he could not relax. Leaving the warlock's study, Garth went to find out if his men had dealt with Morag. With her removed, it would be one less thing to worry about.

Garth found Krif in the barracks. But as soon as his second spotted him, Krif became ill at ease. Garth's stomach tensed. That was not good, and knew he would not be happy after the conversation.

Krif could not look Garth in the eyes and seemed unable to stand still. "Sorry boss."

Garth snarled, his fists clenched. "So, she fecking *slipped* through your fingers?"

Krif shrugged, staring at his feet. "She had her men with her. They killed Landera."

Garth did not care about that. Landera had always been mouthy. If she were still alive, he would send her down to the dark dungeon for her attitude. Krif, on the other hand, had never let him down. That was why he had assigned the task to him. Garth eyed his second, tempted to throw him down there too. "So, we lost one. Your *mission* was to *kill* Morag."

Krif raised his gaze, biting his thumbnail. "We think she has the help of a witch, as we lost all tracks." The large man paused, then added, "If ya want me to do solitary for a couple of nights, I'll go now freely. I let ya down, boss."

Garth shot him a menacing glare but said nothing. He could not have his best man in the dark dungeon, not with Evie and Ulric on their way. "We'll deal with Morag, and your failure to do your job later. We have the more urgent matter of protecting the palace."

Krif appeared concerned. "I understand. What needs be done, boss?"

Garth eyed him. "Not to feck up again!" Krif glanced down, looking guilty. "I need the palace secure. How many men are in the city?"

Krif answered, "Thirty-two."

Garth gestured with his head. That was about the usual number. There was no time to call reinforcements, besides they were dealing with trouble in Adnama.

He sighed. "Well, that'll have to do. I want all on duty. Then we can double the guard and put more patrols in the city."

Krif raised an eyebrow and asked, "Expectin' trouble?"

Garth replied, "Aye, but they won't succeed. It'll be Ulric, a woman and maybe a couple more."

Krif grimaced in disdain. "That drunk couldn't cause too much trouble."

Garth peered at his second in command. "Aye, but from what I have heard, he's sobered up. So don't be complacent."

Krif acknowledged. "I understand. I'll get right on it."

Garth watched him go and cursed inwardly. He had wanted Morag dead and gone already. If she was still hanging around, she could cause issues, and if Bazertari found out, it would not look good for him. He pinched the bridge of his nose, having another flash of Evie's memories. They were not helping matters. He just could not think straight. Garth headed out of the barracks. The first thing he was going to do was see the witch, get this sorted, and then he could deal with the other issues after that.

Nestled in a small alley within the non-human section of Great Oak was the witch's shop. The Sword was aware that whatever he requested here never extended beyond those four walls, which, throughout the years, had been advantageous for him. Garth examined the jars on the shelf in front of him. The musky smell of herbs and incense was overpowering in such a small shop. The shelves covering the walls were full of strange odds and ends, which always drew Garth's curiosity whenever he visited. He leant closer to one jar, striving to unravel what was inside. An eye turned in the liquid within and stared directly at him. Garth quickly turned away.

"Ursula!"

A disembodied voice from the back called, "Just a moment!"

Garth moved to the counter, trying to investigate the back room, but a blue curtain obscured his view. He examined the items scattered on the counter. His attention honed in on a small gold pendant that was like the one he saw Evie wearing. He glanced at the other items and picked up a chicken foot to have a withered hand slap it from his grasp as a woman snapped, "Don't touch!"

He directed his attention to the elderly woman in front of him. Ursula's features showed deep lines, but she still possessed long, jet-black hair and piercing, deep green, elven eyes. "What are you after, Garth?"

He pointed to the pendent. "How much?"

She picked it up and looked at him with curiosity. "Didn't think you were a follower of Rosh."

He shot her an intense glare. "Humour me."

"Three coins."

He snatched the pendent from her grasp, passing her the coins.

She studied him. "I don't think you're here to buy jewellery."

He expelled a profound breath. "I have an issue."

She raised a perfect eyebrow. "I told you to make sure you picked clean girls."

He glared at her. "I do, and that's not the *issue.*"

"Oh," she chuckled.

Garth inhaled deeply. "I had a sorceress share memories with me."

Her eyes focused on him, displaying concern. "That's powerful magic. What memories?"

He gave her a piercing gaze. "Not your concern. I just want them gone."

The witch responded, "Sorry lad, that's too powerful for me. Once in your head, they're there till the day ya die."

Garth sensed a sudden drop in his stomach. "So, I can't fecking get rid of them?"

She tilted her head. "Nay." She clicked her tongue against the roof of her mouth. "Except a good number of ales."

He shot her an angry look, his voice cold, "So, there's *nothing.*"

"Nay, lad, nothing. Over time, they will fade, but they will always be there."

Garth clenched his fists, trying to keep control of the surge of anger. Ulric was right, it had fecked him up. He stormed out of the shop. Garth had hoped he could get his head clear so he could continue with his life, but he was stuck with the memories of someone he never knew. A Moonstar that was not his own. *How am I supposed to live knowing what could have been?* He rubbed his temples; it was making him doubt everything. He made his way back towards the palace, then saw the tavern he liked to frequent. Ale, she said. In the mood he was in now, he needed a good few.

Garth sat in the corner of the busy inn. He had his elbow on the table, the pendant of Rosh held loosely in his hand, and he drunkenly watched it slowly spinning around. Garth remembered worshipping Rosh before he met Morag. He had worn the pendant his father had given him with pride. After his parents died, he tried praying, and it helped. Rosh had given him some comfort, but then Morag had changed everything. He could not even remember what happened to the pendant he had. Then a sudden flash of another memory. It was of Evie holding the pendant. Garth guzzled down a hefty amount of the ale, rubbing his temples again. Her memories were confusing him so much, he could not separate them from his own anymore. He belched and stuffed the pendant in his pocket, motioning to the barmaid for a refill of ale. He just wanted to forget everything.

It was almost midnight when Garth stumbled back to his room. He had tried ale, but the memories were still there. The more he drank, the more persistent they became. Garth slumped onto his bed, cradling his head in his hands. He just wanted them to stop. Garth raised his eyes when he heard movement to see Morag closing his door and strolling over to him.

With an angry look, Garth glared at her and snarled, "Don't test me, Morag."

She snapped, "*Test you?*" She stared angrily at him. "It was *your* men who tried to kill *me!*"

He stood up, swaying a little. "Because Bazertari wants you fecking dead!"

Morag dragged her dagger free from the secret pocket in her skirt and spat, "I think if I deal with you, he'll have nay choice but to listen to me."

Garth looked towards her dagger and then back at her face. "What? Do you think you can beat me?"

She slowly prowled before him, her dagger angled, ready to attack and scoffed. "I should have never listened to that greasy warlock and found you. If I had never found your sorry, snivelling, teenage self, I would be Bazertari's general!"

Garth's temper flared. His dagger was in his hand in an instant, even with his sluggish moves from being drunk. His face scrunched up in rage as he stepped towards her, his dagger up. He lunged towards her, but she dashed to the side, his attack missing its target. Morag countered, but even in his drunken state Garth was quick on his feet and her dagger's blade sliced nothing but air. The Sword snorted in amusement and went at her again. His blade sliced across the bodice of her dress. She cursed, looking down at the torn material.

Garth was already making his next move and he plunged his dagger deep into her mid-section. He stared angrily at her as he felt her blood pour over his hand. "Really? Because of you, it's my life that's all FECKED up!"

Her face was full of astonishment. As her life drained away, she collapsed to the ground like a limp rag. He glared down at her, as she tried to keep hold of her life. Garth kicked her in the side. His hatred for her grew as her blood seeped across the floor of his room.

Garth growled, "I wish I had never laid eyes on you, *bitch!*"

Garth stormed out of his room. He needed to clear his head, and the ale was not working.

TWENTY

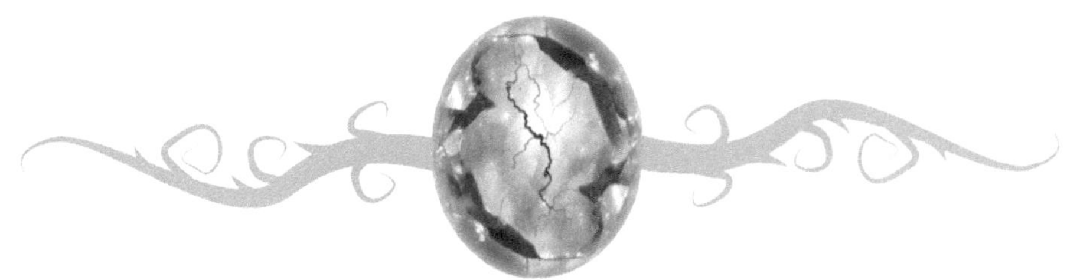

The swirling mass of a portal opened in Garth's dark bedchamber. Bazertari stepped through and regarded the empty bed. His men were right. It seemed his general was out later than normal tonight. An inconvenience when Garth's parasite needed replacement. He surveyed his surroundings and briefly stopped, taking in the sight of Morag's crumpled body on the floor, her blood seeping across the marble surface, staining a nearby rug.

Bazertari stepped closer, but avoided the darkening blood from touching his immaculate boots. Garth's men had failed in dealing with her when he had asked. That was a disappointment, but it was the least of the warlock's concerns.

Turning on his heel, he stepped back through the portal into his study in the palace. He would need to watch his general closely, ensure he was still fit for the position. *Did Garth's behaviour stem from his awareness that his men had failed to carry out his orders? Or was it from investigating Slan?* Bazertari could not quite pinpoint what it was, but Garth seemed distracted on his return. That was the last thing Bazertari needed from his most trusted man. If Garth continued to be distant once the issue of the invaders had been handled, he may have to delve more deeply into the cause. It would be a shame to lose such a valued asset, but

Garth would make an excellent personal guard when the time came.

For the time being, Bazertari would arrange for Garth to have a sleeping draft in his meal in a day or two. He wanted the parasite replaced before the mysterious sorceress and the others arrived. Garth had ensured the city was secure, and he was confident Garth would have them killed before they even reached the palace.

Bazertari rubbed his chin. He contemplated if it would be wiser to capture them, especially the sorceress. She may have useful information. If he could not capture Slan, then perhaps she could be a useful specimen to experiment on with the parasites; see how much control he could wield over a magic user. The warlock who had helped change Moonstar - he could not recall his name - but whoever he had been, he had not survived the process. Over time, Bazertari had improved the versatility of the larvae through breeding. He would consider his options. Of course he could capture the sorceress, but the thrill of controlling Slan was still far more delightful.

Bazertari watched as the two crooked servants strapped the sleeping Garth to the narrow wooden bed. The jailor tightened the straps on Garth's head, to keep it in position. Garth had mentioned nothing of killing Morag, and Bazertari had not either. The past few days his general had been more focused, but he had heard reports Garth had been out most nights drinking. Not the usual routine of his subordinate. Garth's usefulness as his general may soon be at an end.

The jailor raised his gaze with his beady eyes. "He's ready, sire."

The warlock acknowledged with a small gesture of his head and redirected his attention to the glass vials on the side. He picked one up and gazed into the jar. Within the clear liquid, a dark green parasite the size of his little finger moved around. He regarded it, thinking of how many had he implanted in his general throughout the years. Most had remained dormant until they withered and died. If Garth's usefulness was over, the parasite would ensure Bazertari still had control. He could make Garth walk to the dark dungeon on his own accord to await his fate.

Bazertari turned to Garth, the young man fast asleep, unaware of what was about to be placed inside his body. The warlock pressed his lips together. Maybe he should have controlled Morag, made her kill herself. It might have been easier. But the order had also been a test of the loyalty of his men. The warlock wondered if he should stop using the parasites and just turn them all into his personal guards, or possibly servants. There would be fewer mistakes, but he was concerned about exposing himself to that much dark magic. It was already taking its toll. No, he would turn Garth when the time came, the rest he would be more selective. The parasites worked, and if any of the men were disloyal, then the parasite would do their jobs.

He unsealed the vial and, calling his magic, black tendrils slid inside the container and drew the parasite out. The green worm-like creature writhed in mid-air, the black swirls of magic holding it securely. Bazertari directed it towards Garth's face, forcing it up the young man's nose.

Garth's unconscious body convulsed as the parasite crawled up his nasal passage, forcing its way into his skull. The young man thrashed more, the straps straining, but he remained secured. He shuddered violently, then as suddenly as it began, his body stilled. Soon he was sleeping soundly. Bazertari smiled. "A successful insertion." He focused his attention on the servants. "Take him back to his bedchamber."

The silent creatures acknowledged his order by unstrapping Garth. Bazertari briefly directed his gaze towards him. In the morning, his general would be unaware of what lurked at the nape of his neck; ready for him to take control of the Sword's body, whenever he needed to.

TWENTY ONE

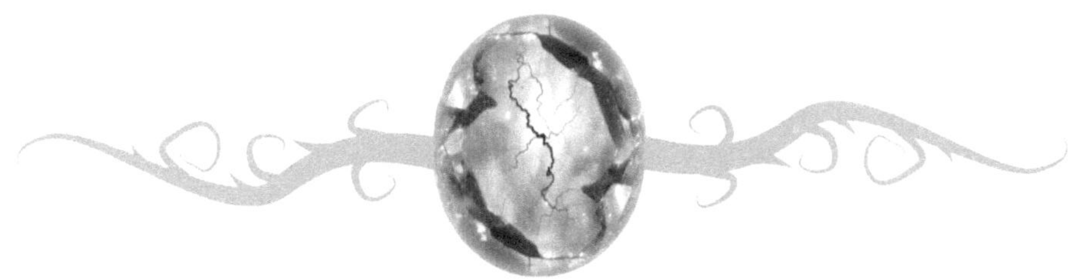

Evie, Ulric and Irric had been travelling for eight days across the country, avoiding the major routes. The two told their new companion about Evie's version of Moonstar as they travelled. The young Sword still found it hard to believe there was a Moonstar at peace, and that Bazertari had been destroyed.

As the light faded, they found an area near some brush to make camp for the night, away from the path hardly known by most. The plant life gave them some protection from the chilly night breeze and would also keep their campfire hidden.

Ulric was setting up a fire after finding some dry twigs in the nearby brush. Irric asked Evie as they brushed down the horses, "So, you and Ulric were close?"

She cast a quick glance back at the large Sword as he set up the fire and turned back to the younger man. "It was just an acquaintance through Garth to begin with, but over time, we became close friends."

Irric gave a silent agreement, brushing the horse down. The stocky Sword pursed his lips. "I see. It must feel strange that, here, you had never met."

"It is, but the Ulric I knew from my Moonstar is still in there."

Irric asked, "Did you ever see me?"

She disagreed with a headshake. "I didn't meet that many of the Guild. To be honest, it was just Garth, Ulric, Corun, Iesha and Slan."

He smiled softly. "I never met Corun. But I heard he was a formidable Sword. When word spread of Garth killing the traveller, he vanished." He patted the horse's neck. "Rumours have it the warlock tortured him, but Corun never gave them anything." He directed a quizzical look towards her. "Who is Iesha?"

Evie stroked the horse's side that she was removing the saddle from. "She was Corun's wife."

Irric showed his curiosity. "Corun was married?"

She answered, "They lived at Garth's farm and Corun helped Garth train me."

"Your Moonstar seems so different from this one. It's so hard to believe it could have been peaceful."

Evie bit her lip, her heart aching again at the fact Corun had been tortured and never had the life he could have had. She sighed, casting her eyes towards the dark sky. "I can't put everything back to the way it was. But I want to make sure everyone gets the justice they deserve."

Irric squeezed her shoulder. "I understand and am grateful for your effort to do this."

She smiled. "It's the least I can do."

The two walked over to the fire where Ulric sat, readying food for them.

Irric said, "I was just asking Evie about your friendship in the other Moonstar."

Ulric glanced at each of them, his eyes lingering a little longer on Evie. "Aye, it seems strange."

Irric took the water bottle from the older man when Ulric dragged his eyes away from the sorceress. The young Sword raised an eyebrow, studying them both for a moment. He then asked Ulric, "So, it must feel odd to know you were close friends, when you have nay memory of it."

The old Sword agreed, "Aye, but the memories were shared with me. I can see what Evie meant and, in all honesty" - he gazed at Evie again - "I know we would still have become friends."

"How?" asked Irric.

Ulric shrugged, looking at the younger man, "I'm not entirely sure." His eyes locked on Evie's. "But there's a sense of familiarity from Evie. The feeling you get with a good friend you have known for a long time."

She studied him. "Yes, I've had that feeling before, when I first came here. I had dreamt of this place and there was a familiarity I found hard to explain."

Ulric agreed. "I believe that's it. Maybe, even though this Moonstar is different, our connection remained."

"I believe so. I came here with no prior knowledge of this land, but now it seems like my home. Anything's possible, I know." Evie sighed, "I must tell you, Ulric, when Garth died, I wouldn't have made it without you. You gave me the support I desperately needed." She glanced at Irric, then back to Ulric. "To be honest, I think we supported each other."

Ulric studied her with deep affection. "I can feel the pain within the memories. With what had happened, we became very close."

Irric eyed the two, watching how they reacted around each other, and wondered what was not being said. "Do you have any happier times?"

Evie smiled. "Yes, there are many." She paused and briefly observed the two men. "There was one that I will always cherish. After we had completed the quest, the days were hot, and we were at the farm in Palasses, having a much needed rest before my return." She chuckled to herself, looking at Ulric. "We had . . . no, Ulric and Corun had drunk a lot, rejoicing in the win and remembering Garth. The next day Iesha and I found them both passed out."

Irric smiled. "We do like a good drink after a battle."

"And they did, so we had to bring them around."

"You threw cold water on us!" proclaimed Ulric.

Evie laughed. "Yes," She gave him a sideways glance, remembering their first meeting in this Moonstar. "Seems to work well."

Ulric responded, "Aye, it sobers you quickly."

Irric regarded Evie. "So, the water didn't go down well?"

She smiled. "No. It started a water fight, one of many. In the end, on that occasion, both I and Ulric ended up in the water trough, together."

Irric laughed. "That would have been a sight to see."

Ulric focused on Evie, his lips curling up in amusement. "I can see the memory as if it was my own. It was the first time we had both laughed in days."

She focused on him, remembering the day fondly. "It was needed."

The two looked at each other, lost in each other's eyes. Irric watched them both, raising an eyebrow again. He took a gulp of his drink and asked, "So, you were just friends?"

Evie and Ulric pulled their eyes away from each other and turned to Irric. She carefully observed the young Sword for a moment, taking note of an expression in his eyes. With the other Ulric, there had been that moment in the trough, but the one she held closest to her heart had been the evening prior to her return home. That had been unforgettable. She turned her head to catch a glimpse of Ulric, a flicker of hope mingling with doubt. She looked away and drank a bit of water when Irric passed her the bottle. *Are we truly meant to be only friends?* Evie shook the thought from her head. It had been over eighteen years ago, and the Ulric here was not the same one.

As silence fell over the camp, all lost in thought, Ulric cleared his throat, glancing at Irric and stated, "We should get some rest. I'll take the first watch."

The other two agreed nonverbally and prepared to sleep. As Evie laid down on her blanket, she glanced across at Ulric as he sat at the fire, and was taken back to the moment of the evening before she had left. The love in Ulric's eyes was hard to forget. There had been that conversation with him and the kiss. Her lips tingled as she thought of it. It made her realise that the day she had told Ulric she loved Garth; she had seen something. Even over the course of many years, she could not mistake a look of someone hurt. Ulric may have been closer to her than she thought, it had been clear there was something that final night. She sensed it, but Ulric avoided the topic. Evie could understand, as within hours, she was gone.

She shut her eyes. *Could there have been something? Would it have developed if I had been there longer?*

She rolled on her side away from the fire. That was in the past. She was here with an Ulric whom she hardly knew. Even if he witnessed those memories, he may not experience the same emotions. But if he did, and she took it further, just to have to go back home, then she would experience the loss of someone else again. She took a long, calming breath and cleared her troubled mind. She shifted on her bedroll, before she let the tiredness of the day pull her into the depth of sleep.

Ulric gazed at the fire for a while, yet once he knew Irric and Evie were asleep, he could not help but look across at Evie. He played the memory over in his mind; she had sensed something that day and with the look his other self was giving her, he would have been thinking it too. But probably because of his friendship with Garth, he would not have pursued it, except in different circumstances. Ulric focused on the memories Evie had shared and saw other moments. He sensed Evie's feelings the evening prior to her departure. They had even kissed, his lips felt the memory. Evie had wanted to ask that Ulric something, but he had stopped her. The expression he could see on his other self, it was undeniable. That Ulric cared for Evie deeply. He wondered if it had been love. He breathed out heavily, gently rubbing his temples. Her memories were mingling with his own, and he was finding it hard to separate them. When his gaze fell upon Evie, he was uncertain if the emotions he experienced were his or hers.

The older Sword pulled his eyes away from her. He experienced a strong attraction towards her and those, he knew, were his feelings. But then he had to ask himself if he could see it becoming more than just a friendship. From the way she stared at him, she cared for him deeply, but it was for a friend she once knew. He inhaled deeply and shifted his focus back to the distant hills. He had to think clearly; they had a task to fulfil and once complete, she would then return home. To have Evie as a friend brought him a sense of satisfaction, and he came to the realisation that perhaps that was all he required. He sighed.

I'm an old, drunkard, has-been anyways. What woman would want to be with me?

At dawn, they packed up camp and carried on. Evie watched Ulric as they rode together and wondered if they needed to talk about the conversation the night before. She was still wondering about what Irric had said. Since he was an outsider, it was possible he noticed something that had not occurred to either she or Ulric. Thinking back to her first time in Moonstar, part of her, years later, had regretted not having the courage to push harder to make Ulric open up to her. Even though there was no time to fulfil it. Although they were about to face Bazertari, Evie contemplated bringing it up before they reached their destination. She pursed her lips. The one thing she had learnt over the last few years was to try not to regret anything. Part of her had the impression that it was perhaps even more appropriate to confront the issue rather than leaving it unresolved.

After they set up camp at dusk, Irric conveniently headed out to gather some wood. Evie walked over to Ulric as he was brushing down the horses. The tall man turned to her and smiled. "We're making good progress."

She responded affirmatively, "We are." She paused, gazing at him. "Ulric, about last night and what Irric said . . ."

He turned to her, his eyes focusing on her green ones. "Aye."

Evie glanced down, experiencing nervousness. Ulric let out a sigh and touched her chin, raising her gaze to meet his.

He said, "You were wondering if there was anything?"

She studied him. "There was something that day, I felt it. Then the conversation, and the kiss before I returned home; it confirmed there was a connection. I know you aren't that Ulric but . . ."

"You want to know," Ulric sighed. "Well, I think there could have been something, but with respect for Garth, I feel that Ulric would have held back and not pursued it."

She asked, concentrating on his mesmerising blue eyes, "And what about *this* Ulric?"

Ulric smiled softly, lost in her gaze. "Well, *this* Ulric is curious." He clasped her hand gently. "But I have only just got my life back from being in a dark place for so long, and you'll go back to your world once this is all over. Would it be wise to pursue something?"

Her eyes met his. "A wise man once said it is better to have loved and lost than not to have loved at all."

His eyes were fixed on her, captivated by her green eyes, his body drawing nearer. "He sounds like a clever man."

Evie squeezed his hand, her chest tightening with the realisation that their bodies were almost touching. "He is."

Ulric leant forward, his lips a hairsbreadth from her own. He paused, then stated, his breath caressing her cheek, "Let's take one day at a time and see."

Evie smiled and glanced back to where Ulric was looking to see Irric and understood why he had paused. Evie was glad she had spoken to Ulric. There was a spark between them and in this version of Moonstar, it could become something more.

Once the horses had been settled, the two joined Irric at the fire and they had something to eat.

Irric regarded the two but said nothing. He had seen how close they were standing tending to the horses when he had strolled back with the wood for the fire. It amused him how they just did not seem to see their attraction to each other. He thought of his lover, and knew she would tell them to find a room and get it done. He breathed in deeply, realising how much he missed the brunette and hoped, if their plan worked, he could keep his promise to her.

After a moment, he said, "So, if we keep at this pace, we may arrive at Great Oak earlier than expected."

Ulric showed agreement. "I think we will. We'll keep to this route which will take us south of Little Stump and then head across the country again. We must keep clear of the deepest sections of the wood, as there will be creatures we wish to avoid. There's an inn we can ride towards if we need food supplies, but I think we may not need any."

Irric nodded his head, looking at his pack. "We'll have enough. It may be wise to keep away from inns until we have reached Great Oak."

Evie said, "Yes, we don't want too many people knowing where we're headed. I know Garth will be prepared, but still think it's best to avoid people if we can. We don't want him being alerted of our pending arrival. If we come across any creatures, I can shield us if needs be."

Ulric responded, "Agreed. Garth could have spies." He cast a sidelong glance at Evie. "It would be wise, as we get closer to Great Oak, that you refrain from using magic. We're all skilled Swords, so we can deal with anything that crosses our path. When we reach the Great Wood, we'll stay away from the primary road, and they won't even know we're coming."

Evie stifled a yawn, and Irric announced, "My turn for the first watch tonight. You both get some sleep."

Once they were done eating, they got comfortable to sleep. Irric sat at the fire and glanced at the sleeping Evie and then Ulric. He wondered how long their uncertainty would continue; they had a connection, and both seemed almost blind to it. He sighed, staring at the flames of the fire. If they did not take a chance soon, he would talk to them, make them see they shared a bond. How deeply, he was not certain, but the way they both gazed at each other when they believed no one was observing was starting to bother him. He wanted them to act. The Ulric he once knew would have acted on such an attraction by now. But with what the older Sword had gone through, he had lost his way over the years, and probably his confidence. Irric would have to talk to Ulric to get him to see he had a chance with Evie. In these dark times, to find love was hard, and he did not want either of them to regret it.

TWENTY TWO

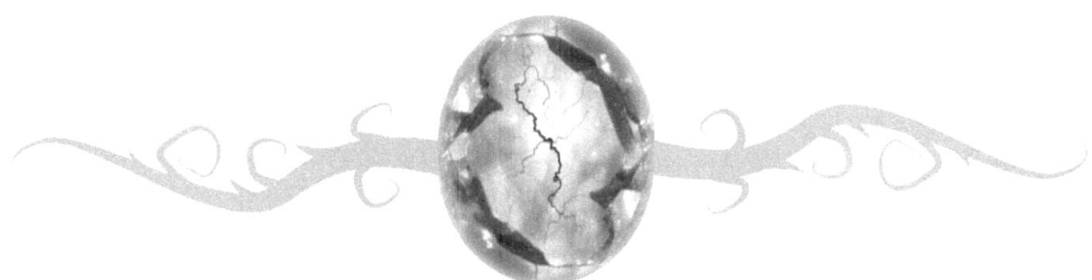

They carried on at first light, and after a few days, Irric had had enough of the two. They talked about trivialities and their past escapades, but they were not acknowledging the attraction between them that was clearly there. He witnessed them both glancing at the other, but they would not take the next step. They both appeared uncertain of each other's feelings, despite it being evident.

On the third evening, after they made camp, the young Sword had had enough of the awkwardness. He walked up to Ulric as he unsaddled the horses and Evie was on duty to gather firewood.

The older Sword glanced towards him when Irric shot him an intense glare and sighed. Ulric ceased what he was doing and asked, "What is it?"

Irric replied, "It's you two."

Ulric frowned. "What?"

Irric rubbed his face in frustration. "What has happened to you, Ulric? I remember when an attractive woman, who's clearly drawn to you, showed any interest, you'd've made a move by now."

Ulric sighed, glancing over towards the trees. "Is she? I have these memories in my head, but I don't know if the feelings from them are a mirror of Evie's or mine."

Irric exhaled deeply, "Ulric, you may have those memories from Evie, but the way you gaze at her, that's you." He rested his hand on the taller man's shoulder. "Take a chance. You always said it was better to have loved and lost—"

"Than to never have loved at all," finished Ulric. He shot a brief glance at Evie as she emerged from the trees with some wood and softly uttered, "But I'm not that man. Not the one she remembers."

The younger Sword smiled at the older man. "So? Let her get to know *you*. Don't try to be *that* Ulric, be the one from here and now. The way she looks at you, she sees you as the same man. Maybe a little unsure of himself, but still the same man."

"But—"

Irric responded sharply, "For feck's sake, Ulric, if you don't do something soon, I'm going to head back to Kerlish. I have a woman there who loves me, and I'd sooner be in a bed with her than watch this uncertainty between you two. You're both driving me crazy."

Ulric smirked. "Sorry. I just . . . and well, she just seems distant."

"Ulric, don't doubt yourself. She may be torn, wondering about you. Follow your heart." Irric glared at him. "And do something before I fecking tell you both to just feck each other!"

Ulric gave a confirming motion and responded, "Alright. I'll talk to her."

"Good."

With curiosity, Evie glanced over at the two men as she set up the fire, wondering what they were talking about. She noticed Ulric gazing over at her and wondered if it had anything to do with their recent conversations and the emotions they had. Since their near kiss by the horses, nothing else had happened, their conversions were just about Moonstar and the adventures they all had had. She wondered if Ulric was conflicted with her eventual return to Earth or if he just could not be the man he once was. She had sensed the old Ulric returning, but there had been something missing. He lacked the confidence he once had. The other Ulric had been so flirtatious, and overconfident. But this one, he was right when he said he was only just getting his life back together. Maybe it was too soon to act on it.

She sighed as she used her magic to get the fire lit. It had not helped that she had been preoccupied contemplating if she even wanted to return to Earth. Regardless of whatever happened between her and Ulric, the important decision she had to make was whether to return to London or stay in Moonstar. There was no one important in her life there. Peter had moved on. She had her parents, and Maxwell and his wife were close friends, but she was doubtful that she would call it home. As she thought about it, she knew deep down that Moonstar had her heart. Earth was no longer the place she wished to be. She could make a full life for herself, be the person she desired to be. With or without Ulric, what she wanted was to stay.

The two men came over, and they sat round the fire. Irric handed out food to everyone. Ulric smiled and said, "We should reach the section of the Great Wood closest to Great Oak in a few days."

Evie agreed, noticing him gazing at her. She felt he wanted to talk to her but not with Irric present. "Once closer, I will direct you to the area where the tunnel is located."

Both men showed their approval. Ulric focused his attention on his food. Evie glanced at Irric as he turned his attention towards the older Sword, appearing frustrated. She wondered if he was seeking to get Ulric to do something. Evie sighed before savouring a sip of the water and passing it to Irric. She would try to talk to Ulric. Maybe, if she told him she was staying, he would be more receptive. Evie wondered if sharing her memories had been a mistake. That could have been what caused his uncertainty, questioning whether he was feeling her emotions or his own.

As they travelled the following day, Evie focused on Ulric's back as he rode ahead, talking to Irric. She would talk to him after they set up camp at dusk and tell him she was staying in Moonstar. Unlike before, she was not required to go back. Moonstar was the place she truly belonged, and she had a deep sense that her parents would understand. With Slan's assistance, she could let them know she was alright and then begin a new life. She gazed skyward at the vivid blue vastness, and smiled to herself, knowing it was what she wanted more than anything. She wanted to belong, and here, she did. This was her home and part of her knew it always had been. As for Ulric, they had proven there was something there with their near kiss, but he had advised to approach it one step at a time. Maybe with her being distant, he had wondered if she was not sure about him. She sighed. To be honest, she was not. This Ulric was not the one who she fought shoulder to shoulder with. But he had the same soul; it was just a little broken.

As they made camp on the edge of the woods, Evie decided to let Ulric know of her plan to stay and talk to him about their feelings. When he went to get some firewood, she followed, saying to the younger Sword she would help. Entrusting the horses to Irric's care, Evie followed Ulric into a small clearing, away from the camp, where he searched for dry wood.

She stopped and gazed at him, as he collected twigs on the ground, oblivious she was there. She walked up to him and said, "Ulric, we need to talk."

He ceased what he was doing and swivelled, startled to see her. Before he said anything, she added. "I've decided that I'm not going to go back to my world."

Ulric frowned. "But what of your life there?"

Evie's throat tightened with emotion, as she reflected on all the moments she had been overwhelmed by a sense of isolation. "What life?" Her eyes filled with tears. "Since I returned from here, I experienced a sense of being lost and unable to fully embody the person I had become."

The clearing fell silent as Evie sobbed. All the emotions of heartache she had endured when she returned came bubbling to the surface.

Moving calmly in her direction, he dropped the twigs. Ulric then drew her close to him and kept her in his embrace. Evie relished his hug as he whispered, "Why didn't you say?"

She stepped back slightly to look up at him, not wanting the embrace to end. "How could I tell you that when I got home, I felt empty? That I could not give a man I thought I loved, a child. That every night, I would fervently wish to wake up here in this land. A place where I could be me, instead of the shell of a person I had become. I had changed so much, I no longer belonged in my world."

Ulric peered down at her, sadness in his eyes. "Oh Evie. I'm so sorry."

She dried her eyes and said, "But when I returned, I felt alive again. I understand I *am* home and I never want to leave."

Ulric smiled, hope in his eyes. "Are you sure?"

She made a dramatic gesture of agreement with her head as she studied his lined, yet still handsome features and savoured his arms that still curled around her. "Yes. More than anything, I know this is the right decision."

Ulric concentrated on her eyes, and was lost in them briefly. His breathing sped a little and then he softly pressed his lips against hers. Evie melted at his touch. She entwined her arms around his neck, Ulric pulled her closer, deepening the kiss. Evie found her body responding to his embrace. It was different from the emotion she experienced with Garth, but she enjoyed it. When they parted, Ulric said softly, "Once we have dealt with Bazertari, I think we need to have some time to get to know each other . . . properly."

Evie smiled, gazing at him, her lips desiring the sensation of his once more. "Once this is done."

"Aye." Ulric glanced back in the camp's direction. "We need to keep our heads clear for what is ahead, but once we succeed . . ."

Evie raised an eyebrow. "Well then, we won't have any distractions."

Ulric chuckled and picked up the twigs he had found for the fire. "We should head back before Irric thinks we've run off abandoning him."

Evie laughed and grabbed some twigs he had dropped. "Come on."

As they arrived at the camp, Irric glanced upwards and exclaimed, "Finally!" Evie frowned, and he added. "I told Ulric if you two didn't start talking and at least kiss, I was heading back to Kerlish!"

Evie said, "Sorry. I promise, we've talked." She smirked. "And kissed."

He gave a subtle nod from his position next to the fire. "So, you two will do something about all of that?" He waved his hand between them.

Ulric replied, "Aye, we will. After we've dealt with that warlock."

TWENTY THREE

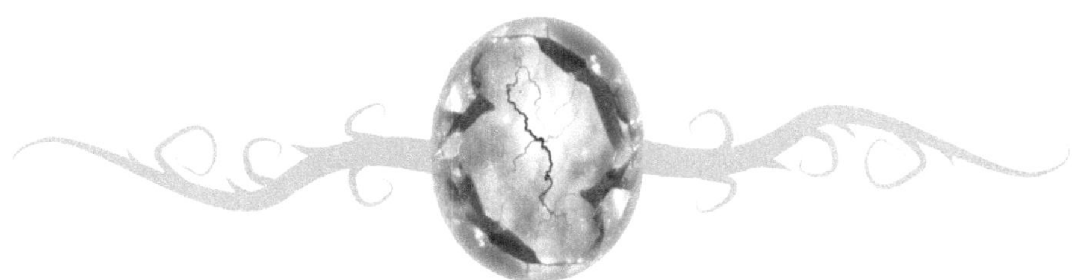

They reached the outskirts of Great Oak after two and a half days. The walled city looked magnificent; the thick, high, grey stone walls were well fortified. Above the watchtowers, which were evenly placed around the wall, fluttered black banners with the symbol of a red skull. In the late afternoon sun, Evie experienced a deep chill of foreboding as her attention was drawn to the palace. It was centred on a hill surrounded by buildings, with views across the city and the Great Wood beyond.

Evie dragged her eyes away from the sight and continued riding, leading the men east of the city; where the tunnel that Garth and Ulric used to rescue her and the royal family was located. Evie was somewhat amazed she still knew where it was. She thought it could be the stone's doing, ensuring that she would remember. However she retained the memory, it was to their advantage.

After reaching the area in question, they all dismounted. The two men kept a lookout while she searched for the hidden entrance near the bottom of the city walls. Evie was getting concerned when she could not find it, worried that someone had bricked it up years before. She was about to think they would need a new plan when she found the concealed opening. It was a lot more overgrown than when Slan had used it, but to her relief, it was still there. She grabbed the vegetation drawing it back and sent a ball of light down the tunnel. Which allowed her to see the tunnel was open and not obstructed.

She approached the two men and said, "We'll make camp near here. Then at nightfall, we'll make our way in."

The pair agreed and they all led their horses to a clearing in the woods, away from the city walls, and made camp. The three sat near each other, deciding not to risk a fire because of patrols. But now they were further south, the weather was not as brisk.

Irric ate a chunk of dried meat and asked, "So when we arrive in the city, what's the plan?"

Evie observed the two men. "That tunnel will get us into the palace directly, and unseen. Once in, the room that holds the bracelet is to the east. That room may have guards, but I hope we can reach it with minimal disruption. If we bump into trouble, you two could cause a distraction while I go in and get it. Once I have the bracelet, we'll face Bazertari. I would prefer the element of surprise. If we alert his men, then he may put up more of a fight."

Ulric responded, "If they're alerted, they'd keep or move Bazertari to the throne room. That's the best place to protect him. That was the protocol for the royal family, and Garth would probably have trained his men to use the same tactic."

Irric agreed. "How many men do you suppose we'll face?"

Evie watched both of them for their reactions. "From what information I could decipher from Garth's memories, I think there may be about thirty."

Ulric gave an affirmative gesture. "Aye, I think he'll split them, half on patrols, the rest in the palace at key points."

Irric raised an eyebrow. "Are you sure about the numbers?"

She gestured with her head. "No, but my gut's telling me it's all we'll have to face. And if things go right, only the ones in the palace."

Ulric responded, "Garth may have thought of reinforcements, but I don't believe he would have had the time to get them. He would've only got back five or six days ago. The other option is Bazertari refused any extra men, not seeing us as a threat."

Evie replied, "That may be the case. I had that impression from the Bazertari I met in my version of Moonstar, and from Garth's memories, it seems Bazertari believes he's invincible. We'll know for sure when we all get to the throne room and face him."

Both men agreed.

Evie studied them and smiled. "Thank you both for agreeing to help me."

Ulric leant forward and clasped her hand. "It is an honour."

Irric glanced towards the city. "How did you know of the tunnel?"

Evie sighed as she observed the pair, struggling to recall all the memories from that night. She dreaded knowing what she must have endured while captured by Bazertari and was glad Slan had wiped her memories of it. "I got captured by Bazertari." She paused as she tried to piece together what she remembered. "Bazertari had me imprisoned in the dungeons, and cast a spell of despair on me. Garth and Ulric used the tunnel and rescued me and the royal family." Her eyes briefly met Ulric's, causing a chill to her bones. Part of her knew that something dark had happened to her. "Most of that time is a hazy memory with the enchantment Slan used to free me of the despair spell, but if they hadn't come when they did, I think I would have died."

Irric gazed at Evie. "Aye, those spells are powerful. Rosh was on your side to survive it." He briefly glanced at Ulric and added, "It's strange to hear that you had worked together against Bazertari, as all we know here is the evil of Garth and Bazertari's rule."

Evie said, "It feels so strange, nevertheless I'm hoping I can at least free this land of evil."

Ulric raised his eyes to the moonlit sky through the trees and announced, "I believe it's time."

The two silently acknowledged, ensuring the horses were secure, and they had their weapons. The group then walked back to the tunnel.

Ulric pulled back the overgrowth and peered inside. "It's pretty dark in there."

Evie smiled. "I can light the way. Let me go first."

Ulric pulled the plants back, allowing Evie, then Irric, to enter. Only a few feet over the threshold, she doubled over in pain. Irric took her arm with concern. "What is it?" Ulric asked the same from the entrance.

She inhaled deeply, resting her hands on her thighs to stop the pain that clenched her chest. Evie shook her head, frowning. "I don't know."

She slowly stood up straight as the pain passed and proceeded to explore further into the tunnel that was illuminated by one of her glowing spheres. Four steps further and even more agony coursed through her body.

Irric tightly grasped her arm. "Feck this," and pulled her from the tunnel and made her sit down on the grassy area outside.

Ulric, who had stayed at the entrance, gave them both a steely glare. "Stay here."

The powerful Sword pulled back the plant growth, crossed the threshold and entered the tunnel. After a few moments, he came back to the entrance and shrugged.

Evie stood up, the pain having subsided, and tried to follow Ulric in. Again, only a few steps in, she doubled over in pain. She drew in a long breath as Ulric gazed at her with concern, about to come to her aid. She gestured with her head in disapproval and forced herself to go further, biting her lip. Evie had got only a little further before her head started throbbing. Within moments, blood trickled from her nose. She tried to continue, but she was doubled over in excruciating pain. The glowing sphere above their heads flickering as her magic stalled. Ulric cursed and hurried over to Evie. Scooping her up in his arms, he carried her out of the tunnel. Once in the open, the muscular Sword examined her pale features, as she remained on the ground with a sensation of dizziness.

"I think there's some type of trap to stop magic users."

Irric cast a gaze towards the city and inhaled deeply. "So, what now?"

Evie wiped her nose, cursing, her gaze on the dark tunnel entrance. Her magic light globe had gone in with no issues, which confused her. But perhaps that was the reason the trap worked. That had been their safest way in. They could not enter through the city, unless . . .

She glanced in the direction of her two male companions. "Let's get back to the camp. I have an idea."

Ulric aided her in getting up, and they returned to the camp. Once they were a distance from the tunnel, Evie experienced a sense of almost being back to normal. They sat near their sleeping blankets and Uric asked, "So, how are we going to do this?"

Evie checked her nose to ensure it had stopped bleeding, a dull ache still vibrated through her body. "We try again tomorrow." She studied the two. "Ulric, I still want you to use the tunnel with Irric. It will still grant us an advantage."

Irric asked, "But with there being a magical trap on it, wouldn't they know it's there?"

Evie shrugged. "Possibly. But that trap could have been set up years ago. The tunnel looked like it hadn't been used in a long time."

"Aye, I think Evie's right." Ulric studied Evie. "I'm gathering you'll enter through the city gates?"

She replied regarding the two, "It isn't ideal, but I think I can sneak in; maybe use a cloaking spell."

Ulric tightened his lips. "Using magic this close to Bazertari, is that wise?"

She sighed, "Maybe not, but it will be easier for me alone to sneak in. If we time it right, you two stir up a distraction, then I gain access to the palace undetected."

Ulric scratched his stubbled chin. "That may work, lass. Then what?"

"We try to keep to the original plan and meet in the throne room."

Both men consented with a gesture of their heads. Evie casually glanced over at her sleeping blanket. "We better get some sleep; I need to enter the city at dawn when the gates open. Then at nightfall, you enter via the tunnel, and I get in via the palace."

The two men agreed. Ulric glanced in Evie's direction. "Just be careful."

She smiled, gently touching his hand. "I will."

TWENTY FOUR

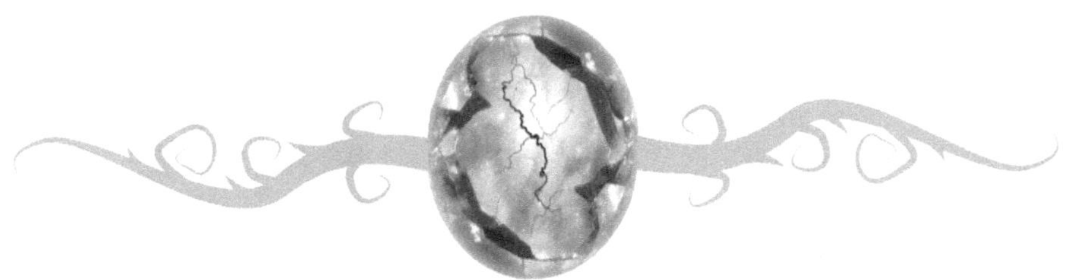

As the sun rose, Evie set off on foot from the camp and made her way towards the stone walls. She walked along the peaceful path from the woods, curious about the level of activity to be found in Great Oak. She recollected the bustling cities to the north, filled with sizeable crowds, mainly consisting of traders. Evie reflected on the city where Bazertari resided.

Would it be the same, or almost a ghost town?

Before Evie reached the main gate, which had just been opened, the noise and commotion of eager traders wanting to enter filled the air. She kept back, watching. The guards, dressed in black uniforms with the same red skull from the banners positioned on the front of their tunics, scrutinised everyone as they entered. She could not sneak in by just mingling with the crowd. Evie looked back at the path she had taken. There had been no side entrances that were not guarded. The main gate was still the best option with the shield of a large crowd.

She eyed the guards as they stopped anyone not showing their features on entry. Garth had indeed instructed them to look out for her and Ulric. There was only one course of action. Even in such proximity to the warlock, Evie had to use magic. She could disguise herself as she had the foresight to infuse an illusion spell on her bracelet. The night she had first returned to Earth, all those years ago, she had made herself resemble more of how she had looked prior to her leaving, and that was with little skill. It should be far easier since she knew more about her powers.

Closing her eyes, Evie concentrated on her appearance. Slowly, her back hunched, her hair began to grey, and her skin aged. Within moments, she hobbled towards the main gate and mingled with the men and women who were waiting to gain entry. As she walked unsteadily towards the entrance, the watchful guards briefly observed her before motioning for her to continue. Evie held her breath. Even though she resembled an old lady, she was still tense, and her arthritic limbs ached from the tension.

Evie walked carefully with her hunched frame, and continued through the impressive wooden gates. Finding herself in the middle of the crowd that moved along the main street, Evie swiftly disappeared among them. When she arrived at a side alley, she took it, and once out of sight, reverted to her normal form. She rotated her shoulders, feeling relief as her body straightened from the uncomfortable form.

Concealing her features once more with her hood, she exited the alley and returned to the main street. Evie glanced ahead, catching sight of the palace. Thoughts of the last time she was at Great Oak came flooding back. Then she had been in chains, but she still had the fear of dread gnawing at her. She drew in a long breath. She could do it, and she was not alone. With Ulric and Irric by her side, they would win. They had to.

As she got closer to the palace, the number of guards patrolling the streets grew. Garth had focused his men where they would be most needed. Unable to use the tunnel, it was her only option. She watched the guards as they strode by.

Could I wait until Ulric and Irric entered the palace grounds and caused a commotion? Would it draw enough guards away to give me access? Or would it cause more issues?

Not wanting to draw attention to herself, Evie ventured away from the palace and wandered around the city streets. She needed to make a plan to get inside the gates while staying out of sight of the patrols until dusk. If she got too close to the palace in broad daylight, she would be spotted. A patrol turned onto the street she was walking down, and Evie quickly stepped inside an old bookshop.

She passed some time gazing at the books and chatting with the old owner about Moonstar's history. Once Evie sensed that the old man was trustworthy, she asked, "There seems to be a lot of patrols of late. Is something happening?"

The bearded man gazed at her. "Aye, the men are tense."

Evie placed the book she was inspecting down. "Oh, so could we be in danger?"

He raised an eyebrow. "I'd be careful, lass. There hasn't been a culling in many a winter. But the men get twitchy if one's close."

"A culling?"

"Aye, lass. Best be careful. There may be a magic user about. They pop up now and then; like to make a name for themselves. But they never last long."

Evie glanced towards the entrance of the bookshop, then back at the owner. She worried if it had been unwise to cast the illusion spell so close to the palace. With the patrols about, she knew it was best to not use any more magic unless she had no choice. "I thought they would keep the patrols closer to the palace to protect Bazertari?"

"Aye, they focus on the main gate. Making sure everyone knows that the warlock is in charge. Then smaller patrols roam the streets. They have talismans that can pick up where spells have been used."

Her shoulders tensed. They could have picked up a trace of her spell at the gate and in the alley. *But what of the tunnel the night before? Would they sense that? Could Ulric and Irric be in danger?*

"How far do the talismans work?"

The old man shrugged. "Nay far. If the magic user is in the city walls, they will find 'em." He eyed her. "Ya seem very interested in this."

Evie smiled, realising she may have asked too many questions. "Oh, just curious."

He leant towards her. "Be careful, lass. From ya accent, ya nay from round these parts. Asking too many questions to the wrong person may get ya into trouble."

Evie acknowledged. "I understand. Good day."

She turned and left. Evie did not think the old man would say anything, but she would have to be careful. The conversation proved useful though, as he told her that the palace gates would be guarded, but not elsewhere. Perhaps she could find another way in. If she waited until nightfall, and ensured she was clear of patrols, she could use a minor spell to make herself invisible and get over the palace walls. It would be a gamble, but it may be her only option.

Evie moved away from the side street, taking advantage of the bustling market crowd. She bought some fruit from a stall as she observed the patrols. Whenever a patrol came too near, she mingled with the crowd or entered a shop to keep out of sight. When the coast was clear once more, she wandered back onto the busy streets, trying to find a way to the palace that was not through the main gate. When another patrol was headed her way, Evie quickly entered a crowded inn. It was early afternoon and a couple of hours of rest would do her some good. It would also give her time to think of some alternatives to sneak into the palace. She ordered ale and food, and sat at a table at the back so she could keep a low profile and watch if any patrols searched the inn.

As dusk fell, Evie left the inn and moved towards the palace, staying hidden in the shadows. If she could find an area of wall that was overlooked, she could get in utilising a spell to help her climb the wall unseen. Once it was nightfall, Ulric and Irric would navigate their way down the tunnel and create some kind of distraction. She just hoped it was enough for her to sneak into the main palace.

When she reached the ornate palace walls, there were guards everywhere; they were not just standing guard at the gates. Even if there was a distraction, she may not be able to get in. Evie cursed. She needed a new plan to gain entry.

Evie took a side street and ventured further along to look at another section of wall. Again, more guards. Garth must have relocated all his men to the palace and stationed them at intervals along the wall. No area was left vulnerable. Evie stood in the shadows, scrutinising the walls. She may have little choice but to risk a larger spell. It would be necessary for her to remain cloaked for longer than just climbing over a wall. Evie nervously bit her lip as she contemplated what would be waiting for her on the other side. Guards were stationed around the wall, similar to her experience in the first

Moonstar. But if Garth was clever, they would be positioned on either side of the wall. She could very well climb over to find a guard standing right below her.

Quietly cursing under her breath, she carefully moved along the narrow street, away from the palace. She urgently needed to find a solution. A small illusion spell to enter the city was one thing, but to get over a well-guarded wall and grounds and into the palace undetected, that would take a lot more magic. In using powerful spells so close to the warlock — he would detect it. She sighed. She needed to come up with a plan fast. Ulric and Irric would make their way into the tunnel in the next hour.

Upon spotting a patrol, she quickly stepped into a side alley to avoid detection.

The streets were emptying, there was probably some sort of curfew, which would make it even harder for her to keep hidden. She cursed. With her gaze fixed on the patrol, she retreated down an alleyway into the darkness, towards another side street. She walked along the wall still looking for a way in, but until the patrol passed, she had to keep hidden. Turning to make her way round the city towards the opposite side of the palace, Evie froze. Someone had blocked her way. She moved to pass the stranger, but her heart skipped a beat when she drew close. It had to be Garth.

He sneered, "*You!*"

Evie tried to turn and run, but he grabbed her wrist, twisting her round as he pulled his dagger free. Even though he seemed unsteady on his feet, his reactions were still fast. His grip on her was like iron, keeping her firmly in place. He brought up his dagger to her cheek, his breath thick with alcohol. "I should kill you where you stand."

She tried to pull free, studying his eyes, seeing the conflict in them. She whispered harshly, "So you will kill me *twice?*"

He scoffed with disgust and went to make a fatal cut but his arm would not move. He cursed, his face full of emotion, and tried again. But he could not do it. He released her and the dagger at the same time. The weapon clattered on the cobbles as the heels of his hands struck his temples repeatedly.

"*Feck!*" He shot her an angry glare, his eyes almost pleading. "What have you done to me?"

Her eyes were fixed on him, her body tense. "I did nothing. I just shared my memories."

He stared at her, tears in his eyes, his fists clenched as he paced. "Everything is so *fecked* up!"

Evie studied him and relaxed. She delicately rested her hand over his closed fists. Her skin zinged with the contact. Garth stopped and stared at his hand, then at her.

When their eyes met, Evie said, "Help me destroy Bazertari."

He let out an abrupt laugh, but his hand did not pull away from hers. Then he asked, "Why?"

"When I shared my memories, I saw yours. The Garth I know is in there, somewhere deep down. Redeem yourself. *Help* me."

Garth pulled his hand free of hers. "I heard that old fool, Slan, telling me to pick a side."

"Then pick one." Evie paused and regarded his features. She ached for his lips on hers once more, but he was not the Garth who had loved her until his dying breath. She glanced towards the palace. "I need to get in there. Help me and we can end this evil *tonight*."

Garth was hesitant. He turned away from her, swearing. He lifted the heels of his hands, hitting his temples again.

Evie stated calmly, "What I showed you was a Moonstar that has been lost. But tonight we can bring this one into the light."

He turned towards her; his eyes filled with tears. He shook his head and said in anguish, "I've *fecked* everything up."

Evie gently retook his hand. "But you can right it."

Garth shifted his gaze towards the palace. Over the past few days, his doubts had doubled, and having killed Morag made him realise he could have had such a different life. He clenched his teeth and gazed at Evie. The memories she had revealed to him confirmed what could have been if that bitch had not corrupted him. His heart ached every time he laid eyes on Evie, but those memories were not his. His life had taken an alternative path, and with that, he was a different person. He averted his eyes from hers and muttered, "I can never be that Garth . . . The one in your memories."

Evie's voice faltered, "I know."

He sighed, bending down to pick up his dagger, "If I get you in, what then?"

"I find the bracelet and defeat Bazertari."

"Then?" he asked as he sheathed his dagger.

"Moonstar is free, and his followers will be dealt with."

Garth swallowed, glancing down at his feet. "That will include me."

Evie's throat bobbed with emotion. Garth sighed, glancing round the street, then turned his attention back to her and smiled sadly. "I'll help you." He paused, taking a breath. "And I'll surrender once Bazertari is dead."

"Thank you."

He looked towards the palace. "I know I'm asking a lot here, but can you trust me?"

She answered, knowing instinctively she could, "Yes."

He stared at her, briefly entranced by her green eyes. "I will take you in as my prisoner. My men won't stop me."

Evie regarded him. It was a good plan, yet if it ended up being a trap, she knew she would have to deal with Garth on her own.

"Keep your hands under your cloak. They will then look like they are bound," he instructed.

Evie smiled and closed her eyes briefly. And a cord materialised over her wrists, making it appear they were tied. Garth quirked an eyebrow and Evie shrugged.

He grabbed her arm. "Just keep close."

The two strolled towards the palace gates. Garth snapped at the guards who were on duty, "Let me in. I have a high-value prisoner!"

The guards instantly stood to attention, the gate opening without questions. Garth pulled Evie in and hurried towards the palace. He casually glanced at her. "Once inside, we need to move fast."

There were shouts from the northern end of the palace. Garth came to a standstill and fixed his gaze on her. "What's that?"

Evie sighed, "Ulric and Irric."

He frowned. "You tricked me?"

Evie grabbed his hand. "*No*, I couldn't do this on my own. There is a secret tunnel to the north. I couldn't enter because of a magic trap. They headed in that way while I tried to find another way in. The plan is still the same; to kill Bazertari."

He studied Evie as they stood near the palace entrance, both of them tense and aware of the potential danger of being discovered. Garth grabbed her arm, escorting her into the building.

He eyed her. "Good plan."

Evie relaxed and followed Garth.

Once inside, Garth stated, "I'll take you to the vault. With the alarm raised, they will take Bazertari to the great hall. Once you have the bracelet, I will get you in there."

She affirmed silently, looking directly into his hazel eyes, noticing they did not seem as cold anymore. "Thank you."

Garth smiled softly, looking ahead. "I just know I need to put things right."

TWENTY FIVE

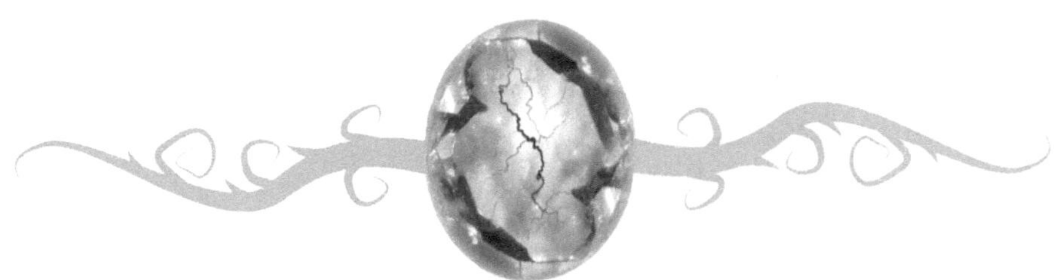

They hurried down a few side corridors, Garth making sure they avoided where his men in the palace were guarding or patrolling. As they made their way along a deserted corridor, the two heard some guards ahead, walking their way. Garth skidded to a stop and opened the door to the side of them, pulling Evie in. He closed the door, listening to the guards outside as they passed. Evie surveyed the large room, they were in the main palace library. She turned her gaze towards Garth as he listened at the door, his hand on the handle.

He cast a brief glance towards her. "They will pass soon. It's best we don't come across any of my men as we aren't heading for the dungeons. And the last thing I want to do is raise any suspicions."

She nodded; her eyes pulled towards the books as they waited. The rushed footsteps of the guards faded, and Garth opened the door and peered out. Without looking back, he beckoned for her to follow. After departing from the library, they pressed on. From the route they were taking and from what Evie could remember of Garth's memories, she was confident that they were heading in the right direction. She felt relieved that she had trusted him, but worried about Ulric's reaction if he knew she was trusting the enemy so implicitly. Garth slowed as they reached another door. Evie recognised it as the one for the vault. The absence of guards made her frown with confusion as Garth unlocked the door with the master key he had in his pocket.

He said, glancing at her and noticing her frown, "Thought it was wise to trick you. An unguarded room wouldn't contain anything of value."

It was a risky move and could have worked, if it was not for the fact Evie had seen it in his memories. They entered the small room; it was filled with magical objects, jewels and books. There were many spell books, some resembling the ones Slan had in his tower when she had visited Moonstar before.

Items covered the floor, the central table and the cupboard on the far wall. There were a couple of chests in the opposite corner, the lids not closed because of the bulging contents within. Evie surveyed her surroundings, noticing several staffs propped against the wall that clearly belonged to sorcerers who had vanished. With a concerned expression, Evie chewed her lip, speculating about what had happened to the owners.

Her fingers tingled, sensing the amount of magic trapped within the items, waiting to be used. Evie paused, a bracelet up high on the cabinet, caught her attention. She moved closer to it, propelled by the attraction of the familiar magic, and noticed her bracelet starting to vibrate. Evie slowed, scrutinising it, and hoped the two stones so close together did not cause a catastrophe.

As she approached, both stones emitted a glow and Evie sensed a buzzing in the air. Garth, who had remained near the doorway, asked, looking concerned, "Should it do that?"

Evie glanced back and shrugged. She slowly headed towards it, hoping there would not be some tremendous explosion. The two bracelets pulsated, and the stones glowed brighter. The one on the cabinet shifted across the surface. The vibrations grew more violent the closer she came towards it. As Evie reached out to touch the other bracelet, she felt a static shock travel up her arm. She gasped, her arm tingling from the sensation. Then a beam of light shot out from the stone into the one on her wrist. The stone in her bracelet grew hotter by the second, then there was a blinding flash. When her vision cleared, the fused bracelet was dissolving into silver dust.

Evie cast her gaze downward as the light within the stone on the cabinet gradually dimmed. As she focused on her wrist, the silver dust floating to the floor, the wounds on her skin had healed. No sign the bracelet had ever been threaded into her, but she could still sense the power coursing through her body. With a slow, steady breath, she reached out for the bracelet on the cabinet. As she took it in her fingers, she had a flash of her grandmother and then Landor. Both smiling and then nodding with satisfaction. Evie swallowed with the sudden surge of emotion and slipped the bracelet onto her wrist. Then the words to the spell that would destroy Bazertari floated into her mind like a distant memory being refreshed. It felt like Landor had whispered them to her only moments before. Evie gazed down at the bracelet, it seemed so strange to see it loose and not welded to her.

Evie turned to Garth, breaking from her daze. "Time to face him."

Garth checked the corridor, and they promptly retraced their steps, then turned right. While making their way towards the royal chamber, he asked, "What do you need me to do?"

She glanced at him. "Keep your men back. Ulric and Irric know to make their way to the throne room or great hall, as you call it. I don't know what their reaction will be when they see you."

Garth sighed, seeing his sadness mirrored in her eyes. "It won't be good. I just hope my actions will show them that I'm helping."

They stopped, out of sight at the last turn of the long corridor, the imposing doors of the royal chamber just ahead. Two guards stood watch. Garth tightened his lips as he peered round the corner. One guard was Krif. There was no choice in what had to be done.

He glanced at Evie and ordered, "Stay here."

She silently agreed, keeping herself hidden. Garth took a breath and strolled towards the door.

Krif acknowledged him with a gesture. "There has been a breach to the north, but Bazertari is secure."

Garth responded, "Good." He paused and sighed. "Sorry, Krif."

Before either could respond, Garth had pulled one of his daggers free. He sliced it across Krif's throat, killing him within moments, then spun around and cut down the other guard before he could sound an alarm. Both bodies slumped to the ground. Blood pooling on the marble floor. Garth wiped his dagger on his black sleeve, gazing at Krif with regret. If he had not acted, his second in command would have killed him as soon as he realised Garth was betraying them. Garth sheathed his dagger and signalled Evie.

She ran up to him, asking, "Now what?"

Garth turned to the door. "Stay behind me." He took a quick peek in her direction, adding. "I hope you can use your magic well, as Bazertari will not hesitate. He will have three of his personal guards with him."

Evie nodded. She would have to act fast.

Garth opened the door, making sure they did not step in the blood pooling on the floor. They entered the large room. Bazertari was sitting on the throne, looking bored. As Garth had stated, there were two helmeted guards on either side of him and one in the middle of the room. All three were as still as statues. Evie knew instantly that they were not human, sensing the evil radiating from them.

The warlock sat up straight and glared at Evie, then shifted his attention to Garth. "What is this?"

Garth responded, "Slan's sorceress, my Lord."

Bazertari stood, but a suspicious expression tightened his features. He frowned, studying Garth. Then he directed his gaze to Evie. "So, you are the person Slan brought through the portal. Where are you from, Barberium? Lost Island? Or further?"

Evie regarded him with disdain. He appeared older than the version she had encountered, but those cold, dark eyes were unforgettable. "Does it matter? I'm here to destroy you."

The warlock laughed as he stepped down from the dais. "I don't think so, my dear." He studied her intently as he stepped forward. "Let me give you an offer. Work for me, and we could dominate this land. Or if you refuse, Garth here, will execute you."

Evie pursed her lips. "Hmmm tempting, but to be honest, Bazertari, in my opinion, you're a bit of a prick." He cast a hostile gaze at her, and Evie added, "Moonstar will be a better place without you."

He turned and stared intensely at Garth, then snapped, "Kill her!"

Garth unsheathed his sword, but remained focused on the warlock and said, "Sorry, but I agree with her. I think it's time for your reign to end."

The three guards suddenly moved as one, turning towards Bazertari, then rushed at Garth, as they drew their swords. He deflected their blows, cutting one down in moments.

Evie glared at Bazertari as he turned back towards her. He smirked. "You aren't just any sorceress, are you?"

She answered, "No. I'm the sole person capable of ending this."

The warlock suddenly shot a plasma bolt from his hand; Evie was ready, and counter-attacked. Moments later, as she sent more plasma bolts at the warlock, Evie saw Ulric enter the royal chamber, but without Irric.

TWENTY SIX

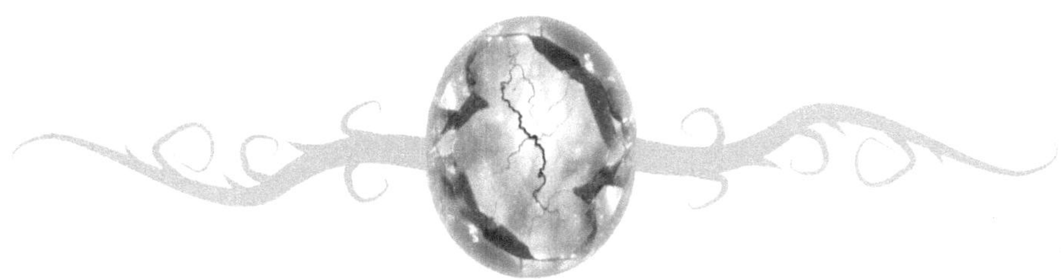

Ulric and Irric had entered the palace undiscovered, but it had not taken them long to come across a patrol. Garth had trained his men well, and the two Swords had a tough fight on their hands. As one small group went down, they soon came across another. It was a continuous fight for the two Swords, then Irric was wounded. After dealing with the last patrol, Ulric inspected Irric's side. He could still fight, but he would not be able to keep to Ulric's faster pace.

The young Sword glared at him and snapped, "You have to get to the throne room."

The older Sword regarded him. "We should stick together."

Irric smirked. "I know, but plans change. I'm capable of looking after myself. Now go."

Ulric glanced around and gave silent approval, then ran ahead to the royal chamber alone. The older Sword hoped it would not be the last time he saw Irric and whispered to Rosh that his companion made it.

Ulric slowed as he turned into the passageway to the royal chamber, seeing the dead guards by the threshold, their throats sliced with precision. His lips curled up slightly, impressed by the skill Evie had used to force her way in. He stepped over the pooling blood and entered the massive room.

The muscular Sword took in the scene as quickly as he could. Evie was at the far end, close to the dais, facing the warlock. Plasma bolts of blue and red light were flung between the two. The air in the room was thick with the vibration of magic. But she was not the only one fighting. Before him, in the centre of the room, were the warlock's personal guards and they were attacking Garth.

Ulric scowled. *Why is Garth fighting the warlock's own men and not helping to protect Bazertari?* Before Uric could determine the reason, one of Bazertari's personal guards ran at him. The muscular Sword quickly brought his sword up, parrying the guard's broadsword. The creature, from its fighting style, had once been a seasoned fighter.

Ulric blocked his assailant's next blow. His eyes flicked towards Garth, who was still focused on the guards attacking him. Ulric briefly wondered if the younger man had turned against Bazertari. The older Sword inhaled as he parried another blow from the guard. He had no time to understand what was happening; he needed to deal with what was in front of him. Then he could confront Garth. Ulric did not care if he may have changed sides, Garth still had to pay.

The inhuman guard swung at him again. Ulric counter-attacked and knocked off its helmet. Ulric's eyes widened at the sight of the mutilated features of what remained of Corun. The old Sword's stomach twisted, as he froze in shock. All that Ulric could see of Corun was covered with scars. His once warm and kind eyes were lifeless in their sunken sockets. Ulric had always feared what Corun's fate had been.

Nay, not him. Not that. Not Corun

The creature that had once been Corun attacked again, no recognition on his grey features. Ulric frowned. He had to end his friend's suffering, even if nothing remained of Corun. They continued to fight, blow for blow blocked by the other. The older Sword observed that even though Corun had transformed into something different, he kept one characteristic from his days as a fighter. Ulric took advantage of it, and in two moves, delivered a fatal blow. Corun dropped to the floor, mortally wounded.

Ulric took a breath, glad he had ended his friend's suffering. The older Sword turned his attention to Garth who was still fighting the other guard. The third guard's decapitated body laid nearby. But movement from the corner of his eye made

Ulric turn. He swallowed as his stomach dropped in fear. Corun stood up when no ordinary human could. Ulric's eyes widened in surprise as Corun came at him again, as if he had never been wounded. Ulric had to use a different tactic. The creature that had once been his friend ran towards Ulric, his sword up, ready to make a fatal blow. Ulric swung his sword high and sliced through Corun's neck.

Ulric whispered as the head dropped and bounced across the marble floor, "Rest now, my friend."

Ulric turned when he heard running footsteps behind him. It was Irric, rushing towards the main doors, with more of Garth's guards following. The old Sword needed to help his wounded companion before he could deal with his treacherous old friend.

Evie's attention was on Bazertari as he sent more red plasma bolts at her. She had noticed some activity from the corner of her eye. Ulric had entered the room and was already fighting one of the personal guards. She could not perceive how Ulric was coping with the constant onslaught of magical propellants hurled at her by the warlock. Another came at her, the red plasma crackling through the air. She dived low to the ground, dodging it, but a second came almost instantly, clipping her thigh. She yelled out, and staggered on her feet as she sent a blue bolt of plasma back at Bazertari.

Evie dared a glance at her thigh to see the smouldering section of her trousers and the skin below. She took a big breath to brace against the pain. Plasma gathered in her hand as she heard a disturbance by the doorway to the royal chamber. She dared a quick look to see Ulric turning to face more of Garth's men. Her eyes scanned the room, seeing that Garth was still fighting the remaining guard of the warlock's private force.

Evie focused on Bazertari again. She had to deal with him now. She sent a forceful blast towards him, sending the warlock flying backwards. His back hit the steps of the dais. Evie sensed the power within the stone, the spell beckoning to her.

Suddenly, Garth turned from the personal guard as it dropped to the floor, lifeless, and ran at Bazertari, shouting a war cry. He was a distraction, giving Evie time.

The warlock recovered quickly from being thrown by Evie and was already getting back on his feet. He scowled as he saw Garth running at him, and forced the young Sword away from him with a magical blast, launching him into the battle at the entrance.

Bazertari then turned to Evie and glared at her, his dark eyes wild. Smirking, he sent a powerful blast of energy her way. Evie had to quickly pull up a shield, but the force of the blast still pushed her backwards. She gritted her teeth as she used her shield to push back against the force the warlock was sending at her. But the warlock pushed again, sending more dark energy towards her. Evie took a deep breath and delved deep into her magic. That was when the pain burrowed into her wrist. She gritted her teeth pulling at more of the magic in her and pushed back, ignoring the pain, but she knew what was happening without looking. The new bracelet was burrowing into her skin like the other one had. Silver vines threaded deep into her, wrapping themselves around tendons, bones and flesh, fusing with her, giving her all its power in the process. The force of the power flew from her, hitting the next wave from the warlock. When the two spears of magic struck each other, the blast wave catapulted them both in opposite directions. Evie hit the far wall next to an impressive tapestry with a bone crunching crack. As she looked up, she saw Garth running at the warlock again, his sword about to find its mark. But with a flick of his wrist, a portal opened, and Bazertari fell through it.

Evie cursed, her head throbbing. She closed her eyes, sensing a wave of dizziness.

Garth ran towards the warlock after being thrown into the brawl near the entrance. As he reached him, his sword swung round to attack, but a portal suddenly opened and Bazertari vanished. Garth cried out in frustration as his sword sliced through space. Then, for a moment, there was silence in the royal chamber. Garth stood there gasping, hearing the remainder of his men die.

Then he heard Ulric snarl, "You're going to die, *Garth!*"

The young Sword turned to see his old mentor scowling at him. Irric was off to the side cradling a wounded side and no longer able to fight. He had not seen Irric since the day he had won the Guardian Tournament and wondered where he had been hiding all these years.

His attention quickly returned to Ulric when the older Sword roared, "*Stand and fight, boy!*"

Garth gripped his sword, his palm sweaty from the fighting, his voice flat, "I don't want to fight you. I helped Evie."

Ulric snorted, glancing across at Evie who lay dazed on the floor. "*Liar!*"

Garth backed away from him and pleaded, "Her memories made me realise what I'd fecked up. And I want to right what I've done."

Ulric growled, "Evie was a fool to share those memories with you. I know you are cold to the core, Garth, and you need to pay. Now *fight!*"

Garth knew Ulric would not listen to him. Garth believed he deserved to be killed by the man he had disappointed the most. Ulric would not just kill him, though; he would want him to fight. It was the honourable way for a Sword to die. Garth wondered why, as he did not deserve an honourable death. But this was how Ulric saw justice to be done, by fighting Sword to Sword.

Garth secured a firm grip on the leather hilt of his longsword and faced the older man. He parried Ulric's blow. Even in his early fifties, he was a formidable opponent. Garth spun his sword, nicking Ulric's arm and the older man sucked in air between his teeth. Ulric glanced at his arm and glared at Garth. He swung at the young man, slicing deep across his mid-section.

Garth cried out, placing his hand on his stomach, as blood seeped through his shirt. With being distracted, Ulric took advantage of it and ran at Garth. Using the pommel of his sword, he hit the young man squarely in the face. A dirty move; one that Garth would have done if he had been wanting to win.

Garth staggered back, losing his balance, landing on his rump. He sat on the marble floor and spat a mixture of blood and saliva from his mouth. Garth was exhausted and ready to die. The young Sword pressed on his wound and stared at his experienced mentor. Ulric firmed his grip on his sword. With pure rage in his eyes, he moved forward to deliver a deadly strike.

Evie slowly came too, her head aching, her vision blurred and realised she must have passed out. Her senses sharpened with the agony from where Bazertari's plasma bolt had made its mark. She could hear fighting, swords clashing. Slowly sitting up, she got her bearings. She turned towards the noise just in time to see Garth stagger back and fall to the ground, his face cut, a stream of blood flowing from his nose. She looked over and found Ulric in a rage, about to strike a fatal blow.

She screamed, staggering to her feet, "*NO!*"

Evie ran as quickly as possible with her injury, stopping between the two men, blocking Ulric. He had to pull back quickly to stop his sword from slicing across her chest.

Ulric snarled, his face contorted in rage, "Step aside, Evie!"

She stood her ground, trying to not put too much weight on her wounded leg. "No!"

The older Sword glared at her. "He *has* to die!"

Evie glanced back to see Garth struggling to his feet. His sword was almost forgotten in his hand. He was gasping for breath, unable to continue.

She faced Ulric again, her voice ladened with sadness, "No. Let him go."

Ulric was visibly frustrated, gripping his sword. "Evie, he is not *that* Garth! How many *fecking* times do I have to tell you? He *murdered* my friends . . ." His voice broke with emotion and rage, "and allies, and he must *pay!*"

Garth spat blood from his mouth and said from behind her, his voice flat with defeat, "Ulric is right."

Evie turned and shot him an angry look. "*No!* Now leave while you still can."

Garth paused, looking at the two.

Ulric sneered. "Let me finish this."

Evie glared at the older man, blue sparks flickering between her fingers. "I can't let you kill him, Ulric."

Evie could hear Garth staggering away. Ulric gripped his sword. He glanced upwards at the ceiling and let out a yell of frustration. Evie flinched but stood her ground. Ulric faced her again. He was breathing hard, his face flushed, his eyes teeming with anger. As he fixated on her, they both calmed. Evie let the magic dissipate, and touched Ulric's tense arm.

"Let him go."

He stared at her, his body coiled up tight.

Evie studied him with affection. "I *know* he's not the Garth I loved. But *my* Garth lost his life. I want this one to live his."

Ulric looked at her, his expression filled with sadness. He pleaded, "But he *killed* so many."

Evie's hand cupped his that held the sword. "I know, but he's not *that* Garth anymore. He wants to make reparation, and I know he will roam this land till his dying day to do that."

Ulric gazed in the direction that Garth had gone. He swore and slowly sheathed his sword, looking around at all the dead bodies. Ulric glanced over at Evie when she exhaled audibly.

He asked, "What about Bazertari?"

Evie shrugged and winced, her leg throbbing. "I don't know. We must find him. Then I can use the spell."

Ulric regarded her, noticing she was leaning. He then saw her singed trousers. "Evie . . ."

She glanced down, seeing the charred flesh. She gripped Ulric's arm as a wave of nausea hit her. "He clipped me."

He took her arm. "You need to have it looked at."

Evie turned her attention to him and smiled softly, noticing his own cuts and bruises. Irric was struggling to get to his feet from where he was resting near the entrance, holding his bloody side. Evie turned to him and limped over to examine his wound. She briefly glanced at Ulric and his wounded arm. "Both of you need your wounds tended to."

The old Sword gestured, walking over, taking her arm again. "As do you." Ulric again glanced towards the side entrance where Garth had run. He tightened his lips and clenched his fist.

She could tell from the residual rage in his eyes that, for now, he would honour her wishes. But if he crossed paths with Garth again, the outcome would be different.

Ulric refocused his attention back to Evie and Irric. He surveyed the room and aided Irric in getting to his feet. "Come on, we must take you both somewhere safe. There may be others still here."

Evie gave silent approval, surveying the room. Her attention was captured by a severed head and she gasped. There was no denying who it was, despite the scars and disfigurement of the features.

Her hand went to her mouth. "Oh god. Corun."

Ulric squeezed her shoulder and muttered, "I couldn't let him suffer."

Evie looked up at him. Her face was full of sorrow as she comprehended what Corun must have endured before he became that thing. "I wonder how many more—"

Ulric cut her off. "There were many."

She nodded, seeing the flash of hate in his eyes. Evie realised even more why Ulric had wanted to kill Garth. But in spite of his past deeds, Evie hoped Garth would become their ally once again. She turned when Ulric's hand left her shoulder. He had moved to help Irric, who winced in pain when he tried to stand straight.

The younger Sword muttered, "We must continue to fight."

Ulric disagreed, "Nay, my friend. Let's get you both healed first."

The large man supported Irric, Evie limping by his side as they eased down the main corridor. Ulric had seen a door close by and said that it had to be the king's study. It would be a secure room where they could rest while Evie healed herself and Irric. Then they could search the palace.

Evie slumped in an armchair in the extensive study, as Ulric helped Irric sit in the one opposite. She winced from the discomfort in her hip and studied the charred flesh. Evie placed her palm on it. Closing her eyes, she concentrated and her hand glowed. After a few moments, the pain subsided and when she looked again; the skin was pink and healed.

She stood up, turning to Irric, and regarded his side. It was a deep wound, and he had lost blood. She raised her gaze towards him and smiled. "Stay still."

Irric observed her hand glowing over the wound until he was healed. He acknowledged gratitude and Evie turned towards Ulric. The muscular Sword was standing by the study door, his gaze fixed on the corridor beyond. She gently touched his shoulder, and he snapped her a look. Being wound so tight, the large man seemed on the verge of exploding. She concentrated on his eyes. "Ulric, relax."

He regarded her. "I will once I have patrolled the palace."

Evie agreed, gently touching his injured arm. As it glowed, she stated, "We'll split up and make sure there aren't any stragglers."

He stared at her intently, touching her cheek. "Just be careful."

She smiled. "And you." She glanced past him, hearing shouts in the distance. "I think once they know Bazertari has gone, they will run."

"Aye, but some will have nothing to lose." His attention shifted towards Irric, who stood and rotated his shoulder. "Let's go now and make sure the palace is secure."

TWENTY SEVEN

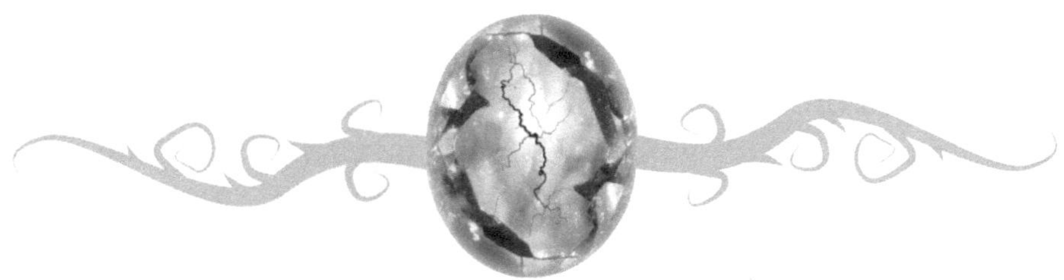

With Bazertari escaping, the palace seemed to fall silent. The three soon realised that most of the remaining army had run. Ulric, who had a better understanding of the layout, provided them with a brief explanation of the palace's structure and areas to search. If they were outnumbered, they were to run back and lock themselves in the study until the others returned. Each having their dedicated areas to explore, they left the safety of the study and ventured into the silent corridors, separating and heading to their appointed locations.

Ulric strolled along the deserted corridor on the east side of the palace. Any stragglers he found were dealt with quickly. Some surrendered, but there were one or two who, with nothing to lose, fought. But they were no match for the experienced Sword who was running on anger and adrenaline.

He was still regretting not defying Evie and killing Garth. Ulric's emotions were conflicted and he could not decide what to do about the redhead who was constantly on his mind. He had told her so many times this Garth was not the same one she had adored. Yet, Evie seemed to hope there was still good in the man Ulric had seen only as the enemy for years. Ulric slowed, rubbing his temples. That was one thing that drew him to Evie, her compassion. But with Garth, it was her weakness. He exhaled deeply. He had searched this section of the palace hoping to find Garth and face him; finish what he had started all those hours before.

As he walked, Ulric replayed the fight in his mind. Even Garth knew he deserved to die. He could see it in the young man's eyes. He was done. Ulric was vexed. *Why had Garth been fighting Bazertari's men? Had he changed sides like Evie had said?* Ulric checked a side corridor. Even if Garth had changed sides, his hatred for him would never go away.

Ulric gazed out the windows on the side of the long hallway at the palace grounds, observing guards running. He had promised Evie to leave Garth be. Perhaps it was about time to let his hatred go, see if Garth repented. Ulric sighed. He was getting soft in his old age. He turned from the view of the grounds and carried on exploring the deserted halls, hoping deep down that Garth made amends for what he had done. If Ulric heard otherwise, no matter how much he cared for Evie, he would put an end to Garth.

Having checked the deserted barracks, Ulric was strolling back from his section of the palace when he came upon the entrance to the dungeons. He knew it had to be checked and ventured down into the bowels of the palace. The stench of decay invaded his nostrils, but it was silent, no one was left alive. It grew colder as he travelled further. He paused at some stone steps that led down into darkness. A chill went down his spine and Ulric tentatively took them. Reaching the bottom he then discovered a tunnel entrance at the end of the corridor.

The old Sword paused. *Had Bazertari made a section to hold more prisoners?* He thought of Corun and wondered what had befallen his friend to turn him into that thing. *Had he been held captive in these dark depths?* The evil he could sense down there would have twisted anything to its will. Ulric shut his eyes, thinking of Iesha. Corun and that kind woman never got the life they could have had.

Ulric swallowed, staring into the darkness, sensing evil in the air. The hairs on the back of his neck raised as he became aware of something watching him. He reset his grip on his sword and took a hesitant step closer. Then the experienced Sword froze. Even he knew it was unwise to venture into the dark depths alone. Ulric stared into the darkness. Goose flesh crept across his arms. The air was thick with evil. He would need to speak to Slan. They had to ensure they sealed this area off as soon as possible.

His breath hitched as a sudden flash of anguish rolled over him, and he could see the very same dungeon through Evie's eyes, although it was fragmented. Ulric recalled Evie mentioning how her time down here had been erased by Slan. But after seeing the tunnel it seemed some of those fragments had remained.

Ulric sheathed his sword, as his mind wandered to Evie. His emotions towards her had grown stronger of late. As he got to know her, it pulled him closer to her. With what had become of Corun, Ulric knew he had to take that leap with Evie. His lips ached remembering their kiss and was glad that her feelings for him appeared to be as strong.

Ulric sighed. Focusing on the here and now. He wanted to be with Evie, but there were more pressing matters that had to be attended to. It was clear that the royal family was gone, with that, the land would fall into turmoil and steps would have to be taken. They will have to inform Slan and see what the sorcerer suggested.

He stepped up the stone steps back into the palace, absorbed in his thoughts. *With Bazertari still alive, would it be wise to pursue a relationship?* From what he knew of the other land, Evie and Garth had pursued their feelings and fought alongside each other. He wondered if they should wait till the warlock was dead. But it could take them months or even years to catch him. Ulric gently pressed his fingers against his temples. The exhaustion from all the fighting was catching up with him, and his shoulders were protesting from age. With years of drinking, his body felt the effects of a battle more than he used to. Then he saw Evie ahead as she walked towards him with Irric. Both looked just as exhausted.

She asked as he reached them, "Anyone?"

Ulric shook his head, seeing dawn breaking in the distance from the corridor window. "I checked the dungeons, all are gone. The royal family is dead."

Evie's free hand played at the damaged material on her black trousers, where Bazertari had hit her with one of his plasma bolts in the earlier fight. As she inspected her wound, her fingers delicately pulled a loose thread, her voice filled with sorrow, "Slan will be sad to hear the news."

Ulric responded, "Aye. Once he arrives, we will know the necessary actions to take."

She lifted her gaze towards him, appraising his features. "You look exhausted."

"Aye, we all need time to recover. The palace is secure. Let's stay in that study and get some rest. It will be necessary for us to check the city and grounds in a few hours."

Evie rubbed her temples as they strolled back. "I think before I rest, I'll try to send word to Slan."

Ulric asked as he followed her, "Do you know how?"

Evie turned back towards him as they entered the room. "He said we had a connection. I'm hoping, if I focus, I can talk to him."

Ulric nodded as Evie sank into an armchair, placing her sword at her side. Ulric glanced round the room, Irric found some alcohol off to the side, and quickly turned to Ulric, acknowledging them. He gestured disapproval by shaking his head. Alcohol was not what he needed. Uric could not relax, he sensed that he had overlooked something.

Ulric glanced over at Evie. Her eyes were closed, and it seemed she was mumbling something. She must have contacted Slan. He turned to Irric and whispered, "I'm just going to take another final look."

Irric raised an eyebrow as he took a gulp of the strong drink he had found. "The palace is empty."

Ulric stated, "Aye, but I can't relax."

Irric regarded him. "Just make sure you get some rest, Ulric."

The older Sword acknowledged with a slight movement of his head, but he continued contemplating Evie and all the events that transpired in the past few hours. His mind was in turmoil while attempting to balance his loyalty to Evie with the deep-seated resentment he harboured towards Garth. As he walked down the corridor, he released a heavy sigh. If he saw Garth again, he would have to make a decision. He worried that could not honour Evie's request. But until he saw Garth again, he could not be sure.

The sun had already peeked over the horizon when Ulric finally returned to the study to find both Evie and Irric asleep. He settled in an armchair and gazed over at Evie. He hoped once things had settled, they could talk.

Ulric exhaled slowly and gazed at the smouldering fire. He was still finding it hard to sleep, his mind wondering; *Where has that warlock gone? Will he return to get revenge?* Ulric sighed. After a good fight, it was hard to wind down, but his body ached, and he needed to recover. There were uncertain days ahead, and he had to be ready. What concerned him more was that there was no royal family left. Moonstar always had a ruling royal line. *Could the land still prosper without one?* He rubbed his eyes, stifling a yawn. When Slan arrived, then they could sort out what they needed to do next.

"Ulric?" Evie spoke softly, gazing at the Sword as he slept in the armchair.

Evie had woken about an hour before and, seeing the Sword sleeping in the armchair, she had told Irric to leave him to rest. She was meditating when she heard him mentioning to the younger Sword he intended to make one last sweep before his repose. He had not returned for over an hour and Irric insisted she rested in the interim. When she had finally woken to see the mid-morning sun pouring into the comprehensive study, she had found Ulric asleep and wondered when he had returned.

She left to patrol with Irric, who had woken earlier and gone to find food. But the palace was empty. They needed to leave the building and investigate the gardens and then the city. But for that, they needed Ulric.

Evie smiled as he slowly opened his eyes and directed his attention to her. He smiled warmly and rubbed his face. "How long was I asleep?"

Evie responded, "A few hours, I think."

He stood up. "We need to search the city."

Evie took a hold of his arm. "Yes, but just take a breath."

His attention was focused on her, his gaze unwavering as he sensed warm affection. "But we . . ."

Evie placed a finger to his lips. "Just stop."

He hesitated, looking at her. Evie rose to her tiptoes and affectionately pressed her lips against his.

She breathed, "I've been wanting to do that for hours."

Ulric intertwined his fingers into her hair and pulled her back to him and kissed her passionately. She surrendered to his touch, and their kiss deepened. Her body melted against his. Her arms slid around him.

Irric stepped into the study. "I think we . . ."

He trailed off, seeing the couple kissing. But his interruption broke their tranquillity and the two parted. Evie glanced over at him, her face flushed. The young Sword pivoted abruptly and muttered, "Sorry."

Evie smirked and turned her head to glance at Ulric, who gazed at her.

He breathed, "Shame we were interrupted."

Evie stroked his cheek and went to move, but Ulric kept his arm firmly round her waist. "We need to check the city," she reminded him.

Ulric grinned. "Aye, but I also want another kiss."

As his lips brushed hers, Evie glanced up at him. They kissed again, his hands pressing into her lower back, keeping their bodies pressed against each other. He then slowly breathed, "Now we can patrol the city."

Evie arched her eyebrow, detecting the bulge in his trousers. "You sure about that?"

He smirked, his hands resting gently on her back, still not letting her go. "Just give me a minute."

She lifted her gaze to meet his. "Promise me you will rest properly tonight."

Ulric softly planted a kiss on her lips. "Aye, if I have company."

Evie mumbled, "I wouldn't call that resting."

He gazed at her intently, smiling warmly. "I wasn't suggesting anything of that nature. Can a man just want to hold a woman in his arms?"

She went on tiptoe, kissing his lips. "Well, seems your body has other ideas."

Ulric kept her close, endeavouring to maintain control over his body. He filled his lungs with air and reluctantly let her go and murmured, "Alright, my body has other ideas. But I promise this eve, it will just be sleeping."

She gave him a look and walked towards the door, stating, "We'll see."

TWENTY EIGHT

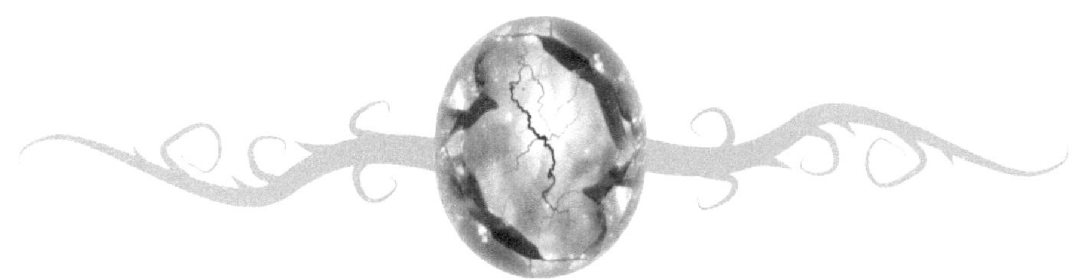

As the sun reached its zenith, the three had diligently searched the palace grounds. Yet, with Garth's men deserting their posts, the Swords realised that they would have to continue their search within the streets of the city.

Evie, Ulric and Irric left through the royal gates, the streets beyond coming to life and the rumours of the attack spreading like wildfire. Whenever they came across any of the locals, they were eager to help and promptly informed the three about the taverns that Garth's men preferred. And it seemed that some were still there, drowning in ale and waiting to surrender. The rest, as they had seen from the palace grounds, had run.

It was late afternoon when they returned to the palace. All were exhausted once more. They found, upon entering the throne room, Slan gazing at the dead bodies. When the three walked towards him, the sorcerer turned to them, his hands causally clasped behind his back.

The wise sorcerer observed them and said, "You did well."

Evie sighed, "But Bazertari escaped."

Slan's nod was slow and deliberate. "Aye, but he will fall."

Ulric surveyed the room. "We should clear this up and get the bodies buried."

The others agreed. Slan stated, "We cannot bury them on palace grounds. We will need help from the locals so we can transport the bodies and bury them in the woods."

Evie's gaze focused on Corun's severed head. "What about any who were once the Guild?"

Slan glanced at the remains of the one who he had named Guardian. "What was once them had died many years ago." He regarded the three. "They may appear to be someone you once knew, but it is just a shell." Slan sighed, "I will also need to place a spell on their graves to ensure they cannot be resurrected."

Evie and Ulric both gasped, "What!"

Slan took a long deep breath, gazing at the bodies. "Chopping the head off has ended them, but if Bazertari can get hold of their body parts, he can use dark magic to resurrect them. I must ensure that cannot happen."

Evie stared at the corpses, feeling sick at what the warlock could do if he had the opportunity.

With Slan's advice, they sent word to the city and soon volunteers had arrived, and they began moving the bodies. It was late evening by the time all were loaded onto carts and ready to be transported into the woods in the morning.

Ulric eyed Evie as they walked back into the palace, both exhausted. He slid his arm across her shoulder and gently planted a kiss on her temple. "I found us a room last eve. We can rest and not be disturbed."

She looked upwards at him; her features grey from tiredness. "The thought of a bed is making my limbs ache."

He pulled her close and squeezed her shoulder. "Come on."

The two ventured through the palace. Ulric, finding the room he had located the night before. When they entered the spacious room in the guest quarters of the palace, the enormous bed covered in deep green covers was inviting. The room had a dressing table with a green velvet stool, and in the space facing the bed, were two luxurious, high back armchairs. To the other far side was an enormous wardrobe, and a side door that was open, revealing an extensive bathroom.

Evie gazed at the bed as she unbuckled the strap holding her sword across her back, leaning it against the nearest armchair, her belt falling to the floor as she then undid her jerkin. She peered at Ulric as he sat pulling off his boots, his eyes dark from exhaustion. Evie walked casually towards the bed and slumped onto it and pulled off her boots, gasping in delight. She wriggled her toes and gazed over to the muscular Sword as he stood undoing his jerkin.

She fell back onto the bed, sighing, "I'm shattered."

He smirked as he laid down next to her. "You have some unusual sayings, lass."

She rolled onto her side and gazed at him. "I could say the same for you."

Ulric locked his eyes on her as he slid his arm under her, pulling her close. Evie cuddled up to him, experiencing the embrace of his arms around her. She rested her head against his chest and sighed, "This is nice."

He tenderly kissed her on her head then rested his head on the pillow and took a deep breath. "Let's just stay here for a while."

Evie placed her palm on his shirt, sensing his muscles beneath, his breath slow and steady. She shut her eyes, listening to his strong heart beating. The steady sound relaxed her.

She murmured, "I like that idea."

Ulric smiled softly, his eyes closed, the weight of Evie against him. The way she rested her head on his chest was perfect. It felt like it had always been this way and he did not want the moment to end. In the morning, they had the hard task of burying all the bodies. Then looking at what needed to be done to restore the land. But, for just a few hours, it would be the two of them, and nothing else.

TWENTY NINE

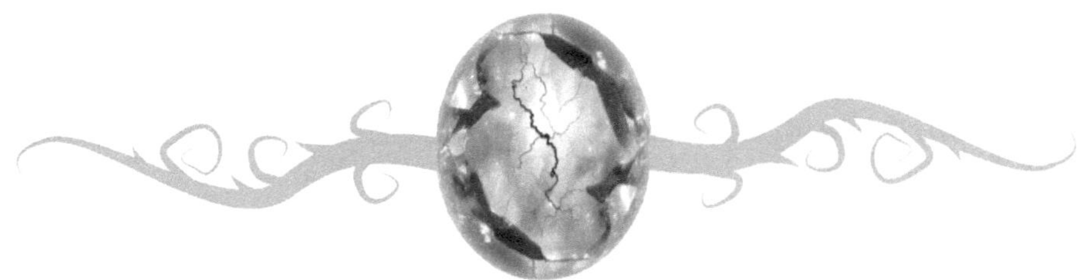

On the following day, the bodies were taken beyond the city wall and into the Great Wood. Once the bodies had been buried in a clearing deep within the woods, the sorcerer placed a protective spell over the grave to ensure any remaining dark magic was eradicated. A group of townsfolk and the three Swords quietly watched, some murmuring prayers to the gods they worshipped. Slan then used another spell to seed the ground with plant growth, and within moments, there was no evidence that there was a mass grave beneath.

As they made their way back to the palace, Evie and Irric socialised with some of the townspeople, while the rest of the group remained quiet, lost in their own thoughts.

Ulric walked with Slan behind the group. He leant close to the sorcerer and whispered, "I need to show you the dungeons. There is something down there."

Slan murmured, "Aye, I perceived the dark presence as soon as I arrived yester noon."

Ulric glanced at the old man. "You know of it?"

"Aye, like Evie, I remember the land as it was before. In that Moonstar, I removed the presence once the royal family had been rescued. Of course, it has been here far longer this time, and I recall, some years before, sensing Bazertari pulling something dark from its depths."

The muscular Sword eyed him. "Then we must ensure it is dealt with as soon as we can."

Slan patted his arm. "Aye, we will."

The two fell silent, both regarding the tall, stone walls as the group re-entered the city. Ulric, Evie, Slan and Irric made their way towards the palace while the city folk returned to their homes in a sombre mood.

When they entered the palace, Ulric returned to the conversation with the sorcerer while they casually strolled down the deserted corridor. The tapping of Slan's staff as he walked echoed around them.

Ulric advised, "I think we should go to the dungeons now. We should not leave whatever is there dwelling in those depths for long."

Evie regarded the two, slowing her pace to join the conversation. "From what I remember the last time I was here, there was some type of evil presence. I remember having this feeling of something watching."

Ulric directed his gaze at her, then shifted his attention to Slan. "Aye, the air seems thick with evil, and I heard a creature of some sort."

Irric, who had also walked up beside Slan, regarded the three. "Wouldn't surprise me, with what Bazertari is capable of. Also, look at what happened to Corun. That warlock must have had something dark to turn him into that thing."

Ulric turned to Evie, his eyes hard with concern when he saw her anxiously chewing on her lip, demonstrating the emotions she was experiencing at the thought of venturing down into the dungeons' depths.

Irric patted her shoulder. "I need help in the armoury. See what we have and what will need to be crafted by myself and the other swordsmiths in the city."

Ulric agreed, glad Irric had noticed Evie's distress about the dungeons. "Aye, we should divide our efforts into bringing order back to the palace. You go with Irric while Slan and I deal with the dungeons."

Her eyes focused on the stocky Sword, her features full of relief. She squeezed Ulric's arm and gazed at him and Slan. "Both of you, be careful."

Ulric smiled. "Aye, we will, lass."

Ulric watched as Evie and Irric walked down the corridor towards the barracks. He turned to Slan as the old sorcerer commented, "It was wise for Evie not to venture down there."

As they walked towards the section of the palace where the dungeons were located, Ulric asked, "What happened to her down there? I have seen Evie's memories, but that time seems to be just a blur."

Slan replied, "That is because I removed most of them. Her time confined in the dark dungeon was not something to remember. Bazertari placed a despair spell upon her. But as I healed her, I saw the genuine horrors of what she had to endure."

Ulric swallowed, his stomach knotting in fear. "By Rosh."

Slan affirmed silently, and as they entered the dungeon, he stated, "That is why I must destroy all that is down here."

Ulric bit at his nail. "Do you think Corun and the others endured such horrors?"

Slan eyed him. "Aye. From the evil source and the dungeon keeper who would have tormented them."

"Dungeon keeper?"

Slan stopped and looked at Ulric. "Never reveal to Evie any of the details I am about to disclose to you. The dungeon keeper was a disturbed man." Slan paused, rubbing his temple. "Let us just say he relished the fact that the prisoners were in his charge and at his mercy."

Ulric clenched his fist. "If I cross that man, he will pay."

Slan gazed around the main dungeon and sighed, "Alas, I believe nothing living is here now."

Ulric frowned. "What of the creature I heard?"

Slan pursed his lips, briefly closing his eyes. "Nay, I sense nothing. Show me the entrance."

Ulric guided Slan further into the dungeon and then showed the entrance. He confessed, "I would have ventured in, but the evil was so thick, I realised it was in my best interest to wait for you."

Slan raised his gaze towards him. "Aye, stay here my friend, and I will see what needs be done."

After parting ways with Ulric at the base of the stone steps, Slan continued to stroll along the corridor and stepped through the carved out entrance and strode deeper into the depths of the tunnel. He emerged into a second dungeon with cells as far as he could see in the dim light. The sorcerer made a glowing blue sphere appear, and it floated above him, illuminating a little further. But the light could not penetrate the darkness, which seemed more like a thick fog.

As Ulric had described to him, Slan could sense nothing but pure evil. He shivered, gripping his staff firmly, sensing spirits from the dark realm. This was far worse than the one he had destroyed in the alternative Moonstar. It was no wonder that nothing human remained if left down there for too long. The sorcerer murmured a spell and a shield of silver light shimmered around him, protecting him from the evil spirits.

Slan walked carefully, his footsteps light, daring not to arouse anything that remained. Ulric had mentioned a creature, but all Slan could hear was the whispers of the dark spirits. But there was a faint smell, and as he walked further, it became more acrid.

As he ventured deeper, the tapping of his staff seemed to be his only company. He slowed, peering over his shoulder as he sensed an evil presence emerge. It seemed he had attracted something to him. Slan closed his eyes, strengthening his shield. This dark dungeon was far deeper and stronger than the other one, but then again, it had many more years to develop.

He sighed, dreading what pain and suffering Corun and others of the Guild must have endured when they were down there. The sorcerer tried not to focus on what cruelty the dungeon keeper would have done, especially to the women. Slan stopped, getting a hold of his emotions. When he had healed Evie and removed the despair spell, he had not expected to see such horrid memories. He knew it was wrong to clear her mind like he had, but if he had let her remember all of it, the quest would have failed, and would have left Evie as a tortured soul.

Slan continued focusing on the present concern. He had forgotten what he had seen in Evie's mind, but now, being here again, it resurfaced. Slan took a breath and cleared his mind as he strolled deeper. He stopped, reaching the source of the stench. The large metal door was bolted. Slan opened it and sent a ball of light in to illuminate the space, as he gazed into a small cave. There were rotting corpses and faeces everywhere. He frowned, seeing a large area mostly clear of debris, and chains in the far wall. An enormous creature had once lived there but, whatever it was, it could not move freely as evidenced by some corpses that were squashed by a heavy weight. Slan tightened his lips, wondering what type of beast had been there. Slan could perceive evil and a sense of something beyond earthly existence. He swallowed nervously, wondering where the creature had gone.

Has Bazertari taken it? If so, what value is it to the warlock?

The sorcerer looked again at the main part of the dark dungeon, sensing the evil as it closed in around him. It was trying to penetrate his shield. He needed to eradicate it quickly before it broke down his defence and devoured him.

Ulric shifted nervously. His eyes were on the tunnel entrance. Slan had been gone too long. He dragged his sword free, gripping the hilt tightly in his hand. The Sword inhaled deeply. He went to step over the threshold of the tunnel, when he saw movement in the dark depths. Ulric's palms became sweaty.

Was the presence trying to break free? Whatever it was, it was getting closer.

Then Slan emerged from the darkness, his features pale, drained. A silver shimmer dissolved around him.

Ulric stepped back and exhaled in relief. "I was worried."

The sorcerer responded, "It goes deeper than I anticipated."

"The creature?"

"Gone. Whatever it was, Bazertari has taken it."

Ulric sighed, "Feck." He glanced in Slan's direction. "And the evil?"

Slan turned his head to see the tunnel. "Stronger than I had expected, and I banished most of it," he said, "but it is too saturated. I must ensure we seal this so nay one can enter."

Ulric stepped further back as Slan turned to concentrate on the tunnel entrance, passing his staff to him to hold. The Sword sensed the rumble beneath his feet as the tunnel collapsed. The entrance filled with rubble, dust pushing through the air towards them. Slan stopped his spell and regarded the blocked entrance.

He glanced at Ulric. "Now to seal it fully."

Ulric watched as the sorcerer mumbled a new spell, his hands moving in circles before him. Strange symbols floated in the air, glowing with a golden light. The sorcerer continued, the light growing brighter as the symbols arranged themselves into a circular pattern. Ulric watched as the circular seal with the strange symbols round the edge floated and settled around the remnants of the tunnel entrance. As it vanished, the entrance turned into solid rock, no evidence of a tunnel ever having been there.

Slan grabbed Ulric's arm for support. The Sword, looking concerned. "Slan?"

The elderly sorcerer directed his gaze towards him as he reclaimed his staff. "I am well. It is just draining to make a seal powerful enough to hold back such evil."

Ulric watched him as he leant heavily on the staff and took Slan's arm. "Let me walk you back to the study where you can rest."

Slan chuckled, patting his muscular arm. "You are a gentle soul, Ulric. I will be well in a moment or two."

Ulric gazed at him. He had never seen Slan look so old and hoped the sorcerer he had known all his life would be well.

THIRTY

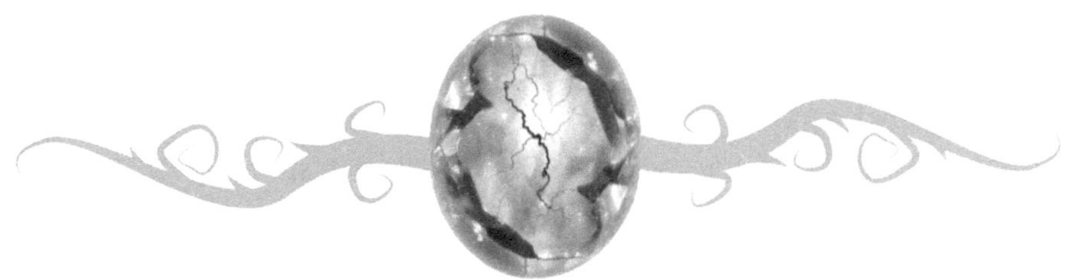

Evie sat in the quiet inn, having ale. Ulric and Irric were at the palace checking on the security with Slan. The last couple of days had been intense with tracking down any of Garth's remaining men and ensuring Great Oak was safe once more. Slan, having permanently sealed a section of the dungeon, also rid the palace of a chill that had been in the air since Bazertari's assumption of power. It had made Evie's skin crawl, wondering what had gone on in the depths of those dungeons and what creature they had imprisoned down there. With trying to secure the city and enlist new members for the royal guard, none of the four had rested. Except that one night when she and Ulric had slept cuddled up together, they had hardly rested properly since. That morning, Ulric had seen how exhausted Evie was, and had insisted that she take a break. He suggested a drink and a meal before she met with Slan later that day to discuss their next move.

Evie went to the tavern where she sat listening to the chatter amongst the customers. Although he had abandoned the city, Bazertari was on everyone's mind, including her own. Ulric had told her to relax, but Evie found it hard to stop wondering about the whereabouts of the warlock and if they could ever destroy him.

The barmaid came over and smiled, breaking Evie's thoughts. As she placed a plate of thickly sliced bread with meat and cheese down, the young girl stopped, studying Evie. Then, glancing around, she passed Evie a note. Evie frowned as she took it, wondering who had sent it to her. She expressed gratitude to the barmaid with a nod and then opened it. She smiled softly, recognising Garth's handwriting.

Meet me tonight.
The alleyway by Old Smith Lane.
G

Evie wondered where he had gone since seeing him sneak away after the fight in the throne room. Evie thought he would have left the city by now. He could have taken his horse and been miles away. Then again, he was pretty banged up and would need his wounds dealt with before he could ride anywhere. Garth may still have some contacts in the city to help him, but that may not last long.

Her eyes locked on the amber liquid of her drink. It would be nice to see Garth and be able to say goodbye. She just hoped he kept to his word. Evie had seen the look on Ulric's face, and he would still kill Garth if their paths crossed again. If that happened, there would be nothing she could do about it without jeopardising her friendship with the Swords.

Evie sighed, placing the note in her pocket. She resumed eating and took a gulp of her ale. She was seeing Slan in a couple of hours, but after that, she could venture back into the city. She would meet with Garth and find out what his plans were.

Evie entered the royal chamber to see Slan studying the impressive tapestry on the wall. She walked up towards it, noticing it depicted Landor's and Bazertari's battle, but Landor's features were wrong, his kind features that she remembered had been twisted with evil. Evie diverted her eyes from the artwork and surveyed her surroundings. There was no evidence of any fight, yet Evie's gaze was fixated on the ground near the dais where Bazertari had vanished. Her

201

stomach twisted in apprehension at the warlock's unknown whereabouts.

Slan turned and smiled. She took in a breath; he looked so frail.

The old sorcerer strolled over to her, leaning on his staff as he moved. "Thank you for endeavouring to protect this land again, Evie."

She announced, "We will find Bazertari, and then Moonstar will be free." She paused. "Do we know where he may have gone?"

He responded, "Alas, nay. I cannot sense him, so wherever he may be hiding, he has a powerful shielding spell. I have sent word to all I know, asking for help."

Evie stated, "We should find him. See if we can locate any of his allies."

Slan studied her, his intense eyes locked onto her green. "Speaking of allies, I hear you let Garth go."

Her eyes shifted downward. "Yes. I couldn't let him die. He helped me get into the palace when he realised what could have been."

Slan stared directly at her. "It was a dangerous game you played, Evie. Ulric said Garth wanted to die."

Evie explained, "He knew he should have to pay for all he'd done, but I want Garth to live. The one I loved didn't."

Slan squeezed her hand. "I understand, and I hope it was the right choice."

Evie asked, "So, what now?"

Slan took a long, deep breath. "With the royal family gone, we need to find a new way to govern. I know of a distant relative who may take over the throne. And with Bazertari out there, they may become a target if they haven't already." He studied her. "Then, when this is all done, I will get you home."

Evie studied him and bit her lip. "Slan, I would prefer not to be sent back."

He frowned, "But your life there."

She briefly averted her gaze and then regarded him. "When I returned, I wasn't the same girl. In that world, I couldn't use my powers, and I felt lost. Moonstar is my home, and think it always has been."

Slan touched her shoulder gently. "Are you sure? You will give up all that you know."

She replied, "I am. I don't need to return like I had to last time." She sighed, looking around. "And to be honest, well, I think I will have a happier life here."

"I understand."

Evie studied him. "As I will be staying, when we have time, can you guide me on how I could connect with my parents? I want them to know I'm okay and not to worry about me."

Slan responded, "Aye. I think you are powerful enough to connect to them and talk with them. I will need to find the right spell."

Evie looked round the room and let out a deep breath, then refocused her attention on Slan. "I have to ask you something."

He glanced in her direction. "What is it? I sensed something troubled you when I saw you at Brak's inn, but with everything at stake, I needed you to focus."

"I know. But I need to know something." Evie paused, squeezing her hands together nervously. "When I returned to my world, I tried to live my life. But there were other things. I wasn't ageing, and . . ." She glanced in his direction. "I couldn't have. . ."

Slan inquired, "Children?"

Evie gave a slight affirmative gesture. "I must know, was it because of the stone? I know that's why my gran died, because of the energy in it."

Slan clasped her hand firmly and sighed. "You are a sorceress, Evie and with that, you will live an almost endless life, but at a cost. Nay magic user can reproduce. It is a solitary life." He studied her with affection. "I have lived over five hundred years and have had many friends and . . . lovers, but the outcome is the same. I will live out my life alone."

"So, it will be the same for me?" Evie peered at him intently. "And if I did return, would it still be the same?"

Slan gave a slow, affirmative nod. "Aye."

Evie drew in a long breath. "I see." She directed her gaze towards him and flashed a smile. "But here, I can be what I'm destined to be. I'll live a long life, but I can be free."

"Aye, you will."

Evie squeezed his hand. It was a lot to take in, but she would still sooner live hundreds of years in a land where she was whole than in a world where she was not.

"Thank you for telling me. I know you mention it will be a life alone, but look at the many people who you have known in your lifetime."

Slan chuckled. "Aye, I have had several drunken nights of conversation with so many."

Evie grinned. "And many more."

Slan concentrated on her eyes. "In the morn, I will have a task for you and Ulric."

"To find Bazertari."

The sorcerer nodded. "Aye, but also to search for the royal family members and bring them back here. But for now, get some rest. It has been a lengthy few days, and I have told Ulric and Irric to rest as well. Irric must return to Kerlish very soon, but he will help me here before he goes. So, you and Ulric will fulfil the task I have for you both." He paused. "But before you leave, I will find the spell so you can message your parents. You will not need me present, but if I tell you what to do, you can then pick the time and place."

Evie looked at him with affection and said, "Thank you, but promise me, Slan, you'll rest as well. You look tired."

"I will, my girl, I will."

Evie was worried to see him looking so frail. She embraced him softly and left. Moving down the primary hallway, she saw Ulric ahead talking to one of the new palace staff.

As he noticed her approaching, he dismissed the young man kindly and turned his focus to her with a smile, asking, "How was the ale and food?"

She directed her attention towards him. "Good, you should have joined me."

"Aye, I think I should have. It would have been far more interesting than checking the security of the palace."

Evie curled her arm through his. "You enjoy it really."

He grinned, staring at her as they walked down the corridor and asked, "Did your meeting go well with Slan?"

"It did. He now knows that I want to stay here. He's also going to find me a spell so I can send word to my parents."

Ulric stopped and turned to face her, placing his arms loosely round her. "I'm so glad that you're staying. We can become more acquainted. But are you sure you want to leave your other life behind?"

She concentrated on his captivating blue eyes. "Yes, I'm sure. This is my home now. It also gives me an excuse to get to know you again. It's odd you are so much like the Ulric I met before. But you're also . . . different."

"I hope that's good."

"It is."

He moved closer to her and gently kissed her on the lips. "These past few days there has been so much going on, we haven't really had time to talk." He let out a sigh as Irric approached them. He cursed under his breath, "By Rosh, I forgot I was going to go over the armoury's inventory with Irric."

Evie smiled softly, unknown to anyone she had a meeting with Garth later. "Don't worry. I have things to do as well. But based on the information Slan shared with me, we will have plenty of time to talk."

Ulric gazed at her intently and kissed her again. He breathed close to her lips, "I can't wait."

She regarded him. "Ulric, promise me you will get an early night. These last few . . ."

He replied, "On Rosh."

They separated, and Evie watched Ulric walk down the corridor chatting to Irric. She smiled softly. She then headed the opposite way, knowing in a few hours she would need to go back into the city unseen.

THIRTY ONE

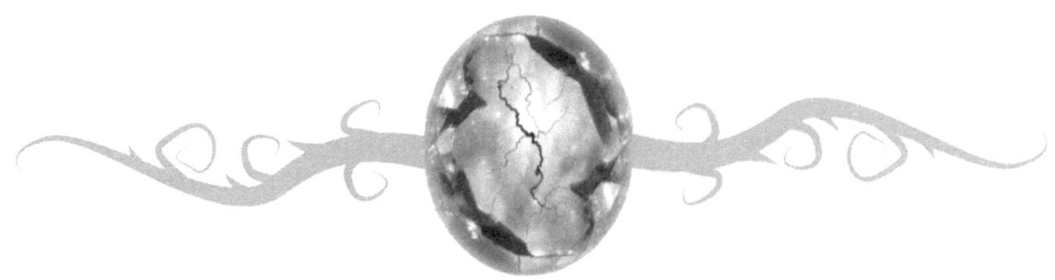

As night fell, Evie left the palace, the hood of her black cloak covering her features. By choosing alternate streets, she retraced her steps and arrived at the alleyway mentioned in the note. As she arrived, she slowed, glancing back behind her, but the street was empty. Evie strolled up the alleyway; she had not walked that far along when Garth emerged from the shadows, cradling his midsection. Even though his hood was up when he turned his eyes towards her, she could see his bruised features.

Evie gently touched his arm. "Are you alright?"

He smiled. "A little bruised, but I'll live." He studied her, his hazel eyes holding a shadow of sadness. "Why didn't you let Ulric finish it?"

She tilted her head, taking his hand in hers. "I couldn't let you die again."

Garth smiled sadly, glancing down at the ground, looking guilty. "But I deserved to."

Evie tenderly placed her hand on his scarred cheek, making him look back up at her. "No, you deserve to *live*. My Garth didn't have that opportunity, but you *do*. All I ask is you do right by your actions."

Garth agreed, sensing the charged air between their hands as they held each other softly. "I will." He paused and studied her. "I will find Bazertari. Then send word to you so you can finish it."

Evie's stomach twisted. Part of her sensed this would mark their final meeting. She studied his eyes, losing herself in their depths. She so desperately wanted to have him hold her one last time. "It seems it's our destiny to never be together."

He smiled sadly. "Thank you for sharing your memories with me. I know I will never fulfil that role for you, but I will care for you, always. I can't help it." He paused, gazing at her. "It has opened my eyes to what I could have been, and I will make every effort to be that man for the rest of my days." He sighed, touching her cheek with affection. "I will miss you."

Evie silently acknowledged, unable to rely on her voice.

Garth glanced down, her pendent catching his eye. "Do you worship Rosh?" She frowned, Garth pointed. "The pendant."

Evie's eyes flicked down at it. "Oh, a little. This was Garth's. I kept it after he died."

Garth touched the pendant with his fingertip. His voice was barely a whisper, "I used to worship, avidly, then . . . Well, I lost faith."

Evie stared at him. "May be time to find a temple again."

He smiled sadly. Garth softly pressed his lips against her forehead and studied her green eyes.

With a deep inhale, Evie asked, "So, what's your plan?"

He said, still holding her gaze, "There are still Bazertari sympathisers out there, so I am counting on my connections to still work. I will ask around to find out where he could have gone. I have some ideas who may know, and when I have found him, like I said, I will send word." He paused. "After that, well, the advantage of being Bazertari's general is I know where all the safe houses are. So, I will track down every one of them."

Evie smiled, studying his eyes, glad to see they were no longer cold and cruel. She sighed and looked down. "I understand you aren't the Garth I knew, but could I ask something?" He studied her and nodded; she raised her gaze to him. "Hold me one last time?"

Garth smiled and enveloped her in his arms, Evie melting in his embrace, and sobbed. When they parted after a short time,

Garth gazed at her and brushed a stray tear from her cheek. "I have to go."

She murmured, "Thank you."

"Will you return to your world once Bazertari is dead?"

She smiled softly. "I won't be going back. My life is here, always has been. So, we may cross paths one day."

"I know we will." He affectionately brushed his lips against her cheek and melted into the shadows, leaving Evie alone with tears rolling down her cheeks.

Evie trudged towards the palace, lost in thought. She had known nothing would come of being with Garth again. But the meeting in the alleyway confirmed it, hitting her heart hard. What she had told Garth was what she knew deep down. Even in the other Moonstar, they had been destined never to be together. Even if he had lived, she would have had to leave him. She let out a deep breath, glancing around the palace corridor. She had been so lost in thought she had not even remembered the walk from the city. Slowly, she walked towards the room Ulric had found for them a few days before. She needed to sleep. Her body ached after the past few days.

"Evie?"

She turned to see Ulric; she expected he would have been asleep at this late hour. He must have been so busy with the palace security and getting some sort of guard organised, that he lost track of time again. Ulric had promised Evie that afternoon to get an earlier night, but neither of them had rested like they said they would.

Evie beamed at him as he strolled over. He gazed at her, and without a word spoken; he held her close to him. It seemed he knew exactly what she needed at that moment. She melted in his embrace. With his arms enveloping her, she had a sense of security and all the emotions from earlier bubbled to the surface and she quietly cried. He kissed her tenderly on the top of the head. Neither spoke, just held on to each other, savouring their closeness.

THIRTY TWO

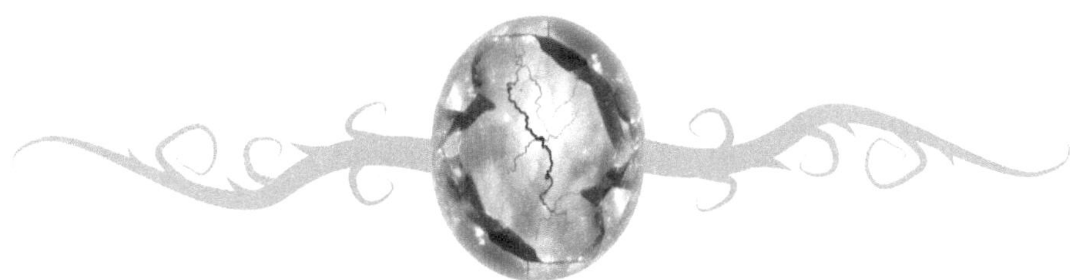

With the sun pouring in through the two large windows, the study was filled with bright, late morning light. The books on the shelves seemed to glow, adding to the warm and inviting atmosphere. Evie observed the room, noting that all of Bazertari's trinkets from the mantelpiece and the shelving round the room had vanished, along with some books that she had sensed darker magic radiating from. She turned towards the far wall, displaying a serene view of open countryside instead of the macabre painting that was there before.

Evie turned her attention back to Slan, who sat behind the impressive oak desk. He, along with the rest of them, had stripped anything that had been the warlock's and destroyed it. But not the books. She pressed her lips together, anything that held dark magic had been sealed away in a vault below the palace itself. Evie had been with Slan when he had performed the spell to cast a powerful magical seal to stop the evil from seeping free, and limiting any that could enter. He had ensured she knew how to maintain it, and what was within the secured room. She still remembered Slan's stern features, and the seriousness in his eyes as he told her how imperative it was to keep the vault sealed. She could understand why; the dark magic in the study just days before had made her skin crawl with dread.

Yet when she asked why the books could not just be destroyed, the sorcerer's response had been blunt. "They can't be. In doing so would release the dark magic held within."

The palace was cleansed of the warlock, but his evil essence still lurked beneath its very floors. It seemed even when they finally rid the world of Bazertari, his presence would always remain.

Evie pulled her mind from her thoughts of the warlock and briefly glanced in Ulric's direction. He stood beside her as he told Slan about the training for the new royal guard. She eyed Ulric's pleasing profile. He had never asked her why she had broken down the night before. He had just held her. Then, after a while, he had whispered they had to sleep, and he had gently led her to their room. Like they had most nights, they removed their weapons and, still dressed, just held each other and dozed off in each other's arms.

When she woke that morning, still in Ulric's arms, she debated whether she should disclose to him why she had been so upset. However, based on his response upon seeing Garth in the royal chamber, Evie decided it was best to remain silent. So, they had eaten breakfast, talking about the task ahead before meeting Slan.

Evie redirected her focus to the present when Ulric asked, "So, where do you believe the royal family members could be?"

Slan responded, "The last I heard, they were at Bay Point. But that was about five winters ago. They might have changed their location if they had the sense of being unsafe."

Evie studied the two. "We will try there first, unless we hear of anything new. Or hear word of Bazertari, then he will take precedence."

Slan agreed. "I have sent word, but up to now, nothing. So, the royal family will be your duty for the interim."

Evie asked, "What if they don't want to take over the crown?"

The sorcerer replied, "That is a possibility. Moonstar has always had a royal family, so if they refuse, or they are all gone, then we may have to consider an alternative. Even with Bazertari still out there, we must get this country back on track. Give the people hope."

Ulric sighed, "Hopefully we find them, and then our land can heal."

Slan regarded them both. "Remember, the land is still lawless and Bazertari will still have some influence, so be on your guard."

They both agreed, and Ulric turned to leave.

Evie stated, "Slan, can I talk to you a moment?"

The sorcerer gave a brief nod, and Ulric departed, closing the door behind him.

Evie glanced towards the closed door then said, "Now that I'm here for good, there's one thing I am curious to know."

Slan studied her and asked, "And what is that?"

"Teleporting."

Slan chuckled. "Ahhh, a skill worth knowing."

She gestured with her hands open before her. "So how? I tried to teleport here some years ago, and it didn't go well."

"You blacked out?" Evie nodded. "To teleport, there are a few factors you need to know. For one, it will require a travel crystal. I will advise you where you can purchase one in the city. But more importantly, you cannot teleport anywhere unless you know where you are going."

Evie squeezed her lower lip in thought and said, "So that means I have to have seen it."

"Aye. Sometimes you can anchor to a person, but most times, young sorcerers and sorceresses will have to get to places the long way for a few years. But the length we live, it is a minor inconvenience to pay. But once you know of a place, then you can teleport there with ease, provided that you have a crystal. It requires a substantial amount of energy to accomplish that, so don't use it too frequently."

"So will it be the same with other lands, too?"

He replied, "To go overseas, it is necessary to have a larger, more powerful crystal."

Evie frowned. "But when I went back to my land, I didn't see you holding a crystal."

Slan rose from his seat and walked around the desk to her. He grasped her hand securely. "That portal was different. You arrived and returned at the same place on Moonstar, it was also the same spot when I brought you here this time. The portal through which you appeared and departed was unique. I did not control it. The stone set in the bracelet is the key. Once I found a crystal that would help me channel into the power, I could bring you here. I had tried with the crystal at Kerlish, and it failed. After more study, I realised that there must have been a crystal hidden below the woods. It is a link between both our worlds, and I believe, with the right crystal, you could travel between the two."

Evie asked, "So others could go to my world?"

Slan disagreed by shaking his head and pointed to her bracelet. "That is like a key to a lock that gives only you entry."

"I think I understand now." She observed him lovingly. "So, I will ride my horse to search for the individuals belonging to the royal family."

Slan agreed, "Aye, and it will provide an opportunity for you and Ulric to become acquainted once more. I think he is very pleased you have decided to stay. I know the one from the other Moonstar had a special fondness for you. He would always talk about you and, when drunk, a little more." Slan raised his eyebrow at the last statement. "And I believe this Ulric has similar feelings for you, maybe more than just a friend."

She studied the sorcerer, wondering what he and the other Ulric talked about. There had been a connection, but knowing she would be leaving and with Garth's death, it remained unsaid. But with this Ulric, it was different; they cared for each other, and that could possibly develop into something.

Evie smiled softly. "Yes, it's hard not to like him."

Slan smiled, patting her on her shoulder. "As for the matter of contacting your parents." He turned, patting an enormous book on his desk, "I have found a spell. Very much how you meditated to me when you had recaptured the palace. But of course, you are connecting further. So, it will demand more of your capabilities to achieve it."

Evie focused on the book and asked, "What do I have to do?"

Slan passed her a small piece of parchment. "I have written what you must say and do. Find a place that is peaceful. You must have nay distractions. Focus on your parents and concentrate. It might require some time for the connection to happen, just be patient. Once you do, you will experience a strong pull. Then you can speak to them. Just be aware the spell requires a significant amount of energy, and it will tire you out afterwards. I suggest you have Ulric close by, as you may lose consciousness for a time."

Evie focused on the parchment. "Thank you."

Slan smiled. "Now, as for the other matter. If you go to the non-human quarter, there is a witch's shop on Wolfs Street. Ask for Menaira. She will supply you with a decent travelling crystal."

"Menaira?"

Slan replied, "Aye, tell her I sent you."

Evie eyed him for a moment. There was a glint in his eye as he spoke the witch's name and she wondered if they were more than just friends.

Evie reached the narrow street she had been informed about by Slan, and halfway down, was Menaira's shop. It was small and unremarkable in appearance; the window was full of trinkets and bottles filled with strange items. When Evie entered the shop, the scents of herbs and incense overwhelmed her senses. A middle-aged woman with striking grey eyes glanced up and smiled. Her light brown hair was left down and cascaded in soft curls across her shoulders. "Can I help ya, lass?"

Evie smiled. "Yes, I'm after a travelling crystal."

She regarded her. "Have you misplaced one?"

"No, I haven't had one before. But Slan informed me you would have some."

Menaira's features glowed with fondness at the mention of the sorcerer's name. "How is that rouge?"

She lifted one eyebrow in surprise. "He's well."

"He's not overdoing it, is he?"

Evie eyed her and asked, "You know Slan well?"

The witch beamed and then chuckled, raising an eyebrow. "Oh, I know him *very* well indeed."

Evie smirked, wondering if this Menaira had been one of Slan's lovers, especially the way Slan had mentioned her name earlier. "Well, he works too hard, and I have told him to rest." She paused, then added. "He's up at the palace. Perhaps you could convince him to relax a bit."

Menaira chuckled and shook her head. "He's too stubborn."

"That's very true," agreed Evie.

The witch stated, "Let me find you that travel crystal."

Evie watched her go into the back and smiled to herself. When Slan had mentioned having lovers, she did not expect to meet one of them.

As she waited, Evie glanced at the items on display, curious about the identity of some of the unusual trinkets. She thought that she should come back and seek Menaira's guidance on things that would benefit her as a sorceress, as well as uncovering more about her connection with Slan.

Evie's thoughts were broken when the woman came back from the back room holding a small blue crystal. "This will suffice for you, lass."

Evie acknowledged, reaching for her purse. The witch placed a warm hand on hers. "Nay need. Just to hear about Slan is payment enough. Let him know that if he needs any herbs, I will give him a discount." The witch winked as she said the latter.

Evie chuckled. "I most certainly will."

Menaira smiled and added. "And follow your heart, lass. Follow your heart."

She glanced in her direction, giving her a puzzled gaze. The witch just winked and patted Evie's hand.

Evie stepped outside, placing the crystal in the pocket of her jerkin, and cast a final glance at the shop. *What did the witch mean?* She had yearned for the Garth here to be something more, but she knew that it was not meant to be. *So, did the witch mean Ulric?* There had been little opportunity to really get to know him, however they had plans to be travelling for a while, just the two of them. They both sensed the connection between them and it would be the perfect time to see where it went.

THIRTY THREE

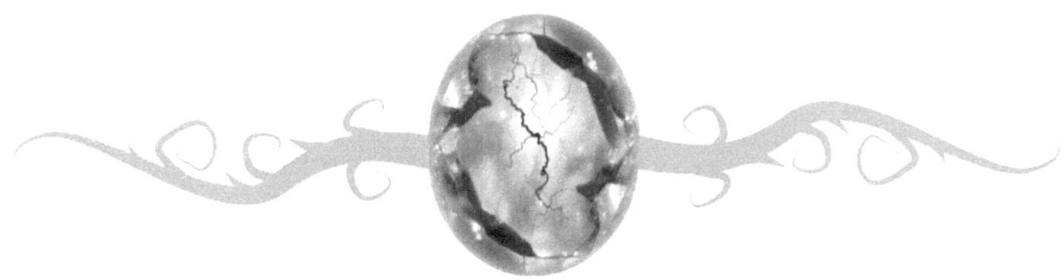

Ulric glanced in Evie's direction as she mounted her horse. Since reaching Great Oak, they had had little time alone together and when they had, both had been so exhausted they had just slept. The idea of having someone lying beside him once more was something Ulric never thought he would relish, or even consider could lead to something more. Ulric chewed his nail. He and Evie needed to talk. But they never had a moment to, and when they did, someone always interrupted them with something pressing from the palace. He hoped, as they rode south, they would be undisturbed.

Ulric sighed, looking ahead as they left the palace grounds. When he saw Evie the night before, his heart had ached. He was clueless as to why she was upset, but just had to hold her. He worried that it was related to Garth. Since he had escaped, she had become distant again. *Is she pulled between her old feelings for Garth and the feelings she's developing for me?* He hoped with all his heart that their friendship developed into something more. He must mean something to her if she wanted to sleep in his arms most nights.

He glanced over at Evie, finding himself torn between his frustration with her over Garth and his other feelings. He had been so distracted by it; Ulric had even spoken to Slan the morning after he had seen Evie. The sorcerer got him to see things from Evie's point of view. It had helped, and Ulric would respect her wishes to leave Garth be. *But what if I run into Garth again?* Ulric rubbed his face. He needed to focus on the task ahead, and his feelings for Evie. Not on revenge that would eat away at him if he let it.

Ulric knew if he could concentrate on the emotions he and Evie shared, he may lay the past to rest. They would be on the road for several days; that would be as good a time as any to talk, and see where this friendship took them.

Evie glanced in his direction, arching an eyebrow when she noticed he was looking at her and asked, "Everything alright?"

Ulric nodded. "Aye. Just thinking."

She rode up beside him as their horses trotted out of the palace gates. "About what?"

He responded, his hand fanning between them, "Us."

She eyed him and grinned. "Slan said this ride would give us time to talk. Think he's playing cupid."

Ulric frowned. "Cupid?"

Evie snorted with amusement. "Cupid. He was a son of a god. In my world, he is depicted with wings and a bow, and would fly round, and whoever he shot arrows at would fall in love."

Ulric burst out laughing, his entire chest rumbling. "I doubt I could see Slan flying round doing that."

Evie chuckled. "Well, no. I don't think that would work."

The Sword looked at her and said seriously, "So, I know I said in the woods we would wait till Bazertari was dead. But we have had moments since, and well . . ."

Evie leaned towards him, gazing into his eyes. "I think we've waited long enough."

Ulric brought his mare to a halt in the crowded street in the middle of Great Oak. He directed his intense gaze towards her and said, "Aye, I agree."

Evie, utterly entranced by his blue eyes, stopped her horse beside him. The bustling of the street seemed to fade away as Ulric's gaze flicked between her vivid green eyes and her delicate, slightly parted, pink lips. Ulric's breathing quickened as his lips ached, longing to experience hers against his once more. Both of them leaned towards each other, Ulric seeing the hunger in Evie's eyes. He licked his lips as his head dipped towards her.

Suddenly, they were both jolted back to their surroundings when a large, burly man with a horse and cart swore at them several times for blocking the road. Ulric quickly apologised as they turned their attention back to riding.

"Get a room," the man muttered.

The two burst out laughing, and quickly rode away before the man cursed them again.

Evie glanced over at Ulric as they rode. When they had stopped, all she could see was him. Her lips tingled in anticipation of his lips pressed against them. If that man had not broken their moment, she knew they would have kissed. Her eyes lingered on his arms as he continued to ride beside her. Her body warmed as she remembered being in his embrace while they slept the night before. It was so perfect. Evie breathed deeply, looking ahead, but her mind would not stop thinking of how it felt to have his arms around her. Ulric had been so relaxed with her and she sensed a pull of tranquillity, as though she was right where she belonged. She had experienced something similar with Garth, but Ulric . . . Ulric; his incredible blue eyes, his charming smile, his strong arms. Evie gripped her reins, trying to stop her body from reacting to the warmth that coursed through her, just by thinking of him. She briefly closed her eyes then glanced up at the sky through the trees.

Leaving Great Oak behind, they headed south-east, through the Great Wood, both lost in their thoughts. Evie could see Ulric glancing her way from her peripheral vision. They were alone at last. There were no excuses, no one to interrupt them. They could finally see where things lead to.

Is he thinking what I'm thinking? Why do I feel so anxious? There's no denying the hunger that was in his eyes.

It was not like she had never been alone with Ulric before. But then again, they had not known about their feelings. But it was happening.

Am I going to regret this? Does Ulric feel awkward too?

Her eyes stole a quick glance his way. No. He sensed it too, and was tense because of it. She had to do something to break the nervous anticipation between them.

"So, how far to Hinerly?"

Ulric shot her a look. Relief flashed across his features. "Oh, erm, it will be about three days from here."

She asked, giving him a soft smile. "And then?"

He took a deep breath, looking ahead, his shoulders relaxing. "Well, we'll then take the ferry across the Great Bay to Fish Crest. Then an additional two days to Bay Point."

Evie watched him for a moment and then looked ahead. "So, with all this time alone, what should we talk about?"

He gave her a big grin. "We'll have nay interruptions."

She responded, "Ulric all to myself. I don't know where to start."

Ulric burst out laughing. Whatever anxiety they had been feeling, it had soon melted away.

The two rode side by side along the road, which wound its way through the large, old forest, and chatted. Ulric told her of his life, going back over fourty years. The variations between the Ulric she had known and the one she was with were actually few. The events in their lives may have differed, but their kind heart and honourable soul were still the same. Then Evie told Ulric about her world and more about the time she had been on Moonstar before.

Ulric listened intently as Evie recounted the night she had met him for the first time.

He chuckled. "It seems we always meet at an inn."

She responded with amusement in her voice, "It seems that way. But at least the first time you were sober, and I didn't have to hit you."

He emitted a deep breath, "It feels good to be back to me old self again. I'd been drinking for so long, I'd become numb to the world."

Evie regarded him, focusing on his hair that was neatly pulled back in a low ponytail. It appeared to be of a shorter length than when she initially encountered him at the inn. "I see you've had a haircut."

Ulric's hand moved to his hair. "Aye, thought since I'm sober again I best tidy up a bit."

She smiled, then eyed him. "Are you sure it wasn't Slan insisting you do something before meeting the royal family?"

The Sword chuckled. "Well, aye, he did kind of hint it needed cutting."

She grinned. "I like it."

They rode in silence until the roadway narrowed because of a large oak. Evie slowed her horse, drawing closer to Ulric. He suddenly let go of his reins and wrapped his arm around her. Evie stared deeply into his eyes and he kissed her passionately. He then let go and smiled.

She eyed him. "What was that for?"

Ulric responded, "I have longed to do that since we departed Great Oak. I saw the opportunity and took it."

Evie gazed at him, her body still tingling at his touch. "I must agree. I have wanted to kiss you again, without interruption, since those woods."

Ulric looked ahead and said, "Well, as we have time together, let us make the most of it." He peered at her, his eyes fixated on her body. "This route can be quiet and nay inns till Hinerly."

Evie quirked an eyebrow and chuckled. "Well, we should ensure we find some suitable camping spots."

The Sword laughed and winked at her.

Evie asked, "So when we first left the city, what were you thinking about?"

Ulric directed a questioning gaze towards her. "What?"

She twisted in her saddle. "On the street we almost kissed. Then, as we left, you seemed lost in thought, like I was."

Ulric arched an eyebrow. "And what were you thinking of?"

Evie blushed. "I'm not . . ."

The muscular Sword burst out laughing and then looked at her mischievously. "The fact you blushed makes me think you were thinking what I was."

Evie flirted, "Oh, you'll find out what I was thinking about later, mister."

He leaned towards her, his saddle creaking. "Hmmmm, I do like a woman who knows what she wants."

She eyed him and smirked. "Do you, now? Well, you'll see."

They set up camp away from the main road at dusk. Ulric went to gather some wood for the fire while Evie dealt with the horses. Once they were settled, she placed out the sleeping blankets and had some food. Ulric returned with wood and built a small fire to keep the night chill at bay.

He sat down beside her and sighed, "It is good to be out of the saddle."

Evie smiled. "When I first travelled here by horse for days, I was so saddle sore. I was irritable as well." She focused her gaze on him. "But this time, it just seemed as if I had come back home."

The large, muscular man smiled; his blue eyes lost in her green. "I think the company helps."

"It does," breathed Evie.

Ulric leaned in her direction and softly kissed her on the lips, his hand sliding across the back of her neck, pulling her closer. She melted at his touch, her loins tightened as his hand slid down her back towards her buttocks. She draped her arms around him, pulling herself against his lean body.

Ulric paused, gazing at her. "I'm liking this trip already."

She giggled and combed her hands into his greying hair, pulling it free of the ponytail and kissed him. She breathed, "I agree."

They kissed more, Evie moved to straddle Ulric where he sat near the fire. He curled his muscular arms around her, pressing her chest against his. Evie felt the bulge in his trousers as his arousal became more apparent. She pulled away, unbuttoning her jerkin. But Ulric grabbed her firmly, locking her in his arms. He stood, carrying her with ease, and gently placed her on the sleeping blankets. He kissed her again before getting up and pulling off his jerkin and shirt.

Her gaze remained fixed on him as she blindly took off her jerkin. She directed her eyes towards several scars on his chest as he bent over to pull off his boots. Evie concentrated on her clothes, removing them as quickly as she could. When she looked up, Ulric was naked and his arousal was plainly evident. Her eyes honed in on his length, pleased by how well-endowed he was.

Ulric knelt as Evie opened her legs for him. Ulric slid over her, their groin brushing against each other as he seized her lips with his. He entered her and Evie gasped at his girth as he filled her.

Their bodies moved in unison as Evie intertwined her legs around Ulric's waist, yearning for a deeper connection. Evie gasped again when their hips met, stimulating her most sensitive spot. Her skin prickled as she closed her eyes and surrendered to all the sensations. Ulric moved to tease her breasts with his soft lips, without breaking his pace. He sucked on her nipples, making them firm as his body moved faster. Evie gazed at him, the endorphins taking over, her body buzzing. Ulric's thighs shuddered along with Evie's as they climaxed as one.

Ulric gazed at Evie as they lay next to each other. His protective arms wrapped around her, keeping her warm from the chill of the night air. His callused hands caressing her back.

He whispered, "That was more amazing than I had imagined."

She showed curiosity. "Than you imagined?"

He chuckled and gave her another peck. "Well, since that kiss in the woods, this was all I've been thinking about."

"Oh, I see." She briefly cast her eyes downward, then brought her gaze back up, a mischievous smile on her face. "So was I."

Ulric laughed, making his enormous chest vibrate. "It seems we both needed this. If we hadn't been so exhausted while at the palace, I would have done it sooner."

She smiled, her hand brushing across his firm chest, tracing a scar. "I think we would have."

He planted a gentle kiss on her forehead as he rolled onto his back, keeping her firmly in his arms, not wanting to let her go. She gazed at his features, and he smiled at her. She focused on the scar across his eyebrow and traced her fingers across it.

He smirked and said, "I fell from a tree." Evie frowned, and he added, "The scar on my eyebrow."

"Oh, I expected it to be from some epic sword fight."

He sighed, "Alas, nay. I was eight and was trying to impress a girl."

Evie chuckled, resting her chin on his chest, gazing at him. "Go on. Did it impress her?"

"Nay, she saw me fall, then all the blood. She screamed, and fainted."

Evie smirked. "Oh, dear."

Ulric sighed, "I was then scolded by my mama and wasn't allowed near the farm where the girl lived again." Evie tried to suppress a giggle. Ulric glanced downward at her and frowned. "It's not funny."

Evie bit her lips. "Sorry, but it is a little. Then again, I doubt it discouraged you from trying to impress the ladies."

He grinned, showing off his gap in his front teeth. "Aye, true. But I have only told you the true nature of this scar."

She raised an eyebrow. "Why thank you. So, what did you tell all the others?"

"That it was some epic battle."

She locked her eyes on him. "I think the true reason is a far better story."

He pressed his lips against her forehead, keeping his arms round her. "I feel I could tell you everything."

Evie glanced into his gaze briefly, then rested her head on his chest, listening to his heartbeat. She whispered, "I feel the same."

Closing her eyes, Evie savoured his embrace. Ulric moved slightly, grabbing a blanket to cover them. He then placed his arms back around her, both keeping warm from the evening chill with the blanket and their body heat. She sensed his breathing slowing as he drifted off to sleep. Evie soon was pulled into the depths with him.

THIRTY FOUR

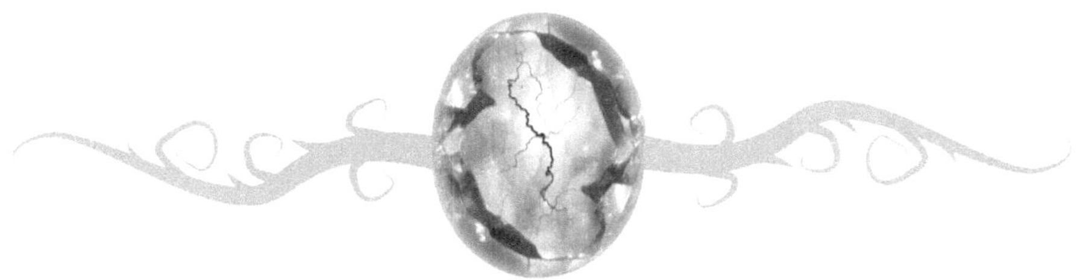

Garth raised his hood as he left the bustling inn in Elms Corner. His target, Bron, was in sight ahead of him. Garth had been tailing the coward all day, but so far, had discovered nothing useful. The Sword thought that the man looked more like a weasel than a human, but he would be the one to lead him straight to any others, especially Tyrak. Even though Bron was only a grunt, he had become firm friends with the large brute. Garth had expected to have found the two together in a tavern, but his luck was running thin. Bron was of no use to him, but Tyrak; he had been given his own unit by Garth and those men under Tyrak's control had infiltrated the north. Intel from them would confirm where Bazertari was hiding. Garth had his suspicions on the warlock's location, but needed some hard proof.

Since leaving Great Oak, he had tracked down several of the men who had been in his army. All having run when the warlock had vanished. Some had not gone far, just to the next town or village, hoping to lie low or wanting to start afresh. The more dedicated were still waiting to get new orders. Garth had come across many and talked to them, some with a little more persuasion, but it got him nowhere. Most told him to ask someone else. Since they were no longer useful, he had dealt with them as he would with any coward. Death.

Garth clenched his fists. He had killed many, but it was not enough. He knew more of his men were out there; from the ones who ran from Great Oak, to his spy network, and those posted on missions. It would take him years to find them all. But his most pressing matter was Bazertari. He had to find the warlock at all cost. After he received new information, he had doubled back to Elms Corner, one of his former men had stated that Bron was alive. Garth hoped he had something useful to tell him and would give him Tyrak's location as no one else seemed to know. Otherwise, he would head for Kerlish, and check in with his spies there.

Garth kept his steps light as he continued to follow Bron down the almost deserted streets. The man was a little unsteady on his feet from the last few hours of drinking. Garth smirked, remembering how Bron could never hold his liquor. He glanced up towards the black, star filled sky; there was no option but to corner Bron and see what he gave him after a bit of persuasion. Once he got the information he needed, and was certain of Tyrak's location, he would then inform Evie.

As Garth trailed Bron down the street, he reviewed all that he had learned thus far. He still had a few ears in the palace, and they had informed him that Slan was attempting to return Moonstar to a peaceful land once more. To do that, Evie and Ulric had gone in search of some distant royal family members. The Sword hoped the two found them, as they were Moonstar's hope of getting back some normality. Several years before, Bazertari had wanted the whole royal line killed off, yet Garth had been unsuccessful in tracking them down. It had been frustrating, but looking back, he was glad he had not found them.

His keen eyes kept a vigilant watch on his objective as they continued down the deserted streets. Bron slowed and looked back. Garth slipped into the shadows. After a moment of surveying his surroundings, the coward walked a little further and then took a side alley.

Garth picked up his pace; it was time to get some answers. He entered the alleyway and shouted, "Going somewhere, Bron?"

The short man froze and pivoted. He laughed nervously. "Garth, I—I didn't expect to see you here."

The Sword responded, "Have to say the same, Bron. Last time I saw you, you were supposed to be on guard duty in the palace."

The man surveyed his surroundings with unease, instinctively raising his hands to protect himself. "The enemy were everywhere."

"Really? All three of them?"

Bronze stammered, lowering his hands, "We—we thought you w—were dead, protecting our lord. With you down, we . . ."

Garth glared at him, making Bron swallow nervously. Like the others, he did not know Garth had changed sides. All that Garth had interrogated prior had thought he had died protecting the warlock. He had concluded that the first couple only said it to survive, but the rumour had taken root.

"Well, I'm very much alive, Bron," responded Garth.

The man jumped nervously when his back hit the solid surface of a building. There was nowhere to go.

Garth sneered at the small man still walking towards him. "I'm in pursuit of Tyrak and I have a notion that you'll know."

The man shook his head, his long neck bobbed. "It was chaos. I have nay idea where any of them went. If we knew you weren't dead, we wouldn't have run. *Honest.*"

The Sword dragged his dagger free, walking up to the man. "Somehow, I doubt that Bron. Where is he?"

Bron shook his head, putting his hands up in defence as Garth came closer. "I—I don't know."

Garth pursed his lips. "Funny, I remember you were both as thick as thieves. I think I need to jog that memory of yours, don't you?"

Bron pushed himself up against the wall, hoping it would swallow him whole. With his hands held high, his gaze swiftly scanned the surroundings in search of an exit.

"I know nothing!"

"Talk, Bron."

The man pushed past Garth and tried to run. Bron had not anticipated Garth's quick reaction, and he was hit in the face with the hilt of Garth's dagger. Bron staggered, blood gushing from his already crooked nose, and fell back on his rump.

Garth straddled him, grabbing one of Bron's ears. The dagger sliced into the skin and he ordered, "*Talk!* Or you'll be known as One-Ear Bron."

The small man panicked. "I know *nothing!*"

Garth pressed harder into the flesh, the ear coming away in his hand. Bron cried out.

Garth snarled, "Where is he?"

Blood poured from the ear as Garth continued to slice downwards, more of it pulling away. Bron whimpered and blurted, "*North.* He went north."

Garth paused. "Where?"

Bron winced as Garth kept the dagger firmly in place. "City of Lights, he went there. Said he had some message."

"Message?"

Bron started to nod then changed his mind as the dagger cut deeper. "Aye, it was asking for anyone who was under your command."

Garth pushed the dagger further. "Who sent it?"

"Some say it were you. But I told Ty I heard you had died protecting our lord. He thought it may have been Bazertari himself."

Garth pulled the dagger free from Bron's ear, half of it dangling free, his hand wet from the blood. As he got to his feet, Garth wiped his wet hand on the side of his trousers as he observed the trembling man and asked, "So he's there?"

"Bazertari? I think so," Bron said from where he sat on the ground, trying to look at his ear that dangled in his peripheral vision.

Garth regarded Bron as he stood back up. "Thanks for the information, Bron. But . . . ."

The small man appeared anxious, his hand holding his ear in place. He quickly brought up his other hand. "But I talked. I told ya what you wanted."

Garth smirked. "Aye, you did. But you're a coward and a weasel, Bron."

The short man went to protest, but his words stuck in his throat as Garth sliced his dagger across it. He turned as Bron tipped over onto the floor, blood flowing from the fatal wound.

Garth flicked his blade to get most of the blood from it, then sheathed it. He glanced back at Bron as he took his final, rattling breath.

At last, he got some good information; he needed to head north. Garth left the alleyway and walked briskly across the town, thoughts racing through his mind.

Why is Bazertari gathering all my remaining men? Maybe he's going to use them to try to find me?

If that was the case, he would have to watch his step or it would not be long before they knew the truth.

It made sense that Bazertari was in the City of Lights; he had his black tower near there in the Dark Wood. But, Garth could not just go by the word of a dead man. He needed more proof. If Bazertari was there, then he would relay a message to Evie and they could confront the warlock.

As he made his way to the stables through the empty streets, Garth pondered how many of his men had headed north. It had been chaos at the palace. When he had been helping Evie in the great hall, Garth had seen several of his men go down. The next day, he heard of bodies being buried in the woods. He was curious as to how many just turned and ran. Or did so after hearing rumours that he was dead.

Garth sighed. Most of his men could not be trusted, but to run like chickens, he would not have believed it. He had killed Krif, but wondered about the others. During the fight, he was sure he had seen some trying to get into the great hall, but that had been such a blur. The ones he had tracked down had been low-ranking officers and the odd spy that he had out on assignment. None were his elite. When he reached the City of Lights, he half suspected he would cross paths with at least one. If Tyrak, who was high in the ranks, was headed that way, then some of his elite could be, too.

THIRTY FIVE

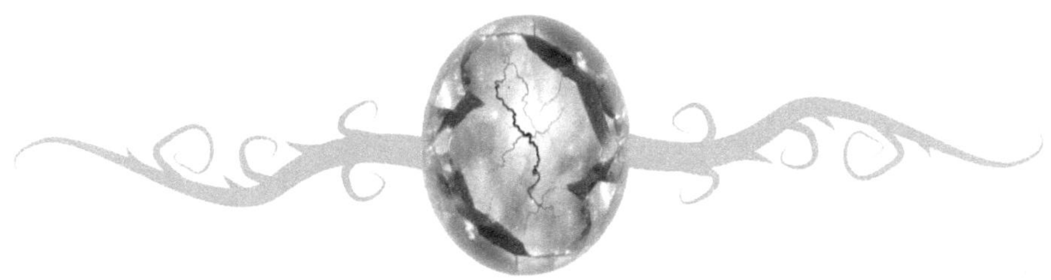

E vie stretched under the blanket as she opened her eyes, concentrating on the trees above her. She smiled to herself as she felt the aches caused by their nocturnal activities, and rolled over to find that Ulric was already up. He was sitting by the fire cooking a couple of rabbits. She rubbed her eyes, wondering how he had got up and gone hunting without disturbing her. Evie held the blanket, moist from the morning dew, securely around her exposed body as she sat up.

Ulric peered in her direction and smiled. "Good morn."

She yawned. "Good morning."

He stood up and sat next to Evie, kissing her firmly on the lips. "Thought after last night, we needed a substantial breakfast."

Evie snorted in amusement; they had both exerted all their energy before falling asleep. She stood, pulling on her clothes, Ulric eyeing her as she covered her slender frame.

She responded, "At this rate, by the time we find the royal family, we'll be exhausted."

The large Sword laughed and lifted his eyebrows. "But it is so invigorating."

Evie moved to sit by the fire, taking some of the hot, cooked rabbit Ulric held out to her. Evie quickly blew on it when the heat became uncomfortable on her fingertips. "Well, true." She flirted, then added. "It was amazing."

He flashed her an enormous grin. "It was. We just—"

"Clicked?"

He tilted his head to one side, gazing at her. She was warming her hands against the fire after devouring the meat he had given her. "Aye, we do. Feels like this is where we're meant to be."

Evie kissed him softly on his lips and focused on his blue eyes. "We are."

His muscular arms embraced her, pulling her against his body, deepening the kiss. Evie ran her fingers through his hair, her body tingling again. She shifted position so she could straddle his lap. Ulric's hands roamed down her back, pulling her shirt free of her trousers. His callused hands stroked her spine. Evie pulled back a little to gaze at his features. "It's going to take us even longer to reach Bay Point if this keeps up."

Ulric chuckled, gazing at her. "I'd sooner be doing this though."

Evie tucked a few strands of his hair behind his ear, regarding him. "The same, but I think Slan may get a little mad at us."

The Sword inhaled deeply, his arms still around her. "Just a little longer."

Evie rested her head against his shoulder. "Not going to refuse."

When the two finally separated, Ulric stood up to pack up the camp. He rotated his shoulder and neck and sighed.

Evie asked, "Are you alright?"

"Aye, but I feel more aches and pains these days."

She eyed him, her fingers glowing. "I can fix that if you want me to."

Ulric seemed a little uncomfortable, his hand enveloping her fingers. "Nay, lass. I think you should still be careful using magic. This land still isn't free of that warlock."

She indicated agreement. When he released her hand, the glowing faded. "I understand. But if you're hurt, I will use my magic."

Ulric's lips turned up softly. "I gather from that tone, you won't give me a choice."

Evie eyed him. "No, I won't."

He chuckled as he placed the remaining cooked rabbit in his pack. "I learned from an early age not to argue with a woman."

Evie laughed and started rolling up the sleeping blankets.

Ulric eyed her and stated, his tone serious, "I know this land is freer than it was a few weeks earlier, but we should still tread with caution."

"Understood."

As Ulric placed his saddle bags on his horse, he tightened his jaw and then said, "But in this cold weather, a soothing hand wouldn't be too terrible."

She eyed him. "I *knew* it."

He grinned as he strolled over to stamp out what was left of the fire. Not long after, they were on the road again. They talked about their lives and Ulric shared more tales about his youth.

As they rode, Evie began thinking of her parents. She had the belief that the best time to contact them would be as they travelled to Bay Point. There may not be as good as an opportunity once in the city. When they made camp that night, Evie regarded the small clearing, and knew it was the perfect spot.

She turned to Ulric. "I need your help with something."

He responded, raising an eyebrow, "Well, if you desire me to give some extra special attention to your—"

Evie playfully hit him on the shoulder. "No, nothing like that."

There was a hint of sadness in his expression. "Oh."

She kissed him softly. "Well, not yet anyway. But at the moment, I want to send a message to my parents to tell them I'm okay. I feel I should do it tonight."

Ulric nodded. "I understand. What is it you want me to do?"

She eyed him. "Well, for one thing, don't distract me." He gave her an innocent look. She giggled and continued. "I must concentrate and focus on them. It will take a lot of my power, so I may be weak for a while afterwards."

Ulric said, as he unsaddled the horse, "Aye, I can be there for you."

Evie acknowledged her gratitude while arranging the sleeping blankets.

Ulric made a fire and gave her something to eat. "If you are going to be using a lot of energy, make sure you eat first."

Evie gazed at him. She liked the caring side of the formidable Sword. Once done eating, Evie settled down on her comfortable blanket and read Slan's note, committing the spell to memory. She briefly glanced over at Ulric. He had removed his sword and was cleaning it with an oiled cloth.

She stated, "Won't be long."

He directed his attention towards her and beamed warmly. Evie shut her eyes and whispered the spell, focusing on her parents.

At first, nothing happened. Evie heard Ulric softly humming a merry tune as he cleaned his sword. She opened one eye, looking across at him. He seemed oblivious that he was doing so. She adjusted a little, getting comfortable and shut her eyes, trying to zone out the sounds of the forest and Ulric, focusing on her breathing.

Evie experienced a subtle tug and discovered herself in a dark abyss. For several minutes, there was nothing but silence. She focused on her parents but she was still alone, floating above still water. In the far distance she could hear Ulric still humming, and then an image of him cleaning his sword appeared, the cloth grated loudly against the blade. Mingled in that sound, she caught her mother's voice. It was faint, but it was hers. Evie calmly took a breath and focused on the voice. It sounded like she was talking to her father.

Then Evie dropped into the waters, and she passed right through, pulled down at a phenomenal speed. She gasped, in shock, trying to keep focused. Evie crashed through a ceiling and her feet hit the floor. She snapped her eyes open to find herself standing before the startled couple in their lounge.

Her father jumped back in his seat and gasped, "What on earth?"

Her mother looked up. "Evelyn!"

Evie pressed her teeth against her lip. She hated when her mum called her that. She took a long, slow breath. Now that she was there, Evie was unsure of what to say.

Her father regarded her. "Hun, how did you get in here?"

Evie's mother frowned as she slowly stood. "What's wrong?"

Evie experienced tears welling up in her eyes, astonished by the fact that she could see them again. Her mother walked over to her, and to Evie's surprise, the older woman embraced her. She had fully expected that she would have appeared much like a hologram, the same way she talked to Slan. But she was there, in her parents' house, standing right in front of them. It was real. Evie was nearly overwhelmed by the sensation of her mother's embrace. She had not prepared herself for that.

Her mother concentrated on her eyes and asked, "What is it?"

Evie inhaled with uncertainty. "Mum, dad. I must tell you something."

Her father stood, making his way over to her. He regarded what she wore and mumbled, "You went back."

Evie frowned. *How could he know?* She had erased their memories. "How?"

The couple glanced at each other. Her mother admitted, "I'm not sure. We just know."

Evie took her parent's hands and bit her lip. "Yes, I have gone back. They *need* me. I must save them from the evil that's returned."

Her mother gently touched her daughter's hand and took a shaky breath. "You aren't coming back, are you?"

Evie focused on her mother's green eyes to see tears welling in them. "No. I think it's my true home. I b—"

Her mother interrupted, "Belong there."

Evie's eyes became teary again. "Yes. I can't explain it, but I'm happy there."

Her mother sniffed. "That's all we ever wanted for you."

Evie smiled, unable to trust her voice. Her father gazed at her and said, "We will miss you, honey."

She quietly affirmed with a hard swallow.

Her mother squeezed her hand and stated, "This will also be the last time we will see you, isn't it?"

Once more, Evie simply agreed with a nod. She was too overwhelmed to say anything. She took a long, deep breath. "I will miss you."

The parents observed her. Her father, then mother, embraced her tightly. Her mother asked, "Is it like what your gran described in her dreams?"

Evie replied, "It's beautiful, mum."

The older woman patted her daughter's hand affectionately. "Sorry, I was so hard on you. All I wanted was for you to be happy."

Evie focused on her features. "I know, and now I am. I think I will be very happy."

Her mother smiled. "Find yourself a nice man, won't you?"

Seemed her mother still wanted to marry her off. "Oh, I think I already have."

Her mother beamed. "Good."

Then the older couple's demeanour changed. Her father called, as his hand passed through hers, "Evie?"

She gazed downwards, noticing herself gradually disappearing, her vision blurring. She quickly added. "I can't sustain this much longer. I love you both. Tell work . . . I don't know . . . that I have decided to travel or something."

Her mother chuckled, "Don't worry. Now go. Be happy."

Evie nodded, the image of her parents fading. She was back in the black abyss. Again, she was falling, then she hit the forest floor, hard. She gasped and saw Ulric looking up at her. Just as he leapt to his feet, she lost consciousness.

Ulric glanced toward Evie as she closed her eyes to begin her spell. He turned his head and started wiping down his blade, humming to himself. He could not get the tune out of his head ever since he had visited a tavern a few days ago, searching for new recruits with Irric. The bard there knew how to make a tune stick in your head and now he was finding himself humming it. Ulric glanced back, remembering how Evie needed to focus and realised he could be distracting her. The song froze on his lips when he saw Evie floating mid-air. He abruptly rose to his feet as she collapsed to the floor, resembling a discarded rag doll. He rolled her over to see her face, blood pouring from her nose.

"*Evie.*" He shook her gently. "Evie?"

She was out cold. *Had the spell not worked?* She had only just closed her eyes. He looked at her with apprehension, wondering how long she would be unconscious for. He admired her features, kissing her lips gently. "Come back to me, lass."

Her breathing was shallow, her features pale. Ulric rested his hand on her chest, relieved by the sensation of her heart pulsating. He briefly cast his eyes upwards at the sky to thank Rosh that she was still alive. He held her gently in his arms, wiping the blood from her nose, and whispered, "Don't leave me, lass. I've only just found ya."

Evie experienced the presence of an arm around her, a hand delicately caressing her cheek, then the throbbing of her head. She gently lifted her eyelids and focused on Ulric gazing at her.

He smiled softly, brushing a loose strand of hair away from her face. "Glad to have you back."

She croaked, "How long?"

He raised his eyes to the dark sky. "A few hours. I was worried you'd nay wake up."

Evie smiled softly, cupping his cheek with her hand. "You can't get rid of me that easily."

She attempted to stand, but dizziness overwhelmed her. Ulric reacted instantly and caught her with his arm round her, almost frightened she would collapse again. "Take it slow."

Ulric quickly offered Evie some water. While she was drinking, he asked, moving around to face her. "So did it work?"

Her eyes locked onto his, a rush of emotions flooding over her at the thought. "Yes. I spoke to them both." She sighed, focusing on his blue eyes. "It was hard, but they seem to be happy for me."

Ulric responded, cupping her cheek in his large hand, "I'm glad you could talk to them."

She slowly nodded, tears spilling over her eyes. Ulric pulled her into his arms, and held her close as she sobbed, realising she would never see her parents again.

THIRTY SIX

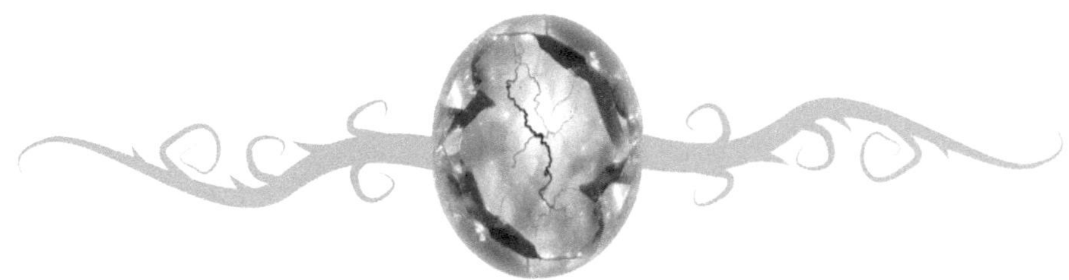

By remaining on the major route, they reached the sizable town of Hinerly after three days. It was busy, even with the sun already setting after a long day for the fishing town. As the two travelled down the main street, the locals regarded them with suspicion, but Evie could sense the atmosphere of fear was already dissipating. As they rode along the main street, she wondered how far word had spread of Great Oak being freed of Bazertari's grip. Even though hopeful, Evie feared that there would be another town or city that would soon experience his wrath once he had recovered. She took a moment to glance at Ulric, wondering if it would have been more prudent to find the warlock and not the royal family. But in giving the land hope, the warlock would soon find his hold over the cities diminishing.

When they reached the nearest inn, they dismounted their horses, tied them to the hitching post, and entered while carrying their swords and saddle bags. It was crowded, yet all within had stopped talking and turned towards the door. Ulric and Evie, having kept to the habit of keeping their hoods up since they had left Great Oak, took two steps in, then paused. After a moment, the crowd turned as one, and the chatter resumed. Ulric approached the main counter while Evie sought out a place to sit.

Evie found an open spot that had occupied tables all around them. It was not ideal, but it had to do. She watched Ulric as he came over carrying two mugs. Evie saw his hood moving slightly as he walked and knew he was observing the customers scattered around the large room. She half wondered if the Sword ever relaxed. He sat opposite, placing a mug before her. As Evie took it to take a sip, she noticed that his was full of water, not ale. It seemed his taste for ale was behind him for the time being.

The Sword leant forward and muttered, his head in shadow under his hood. "The table at the back. See the lone drinker?"

Evie peeked over his shoulder from under her hood, taking a sip of her ale. She looked again at Ulric. "I do. Who is he?"

Ulric responded, "One of Garth's men."

She arched her brow. "Do you think he's followed us?"

Ulric shrugged. "Not sure. He could be looking for the same people we are. Or, as Garth had many stationed over Moonstar as spies, he may be trying to keep a low profile with what has happened."

Evie gazed past Ulric's muscular shoulder, watching the man. "What do you want to do?"

Ulric glanced up at the barmaid as she placed down their meal of sausages and potatoes. He extended his thanks to her and then directed his gaze towards Evie. "We'll eat our food. But if he leaves, we need to follow him."

She started eating; the smell made her ravenous. As they ate, Evie would occasionally glance over at the table in the corner, where the lone man still sat, drinking his ale.

As the evening progressed, the man did not move. He gazed round the inn, looking towards Evie and Uric a few times.

She leant towards the Sword and said, "I don't think he followed us, but he is suspicious."

Ulric responded, not looking, as it would have been too obvious, "Are you sure?"

"No, but he keeps looking our way. Almost mirroring us. Like he's waiting for us to do something."

Ulric tightened his mouth and stated, "I'm going for a walk. See if he takes the bait."

Ulric stood, strapping his sword back on his back, and departed from the inn. Evie remained in her current position, drinking her ale. She was thinking she may have been mistaken when the man drained his tankard and stood. Evie cocked her head to watch him discreetly. She expected him to follow Ulric. Instead, he strolled over to her table and sat down.

Scarred heavily, and with cold grey eyes, he leaned forward a little and leered at her. "We don't get many strangers this far south."

Evie peered up at him, keeping her face in shadow. "Just passing through."

She paused, regarding him. She had not seen a sword, but there were two long daggers fastened to his belt. Her sword was leaning against the bench she was sitting on, but could get to it quickly if needs be.

He smirked, focusing on her features that were in shadow. "Where'd your friend go?"

"Not far," stated Ulric, surprising the man as he slowly sat down beside him.

The scared stranger froze a moment before glancing at the muscular Sword as Ulric patted him hard on his back.

Evie regarded the man. "So, why are you here?"

He examined Ulric and then shifted his attention to Evie. "Just passin' through."

Evie lifted her eyebrow in scepticism. Ulric continued to hold his hand against the man's back and slapped it hard again. "Well, my friend, I believe we require some fresh air, don't you?"

The man glanced between them both, sucking air between his crooked teeth. "Aye, I think we do."

The scared man staggered forward as Ulric pushed him into the side alley. The Sword scowled as he towered over him. "So who are you?"

The man glanced at them both and sneered. "Curious why an old drunkard is suddenly on the move again." He paused and regarded Evie. "I'm also wondering who you are."

She stepped forward, glancing at his hand as it twitched, edging towards one of his daggers. "Well, if you answer our question, you may get some answers."

He stood his ground, glaring at them, then laughed.

Ulric moved fast, his fist finding its mark. The man staggered back, falling on his backside, blood streaming from his nose. Ulric snarled, "I asked you a question!"

The man glared up at him, spitting blood from his mouth, and just grinned. Then slowly got back to his feet.

Ulric's posture was tense, his fist clenched. "Well, boy?"

The man stared at Evie, then back at Ulric. Then slowly unsheathed his dagger. "You think I'll tell you anything? Garth told us how you're just a has-been Ulric. Let's see what ya got."

Ulric smirked, pulling off his cloak and drawing his sword. "You'll be eating dirt, boy."

Evie pulled her sword free, pushing her hood back, ready. But Ulric was fast and lunged at the man. The stranger pulled his other dagger free and used them as dual weapons. He was fast, dodging Ulric's advances. Metal clashed as they parried each other's move. Evie kept back, looking out for anyone appearing, but it seemed the scarred man was alone.

He was a good fighter, but Ulric, even though older and bigger, was skilled. He sliced the man across his thigh. As his hand went to cover his wound, Ulric struck again, the blade slicing across his arm. Then in one swift motion the pommel of Ulric's sword hit the man in the face. The man staggered back, dazed, and fell to the floor. His weapons fell free of his grasp.

Ulric stood over him, placing the blade of his long sword across the man's throat. "Talk!"

The scarred man spat blood at Ulric. The Sword pressed the point of his blade against the scared man's throat, cutting into the skin.

Evie came up behind them and added, "I suggest you talk."

The man's gaze locked onto her, then Ulric, "Even though you killed Garth, we still honour his orders."

Ulric cast a quick glance at Evie, both puzzled, but he said nothing and turned back to the man.

Evie questioned, "What orders?"

The man remained silent, so Ulric pressed his blade further into the wound. The man just smiled.

Evie knelt behind the man's head and glanced at Ulric. "Keep him still."

Ulric sheathed his sword and pulled a dagger free as he lowered to the ground. He pressed his knee on one of the man's shoulders. Firmly held the other with his hand, while his free hand held his dagger at the man's throat.

Evie placed her fingers on the man's temples. He glared at her. Evie shifted her focus onto his eyes. The man struggled to break free of her, but Ulric applied more pressure on the blade of his dagger. Evie shut her eyes and saw flashes. A note. A meeting with other men and a woman. Then —

Suddenly, the man yanked his head up, cutting his own throat on Ulric's blade. Evie fell back, the connection lost. Ulric glanced at the man, his features filled with astonishment as their captive drew his final breath, blood spilling onto the ground.

Ulric whispered, "He'd sooner take his life than to talk."

Evie stared at the man's lifeless eyes and sighed, "Well, not until I saw something."

Ulric stood upright, sheathing his dagger. He turned to Evie, aiding her in getting back on her feet. "Let's talk in our room. I don't think it advisable to be seen here."

In their first floor room at the back of the inn, Ulric sat on the bed cleaning his sword while Evie walked back and forth by the small fireplace. "I saw him talking to a group of men and women. They resembled skilled Swords, but before I could clearly see what they were doing, the image vanished as he sliced his throat." She turned, facing Ulric. "But I saw something else."

The Sword glanced upwards and hesitated, the oiled cloth in his hand forgotten. "What?"

Evie came and sat beside him on the bed. "It was a note. The handwriting appeared to be Garth's."

"And?"

Evie pursed her lips. "But I doubt it was from him. It couldn't be."

Ulric tensed, but bit his tongue, remembering what Slan had told him. Evie trusted Garth, yet, despite his efforts, Ulric still could not. He kept his voice calm, "What did the note say?"

Evie shifted her attention to his eyes. "Royals south. Kill them." She shook her head. "But Garth assured me he planned to make amends. Help us find Bazertari."

Ulric asked sternly, frowning, "When?"

She averted her gaze from his eyes. "A few days after we took Great Oak." She gnawed on her lip. "Our last night there, you saw I was upset, but you never asked why, you just held me."

Ulric let out an exasperated breath, tossing the oiled cloth towards his saddle bag. He had wondered what she had been upset about, but if he had known . . .

He snapped, "For *feck's* sake, Evie."

Evie stared angrily at him. "He has *changed*. I *know* him."

Ulric put his sword to one side, then clasped Evie's hand. "Evie, I care for you, deeply. Yet, you seem unable to make a clear judgement about Garth."

She responded, "No, it's you whose judgement is clouded. You didn't see what I saw, Ulric. Garth felt torn. Broken. He was distraught over what he had done."

"I have witnessed him act like your friend and then suddenly turn and slaughter. You were a necessary step towards an objective. He saw your weakness for him and he *used* it."

She yanked her hand out of his grip, standing. Her expression filled with frustration. "*No*. I trust Garth."

Ulric rubbed his temples. No matter how hard he tried, he could not get Evie to see. He gazed up at her, lost in her eyes. He would have to bite his tongue. If he continued down this path, he would lose her before they had even started. He stood, placing his hands on her shoulders. "Alright, say he has changed. Why the message?"

Evie looked up at him and shook her head. "I don't know."

Evie anxiously chewed on her lip, studying Ulric. She could see he wanted to believe her, but doubt lingered in his eyes. He had seen the dark side of Garth for too long and could not see how much he had changed. She inhaled deeply; she did not want to jeopardise what they had just found, but she also had to make Ulric see that Garth had changed.

"We head for Bay Point and find the family. But be on guard in case there are others."

Ulric rubbed his temples again and sighed, "Agreed, but it's late. We both need some sleep. We'll go down to the ferry at dawn."

Evie placed her hand on his cheek, then kissed him. He enveloped her in his embrace and they hugged. He gave her a passionate kiss and gazed into her eyes.

Evie softly smiled, enjoying the sense of safety in his arms. "I just want you to hold me."

His arms tightened around her. "I'll never let you go."

THIRTY SEVEN

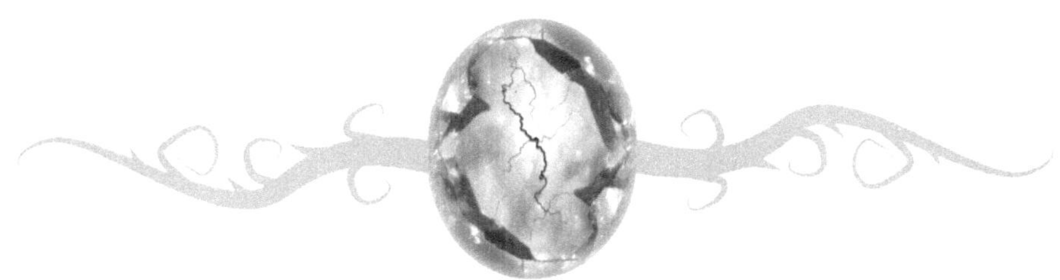

Evie and Ulric reached Bay Point after three days. The coastal city, from their high vantage point, looked picturesque. Watchtowers were strategically placed around the high sandstone walls, and attached to the roofs were green banners. More of the banners could be seen on the taller buildings within the city itself, all fluttering in the sea breeze. As the city came into view, it reminded Evie of Palasses, when it had been a more prosperous city in the Moonstar she had first visited.

Evie dismounted just off the main road, the wooden gates of Bay Point ahead. She stood next to her horse, and closed her eyes. Then she focused on Slan while Ulric waited patiently. They had a contact to meet and did not know where to go. Slan had thought it best to withhold the location until they arrived. Now, on the outskirts of the city, and with her stronger link to the old sorcerer, Evie concentrated on projecting herself to him.

Slan lifted his gaze from his desk in the study when Evie appeared before him. He smiled. "This is a stronger link compared to your first attempt."

Evie smiled warmly. "I believe I'm getting the hang of it now, but it still feels odd. My fingers keep tingling."

The sorcerer chuckled. "You get used to it. What news have you?"

"We are on the outskirts of Bay Point."

Slan asked, "Any trouble on route?"

"A little."

Slan raised an eyebrow. "Go on."

"There was a scarred man at Hinderly. It seems he was looking for the royal family, too."

"Are you sure?"

She replied, "He wouldn't talk, but I probed his mind and saw images. I believe we should proceed with caution."

"I thought as much. I know Garth had sent many scouts to find them over the years."

Evie responded, "So, this man may have been looking for a while?"

Slan gave a quick nod. "Aye. Many were loyal to him and Bazertari, and even though we have Great Oak back, their orders still stand. You will find the same in many towns and cities. Men loyal to Garth and the warlock still have a duty to uphold their orders. There will be others who will run, but one's like the scarred man will remain committed till the bitter end."

Evie nodded, glad that her trust in Garth had not been broken. The letter was an old command. She sighed, "So where now?"

Slan observed her. "If my information is correct, they have lodgings to the south of the city, on Bakers Row. They are above a bakery that belongs to a man named Lance Hormwood. If they have moved, then he may know where to."

"We will go there now."

Slan reached out his hand and ordered, "Wait."

She focused on him. "Yes?"

He gave her a warm gaze and asked, "You and Ulric. Is it going well?"

Evie glanced down, blushing. "Yes, very well."

The sorcerer chuckled. "I knew it would. The Ulric from the other Moonstar always regretted that he never expressed his feelings to you. Even if it amounted to nothing."

Evie looked at the ageing sorcerer. "So, he had feelings?"

Slan replied, "Aye he did. By the end, he truly loved you. But, the . . ."

Evie smiled sadly. "The timing wasn't right."

Slan gazed at her. "Aye. He acknowledged the connection you had with Garth and believed it wasn't the right course of action."

"I sensed there was something with Ulric. My last night on that Moonstar, it had been undeniably in his gaze, but he told me to say nothing and leave it be. I realised it was his friendship with Garth that he had kept his heart hidden." Evie smiled softly. "But here and now, we are enjoying each other's company."

Slan chuckled. "Good. I'm glad things are progressing this time. You both deserve happiness. Now go. Ulric will wonder why you are blushing."

Evie ended the connection, aware her face was flushed. She casually glanced at Ulric to see the Sword giving her a quizzical look.

Then he chuckled. "I gather Slan was asking about us."

Evie nodded. "He was."

Ulric smiled. "He can never keep his nose out of things."

"He means well."

Ulric said, "Aye, he does." He paused, then asked, "So, where are we to go?"

"Bakers Row, a bakery owned by a Lance Hormwood."

The Sword remounted his horse. "I know the street, but not the baker." He directed his attention to the mid-afternoon sky. "We'll find it now, then look for an inn."

They rode into the busy city. The walls were similar to that of Palasses, but not as big, despite having a large port. They navigated through the maze of streets, reaching the south section of the city. Ulric led the way to Baker Row. The street was short and narrow, so they tied their horses up outside a blacksmith that was a little ways back on the route they had taken. Ulric asked the dwarf to check the horses' shoes, then they walked the remainder of the way.

The smell of fresh bread and cakes invaded their nostrils as they strolled down the narrow street. The buildings were tightly packed, making it appear like they were leaning towards the street. Halfway down was a bakery with an impressive shop front. Ulric glanced at the sign, his eyebrow arching, Hormwood Bakers. It seemed they had found the right one. The shop was not too busy, with only one other customer. As they entered, Ulric and Evie greeted the large plump man behind the counter with a nod, taking off their hoods.

Once his customer left, he regarded them and said, "Don't get business from Swords that often. What can I do for ya?"

Evie smiled. "We wish to talk to the owner of this establishment, Lance Hormwood."

He eyed her with suspicion. "Who's askin'?"

Ulric smiled. "Friends from Great Oak."

Evie added. "We have an acquaintance, an ancient one."

He walked from behind the counter to the shop's door, opening it. "Nay clue what ya after, and I suggest ya leave."

Evie stated softly, "Slan sent us."

He directed his gaze towards them and shook his head, indicating towards the door. "I'd like ya to leave."

Ulric directed Evie over the threshold. "As you wish."

The two Swords left, the baker closed the door behind them and locked it.

Evie gazed back at the building and sighed, "Now what?"

Ulric observed the shop and then retraced their steps. "We find an inn."

Evie caught up with him. "And then what?"

"Wait for them to contact us."

She frowned. "What?"

Ulric stopped and smiled. "He will now tell them we have been by and what we have said. Whoever was watching from the back will send someone to follow us, see which inn we will stay at, and then contact us."

Evie, still frowning, asked, "How do you know?"

He chuckled, grabbing her hand gently in his, pulling her down the street. "It's what I would do."

She glanced back, not seeing anyone in the street. If they did not get approached, then they would have to keep trying until the baker speaks to them.

The two sat in the not too busy inn, finishing their evening meal of stew and dumplings. Ulric was telling Evie about one of his visits to the city and how it entailed a dark-haired beauty and a hired Sword. She smiled as he reminisced, and Evie wondered how many women he had left with broken hearts in his youth. Evie leant back, savouring her ale, noticing Ulric was still only drinking water, and questioned if he would ever have alcohol again. She paused drinking when she noticed a hooded figure a few tables away looking their way. Both she and Ulric had removed their cloaks. Ulric advised that in the event they were going to be contacted, it would be easier for them to be found. It helped that in Bay Point, they also felt less of a need to keep their features hidden.

Evie shifted her attention to Ulric, who sat opposite her, his back to the hooded figure. "We seem to have an interested party."

He arched an eyebrow. "Can you see what they look like?"

She savoured a taste of her ale, taking another look over Ulric's shoulder so it did not come across too obvious. "No, hard to say. Their features are in the shadow of their hood."

Ulric pursed his lips. "Alright. Finish your food and we will see if they venture over."

Ulric signalled to the barmaid for more drink, and they continued to talk while Evie kept a close eye on the figure. It was a good while before the stranger suddenly stood; then paused a moment before picking up the pint and walked towards the two.

Evie displayed her curiosity through a raised eyebrow. "They seemed to be done waiting."

Ulric fixed his gaze on her, but his hand had moved slightly so he could access the dagger on his belt quickly. Evie glanced upwards when the hooded figure halted at their table.

The voice was low and seemed young, "So, Slan sent you?"

Evie raised her gaze towards them and enquired, "Who's asking?"

The hooded stranger remained standing, holding his ale casually. Ulric watched the interaction with caution.

The person leaned closer and declared, "In the morn, return. There will be some loaves ready to collect."

Then he downed the ale, placed the empty tankard on the table, and left.

Evie went to follow, but Ulric touched her hand gently. "Nay. We'll go back in the morn."

She averted her gaze from the inn entrance where the figure had gone. "Do you know who that was?"

Ulric shrugged. "Nay clue. But methinks we'll get answers in the morn."

She shifted her attention to his eyes, raising an eyebrow. "Early night?"

He winked. "Not going to say nay to that."

They walked to their room and as soon as the door locked, Ulric was undoing Evie's black jerkin. She grabbed his neck, pulling him towards her lips, making it difficult for him to continue undoing her top. He abandoned his first objective and ran his fingers through her red hair as he deepened the kiss. He sucked on her bottom lip and gazed at her momentarily, then he lifted her, sweeping her into his embrace and carried her to the bed. Evie giggled and kissed him again as he climbed onto the bed still holding her.

Ulric leaned over, putting her down, not letting their lips part. He then pulled back, to gaze at her again. His hands returned to his initial job of undoing her jerkin. He made swift work of the buttons on her shirt and pulled it off as he caressed her breasts. Evie closed her eyes in pleasure. Ulric leant forward, his lips brushing over her breasts and sucked her nipples, until they grew into hard peaks. He glanced up at her as she laid back, her eyes closed, savouring his gentle caress with his lips. He started placing gentle kisses down her chest and across her stomach. Her body tensed in anticipation as he ventured further. His callused hands roamed down to her trousers and as he kissed her abdomen, he undid them. He pulled them down, over her hips, maintaining his kisses as he crept down to the apex of her thighs.

Evie's breath caught as she experienced his lips moving further down, causing a delightful tingling sensation in her loins. She bit her lip, as he continued to explore, his tongue warm and welcoming. She arched her spine as her body lost control. Ulric's large hands gripped her hips, making her body spasm, almost violently.

She gasped, "Ulric—"

He did not stop. Evie's entire body quivered, its reaction beyond her control. She was unable to do anything but submit to him as he continued between her legs. She cried out in pleasure, her body vibrating. Then he suddenly stopped. He yanked down his trousers and entered her. Evie gasped as he thrusted hard inside her, his sizable phallus going deep. Evie was still high from her orgasm and gazed at Ulric as he skilfully moved his hips, guiding her to her second peak. He leaned over her, capturing her lips with his as his hips continued to rock into her, their bodies moving as one. Evie struggled to concentrate as Ulric's movements grew erratic and his thighs trembled. He was about to orgasm, and she was on her third. She gripped his shoulders. Her legs were jelly. She could no longer control her body, and they climaxed together.

Ulric looked at her, breathless. She could still sense his presence pulsating inside her. He smiled softly and kissed her again. He took a hold of her and rolled over so Evie rested on top of him. Her body shivered in delight.

She gazed at him, panting, "Don't ask me to go anywhere. I think my legs are broken."

He chuckled, gazing at her flushed features. "All you have to do is stay in my arms."

She whispered, her body shaking from the endorphins. "I can do that."

He delicately brushed his lips against her temple and sighed, keeping his arms around her.

They remained in that position for some time before Ulric said softly, "Think you have stolen something from me."

Evie stayed where she was, her cheek against his chest, her fingers caressing the dark hairs there. "What?"

He whispered, "My heart."

Evie glanced up at him, catching his intense gaze fixed on her. "Ulric—"

He brushed an unruly hair from her face. His attention was solely on her, the love clear to see. "I don't fall for many women. But I—I'm powerless to prevent it. The thought of not having you here with me. . . well, it hurts."

She gently kissed his lips and smiled softly. "I feel the same. These last few days I don't know, I just—"

He stopped her with a kiss and wrapped his arms tightly around her. "Let's just stay like this."

Evie smiled and savoured his embrace. "Gladly. Do not expect me to move for the next few hours."

Ulric scoffed, his chest rumbling from the laughter. "Seems I have found what to do to keep you still."

Evie giggled and stole a quick glance up at his features. "I'll have to return the favour."

He kept his arms wrapped around her and said, "Not tonight. This one was for you."

She quirked an eyebrow and snuggled up against him. The large brute had a gentle, selfless side, more than she had realised.

THIRTY EIGHT

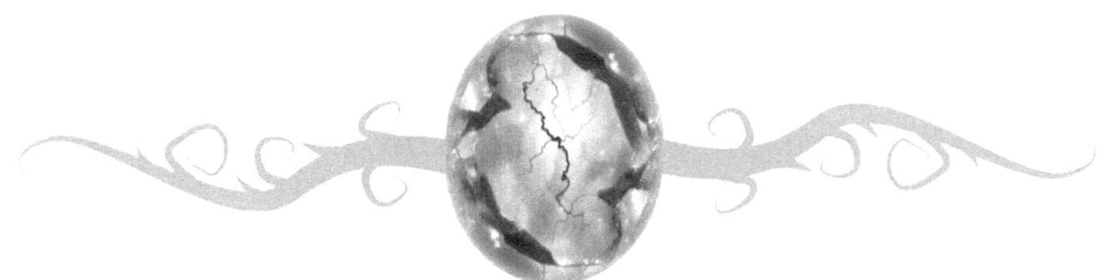

It was mid-morning when Ulric led the way back to the bakery. Only a few people casually strolled past them on the street, and the store appeared deserted. When Ulric and Evie crossed the threshold, the large man behind the counter raised his gaze and regarded them with suspicion.

He said, "If ya come for ya loaves, they're in the back."

They both gave a sign of approval and proceeded to accompany the large man into the back room. There, standing by a sizable table, was a young man of about sixteen. By his side, with a similar jaw line and hair colour, was a man in his late thirties. Both wore finely made blue jerkins and black trousers. It was apparent that they had previously experienced a lifestyle characterised by wealth and influence.

The boy observed the pair, his hands clasped together before him, and said, "So, Slan is searching for members of the royal family?"

Evie answered, recognising the voice from the night before, "Yes, and you are?"

The older man stated, his voice full of authority, "I am Terian Cloudbane, and this is my eldest son, Ellan."

Ulric bowed his head slightly. "An honour to meet you, Your Highness."

Evie's eyes widened, and she quickly bowed her head.

Terian studied them, his arms folded across his chest. "Nay need for such formalities. We have nay intention of taking the throne."

Ulric's features paled. "But Moonstar needs a royal family to lead."

Terian responded, "I have nay interest in the duties that may be put upon me. My family are distant cousins and nothing more."

Ulric insisted, "But for the sake of Moonstar."

The would-be king regarded them both, his stance still defensive. "I feel that you have made your journey for nothing." He glanced at his son. "I have to think of my family before duty."

Evie added, "Before you make such a decision, will you talk to Slan?"

Terian regarded her. "From your accent, why would someone not from these parts have such an interest in what becomes of this land?"

Evie responded, "True, I wasn't born here. But my heart was, and I have a deep connection with this land. When I met the royal family, they were very honourable, and this Moonstar needs stability, and we think you can give it that."

Ellan frowned; his young features were full of suspicion. "You said you have a connection with our land. But why would you say *this* Moonstar?"

Evie arched her eyebrow regarding the young man, she was impressed by the boy's sharp listening skills. Not many people would have understood the depth of what she had just said. "It's hard to explain, but I have been to Moonstar before and freed it from Bazertari. *This* Moonstar isn't the one I remember, but I want to ensure it can have the same freedom I gave the other."

Terian's features turned dark and walked towards her. "Who," his voice stern, demanding, "*are* you?"

She rolled up her sleeve, revealing the bracelet. "I am the traveller."

Ellan snorted as he peered over the table to see the bracelet. "That tyrant, Garth, killed her years ago."

Ulric responded, stepping closer towards her, his shoulders tensing as he regarded Terian's aggressive approach, "Aye, he did. But Evie *is* the traveller. Slan pulled her through a portal from another land, as he knows she is the sole person to free us. But we also need a royal family to rule. To bring hope to the people."

Ellan glanced at the pair and shrugged. His voice was full of authority, like his father's. "But is that a guarantee? I heard the warlock escaped."

Evie's eyes glanced downwards in guilt. "He did." She regained her focus on the two men. "But when we find him, he will be destroyed. I am the only one who can and his days are numbered."

"Unless someone kills you," stated the teen, scepticism in his voice.

She directed her gaze towards Ellan and responded, "He can try, but as before, he *will* fail."

Ulric paused briefly and implored, "Listen, before you make your decisions, will you please talk to Slan?"

"And how," asked Terian, folding his arms across his chest and looking at them both with disdain, "are we to do that?"

Evie replied, "I can contact him."

Terian regarded her sternly and ordered, "Then do."

She looked at the would-be king; he did not believe her, but she hoped deep down that Slan could persuade them. She pressed her lips together and closed her eyes. Then, like she had the day before, she contacted Slan. Once a couple of minutes had passed, he responded, and Evie turned to the Cloudbanes. "He said he will talk to you in private. Ulric and I will wait outside."

Both nodded and eyed Evie and Ulric as they left the room, just as Slan appeared as a projection.

Ulric glanced back as the door closed and said, "I hope this works, or we have ridden here for nothing."

Evie fixed her eyes on him and took his hand. "Let's get some fresh air. They may be talking for a while."

Ulric paced in the narrow street, while Evie was resting against the wall of the building opposite the bakery. They had been out there for hours. Evie watched the passersby with curiosity, her gaze flicking towards the bakery now and then. She turned her attention to Ulric, noticing how tense he was.

"Just relax, Ulric."

He continued to pace, looking towards the bakery. "Why are they taking so long?"

Evie pushed herself off the wall with her shoulders and said, "They have doubts, which is understandable. They have lived in hiding for years, their entire family line was hunted. I can understand their trepidation."

Ulric stopped and pivoted towards her. "But it is their *duty.*"

She gazed at him with affection. "Yes, it is. And Slan will get them to see. I know it."

He started pacing again. "Well, they better make their minds up fast."

The door to the bakery opened and Lance, the baker, gave a low whistle, to get their attention. Ulric froze mid step and turned, then moved towards him with Evie.

Lance regarded the two and said, "They want to talk."

They nodded and proceeded to follow Lance back inside to the back room. A woman, with a newborn of only a few days cradled in her arms, had joined Terian and Ellan. Evie noticed how Ellan's eyes matched the woman's and surmised that she was the queen-to-be.

Terian observed the two and said, "We have spoken to Slan and he is very convincing." He glanced in Evie's direction. "He informed me of who you are and I am holding you to your promise of freeing this land. I want to return Moonstar to what it once was."

Ulric replied, "So you will rule?"

He answered, "Aye, I will. My son, Ellan, is a little reluctant. But I know where our duties lie, and they are for the people of Moonstar."

Evie smiled. "Thank you."

He gave a silent sign of approval. "My wife, Estra, and our son, Dion, will remain here, as she has given birth a few days ago. But Ellan and I will accompany you both back to Great Oak."

Ulric responded, "Understood. We will ensure your safety, but you must do as we ask."

Terian said, "We will. Slan has told us what an accomplished Sword you are, Ulric, and we will follow your lead."

Evie nodded in approval. "How long do you need to prepare?"

"Not long," stated Terian. "We will require horses, but Lance will have a talk with Gron, the dwarf blacksmith. He usually knows where horses can be purchased quickly, with nay questions asked."

Ulric asked, "Then we will leave in two days. How skilled are you both with the sword?"

Terian replied, "Well trained. I ensured Ellan was from a young age."

Ulric gave a confirming gesture. "Good. I do not expect we will have trouble, but it is best to be prepared."

The king-to-be said, "We will meet you at dawn in two days at the city gates."

Ulric and Evie agreed, leaving them to prepare.

Evie glanced towards Ulric as they walked back towards the inn. "So, what do we do while we wait?"

"Get supplies and prepare to have to babesit."

Evie frowned, "Babesit?"

"Aye, Terian said they are trained to use the sword, and they may be, but I suspect they have not used a sword in an actual fight. They both have an air of confidence, but when faced with danger, I can see they will both freeze."

Evie sighed, "Understood. Let's hope we don't have any trouble."

His gaze shifted towards her, raising an eyebrow. Evie remembered the scarred man they encountered at the fishing village, and she had to agree with Ulric. The journey back probably will not be easy.

THIRTY NINE

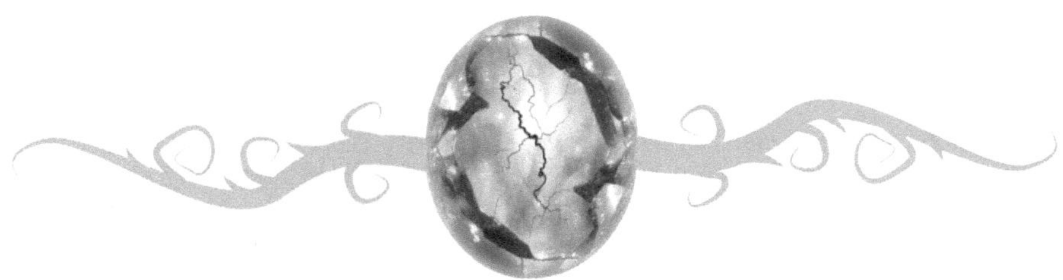

Garth sat towards the rear of the bustling tavern in the City of Lights. The air was thick with smoke from the two men near him as they drew on their pipes talking about their day at the market. It had taken Garth several days to get here and another couple to track down anyone from his army.

By obscuring his features with his hood, he maintained his hazel eyes on the two individuals he had trailed earlier. They sat chatting and drinking, but with the noise of the tavern, and a local bard bellowing out a jolly tune that many were singing along to, Garth could not hear them completely. Luckily, Ulric had taught him when he was a boy how to decipher a conversation from reading lips. It was not foolproof, but he had worked out that they were waiting to meet Tyrak. It seemed they had also received the message to head north and they mentioned his death. The rumour was widespread, and for him, it was beneficial. He still had not found any of his elite and wondered if they had all been killed or were in hiding.

Garth took a quick sip of his ale as some people left and blocked his view for a moment. *Were they discussing Bazertari?* He had missed them mentioning the name, but from what he had picked up, Tyrak was going to take them to a base of operations. If he followed them, he may find his men and the warlock. When he did, he could then let Evie know.

Garth knew of a witch in the non-human quarter that he could trust, and with a bit of coin, she could send Evie a note magically.

He glanced towards the door when a hooded figure entered. *Could that be Tyrak?* The two he had been watching were not hiding their identity. Tyrak was too cocky and would make more of an entrance. That was one reason he never used Tyrak for spy missions; he would have been easily spotted by appearance and mannerism.

Garth leant back a little, realising he could be here for some time. He went to take another sip of his ale when his view was blocked. Garth lifted his eyes and observed a slightly stooped, hooded figure giving off the impression that he was after something.

Garth snapped, motioning with his hand to move. "Not interested."

Ignoring Garth, the uninvited guest sat down opposite him, blocking his view entirely. Garth gave the stranger a fierce look and went to leave, but found he was frozen stiff, unable to move.

The hooded figure leant forward, and a familiar voice menacingly said, "I think we need to have a little chat, don't you?"

The figure moved slightly, allowing Garth to see under his hood. His eyes widened as Bazertari glared at him. Garth tried to say something, but, like his body, his throat was not working, it was clamped shut, no sound was getting through. He tried again to move but was still frozen in place. All he could do was blink.

The warlock chuckled, regarding him as he tilted his head. "There will be time to explain your treachery later. I am curious why *my* general would turn on me."

Bazertari's expression changed and he scowled, leaning closer, inspecting Garth's frozen features. Black wisps of magic seeped from the warlock's fingertips and slithered across to Garth's hand that held his tankard. Like strings, they attached to the Sword's hand and pulled each finger back, and then lifted the hand from the tankard. Garth's hand was raised into the air and then slammed down onto the table, the tendrils of smoke pulling the fingers taut so the hand laid flat. Garth watched the whole thing with fear in his eyes. In one swift motion, he had made Garth into a puppet.

The warlock pressed his hand onto Garth's and sneered, "So let's see how she did it."

Bazertari's eyes turned black as Garth felt the warlock's dark magic seep into his mind. It was painful as it clawed at the Sword's memories. A muffled grunt escaped his throat while attempting not to cry out in pain. Garth desperately tried to stop the warlock from looking. But Bazertari's black gaze intensified, and he delved deeper, breaking Garth's resolve. Garth's hazel eyes brimming in tears from the excruciating pain.

The warlock sneered, "So you and her had a *destiny*. That explains the strong connection." He paused, smirking as he delved further. "Interesting."

Bazertari reclined and released the connection. The darkness faded from his eyes, revealing his amber irises speckled with black. Garth's own eyes still watered from the pain.

The warlock scowled. "You weak *fool*."

Garth tried to move, his hand shifting slightly on the table, his eyes teeming with rage. The warlock let out a deep breath, then the two men that Garth had been following approached the table, glaring at him. The Sword cursed inwardly. He had walked right into a trap.

Bazertari regarded him and smiled. "Perhaps it is time you had your punishment, Garth."

The Sword glared at the two men, frantically trying to move. His hand moved a fraction more, but he still had no control. Bazertari rose to his full height, glaring at Garth before he snapped his fingers. Garth slumped forward on to the table unconscious.

The warlock turned to the men. "Bring him."

Garth spat blood onto the damp dungeon floor as he dangled from the ceiling. He had lost sensation in his hands some time ago, and his body was a wall of pain. He was on tiptoe, but even though he could sense the damp floor against the balls of his bare feet, it did not alleviate the pain in his shoulders.

A fist made contact with his side again, pain vibrated up his spine. He glared at Tyrak; the large brute's fists had hit him so many times he had lost count. Then he was hit again against the rib cage, and a weakened rib finally snapped. Excruciating pain burned through his body.

Garth peered past Tyrak through swollen eyes and wheezed. The large brute punched Garth again in the side, pressing the broken rib against his lung. He heard a chuckle, and saw Bazertari walking towards him in the dull light. At that moment, Tyrak landed another powerful hit to Garth's torso.

In spite of the pain, Garth noticed that Bazertari was limping, his stance slightly bent. *Did I hit the warlock before he vanished through the portal at the palace? Or is it from the effects of using too much dark magic?*

Garth grimaced, trying not to show how much agony he was in. "So nay chat?" The bearded man glared at him.

The warlock chuckled some more as he regarded the battered and bruised Sword from where he dangled in the dungeon cell. "We will, but this is far more entertaining." He paused, moving right up to Garth, digging his finger into his side where the broken rib was. Garth could not prevent the sharp cry of pain from leaving his lips. The warlock added, "Unfortunately I don't have my dark dungeon that I had at the palace. So, here, your punishment will have to be somewhat rougher."

Garth shot him a fierce glare, spitting more blood from his mouth. "Well, I could do this all day."

Bazertari regarded him, stepping back and signalling for Tyrak to punch Garth again. The brute happily complied.

The warlock rubbed his chin, seeing the pain etched across Garth's face. "We will see." His icy gaze assessed Garth from head to toe. "Well, revenge is never idle. I have more to do to ensure the *bitch* who corrupted you pays."

Garth angrily pulled against his bonds. "You fecking werewolf arse!"

Bazertari turned, glancing back at him, raising an eyebrow. "So you are fond of her. Interesting." He smirked and turned away. "Rest assured; you will have company soon."

The Sword stared menacingly at him, and with sudden strength, tried to break free of his bonds. Tyrak was ready, and punched Garth across the jaw. The Sword's vision turned white then black when the second punch knocked him out cold.

Slan was pleased that the Cloudbanes had agreed to rule. But until they arrived, there was a lot of paperwork to deal with. With tired eyes, his gaze shifted towards the night sky through the study windows. He should really get some rest and look at these papers in the morning, but this also kept his mind occupied with matters other than Bazertari. Since his disappearance from the palace, Slan feared the worst. He knew Bazertari would seek revenge.

Slan froze when a hand clamped down on his shoulder, then there was a sharp pain in his side. The point of a dagger penetrated through the cloth of his robe.

A bitter voice murmured in his ear, "Missed me, old man?"

Slan craned his head round to see, unable to turn with the warlock clasping him. The blade pressed harder into his side. "So, you live."

The warlock spat, "Aye. That bitch of yours won't get to use that spell on me again."

Slan responded calmly, realising that he may not see another dawn, "Your overconfidence will be your downfall."

Bazertari pushed the dagger further into Slan's side, the blade slicing through his robe into his skin. "Maybe so, but you will never live to see it."

The sorcerer grimaced in agony as the weapon cut deeper. Something was wrong.

Bazertari sneered, answering his thoughts, "Oh, and the blade that I am digging into your side is made out of devil stone. I want you to suffer, Slan. Live long enough for that *bitch* to find you."

Bazertari yanked the dagger at an angle, snapping it. The piece of stone in Slan's body moved with a mind of its own. The sorcerer cried out in pain. He had read about the devil stone. It was used as a torture device. It wormed its way through a body, inflicting as much damage as it could, making the victim die very slowly.

The warlock stepped back as Slan fell from his chair and curled up in agony. He said, his voice full of bitterness, "I am hoping this will give her a message. I am aware that you are linked and when she teleports here, I will instruct her on what to do."

Slan glared at the warlock, his body convulsing in pain. "Y—You w—will pay."

Bazertari smirked. "Maybe so, but I will go down in a *blaze of glory.*"

The warlock then opened a portal and vanished. Slan clawed at his side, feeling the devil stone move through his body agonisingly slow and painfully.

He gasped, "Evie . . ."

FORTY

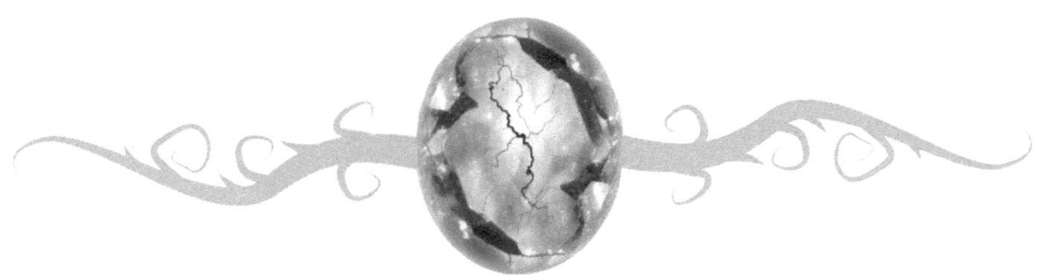

Evie jolted awake. The pain in her side was excruciating. Images of Slan being stabbed by Bazertari flashed through her mind. She sat up gasping; it seemed so real. Too real.

A hand gently touched her shoulder. Evie glanced upwards and found Ulric kneeling beside her, he had been on watch by the fire. Terian and Ellan were still asleep.

"What is it?"

Evie frowned. "I'm not sure, I—" Pain burned in her side again, and she inhaled sharply.

Ulric gripped her arm. "Evie?"

She raised her eyes to meet his, tears welling in her eyes. "It's Slan. I think . . . I think he's . . . dying."

Ulric walked back and forth near the fire, Terian and Ellan stood to the side, looking on in concern.

Ulric turned back to Evie. "It could be a trap."

Terian stated, "It *will* be a trap."

Evie glanced at both of them as she strapped her sword onto her back. "Yes, I know it is, but Slan is in great pain. I must go."

Ulric stopped pacing; his arms folded. "I don't like it. I should go with you."

She sighed, glancing towards the king-to-be and his son. "No, you have to make sure they get to Great Oak safely."

"Then we all go," said Ulric, determination etched on his features.

Evie firmly shook her head. "I haven't teleported before. I would rather not take a chance. If I end up in a wall, so be it, but I can't risk you or Their Royal Highnesses." She sighed, "I don't know if I can even do it."

Ulric walked up to her, taking hold of her shoulders gently. "I definitely don't like it."

She looked up at him and planted a gentle kiss on his cheek. "I know, but I have to."

Ulric embraced her tightly. "Be safe, please."

Evie savoured his embrace. "I will." Her gaze met his as she raised her eyes. "I can take care of myself."

"I know you can. I just don't want to lose you, now that I've found you."

She lovingly tangled her fingers in his hair and kissed him passionately. "I'll be alright."

Ulric nodded, reluctant to let her go. "We'll get to Great Oak as fast as we can."

Evie stepped back from the men and drew in a deep breath, her eyes closed. Ulric observed her closely as her features furrowed with concentration. Slowly, blue swirling smoke appeared behind her. Ulric experienced static in the air as the portal grew larger. The volatile vortex of glowing smoke flickered wildly, the portal was unstable.

He gripped his fist, murmuring, "Let it hold."

Ulric's eyes remained fixed on Evie as she inhaled deeply, and the mass behind her grew steady. An image of the study appeared in the smoke. She turned towards it, then she swiftly glanced back at Ulric before stepping through. Ulric moved closer as he watched the woman he loved vanish into the swirling mass. Then the portal snapped shut, leaving the three men at the campsite with only a small fire illuminating the area.

Ulric whispered, "Stay safe."

Evie stumbled into the study, the portal closing behind her. She experienced dizziness as she dropped to her knees and vomited. Wiping her mouth, she took a brief pause to get her bearings, her stomach still doing somersaults. Evie quickly turned when she heard Slan.

He gasped through gritted teeth, "Evie."

Slan was on the floor, coiled up in a ball, pain etched across his pale face. She gasped in fear and worry. Scrambling to her feet, she rushed over and fell to her knees beside him. Her eyes filled with tears.

"Who did this?"

Slan grimaced and coughed up blood. "Bazertari." He paused. "I don't have long. You must be ready."

Evie assessed his body, her eyes focusing on the wound on his side. "I can heal you."

Her hand glowed, but Slan grabbed it, shaking his head. "Nay. It will not help. The warlock is seeking revenge. He knows he can not kill you, so be wary; he will trick you."

Evie gazed intensely at him, cradling his hand, his skin already cooling. "I won't let him trick me like last time."

Slan stared up at her and winced in pain as the shard twisted closer to his heart. "You must destroy him. Whatever he does to try and stop you, keep yourself focused. He will know your weaknesses. Do not let him use them against you."

"I won't."

Slan smiled at her. "You have become a fine sorceress, Evie."

She nodded, tears spilling over her eyelashes. Slan grimaced again and gasped as the shard found his heart. He locked eyes with her and smiled. "Live a long and fruitful life. Leave as many broken hearts behind you as you can."

Evie smiled sadly. "I will follow your example."

Slan clenched his chest, his last breath escaping from his parted lips. Evie sniffed, still holding Slan's cold, limp hand. She pressed her lips gently against his forehead and sobbed.

"What a touching sight," stated a cold, familiar voice.

Evie looked up sharply and sneered when she saw Bazertari. A plasma ball shot from her hand, but it flew straight through him, and the books behind him exploded into shreds of paper and leather.

The warlock laughed. "Do you think I would be foolish enough to teleport there?"

Evie snarled as she stood, "Why don't you grow a pair and find out!"

He tightened his lips and scoffed. "Well, you are a fiery one, aren't you?" He took a brief look at the body of Slan. "I can see why the fool brought you here."

Evie shot him a hostile look. "So was this to get my attention? It has."

"Good. Now to fulfil my plan."

"And that is?"

The warlock walked towards her, looking her up and down. He pursed his lips. "Let us meet face to face."

"Where?"

Bazertari shut his eyes briefly and an image of a field, with mountains in the distance and a forest, appeared in her mind. Followed by a second image of a circular tower made of black stone.

The warlock added. "You need something to focus on to teleport. That's my tower. Before you leave notes for the drunkard to find, know that it is in the heart of Demon Forest. Any who enters *never* leaves." He paused, tilting his head to one side. "Well, not how they entered, anyway."

She gave him a piercing look. "And then what?"

He smiled. "Well, let's see . . . you join me."

Evie laughed. "Join you?"

"Well, should you desire for the drunkard to remain alive, then, aye." He brought up a finger as if suddenly remembering something. "And, I have a bargaining chip at my end as well."

Bazertari turned and grabbed something to the side of him. He yanked a battered and bruised Garth into the vision, his face swollen almost beyond recognition. Evie gasped.

The warlock smirked. "It seems you are both linked by destiny. You might have a fondness for that drunkard, but this fellow, well, I think you would do almost anything to keep him alive."

Evie clenched her fists and snarled. "You *fucking* bastard!"

Bazertari smiled without emotion. "Don't take too long, my henchman Tyrak is enjoying beating up his old superior." The warlock gazed at her, his eyes remaining on her longer than she liked. "I have a feeling we will make a formidable couple."

Evie sneered at him and screamed in frustration when he vanished. Her attention shifted to the body of Slan, a sob escaping from her lips. Ulric was right, it was a trap, a lure to bring her to Bazertari.

Evie paced the study, biting her lip. She was going to deal with the warlock, but she needed to think clearly. Bazertari had one thing right, she would do anything to stop Garth coming to any harm. The same with Ulric. She paused. *Were we followed from Bay Point?* She had to warn Ulric. He would be about six days from here. She yanked open the study door; she needed help.

The guard in the royal green uniform studied her as two others carried Slan's body out of the study. "You sure it's the warlock?"

Evie paced before the desk. "Yes, and I'm going after him. But I need your fastest riders to head to Hinderly. You must get word to Ulric."

The uniformed man asked, "Where are you going?"

Evie passed him a note. "Best you don't know. Everything is in this. It's for Ulric's eyes *only*."

He took it, leaving Evie alone. She inhaled and concentrated on the images Bazertari had shown her. *Can I do it, go somewhere I have never been to?* Slan had told her once she had seen a place she could teleport, so it should work. She shut her eyes and focused on the image of the tower. Moments later, a portal opened. She knew it was a trap, but she had to do something. Evie stepped into the light.

FORTY ONE

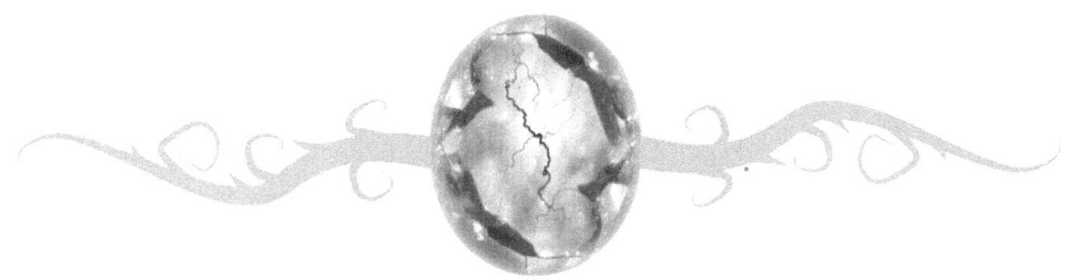

For the past two days, Ulric had been distracted. Since Evie had stepped through the portal, he had been worried about her. His duty was to keep the two royal family members safe. But if he could leave them and be with Evie, he would do so in a heartbeat. Terian had tried to ease his concerns by keeping him distracted with conversation, but Ulric found his mind wandering back to her repeatedly. The three rode on in silence as the soon-to-be king realised his efforts were futile and left Ulric alone with his thoughts.

The rhythmic sound of pounding hoofbeats resonated through the peaceful forest. Ulric pulled his horse to a stop and took a moment to assess the route in front of him. He redirected his gaze towards his companions as his hand inched towards the hilt of his sword. Terian and Ellan did the same. If it was an attack, he hoped to Rosh the two held their ground.

Ulric stared ahead once more, his shoulders tense. His keen eyes focused on the three riders in the royal green uniform as they came galloping into view. They had a gold sash across their uniform, which made them royal messengers.

He eyed the riders as they came closer and speculated it had to be news about Slan. His hand reached for his dagger, which held the insignia of Rosh, and prayed for good news. Ulric recalled the night Evie had left and how she had sensed

Slan was dying, but he could not believe it, not that stubborn old man. His stomach twisted more. *What if it's about Evie? Had the teleport gone wrong?* He looked back at his two companions, their expressions mirroring his own.

The riders, drenched in sweat and their green uniforms covered in dust, came to a stop. The horses, visibly exhausted, snorted and panted after a challenging ride. One rider moved forward. He regarded Ulric for a moment, then pulled a note from his official satchel.

With a breathless voice, the young man passed it to Ulric, "From Evie."

Ulric snatched it from the man's sweaty hand and ripped the note open.

My dear Ulric,

I'm so sorry, but Slan died from his injuries. My magic could not heal him. The weapon Bazertari used to murder him was a devil's blade. All I could do was stay by his side in his last moments.

Soon after Slan died, Bazertari confronted me via projection and wants to meet.

I am truly sorry, but I have gone alone to face him in the Demon Forest. He needs to be held accountable for what he did to Slan and this land.

Go on, swear your head off, as I know you will. But please, do not do anything foolish, it's not safe.

Once I have killed Bazertari, I will return. I promise.

Love you always, Evie xxx

Ulric cursed, and then cursed again. He crumpled up the parchment and turned to the rider. "When did she leave?"

The rider responded, "Over two days ago."

Ulric cursed, "*On Rosh, Evie.*" He glanced again at all the riders before him and gestured towards his companions. "This is Terian and Ellan Cloudbane. Get them to Great Oak. Safely."

Terian asked Ulric, concern etched his features, "What happened?"

Uric replied, "Slan has been murdered." Terian gasped as Ulric continued, "You must make your way to Great Oak with these guards."

The future king frowned. "Where are you headed?"

"North."

Ulric did not wait for a response. He nudged his horse forward and left the main road, away from Great Oak. Riding as fast as he could through the Great Wood, he headed towards the one person who could help him. He had to assume that she still had her home in the same clearing, if he could find it. He had not seen her in such a long time, Bazertari's men could have killed her or, like many others, she had left Moonstar behind. The Sword hoped she was there. The Demon Forest in the north would take days to get to. Days he did not have. He needed to be teleported. With Slan dead, and no other sorcerer around, Handrea was his only chance.

Ulric forced his mount to weave through the trees, not letting it slow. The stallion panted, Ulric trusted its strength but prayed it would prevail. He looked ahead through the trees; he was going by instinct now, having ridden hard for hours. Ulric had not the time to ride with caution. Every moment counted. Then he caught sight of a clearing ahead in the dappled light and slowed. That had to be it. Ulric pulled his mount to a stop, the animal breathing hard. He quickly dismounted, peering through the trees. He took hold of the reins, and walked his horse the remainder of the way.

He patted the stallion's neck. "I think we're here now. I promise to let you rest."

His steed's nose butted his shoulder as they entered the clearing. Ulric smiled, glancing at the animal, making a mental note to ensure it got a pleasant treat.

Ulric turned his attention back to his objective. In the centre, stood a small cottage with smoke drifting from its chimney. Someone was home. It surprised him that he had remembered the way. Most people would have been lost if they took the same route he did into the depths of the Great Wood.

Stopping in front of the building, he fastened his steed to a hitching post and patted the stallion's neck again. Ulric then knocked on the old wooden door. *Would she even help?* After all, Ulric had not seen the witch in sixteen years. If she refused, he was at a loss for what steps to follow. He could ride, but it would be too late. If he was not already.

Once the never-ending wait was over, the door swung open and an aged woman with remarkable blue eyes briefly looked up at him.

She snapped, "What're ya seeking?"

Uric smiled. "Handrea, I need your help."

She observed him briefly, then a broad smile crept across her wrinkled features. "Ulric, my boy, how are ya? Come in. Come in."

She stepped back, letting Ulric enter. He could never comprehend how she achieved it, but from an external perspective, the cottage appeared very small. But once you walked past the doorway, you found yourself in an enormous cavern, with tunnels leading from it. Maybe that was how she had evaded Bazertari. The cavern could be on a different plane.

He followed her to a large table in the middle of the room. "I feared you may have gone."

She stole a quick glance at him. "That warlock will never find me. He's a twit."

Ulric chuckled. Handrea was always to the point. He let out a sigh and glanced in her direction. "Handrea, you're the only person who can help me."

The witch smiled. "I know. But first, how are ya, me boy? I feared for ya when ya lost yar way." She waved her arm before her, gesturing to his appearance. "But it seems ya have found it once more." She eyed him. "I'm thinking a fine woman has stolen yar heart."

Ulric shuffled awkwardly. He and Evie had only just told each other how they felt. Then again, she could always tell things before others could. Because of his new-found love, he could not lose Evie, not now. He took a long breath and focused. "I have to reach the Demon Forest, and quickly."

She stared up at him, patting his arm. "As I suspected. Smitten." Then her features turned serious. "The Demon Forest is a dangerous place. Any that enter don't return."

Ulric nodded. "Aye, I've heard the stories. But I have nay choice. She's gone there on a fool's errand, and I need to help her."

Handrea asked, "How did she get there?"

"Teleported. She's a sorceress. But she's in way over her head. Facing Bazertari alone."

Handrea shook her head. "Unless she's the traveller, all hope is gone."

Ulric leant forward. "She is the traveller, and the only person who can destroy him. But not *alone.* I already fear something has gone wrong as two days have passed already and nay a word."

Handrea chuckled. "So he did it."

Ulric regarded her and asked, "What?"

"Slan. The fool did it."

"You knew Slan would do this?"

She answered, "Aye, he told me all about how Moonstar had changed and how the traveller had freed us. I had wanted to help him, but I didn't have the skill he needed. But it seems he handled it."

"Do you know he has died?"

Handrea glanced down, sadness in her eyes. "Aye, I sensed his suffering, and then his presence departed from this world. He will be missed." She squeezed Ulric's hand. "To the matter at hand. I must get ya to the Demon Forest as fast as I can. But ya will need a talisman to protect ya in that forest. I believe that twit has a tower there in its depths, but not knowing precisely where, I will have to teleport ya to the outskirts of the woods." She paused, glancing towards her bookshelf. "But I will also give ya something to guide ya."

Ulric nodded, smiling softly. "Thank you."

She replied, "Get what ya need from yar horse. Ya will go by foot. And to be honest, that poor animal needs to rest after ya pushed it so hard to get here." She paused, passing him some ginger root. "Ya also need this. My portals aren't as stable as a sorcerer's, so ya may experience some discomfort."

Ulric had not teleported often, but he was always sick afterwards. He gratefully took the root and placed it in his pocket. Then he went out to his horse, taking what he required. He grabbed food and a few other items, placing them in a satchel. He paused, looking at the stallion, then retrieved an apple from his pack and held it out to the horse. It crunched down on it, snorting a thank you.

When he went back inside, Handrea was busy at work mixing a few potions to make the talisman. As she worked, she pointed to an amulet on the table.

"Take that. It will direct ya to what ya desire and, as it's the girl, it will take ya to her. It will glow bright and pulsate when she's close."

Ulric nodded, placing it around his neck. He then watched as the witch started on the talisman.

She eyed him and remarked, "Drumming those fingers on the table will not make me move any faster."

Ulric glanced down, having not even noticed how tense and impatient he was acting. He quickly stopped and began pacing, but paused when Handrea shot him a piercing look.

He exhaled heavily, "I'll wait outside."

He lay on the ground, staring at the early evening sky, trying to relax. Ulric needed to be focused and not to worry. Evie was capable of looking after herself. But his stomach still twisted, hoping she had not come to any harm. If she had, he was not sure he could take it. He closed his eyes and prayed to Rosh, although he had abandoned the warrior god years ago. He wondered if the god would hear his prayer. But he needed Rosh to protect the woman he loved more than anyone before. If Bazertari harmed her, he would not be responsible for his actions. He would make the warlock pay. He could not continue his life without her.

FORTY TWO

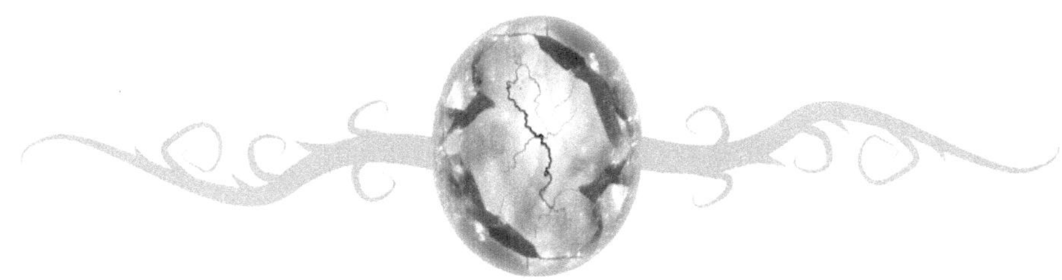

Evie spat on the ground, trying to rid the acidic remains of vomit from her mouth. She hoped she would not get sick every time she teleported. Standing back up straight, she looked around at the tall, densely packed trees as she wiped her mouth. The Demon Forest was ancient. As she scrutinised it in the low light, she shivered, the air was thick with the sense of evil. It was not a place to venture into if it was avoidable.

A sigh escaped her lips as she turned back to the ominous ebony tower that loomed in front of her, beginning to regret her decision to come alone. The tower was so tall, the top of it vanished into the darkness of the trees above. She experienced a strong desire to create a light globe to examine it more closely, but Evie did not want to attract anything unwanted. She stared up at it. The dark stone was spelled to absorb the surrounding light.

Evie squinted upwards, she could not detect any windows or signs of life. She twisted sharply, gazing towards the trees again, when something inhuman growled in their dark depths. Deep in thought, she chewed her lip, considering if she should just make a portal back to the palace and wait for Ulric. She shifted her concentration back to the tower. She would do it by herself.

As she roamed around the perimeter of the imposing structure, she searched for an entrance. After walking several metres round the base towards the opposite side, she discovered a large oak door. Her stomach twisted. She was alone and about to walk into what was clearly a trap. She approached the door and as she reached it; it creaked open.

Tentatively, she passed through the doorway. Evie entered a dark hallway with one torch on the wall to her left, the flickering flames lighting the area. Standing before her was a statue. It was of Bazertari looking ahead, one hand lifted slightly in a becoming gesture. She sneered at the marble features of the warlock. She was not surprised that he would have a statue of himself.

She turned to the flaming torch, seeing an entrance with stone steps curling upwards. After drawing in a long breath, she went up to them. Evie had expected some sort of welcoming party, but it seemed like the tower was deserted. Her gut tightened knowing it was a trap she had just willingly ventured into, yet she felt she had no choice. Bazertari needed to die, and confronting him was the only way. As she climbed the stone steps, she glanced back when the door clicked shut. There was no turning back.

A good way up the enclosed stairs, she came upon a door on her right. Like the one below, as she reached it, it opened. All she could see were bookcases crammed with ancient texts that covered the walls.

Evie paused, then a familiar voice called out, "Enter."

She walked across the threshold and into a circular study. Near the centre was Bazertari, sitting at an impressive obsidian desk with demons carved into its thick legs. The surface was covered with scrolls and strange objects. The warlock's attention was focused on the enormous book he was reading.

She murmured, "Bazertari."

The warlock glanced up and raised an eyebrow. Evie shot him an angry glare and attempted to throw a plasma bolt, but suddenly found herself paralysed, unable to move any of her limbs. Only able to move her head, Evie directed her gaze downward to see she was trapped in a pentagram. She tried to force herself to step forward, but to no avail.

Bazertari laughed wickedly as he stood and stepped from behind his desk. "Did you think I wouldn't be prepared?"

Evie glared at him. She had neglected to be cautious and observe her surroundings before entering. She attempted to move again but found herself frozen solid. Bazertari walked up to her. His intense focus was on her, licking his lips. His leer made her feel uncomfortable.

"After the last time we met, I wanted to ensure you didn't destroy my study." He pressed his lips together and walked around the outskirts of the pentagram, studying her. "So, you are the traveller. Garth had described a naive girl when he killed the one here. But you . . ." He paused, his lips curing in a sneer, "But you are nay, girl."

Evie strained to follow him, frustrated with being unable to move. She turned her head the other way, watching him with her peripheral vision. "I killed you once. I can do it again."

"And so you may. But with such power at your disposal, you could do *anything*. Be *anything*. You could rule this land and nay one could stop you."

He stopped and slowly moved his hand up and down, touching the invisible shield that surrounded Evie. She gasped as hands touched her, creating a physical feeling in her body.

The warlock chuckled. "*So* responsive."

Evie sucked in a breath, and glared at him. But he moved his hand again, and Evie reacted. The sensation was a combination of Garth and Ulric touching her. Biting down on her lip, Evie's body took over, quivering in response. She closed her eyes, attempting to prevent her body from betraying her.

She breathed, "Stop it."

Bazertari stared at her and moved his hand away. The sensation stopped instantly.

He smirked and walked back to his desk, "I think we could work well together. Rule side by side." He gazed back at her. "Be . . . lovers."

Evie snarled, "*Never.*"

The warlock glanced back at her, raising an eyebrow. "I have a different opinion."

Evie inhaled deeply. She could not succumb to him, but in his trap, she was powerless. "Am I to just stay in this as a plaything for you?"

He stared at her, a sly smile on his face. "Oh, nay." Bazertari sat back down at his desk and regarded her, his features cold again. "I believe you require time to consider your options." The warlock snapped his fingers.

Suddenly, Evie was falling. She cried out as she hit a cold, damp, stone floor. Dazed, she slowly sat up, looking round in the dull light. She was in a dungeon, behind bars. She rubbed her temples and cursed. Tears welled in her eyes; he had tricked her again, casting doubt on her decision.

She quickly turned as someone wheezed in pain and shuffled about. She moved towards the cell next to her when she heard someone whisper, "Evie?"

As the figure struggled closer, she gasped in shock. It was Garth. His features were cut and swollen. Blood and bruises covered his bare chest. "Garth!"

His fingers curled round the bars as he forced his battered body to move into a seated position. A gasp of pain escaped his lips. He pleaded with her, "Why did you come?"

She gazed at him intently. "Because I'm a stupid, stubborn fool."

He said, his left eye swollen shut, the other bloodshot, "Oh, Evie."

She sighed, "I thought I could face him. I knew it was a trick, but I still came." She glanced down, tears escaping her eyes. "I fucked up."

Garth's blood stained fingers slid between the bars and shakily wiped a tear from her cheek. "Ulric should have stopped you."

She gazed at him. "He wouldn't have been able to." She sighed, "Bazertari killed Slan, threatened you and Ulric. I couldn't stand back and do nothing."

"He finds what your weaknesses are and uses them. I used to do the same."

Evie eyed him. "Ulric thinks you did that with me."

Garth sighed, leaning against the bars, looking exhausted, "Ulric will never forgive me. I know that." He casually glanced at her, his head resting against the bars. "But you. You saw there was hope, and I will never forget it."

She gently touched his swollen cheek. "I care too much for you." She glanced down. "I—"

Garth clasped her hand. "I'm happy for you both."

Evie lost herself in his eyes. "You are?"

He started to chuckle then stopped as pain etched across his face. He breathed in slowly and said, "I can't give you that, but Ulric can."

Evie wondered how Garth had known. She sniffed and glanced around. "How long have you been down here?"

He emitted a grunt while attempting to move. "Can't remember. Feels like weeks, but may be less."

Evie regarded him. "Have you seen anything that may help us escape from here?" He shook his head. She bit her lip. "Then we need to figure something out."

Garth responded, "I can't help you. I can barely sit, an' can't stand."

"Then let me see what I can do."

She gently touched his shoulder through the bars and concentrated. Her hand glowed, but pain suddenly shot through her head, and she cried out, pulling her hand away.

They both turned when they heard Bazertari tutting. He stepped from the shadows and regarded them both. "Oh, nay my dear. Nay using magic."

Evie growled, "Garth's in pain."

"So?" The warlock glared at Garth. "He betrayed me, and needs to be punished."

Evie stood up and moved towards the bars that divided her from the warlock. "Why don't we end this now? You and me."

The warlock moved his hand towards her, and Evie jerked her head away from his touch. "And lose such a wonderful opportunity? I don't think so. After some time down here, you will understand what the best cause of action is for you."

She stared angrily at him. "It won't work."

He chuckled as a large man walked up beside him with scars marring his cruel features. The warlock gestured towards him. "This is Tyrak. You would have seen his handy work on Garth already. I believe if you see him beat Garth to near death every few days, you will soon reconsider." Evie shot him a disdainful glare. Bazertari pursed his lips. "Maybe Ulric would be a better target?"

Evie spat at him, the spittle hitting him full in the face. The warlock wiped it away and sneered, "So be it."

Tyrak opened Garth's cell and strode towards him. The young Sword was too weak to move. The large man grabbed him, dragging Garth into the middle of the cell, and started kicking him in the torso. Garth hunched into a ball, trying to protect his already battered body.

Evie yelled, "*Stop it!*"

The warlock laughed as Garth was beaten unconscious. He then signalled to Tyrak, and the brute left the cell. Garth lay still on the floor, his breathing shallow.

Bazertari said, "Don't worry, he won't die. He's much too valuable. I ensure he's healed enough to take another beating." He observed Evie. "And when that drunkard gets here, you will have two companions to watch as they get beaten repeatedly. Never granted the gift of death from their suffering. Then you can consider your options. You cooperate; they live. Well, I say live, but they *will* suffer. I just won't let them die." He smirked, gazing at her. "I have to ensure that you remain compliant until I've bent you to my will and they are nay longer needed."

Evie glared at him. The warlock chuckled and walked back into the shadows. Evie stepped back, slumping onto the floor, and sobbed. The one thing she never thought would happen, did. She was a prisoner.

What am I going to do?

Slan was gone and Ulric was at the other end of Moonstar. Part of her wanted him to rush in and rescue her, but if he did, then his fate would be sealed. She wondered if she could trick Bazertari, get close, and then kill him. Her skin crawled at what she may have to do if she chose that path.

But is it a price worth paying to rid this land of evil?

Her eyes were pulled back towards the battered Garth. He was wheezing, struggling to breathe. She wondered how many of his ribs were broken, and worried that at least one might have pierced his lungs. Evie sighed, gazing into the shadows. She could not let Bazertari win. She regarded the bars.

Can I break them with my powers?

Evie stood up and concentrated. Her fingers tingled as she sensed the formation of plasma in her hand. She calmed herself and threw the bolt at the bars. It just dissipated. Then suddenly, pain burned through her and something catapulted her backwards. She slammed into the stone wall with an agonising crunch. She gasped in pain and heard the disembodied voice of the warlock.

"Oh, my dear. Any magic you use will just cause you pain. The cells are enchanted. Nay magic can be used, except mine."

Evie gasped in astonishment as she experienced the sensation of being healed. She looked around, but the warlock was nowhere in sight. She stared at the cell. Then over at Garth, hearing his breathing improving. The warlock was right. She could not use magic, but the cells possessed the ability to heal the occupants, just like the warlock had said. It would be enough to mend Garth so he would not die.

Evie slumped against the damp wall and sighed. She was well and truly fucked.

FORTY THREE

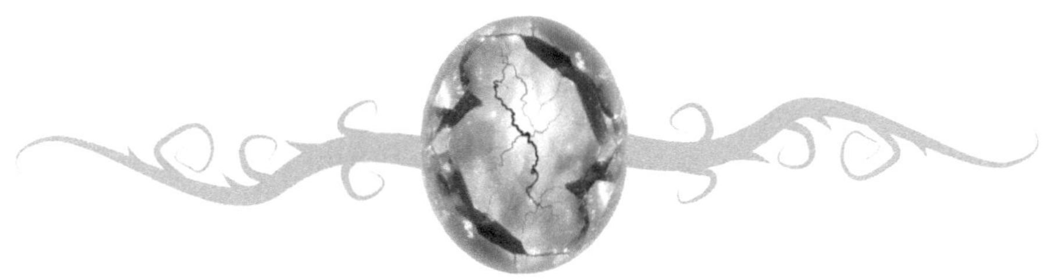

E vie sat, leaning against the stone wall, lost in thought. With her plan of escaping foiled by the enchanted cells, she had to come up with a solution before Ulric showed up and got trapped as well.

Could I trick that brute, Tyrak? He has an intimidating appearance, but would it be simple to deceive him? Get him to let me out, maybe tell him I want to see Bazertari?

She stiffened when she heard movement. Tyrak snorted and fixed his gaze on her. He strolled up to her cell and shoved a bowl of something like porridge under the door. He then did the same at Garth's.

The brute snarled, "Food up."

Evie cast her gaze across at it and grimaced. Then looked over to Garth as she heard him wake. He shuffled across to the bowl and shovelled the food into his mouth. She leaned over and took hers, sniffing it. It smelt foul, yet it must have been edible.

Garth glanced in her direction. "Eat. Doesn't come regular."

She gave a silent agreement, dipping her fingers into the cold gulpy substance and putting some in her mouth. It was vile. But she also needed to eat.

Evie slid the empty bowl away, wiping her mouth. While the slimy substance was not enjoyable, she could sense her body appreciating the small comfort of having some food. She heard Garth sliding his bowl away, and she turned towards him.

The Sword leant against the bars, his eyes closed. She moved closer when he whispered, "What's your world like?"

Evie leant on the cell bars next to Garth and glanced at him. It felt strange telling him about her world again.

"Very different than this world."

He turned slightly towards her. "Do you have Swords?"

Evie smiled warmly, remembering that the Garth she loved had asked the same question back then.

"No, not like you or Ulric. What we have are armies and they don't use swords. We use weapons called guns. They propel bullets, like small stones, at great speeds and distances."

"Sorcerers can propel—"

Evie grinned. "Objects?"

He locked eyes with her. "How?"

Evie responded, "My Garth asked and said the same things."

The young Sword chuckled, then winced in pain.

"*What* a touching sight."

Evie quickly turned to observe Bazertari standing by her cell, watching them both. The large brute, Tyrak, yanked open Garth's cell and strolled in. Garth struggled to rise to his feet, glaring at him. He tried to look as strong as he could, anticipating what was about to happen.

Evie stood up and ordered, "Leave Garth out of this."

Bazertari regarded the bars and then focused on Evie. "Then join me."

She sneered. "No."

Bazertari turned to Tyrak, and the brute slammed his fist into Garth's mid-section. The already battered Sword doubled over. Tyrak then grabbed the winded Garth and shackled his wrists and then hooked him up on the ceiling. The Sword's dangling feet just barely reached the floor. Tyrak stood in front of Garth, waiting. The young man slowly pulled himself up and spat at the brute who snarled at him.

Bazertari turned back to Evie. "Join me."

Casting a brief look over at Garth, Evie saw him grunt as he tried to turn towards her. "Don't Evie."

She glared at the warlock. "No."

Tyrak punched Garth in the stomach.

Bazertari repeated, "Join me."

Evie snapped, "No!"

Garth was hit again. The battered Sword vomited up the food he had recently eaten. Evie shut her eyes, hearing Garth's grunts of pain as Tyrak pummelled him.

Again, Bazertari said the same thing. Evie paused, biting her lip. She glanced at Garth.

The Sword struggled to look towards her and whispered, "Don't Evie."

She turned around to face the warlock, tears flooding over her eyelashes, and murmured, "No."

Evie flinched as she heard Garth being hit again. He cried out in pain as a rib cracked. She closed her eyes, pressing her palms against her ears, afraid to look as he was beaten. Bazertari repeated the request again and again. Each time, it took her longer to respond, fearing the next punch would be too much. Then Tyrak punched again and Evie heard nothing from Garth. She spun round. Garth was hanging from the shackles unconscious, blood seeping from his slack mouth.

Suddenly, Bazertari's lips brushed Evie's ear as he whispered, "Once he's healed enough, we will try again."

Evie spun swiftly to find the warlock smirking beyond the bars. She stared angrily at him. *Why had he seemed so close?*

"Let Garth go."

Bazertari gazed at her. His eyes lingered on her longer than she liked. "Nay, my dear, the fun has only just begun. But I believe that once I have your Ulric, then you will reconsider. You may have a destiny with this one, however, I sense that your heart nay longer belongs to him."

She sneered and spat towards him. Bazertari chuckled, her spittle missing him. He turned on his heel. Tyrak left Garth's cell, leaving the unconscious Sword where he was, hanging by the shackles.

Evie moved to that side of her cell. "Garth? *Garth?*"

There was no response. He was out cold. Blood dripped down his face onto the floor. If Bazertari tortured him again, she was uncertain of her capacity to endure hearing it, watching it. She slumped on the ground, wiped her eyes and sniffed. She did not want to accept that she may have no choice but to give in to Bazertari just to get Garth out. She wiped her nose on the back of her hand. The warlock would not kill her, but he may do something again. She remembered the trap in his study; she had been completely helpless. She wondered what she could possibly do to free them. Evie leant against the bars. She had to think of something. She closed her eyes, experiencing exhaustion. Sleep quickly pulled her into its depths.

Bazertari strolled out from the shadows of the cells and observed the sleeping Evie as he muttered the last part of the spell.

He smiled and turned to Tyrak. "Take her to the room below."

The brute gestured with his head, unlocked the cell, and effortlessly lifted the unconscious Evie. He carried her from the cell to a side door. Then descended the steps, followed by the warlock. They entered a small, dimly lit room, a wooden bench in the centre with straps secured to it. Tyrak placed Evie on the bench and fastened the straps to her arms, legs and head. Bazertari strolled over to the far side of the room to a table with several glass vials.

Bazertari regarded them and then turned his attention to a large vial. He picked it up, studying the green-coloured parasite within it. It glowed and squirmed in the clear liquid inside the vessel. Within days of leaving Great Oak behind the warlock had been able to teleport the devil worm to below his tower. The stocks of larvae they did have had been lost in the dark dungeon when Slan had sealed it tight. But the larvae he had been nurturing with dark magic had been stored in his tower, so not all of his work had been lost. The warlock's mouth twisted into a subtle grin. "Now to see if my use of magic will make you pair with this sorceress."

The warlock gazed at Evie's sleeping face. He may not have her willing, just yet, but with the magically enhanced parasite, he soon would.

He had experimented on other magic users, resulting in their deaths. Bazertari had then taken measures to ensure that he nurtured the parasite for a longer period with a stronger spell. He needed to be certain his hold would remain permanently. As for taking back control of Moonstar; provided he could acquire enough parasites, and that his victims did not reject them, he could have an entire army under his control. Then he would rule the land, the people living in fear of him, and Evie willingly at his side.

Bazertari's hand tingled as Tyrak strapped Evie's head into position. He turned to the brute. "Leave."

The large man obeyed, and promptly left the room. Bazertari turned to Evie. He opened the vial and removed the parasite with magic. The small creature squirmed in the air as Bazertari's black tendril directed the creature to Evie's face. The creature landed on her top lip, then crawled up her nose.

Evie's body convulsed as the creature entered her head. The strap kept her head from moving as she shuddered, her body trying to reject the parasite. The stone on her wrist glowed. Bazertari cursed. He could not let the creature be destroyed before it had taken hold. Bazertari mumbled a spell as her convulsions increased. Then her body slowed and relaxed, the glow of the stone fading. He may not be able to destroy the stone, but he could manipulate it.

Bazertari grinned, sensing the parasite's progress deeper into her head, winding its way into her brain. He drew in a deep breath as he experienced the connection. It was weak, but in time, he would have control. Evie's unconscious body twitched, and she let out a moan.

The warlock stared at her with intensity and whispered, "Soon you will be all mine."

FORTY FOUR

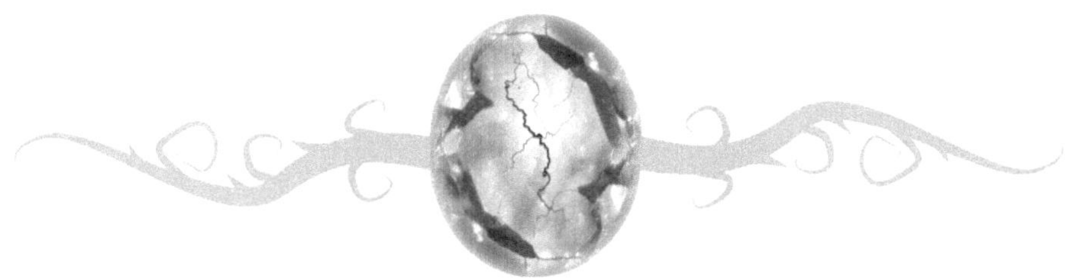

Ulric walked through the portal, out onto an open field and placed his hands on his knees as nausea flowed over him. He hated portals. As he glanced back, the swirling grey mass flickered and snapped shut. Ulric pulled the ginger root Handrea had given him from his satchel and quickly chewed on it. Taking a few deep breaths, he slowly directed his attention upwards, establishing his bearings.

Ahead of him was the Demon Forest. The tall, ancient trees made it a foreboding place. He spat out the masticated root and breathed deeply. He just hoped he was not too late.

Taking large strides, he reached the outskirts of the forest and paused pondering which direction to go. He pulled the amulet from under his shirt, holding it in his palm. He moved from side to side. There was no sign of anything occurring. He cursed, then remembered what Handrea had told him. He cleared his mind, focusing on Evie.

He whispered, "Please work."

He faced towards the west, and the amulet pulsated. He moved away, and it stopped. It pulsed again when he turned back in that direction. He observed the forest and touched his fingertips to the warding talisman in his jerkin pocket. Ulric hoped it would protect him like the witch promised. Otherwise, as soon as he stepped within the trees, he would have demons on him.

Ulric was only a few steps within the Demon Forest when darkness fell all around him. He swallowed, hearing inhuman sounds and wondered what creatures lurked in its depths. There were rumours of a safe way through the forest, but none had ever dared to try. He walked carefully ahead, the pulsation of the amulet against his chest under his shirt being constant. Hearing movement nearby, he pulled his sword free and observed the surroundings. Nothing ventured towards him. The talisman was working.

Weaving between the tall trees and stepping over thick black vines, he thought about Evie. It had been over three days and no word from her. She had known it was a ploy, but she had still gone alone. He wished she had waited. They could have then faced the warlock's threat together. Ulric shook his head in frustration, thinking she was just too stubborn.

He smirked. That was what he found attractive about her. And, he had to admit, he was just as bad. But he could not deny his frustration with her. When he rescued her, he will have a stern word. *Well, after I kiss her first.* He lost himself for a moment, thinking of her soft lips, and his instantly ached, wanting to feel them once more.

Ulric paused, seeing movement ahead, he forced himself to the present. He squinted, trying to make out what it was. A demon. The spider-like creature was roughly as big as a pony and as black as the surrounding trees, but he could still make out its crooked body. Ulric crouched, his grip firmly on his sword, as it passed by.

Thinking back, Ulric wished he had asked Handrea to enchant his sword with runes. At least he would have more of a fighting chance. But then again, he had just jumped into action, not thinking everything through. He sighed, pressing the bridge of his nose. Ulric had not been thinking straight for days, his worry for Evie clouded his usual sound judgement. His thoughts drifted to her again. When he found Evie, she would moan at him, telling him what a fool he was. He shook his head. Then again, he would just say the same to her. They had both jumped in with no preparation. If they made it out, it would be in the lap of the gods. Ulric glanced up through the dense foliage, unable to catch a glimpse of the sky.

He murmured, "Guide me Rosh." Ulric refocused his attention on the demon and watched as it wandered out of sight. He then slowly stood and carried on.

Ulric had been walking for what seemed like hours to him when the amulet started to pulsate rapidly, and glowed through his shirt. The Sword stopped and peered through the trees. Not believing his eyes, he hastened his steps and entered a small clearing. A tall ebony tower stood before him. Ulric arched his eyebrow. It was Bazertari's lair.

Ulric tightened his lips and walked round the perimeter. He had expected a castle. That would have been easier to get into. Ulric stopped at a large door and regarded it. A tower with only one entrance meant sneaking in was out of the question. He sheathed his sword and raised his eyes up at the structure. The smooth stone left no way to climb it. Ulric cursed. Without a plan, there were few options to try.

He stepped forward, shrugged, and knocked. Nothing happened. Ulric looked towards the forest; he did not fancy staying there too long, but he was not about to turn back, either. He positioned his hands on his hips as he scrutinised the door and pursed his lips. Then he turned the handle, and the door opened. Ulric expressed scepticism with a raised eyebrow.

A definite trap. But how else am I going to get in? Ulric took a deep, bracing breath and crossed the threshold.

Inside, positioned directly in front of the doorway, was a statue of the warlock. The Sword snorted with disdain. The warlock was as pompous as he had thought. He peered up at the marble features, surprised that duplicates of the statue were not at the palace. If there had been, it would have been satisfying to watch Slan destroy them. Ulric sighed, thinking of the deceased sorcerer. He was going to miss the old fool.

The amulet pulsated faster, bringing Ulric back to the present. When he turned to his right, he saw an entrance to some stairs heading down. Pulling his sword free, he took them. The deeper he went, the damper it became and the vibrations of the talisman intensified. He knew the stairs led to the dungeon, to where Evie was located. He hoped Evie was unharmed, but then remembered the other Moonstar and the despair spell. He hoped to Rosh the warlock had not used it on her. As he ventured onward, he heard someone in distress, and then Evie shouting. He quickened his pace. Whatever was happening, he needed to stop it.

At the bottom of the stone steps, there was a doorway. When Ulric entered the dungeon, he found a row of four cells, and to his left was another door that was closed. Ulric's focus returned to the cages. In one, a large brute was beating someone unconscious. He turned his gaze to the next and found Evie holding the bars, looking on and pleading. The Sword inhaled deeply and ran to the open cell.

Ulric raised his blade to deliver a powerful strike to the brute's back, putting an end to the vicious assault on the defenceless victim. When the man turned, Ulric could hardly recognise the battered Garth. He looked up as the beast of a man threw a punch, seemingly unaffected by the wound on his back. Ulric struck again, his blade slicing through the large man's arm. The man sneered and swung his other fist at him. Ulric jumped back out of reach, but had little space to move inside the cell. He pulled a dagger free and threw it, but the brute batted it away, the blade skidding across the floor.

Ulric's gaze followed the path of the deflected steel then looked back at the brute. Few would tower over Ulric, but that man did, yet, he was slow. It seemed to be the only advantage in the situation, and Ulric knew he had to use it. He shifted from foot to foot, dodging the powerful fists. Then an opening appeared and Ulric slashed with his sword again. His blade struck, cutting the flesh deeply. The giant came to a stop and directed his gaze downward, cradling the wound.

Ulric used the moment to attack again, his blade nicking the man's side. Then the brute grunted in surprise, and his shoulders flinched. Ulric had moved to the side to avoid a punch that did not come and looked past the large man. Evie had her arm through the bars, staring intensely at the giant. Given the position of her hand, Ulric knew instantly that she had taken his dagger and flung it. The old Sword had not the time to give thanks as the large man growled in anger and ran at him. He brought up his blade, but not in time to defend himself.

Ulric was hit with full force by the giant, and slammed hard into the wall. The Sword tensed, ready for a fist to find its mark. Ulric stilled when his eyes regained their focus. The brute's face was filled with astonishment. Then the man coughed, and blood poured out of his mouth. Puzzled, Ulric glanced down. The steel was in the man's chest, buried up to the hilt. The old Sword breathed a sigh of relief at the fortunate position his blade was in when the brute came charging at him. Feeling the weight against him, Ulric used the wall as leverage and pushed with one of his legs. The dead body of the giant slid off his sword onto the dungeon floor.

Catching his breath, Ulric finally took in his surroundings. Laying on the floor was Garth, looking in a bad way and barely breathing. Then his gaze locked onto Evie. She was gazing at him, relief on her tear-stained features. Ulric swiftly sheathed his blade and extracted the cell keys from the lifeless body. Then he recovered his dagger that was embedded in the brute's back. He moved towards Evie's cell and when he unlocked it, she ran into his arms. He curled them around her, never wanting to let her go, then kissed her.

She gazed up at him. "I'm sorry."

He stared intensely at her. "You are one fecking stubborn woman."

She smiled softly and sniffed. "I should have waited for you."

He wiped the tears from her cheek. "Then you wouldn't be the woman I love."

She focused on his eyes and kissed him passionately. His arms curled round her tighter.

She whispered, her lips hovering over his, "I love you too."

He closed his eyes, enjoying their embrace. Ulric's focus shifted to the current moment when he heard Garth grunt while struggling to get to his feet. The two parted, and Evie left the cell to check on Garth. Ulric was close behind.

He regarded the younger man and asked, "What the feck have you got yourself into, lad?"

Garth sat, gasping in pain. He peered up at Ulric. "You know me and trouble."

Ulric sighed, kneeling next to him, Evie by his side, "Can you walk?"

Garth shook his head, cradling his arm that rested at an unnatural angle. His whole body was broken.

The older Sword pursed his lips and turned to Evie. "He needs a healer."

She requested, "Can you ease him from the cell? I can help him but not while in these, they are enchanted."

Ulric gave a quick nod and helped Garth to his feet. The young man let out a painful gasp. Once outside the cell, Ulric helped him to sit. Evie gently laid her hand on Garth's shoulder. Her hand glowed. Garth's wounds began to heal. But Evie suddenly stopped, panting.

She gazed at Garth, then Ulric. "I can't heal him anymore. I don't have the power to do it." She took a quick look back at the cells, a puzzled look on her features.

Garth placed his hand on hers. "It's enough. I can stand now. You need your strength to face Bazertari."

Ulric responded, "I agree." He took a brief look over his shoulder in the direction he had just come from. "Do you know where he is?"

Evie shrugged. "I think up in his study." She paused, gazing at his blue eyes. "But how did you get in?"

Ulric replied, "The door was open."

Garth and Evie stared at him.

Garth wondered, "So, you just walked in?"

Ulric shrugged. "Aye. What else was there to do?"

Evie chuckled. "And you think my coming here was foolish?"

Ulric glanced in her direction and flashed her a toothy grin.

Garth released a heavy sigh as he rested against the wall. "We must find Bazertari and end this. He's gathering all my remaining men in the City Of Lights. He's planning something."

Evie nodded. "He was trying to get me to join him."

Ulric expressed his belief in her. "Well, we know that won't happen."

She gazed at him with a slight smile. Ulric frowned, wondering if she had been imprisoned long enough to become weakened. Ulric turned to the stairs. He did not have time to consider what could have happened.

He announced, "Let's get out of here and then find him."

Evie went to help Garth as he struggled to walk. Ulric turned to see Evie struggling and wrapped his arm around the wounded man.

"I'll take him. You scout ahead."

She gave a silent agreement, leading the way. She found her sword propped against the wall near the steps, along with her daggers. She grabbed them, then made her way up the steps.

Garth glanced up at his old mentor. "Thank you."

Ulric directed his gaze towards him. "You still have plenty to make up for, lad. But I believe you are striving to make amends."

Garth winced as they started up the steps. "I am, and will do so till my dying breath."

Ulric took Garth's weight when the injured Sword faltered.

He asked, "So you think Bazertari is in the City of Lights?"

Garth replied, "Possibly. I heard him talking to Tyrak days ago about having business elsewhere. His overconfidence has always been his weakness."

Ulric nodded as they reached the ground floor. He glanced at the statue. "As well as being a self-centred arse."

Garth chuckled. "Aye."

Leaving the tower, Garth stumbled, his breathing laboured. Ulric regarded the young man's battered features, seeing how pale he was. The older Sword knew Garth was far worse than he would admit. He needed a healer, and fast.

Ulric encouraged, "Come on, lad. Just hold on a little longer."

Evie came up to him, placing her hand on Garth. It glowed, but she staggered slightly. Ulric grabbed her with his spare hand.

Ulric said, "Nay. I can't have two of you down."

Garth said in a low voice, "I'll be alright. I just need to rest."

Ulric moved Garth's battered body round and hefted him over his shoulder. Garth cried out in pain.

Ulric stated, "Sorry lad, but we need to get out of here as quickly as we can."

Evie gazed at Ulric, her eyes mirroring his own concern.

She whispered, "I can't get us to the City of Lights. I've not been there. I might try Kerlish. But I haven't teleported more than myself."

Ulric squeezed her hand. "Don't worry. I have a plan. We just need to get Garth seen to first."

She glanced at Garth, who was barely conscious and hoped they had time. She turned her gaze towards Ulric as they moved swiftly, but with caution, through the forest.

"Will we be safe getting through here?"

Ulric looked at her, keeping a firm hold of Garth's body, which was almost a dead weight as he lost consciousness. "I have a talisman. Just hope it's strong enough to mask the three of us."

Evie focused her attention ahead. There was movement in the shadows, her features filled concern. "What was that?"

Ulric grunted as he shifted Garth's weight slightly on his shoulder. "Demon."

"*Demon?*"

Ulric glanced at her. "Aye." He quickly grabbed her arm, pulling her down low, himself crouching too.

Ulric looked ahead, seeing what could have been the same crooked spider demon he had seen before, but then he saw another. He swallowed. That was not good. They needed to hurry, but with Garth out, he had to carry him and the young lad was heavier than he appeared.

He turned to Evie and whispered, "Lass, do you think you could make a distraction? Towards the warlock's tower. We need a clear path."

Evie glanced back the way she had come. Although she had not sense anything that could cause such weakness, attempting to heal Garth moments earlier had made her dizzy. Something like a plasma ball would take, she hoped, less power.

"Yes, I can."

Ulric gave her a warm grin. "Good. Get ready. I'll tell you when."

Ulric kept his eyes on the forest ahead of them, peering into the trees, watching the demons. He then stood, taking Garth's weight again and signalled to Evie to stand as well.

He said quietly, "As soon as you send that distraction, run east. I'll be close behind."

Evie nodded, turning towards the direction Ulric pointed in. She focused on making a plasma ball. The energy crackled across her fingers as the blue ball of light developed.

Ulric whispered, "Now."

She shot it as fast as she could, back the way they had come. The ball lit up the dark forest, leaving a glowing trail in its wake, then exploded in the trees near Bazertari's tower. Evie and Ulric had started running as soon as the light hit the trees. The Sword was slowed with the dead weight on his shoulder, but he was a powerful man and he kept to a quick pace.

Evie's lungs were burning, but she did not stop. She could suddenly see moonlight ahead of her, then she burst out of the trees into a large field. Moments later, Ulric stumbled out after her. He staggered and stopped, almost dropping Garth, but regained his balance just in time. Evie turned her head towards the trees to see dark eyes watching them. But none of the creatures ventured past the tree line.

Evie turned to Ulric. "Now what?"

He glanced in her direction and grinned.

FORTY FIVE

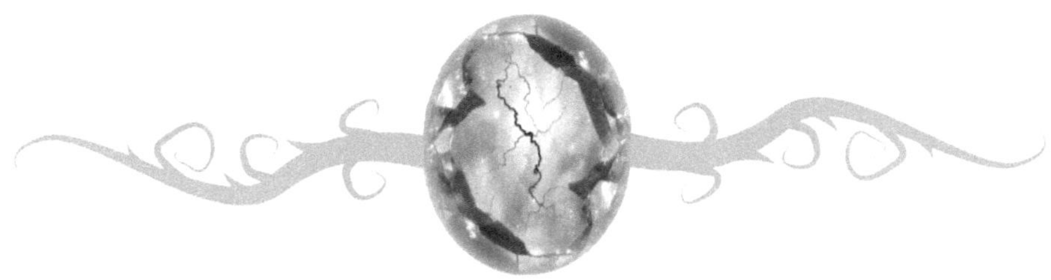

Handrea swiftly cleared the large table in the centre of the room as Ulric and Evie entered her home through the portal. Her eyes were on the unconscious Garth being carried over Ulric's shoulder. Carefully adjusting his position, the older Sword gently placed Garth onto the wooden surface. The battered young man groaned in pain but did not stir.

The old woman looked at Garth, then at them. "He's in a bad way."

Ulric responded, his voice full of concern, "Do everything you can."

The witch nodded, turning to Evie. "Ya need rest. To try to heal someone this injured will take its toll. More so if ya've been in an enchanted cell."

Evie frowned. "How?"

The aged woman beamed. "Slan mentioned how compassionate ya are, so ya would not want the lad to suffer. I'm also aware of what that twit is like. He's known to use enchanted cells. Looking at this poor lad, he's been beaten to near death. And more than once."

Evie agreed, "Yes, but how would it have affected me? I couldn't use magic, it physically hurt when I tried. So, I stopped as soon as I realised."

The witch gazed at her, softly placing her hand on her shoulder. A flash of concern crossed her features. She said, "The cells would have needed some source of power to keep this one from dying. I have a feeling that twit was using yars. Ya wouldn't have noticed until ya tried a powerful spell. Like healing or attempting to kill the twit."

Evie regarded her. She realised that the cells were yet another trap. Trying to trick Bazertari while inside the cage would have rendered her powerless, and she would have become easy prey for him. She cursed.

The witch chuckled. "Ulric said ya were a fiery one."

Evie glanced at Ulric, who shrugged, looking confused.

The witch chuckled. "Lass, he didn't say it in words. But I could tell." Handrea turned to Ulric. "I'll help yar friend here. There's a room in the back. Make sure this one gets some rest. Imprisonment in an enchanted cell for a few days will have drained her more than she realises."

The older Sword gestured with his head, taking Evie's hand in his, pulling her away from Garth and the witch. When they entered the room, Evie fell onto the small bed, feeling completely drained.

"Will Garth be alright?"

Ulric sat beside her, his arm curling around her. "Aye, Handrea's a talented healer. She has nursed many back from the brink. Even me."

"You?"

"Aye. I was young and foolish. Thought I was invincible."

She sighed, glancing away from his eyes, "I'm sorry."

"Sorry? You weren't there."

She directed her eyes towards him and smiled. "I mean, about going on my own to confront Bazertari. I should have been patient. Prepared more."

He gently kissed her. "Evie. You did what you thought was right. To be honest, even though I cursed several times, I still think you did what you believed was the wisest decision."

She smirked. "So I was right. You cursed."

Ulric chuckled. "Aye, and then panicked." His intense blue eyes concentrated on her green. "I can't lose you Evie."

She kissed him, savouring his embrace. She stifled a yawn. "What you said at the inn; you told me I had stolen your heart, but I hadn't thought it was even more. But then in the tower you said I was 'the woman you love'. When did that change?"

He pulled her close, resting his chin on the top of her head. "After Handrea kicked me out of her house, I was left alone with my thoughts. I was so worried for you, I prayed to Rosh. I realised it then, that I love you. And more than anyone before."

She smiled softly, her eyes closing. "Same."

Ulric held her, noticing her body relax as exhaustion took over. He gently kissed her and lowered her onto the bed. He brushed the stray hair from her face and observed her. So much relief had flowed over him when he saw her that he experienced a sense of giddiness. Safe at Handrea's, he never wanted to part again. He covered the sleeping Evie with a blanket. Then sat in silence for a while, contemplating what they would need to do next. He took a deep breath. The first thing was to find out if Handrea could heal Garth. Ulric got to his feet and left the room, strolling back up the corridor to the main part of the witch's home.

Garth was lying on the table, his chest moving gently, his wounds covered in a green paste.

Ulric gazed at him. "How is he?"

The witch replied, her voice despondent, "He has several broken bones, as well as internal injuries. He suffered a lot of beatings. On multiple occasions he had been brought back from the brink. From my understanding of the healing spell, it was crude and not fully finished, just enough to keep him alive. I'm amazed that he's alive at all with how many times they've brought him back."

"He's stubborn."

Handrea regarded the older Sword. "I'd've thought with all that he had done, ya'd want him dead."

Ulric sighed, "Aye, I thought so too. But when I saw him, I— I just couldn't."

She smiled at him, placing her hand on his forearm. "He's still a good man. Something Evie saw, and I think ya know as well."

"Aye. I hated him for years and imagined killing him. I nearly did when we retook Great Oak."

"Yet, in yar heart, ya knew."

Ulric regarded the old woman. "You just know people's inner thoughts, don't you?"

She shrugged. "Not sure if it is a gift or a curse. But, aye." She gazed towards the room in the back, where Evie was sleeping. "Have ya told her how ya feel?"

Ulric raised an eyebrow. "You even knew that?"

She chuckled. "Get some rest." She briefly glanced in Garth's direction. "It will be wise to leave the lad here. It will be several days before we can move him." She returned her attention to Ulric. "That warlock won't be happy, and there will be a battle. Till then, ya both need to rest."

With a weary expression, Ulric rubbed his temples. "Aye, I'm not as young as I used to be."

"None of us are. Now rest."

Evie woke with a gentle kiss to her lips. She smiled, stretching her stiff limbs and opened her eyes. Ulric gazed down at her. Then his arms encircled her, instilling a sense of comfort within her.

He smiled. "Good morn."

She replied, "I could get used to waking up like that."

He grinned and brushed the hair from her cheek. "You can count on it."

Evie snuggled against him. She knew very well what was to come, and wanted to take advantage of the tranquillity.

He stroked her hair and said softly, "Garth is doing well. But will need time to recover."

She gazed up at him. "Thank you for helping him."

He sighed, "I know I've been stubborn regarding him. I'm sorry for that, and what I've said. You saw the good in him. My bitterness blinded me."

Evie sat up a little, regarding him with affection. "Don't be. I should have been more understanding. I know I was blinded by what I once felt for him. But the love I have was for the Garth I *knew*. It was unclear at first, but I came to realise, I care deeply for him, but more . . . I don't know, like family. Does that make sense?"

Ulric lost himself in her eyes. "Aye. I understand."

She smiled, concentrating on his handsome features. "What I feel for you, Ulric, is what I want now. You, and you alone."

They kissed passionately. Ulric pulled her close, Evie desiring to experience him inside her again. But a movement behind them killed the moment.

Handrea stated, "Sorry I didn't mean to . . ."

The two looked across at her, and they parted. Ulric drew in a deep breath to regain control of his body.

Evie said, "No. We were just—"

The witch smirked. "Young love. But unfortunately, it will have to wait."

The two stood. Ulric asked, "What happened?"

"That twit. Seems he wasn't too pleased about the rescue."

Ulric moaned, "What is that warlock up to?"

When they reached the main room, Evie glanced across at Garth, who was sound asleep.

The witch eyed her and said, "He's healing well."

Evie asked, "So, where's Bazertari? At the tower, Garth told us he thought he was in the City of Lights."

"Aye, he's there and has taken control of it."

Ulric cursed, "Are you sure?"

Handrea nodded, passing him a note. "This was on Garth's chest this morn."

The Sword opened the parchment. He turned his eyes towards her. "From whom?"

"A witch I know in the north."

"Are we still safe here?"

"Aye, we are. She's a trusted friend, and I asked her, after ya had left to find Evie, to let me know of any news about that twit." She pointed to the note as Ulric read it. "As ya can see, he wants all yar heads. And is challenging Evie to confront him."

Evie snatched the note from Ulric's hand, reading it. She directed her attention to the two. "Then we face him."

Ulric sighed as he regarded the map Handrea had of the city. "As you can see, the city is walled, but if Handrea can teleport us somewhere here." He directed his finger to a place within the city itself. "We can then make our way towards him." He glanced up. "If the note is correct, and he is situated at the temple of Rosh, it's in the centre of the city near the main square."

Evie said, "From what Garth told us, Bazertari was rounding up all his men that were still loyal. But how many, I don't know."

"Aye," replied Ulric, "so, he may have them patrolling the streets and guarding the temple."

"Is there a back way in?" Evie asked, gazing at Ulric.

Ulric paused, considering briefly. "It's been a while since I've been there. But aye, I think so."

Evie lifted one eyebrow. "Could we get in undetected?"

He shrugged. "Depends how well he knows it."

Evie turned to Handrea. "How well do you know the City of Lights?"

The witch smiled. "I can teleport ya within a few streets."

The redhead nodded. "Good. We go tonight."

Ulric directed his intense gaze towards her. "Stealth attack. I like it."

She grinned, meeting his eyes and gave him a quick kiss. Then she glanced over at the sleeping Garth, then back to the witch. "Don't let him know if he wakes, as he'll want to help."

Handrea smiled. "I'll keep him sleeping for a few days. He needs it to heal anyways."

Evie turned to Ulric. "Ready to face Bazertari again?"

He replied, "Aye. This time, we do it together."

Evie firmly clasped his hand. "Definitely."

FOURTY SIX

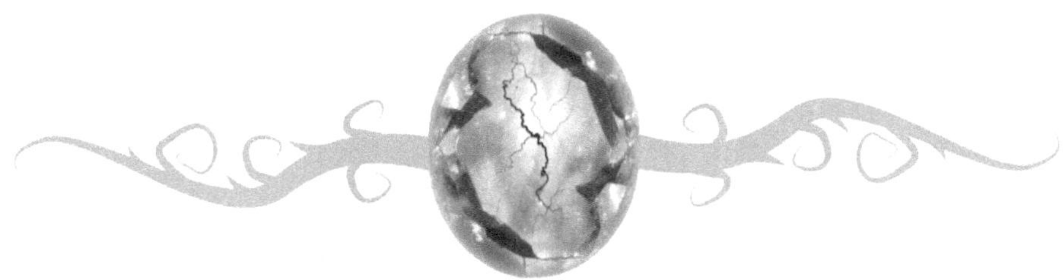

Ulric and Evie crouched low, peering at the back entrance of the temple. There was only one man on guard. Bazertari was expecting them. They exchanged glances, then silently moved through the shadows, reaching the entrance. Out of sight, Ulric threw a dagger. His aim was precise, striking the guard's throat, leaving the man unable to cry out for help. With agility, Ulric rushed forward and caught the falling guard. With a forceful tug, Ulric brought the man into the shadows and executed him by removing the blade, and letting the blood pour from the wound. The Sword then wiped his dagger clean and cracked the door, glancing in.

Inside the temple were six guards, but no sign of the warlock. The two crept inside, keeping out of sight.

Evie whispered, "Are there any other rooms?"

He replied, "At the back. It holds some of the texts on Rosh. He could be in there."

Evie glanced around the base of the small statue they were hiding behind and watched the guards. As soon as they attacked any of them, the others would be alerted.

She eyed Ulric. "So, how do we do this? Go in guns blazing and make Bazertari come out?"

Ulric frowned. "Guns blazing?"

Evie chuckled. "Sorry, a saying from my world. I mean rushing in, not stealthily."

He pursed his lips and pointed towards the middle of the room. "Nay, with stealth. We take down those two with our daggers. Then we go in and fight the ones that remain."

Evie agreed, yet she froze when a voice whispered close to her ear.

"You came at last."

She glanced behind her, but no one was in sight. Evie frowned, wondering if there was someone watching them. She worried there were more guards, maybe cloaked by a spell. She flexed her fingers, attempting to sense if there was anyone nearby, but she sensed nothing. Ulric's voice pulled her back to the sight before them.

He murmured, "We'll split up. Keep low, and get closer to those two."

She nodded, rotating her shoulders. Why did she still sense that they were being watched? Then the sound of the voice returned, causing a prickly sensation, and goosebumps raised up on her skin.

"Come to me Evie. Come to me now."

Evie's head felt fuzzy as her gaze shifted towards Ulric's direction. He was crouched low, moving behind the statues ahead of her. He glanced back, beckoning to her to follow, frowning. Her vision blurred. Something was wrong. She sensed a light-headedness, her body lacked energy.

The voice was in her head again, louder this time, *"Come now!"*

She squeezed her eyes shut, trying to refocus. Ulric was moving back towards her, looking concerned. Evie wanted to tell him about the voice and feeling strange. Then, as if strings from above were pulling at her body, she slowly stood, unable to stop herself.

Ulric hurried back to her, and struggled to keep her from rising. "Evie, what the *feck* are you doing?"

She stared at him, experiencing a sense of confinement washing over her. Evie desperately wanted to tell him she did not know what was happening. With all her willpower, she tried to stop herself, but her body was still moving, breaking loose from his grip. Ulric's features were full of shock and concern. He grabbed her again, trying to stop her without alerting the guards. But with unknown strength, she broke free and continued. Her movements were stiff and robotic. She wanted to turn back to him and beg him to help her; yet Evie stared straight ahead. It seemed to her as though she was in a dream, a blurry haze surrounded everything.

What's wrong with me?

Evie could hear Ulric muttering her name, then it was cut off. She desperately wanted to turn to see if he was alright, but she continued forward. She walked stiffly out into the open, all the men watched her, but none of them reacted. Evie tried to stop herself, but it was as if she was being controlled like a puppet. She could not do anything. She was a passenger in her own body.

She approached the door to the back room.

The voice urged, *"That's right, come to me."*

When the door opened, she found herself facing Bazertari. He gazed at her intently with a smile on his face. "Good."

She halted before him. Evie was desperate to speak, but only a murmur escaped from her lips. The warlock smirked, leering at her, licking his lips. Emotion overwhelmed her, causing tears to fill her eyes.

Why can't I move?

The warlock stepped closer. "I can see you are attempting to comprehend why you came to me so willingly." His fingers brushed against her cheek, Evie was disgusted by his touch, yet she remained motionless, like a statue. He smirked. "It was a very simple spell. One you would never have detected happening. It may require a few more days until you are fully mine, but a persuasion spell was useful for the time being. The magically enhanced parasite I implanted inside your head will soon take over. You won't be able to resist me."

With a fierce gaze, she tried to scream at him.

Bazertari leaned in, his lips hovering over hers. "At the tower, you always seemed so peaceful while you slept. As my magic slowly seeped into you."

Tears rolled freely down Evie's cheeks. She wanted to use her powers and kill the warlock where he stood, but her body would not react.

The warlock peered intensely into her eyes and took a deep breath, his lips brushing hers. "Once you belong to me, you will be mine *forever.*"

Another grunt escaped her lips as Evie internally sobbed with anguish.

Bazertari stepped back, regarding her. "Now sit."

An invisible force made Evie step to the side and slump into the chair near him.

The warlock puckered his lips, gazing at her, then chuckled. "When that Sword tries to rescue you, he will fall into my trap. Once I possess you, I may allow you to have him as a plaything."

Evie could only stare ahead, her body solid like stone. She tried with all her might to move, but Bazertari's hold was just too strong.

Ulric turned back to see Evie frozen where she was crouching, concern etched across her features. He frowned and moved back towards her. As he got closer, she suddenly stood, exposing their position. Still crouched, Ulric attempted to bring her back down.

He said urgently, "Evie, what the feck are you doing?"

She yanked her hand free, her features blank, and began walking further into the temple.

Ulric remained where he was hiding, whispering sharply, "Evie. *Evie! Ev—*"

He tumbled through the floor when a portal opened below him. Ulric landed with a thud and glanced around, spotting Handrea.

He snapped, "What the feck! Send me back. There's something wron—"

She finished his sentence, "Wrong with Evie. Aye, I know."

Ulric rubbed his lower back where he had landed, getting to his feet. "Handrea, what the *feck* is going on?"

The witch regarded him. "When Evie arrived. I sensed something."

Ulric frowned. "What?"

"I wasn't sure. I thought it was because she was exhausted from being in an enchanted cell. But—" she paused. "Let me show ya."

Ulric followed her over to the sleeping Garth. He observed the young lad, his body still swollen and battered.

Handrea gently raised Garth's limp arm. "Look at his fingers."

Ulric glanced in the direction of Handrea and then shifted his gaze towards Garth's dirty hand. "What am I looking for?"

Handrea pointing to his nails. "There."

Ulric observed a light blue hue under his nails. "They look a little different. So?"

Handrea put Garth's arm gently back down and regarded Ulric. "That's evidence of an infestation."

He stared at her, becoming frustrated. "What the feck has that to do with Evie?"

Handrea exhaled heavily and set a bowl directly in front of him. Lying dead in it was a brown, worm-like creature.

Ulric pulled a face of disgust. "What the feck was that?"

Handrea glanced back at Garth, who slept soundly. "Warlocks use parasites to enhance spells. Especially a persuasion spell."

"Persuasion spells?"

"Aye. They are simple, but powerful. And if the warlock can manipulate the parasite, they become permanent after a time."

Ulric swallowed. "What are you trying to tell me, Handrea?"

"Garth had that." She pointed at the parasite. "At the base of his skull. Although Garth possessed free will, if the need arose, that twit could have taken control of him. What I sensed from Evie had a different impression than the one in Garth. I think that twit has magically enhanced her parasite so it will fully take hold. The twit must've used a persuasion spell on her as I don't believe the parasite is strong enough to take hold . . . yet."

The colour drained from his face. "How long?"

Handrea gazed at him. "It's necessary for us to be quick, but I've a plan to get the lass back." She glanced at the still unconscious Garth. "I don't think there was a spell on the lad, but from what I can tell, he's had a few parasites in him over the years. Probably in case he turned on the twit. The warlock could use the parasite to control him. Not as powerful or permanent as a magically enhanced one, but still effective. It takes a lot of magic to do that spell, so the twit would use it sparingly. But, I'm certain that I can break it. So if we can get Evie back here, I'll free her."

Ulric bit his lip, staring at Garth, his chest rising and falling steadily.

The old Sword said, almost to himself, "I can't lose her."

Handrea patted him on the back. "Ya won't. Now come with me."

Ulric followed her in a daze. "You can break it?"

"Aye, but ya need to get a talisman on her. Then get her back here."

Ulric sighed, "He knows I will be coming."

The witch chuckled. "I didn't say it would be easy."

Handrea entered a study full of books and papers; she strolled up to the cluttered desk and picked up a silver pendant. She looked back at him and grinned. "Now ya need to get this round her neck. This will break the control Bazertari has. But only enough for her to go with ya. Depending how far along she is, she may not be lucid. If so, just get her back by any means ya can."

"Lucid?" asked Ulric with concern.

Handrea smiled. "Don't worry lad. She just may not be fully herself. So don't get too worried."

He sighed, "So how am I to get in there? The element of surprise has kind of gone."

"Well, ya could surrender to them."

Ulric snapped, "What?"

The witch chuckled. "It's the quickest way in, lad. But don't worry, ya will have a talisman too. The twit won't be able to harm ya. However, I am optimistic that my friend will keep him occupied."

He gazed at her, puzzled. "What?"

Handrea eyed him, patting his cheek. "Catch up lad. Ya head's in the clouds over this sorceress. The note that told us that twit was in the city is from my friend. She's powerful and has a few tricks up her sleeve."

Ulric nodded, realising he was not thinking clearly; he was too concerned about Evie. His eyes focused on the witch. "Promise me, Handrea, that Evie will be alright."

She glanced up at him and squeezed his arm. "Aye lad, she'll be alright." She paused. "Just don't feck this up."

Ulric smirked and observed the elderly woman, hoping that the plan would be successful.

FORTY SEVEN

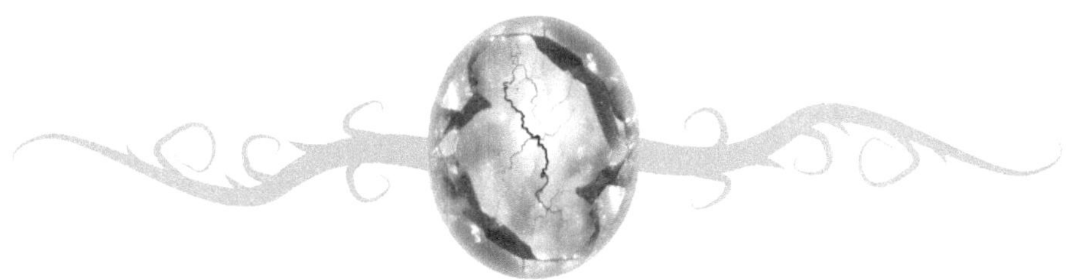

Ulric stepped through the portal and quickly crouched out of sight, looking at the unguarded back entrance. He pressed his lips together. This was most certainly a trap. Handrea had promised a distraction so he stayed where he was, and regarded his surroundings. His expert eyes focused on the back door. *Will the men pounce on me as soon as I cross the threshold? Or will they wait till I'm further in?* His fingers twitched over the hilt of his dagger. Then he heard shouting at the front of the temple. That had to be his signal.

The Sword moved quickly and quietly to the entrance, opening the door carefully. He was supposed to surrender, but Ulric decided to sneak in. Should he be able to make it to Evie with no one catching sight of him, he would feel better. As he made his way into the temple, he assessed the situation, keeping low. He watched Bazertari storm out the main entrance, and the four guards that followed him. That left only four in the temple. One of which stood outside the door in the back. That had to be where Evie was. He advanced slowly, staying in the shadows.

Ulric crept round the statues, getting closer. The three guards by the main entrance were watching the argument outside. The voices were rising, and Bazertari was getting impatient. Ulric needed to be quick. He moved towards the lone guard by the back room. The man's attention was on the events outside as well. The old Sword came behind him and knocked him out cold. Ulric moved the body out of sight and then entered the room.

Ulric froze on the threshold, seeing Evie. She was in a chair, her eyes closed, her features looking drained.

He dashed over to her, calling, "Evie?"

With a flutter of her eyelids, her eyes opened. Her body was rigid and unmoving. Tears welled up in her pleading eyes, yet her face remained devoid of emotion as a moan slipped from her lips.

Ulric brushed her cheek. "I'm getting you out of here."

He pulled the pendant from his pocket and went to place it around her neck. Suddenly, her arm snapped up, her hand gripped his wrist with unnatural strength. He could not reach her head.

He pulled at her grasp. "Evie, I'm here to help."

A single tear trailed down Evie's cheek, her eyes on her clenched hand. She tried desperately to say something, but no sound would come. Ulric understood. Evie was not in control of her own body.

Is Bazertari commanding her or is it the parasite trying to protect itself?

Ulric had to get the amulet on her or he had no way of getting her out. He grabbed the pendant with his other hand. Evie's other hand snapped up, but Ulric was aware of the motion, and avoided the hand reaching for him. Then in one swift move, the necklace was over her head. The paralysis was broken almost instantly.

Evie blurted out, "... rap! It's a trap!"

Ulric gazed at her. "I know, but he won't get us."

Evie struggled to stand, her legs still seemingly not fully under her control.

Ulric supported her as she got back on her feet. "It's like you've had too many ales, lass."

Evie snorted with amusement, gazing up at the man she adored. "Bazertari. He did something to me."

Ulric held her tightly, taking most of her body weight when she was fully upright. "Don't worry, Handrea knows what to do."

Maintaining a firm grip on her, he rubbed the stone in his pocket to let Handrea know to make a portal. As they stepped through, Ulric heard shouts behind. Bazertari's men had found the knocked out guard.

Handrea regarded the two as Ulric supported Evie through the portal which snapped shut behind them.

"Quick in here." She led the way to a side room and pointed to a wooden chair. "Sit there, lass."

Evie slumped down in the chair when Ulric let go of her. She could not understand why she was experiencing such extreme fatigue.

The witch turned to Ulric, passing him some leather straps. "We have to secure Evie down."

Evie directed her gaze upwards at the two. "I'm in control now."

The witch glanced at her. "Nay, lass, that pendant is giving ya some movement, but that parasite is still in control. And when it realises what we are doing, it will try to rip that pendant from ya. So it can use ya to kill us."

Evie paled, swallowing, then slowly agreed, letting the witch strap her arm onto the chair's armrest. Ulric came up beside her, doing the same to her other arm.

He fixed his eyes on her. "Sorry lass."

Evie gazed at him. "No, this has to be done."

Her legs were also secured in place, and then the witch observed Evie and said, "Sorry lass, but this will fecking hurt."

Evie was anxious; her hands gripped the chair, her knuckles white. "Do it."

Handrea took a mug off the side table and put it to Evie's lips. The redhead grimaced at the smell.

The witch remarked, "Aye, it tastes foul as well, but ya need to take all of it."

Evie raised her eyes to the old woman's, her piercing blue irises full of kindness. Then she gulped down the thick green liquid. The witch was not wrong; it was disgusting.

Once the green liquid had been swallowed, Handrea put the mug down and focused on Evie. She took a steady breath and began to chant a spell. Ulric looked on anxiously. A turquoise glow seeped from Handrea's fingertips, filling the room with the buzz of powerful magic.

Evie kept her eyes on the witch as the magic glowed all around her. Her skin tingled as the spell penetrated her body. It flowed through her; the energy moving towards her head. Then there was pain at the base of Evie's skull. She gasped as the pain intensified. Evie experienced her limbs resisting the straps as Handrea continued to chant, but she understood it was not her own reaction, but rather the parasite's influence. The pain grew worse, radiating throughout her body. Handrea repeated the spell, her voice getting louder as Evie's body thrashed in response. The parasite was determined not to release its hold. It was fighting the spell. Evie's eyes filled with fear that the witch's spell would not be strong enough.

Ulric paced the room. Evie's screams for the last hour were pure torture. He kept looking at the witch and then at Evie as she thrashed about in the chair. The redhead was drenched in sweat; Handrea looked exhausted. Evie released a long, shaky breath. Her face etched with so much pain, he wanted it to stop. He clenched his fist, looking at Handrea with concern.

How much longer can either of them last?

His eyes roamed towards Evie's neck, seeing something twisting under the skin on the side of her neck. The parasite was fighting hard to stay connected. Ulric observed the woman he loved; it seemed that Evie could not take much more. As Handrea continued chanting, Evie retched. He drew in a deep breath, a nauseating sensation in his stomach at the thought of what that parasite was doing to Evie to stay put.

Handrea paused her chanting and glanced at Ulric. Her voice was strained as she ordered, "The bowl! Grab it."

He picked up the grey medium-sized bowl from the side counter and held it with apprehension. Handrea began chanting again. A faint, black mist drifted from Evie's lips, floating towards the witch's glowing fingers.

Evie retched again; her whole body convulsed. Then something slithered between her lips. A thick, green worm squirmed in her mouth. Handrea moved her hands towards the thing and the black mist trailed from it. She rippled her fingers as she enticed the mist forward which, like strings, pulled at the creature. Evie retched again and then the worm landed in the bowl Ulric was holding with a splat. He jumped back in disgust, dropping it, frantically stamping on it as it writhed about on the floor.

Handrea stopped her chanting and after a moment, all they could hear was Evie panting and sobbing in relief.

Evie sensed a gentle, callused hand on hers as she lifted her gaze, focusing on Ulric's loving gaze.

He crouched before her and murmured, "You alright, lass?"

She carefully moved her head in agreement as he released the straps. As soon as her hands were free, she flung her arms around him, burying her head in his chest and sobbed. Ulric ignored the straps on her ankles and held her close. Handrea quickly finished the job and he pulled her from the chair as he stood, not letting her go.

Ulric picked Evie up in his arms as she continued to cry and strolled to the room they had slept in the night before. The witch ordered him to take Evie to rest.

As he sat slowly on the bed with Evie's arms still firmly around him, he whispered, "You need to get some rest."

She said, her voice muffled against his chest, "Just hold me."

He sighed, closing his eyes, relishing the embrace, "Alright, lass."

After a while, Ulric sensed Evie relax against him, her breathing steady. He gently laid her on the bed, pulling a blanket over her. Ulric regarded her pale features, wondering what Bazertari would have done to her if they had not got there in time. He knew he would have lost her forever.

He stood up, his eyes lingering on her sleeping features. His body full of relief. Closing the door quietly behind him, he strolled back to the room where he had left Handrea.

When he entered, the old woman was examining the remains of the parasite.

Ulric walked over to her and grimaced at the squashed creature. "Well, at least it's dead."

Handrea eyed him. "I've never seen such a formidable man so jumpy over a little critter."

Ulric straightened his shoulders, clearing his throat. "It just surprised me with how quick it came out."

Handrea chuckled, looking at him for a moment, then redirecting her attention to the parasite. "It would have died within moments of being extracted from her body. This one is far larger than the one in Garth. Magic has manipulated this one."

Ulric gazed at the witch. "So, is Evie free of him now?"

She directed her gaze towards him and patted his arm. "Aye, ya lass is nay longer bound by him. She just needs some rest."

"What of Garth?"

"He's healing nicely. I'm going to keep him asleep for a few more days. Need to ensure he recovers."

Ulric asked, "And the warlock? We have to confront him."

She arched an eyebrow. "Aye, but ya need the traveller at full strength. She has had a lot thrown at her these last few days. The twit won't be going anywhere. Now that he knows she's gone, he will prepare to fight her." She paused. "I have also sent word to my friend in the city. She thinks she can find some of the city guards who are in hiding."

"She can?"

"Aye. If she can convince them. Then you will not be alone."

Ulric responded, "If she can get them to help it will distract his men. Give Evie a chance to face him."

Handrea smiled. "Then the twit will be destroyed."

With a sigh, Ulric gently rubbed his temples. "Good."

The witch gazed at him. "Go sleep with yar lass. I will sort what will be needed."

Ulric glanced at the dozing Garth, then wandered back to the room. Carefully, he laid down behind Evie. She murmured, snuggling up to him. He embraced her with affection, locking his arm around her. Taking a slow, deep breath, he closed his eyes, cherishing the woman he loved in his arms.

FORTY EIGHT

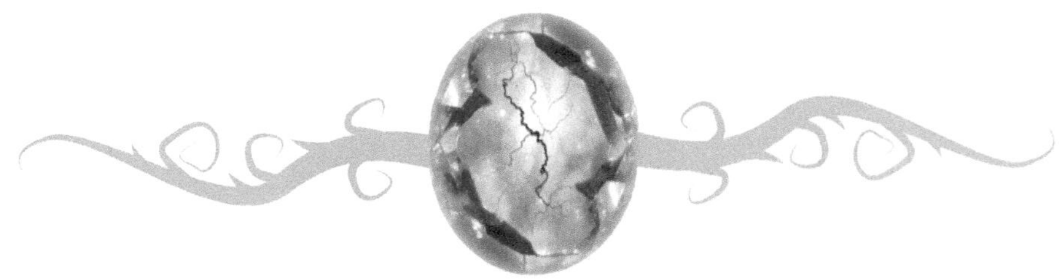

Evie woke up, aware of Ulric's strong arm resting on her waist. She faced him and smiled. Even fast asleep, he wanted to protect her. She gently lifted his arm and slid from beneath it. Evie quietly stood and gazed back at the sleeping Sword. She kissed him on the forehead, then left the room.

The cavern seemed so quiet in the early hours. She entered the main room to see Garth sleeping. She strolled over to the table where he lay. Evie sat on the chair close to him and gently held his hand. She took a deep breath as she looked at his bruised features.

She murmured, "I will kill Bazertari. Make him pay for what he did to us. And this land."

Evie fell silent, lost in thought. So much had happened recently she was still trying to process it all.

"Don't worry, lass, Garth will live and will be well soon," stated an aged voice.

Evie glanced round as the witch walked in from a side corridor. "Thank you for helping him."

Handrea pulled up a chair and sat next to her, regarding Evie's features.

The younger woman asked, "How did you know what to do with me?"

The old woman smiled. "Garth had a parasite as well."

Evie briefly glanced at him, then returned her focus to the witch. "He had one?"

The witch nodded. "Though it hadn't been manipulated with magic, I believe it was a precaution, in case Garth went against him. The twit could have rendered him frozen, or controlled his body. From what I could tell, he must have had a few over the years. When they are small and unmanipulated, they die off after a year or so."

"And with me?"

Handrea smiled softly. "The parasite within you was considerably larger, but young. So I think it must have been inserted while ya were his prisoner. Magic had manipulated it, made it grow at a rapid rate." She focused on Evie's eyes. "Did the twit do anything to ya?"

Evie anxiously wrung her hands together, recalling the sensation of the parasite being extracted from her. "He—"

Handrea rested her hand on Evie's, stopping her from wringing her fingers. "What did that twit do? Did he recite any spells?"

Evie looked to the woman, tears in her eyes. "He—he told me that every night when I was in his tower, he used his magic on me. Then when I was at the temple, before Ulric came for me, he stood before me and mumbled something in a language I didn't know."

Handrea gazed at her. "That twit used a spell to ensure the parasite fed off your power. Only a little, not enough for the stone, or ya, to realise till it was too late, and by then ya would be fully under his control."

Evie anxiously gnawed on her lip. "When at the temple, I had the sensation of losing myself. I think if Ulric hadn't come—"

Handrea cupped her cheek in her withering hand. "But he came, and all is well now."

Evie acknowledged her and responded, "I understand, but I fear what could have happened if Bazertari got me under his spell."

Handrea smiled. "But it failed and ya are here, and free of it." Handrea gestured with her head towards the back room.

"That kind soul back there sleeping, well, he's smitten. Lass, ya captured him, heart and soul. He couldn't rest until ya were safe."

Evie smiled and regarded the witch. "Why do you never call Bazertari by his name?"

She made a small pout with her lips. "Because he's a twit."

Evie chuckled. "I have to agree."

Handrea patted her hand and said, "Now go back to bed before Ulric wakes. He'll panic if he finds ya gone. He was fretting so when he had to leave ya."

Evie stood up. "Thank you, Handrea."

The old woman smiled warmly. "Sleep well, lass. Ya have a long few days ahead of ya."

Evie strolled towards the rear room and climbed back into bed next to Ulric. She laid down and shut her eyes. As she drifted off to sleep, his arm gently curled round her, keeping her safe once more.

Evie experienced the sensation of lips on her ear as she woke. The Sword's muscular body was pressed against her back, his arms cradling her gently. She smiled softly and turned slightly to see Ulric.

He smiled. "Good morn."

Evie shifted her weight so she could study him more easily. "Good morning."

He nuzzled his nose into her hair, breathing in deeply, and kissed her softly on her neck. "It feels so good having you in my arms again."

Evie's hands stroked his muscular arms that were curled around her. "I share the same feeling. I feel safe."

Ulric spoke into her hair as his lips caressed her shoulders and neck. "I will protect you, always."

Evie raised an eyebrow as Ulric's body betrayed how much he was enjoying their closeness. She smiled softly, her body zinged as she recalled the conversation Handrea had with her in the early hours. She turned in Ulric's grasp and tenderly pressed her lips against his.

Ulric stared into her captivating eyes and kissed her back, deepening it. Evie combed her fingers into his medium length hair, not wanting the kiss to end. She shifted her body, her leg hooking around his waist, locking their bodies together. His hands roamed down her spine, pulling her shirt out of her waistband, then his callused hand stroked her soft back. Evie's skin prickled in reaction.

He tenderly kissed her and slid a hand round towards her front. Evie moaned as his fingers crept into her waistband and edged toward the junction of her thighs. Her skin tingled as his fingertips played with her nether lips, making them moist. They continued their kiss as he explored her more, his groin becoming engorged with his own arousal.

Ulric leaned back from her and unbuttoned her shirt. He pushed it off her shoulders, exposing her breasts. He moved down, kissing them gently, his tongue playing with her nipples. Evie gasped, her head tipped back, her eyes closed, her body buzzing with delight at his touch.

The large man suddenly grabbed her, pulling her under him and he straddled her, gazing at her. He smirked, then shifted his body as he brushed his lips across her torso, roaming further down with every caress. Evie stretched out, putting her arms above her head, relishing how her body reacted to his gentle touch. She arched her back as he pulled down her trousers and his tongue found her pearl, making her thighs quiver.

She murmured, "Don't stop."

Ulric continued to play, his tongue was warm and welcoming. Her legs began to spasm, as an orgasm developed. He grabbed her thighs, keeping them still while he proceeded to drink her. Evie gasped as the orgasm took hold, and Ulric brought her over the brink. Ulric slowly moved his lips back up her body as she continued to buzz. His lips closed over her nipples, making her gasp from their tenderness. He gazed deeply into her eyes as he blindly took off his trousers, never breaking contact as his enormous penis gently entered her.

Ulric moaned as she enveloped him; he pushed into her harder, deeper. Their hips moved rhythmically as he got closer to climax, Evie about to have a second. Ulric then slowed, just before they peaked, wanting to delay their release. He locked eyes with her and gently kissed her, his hips moving slowly, just enough to sustain their arousal without reaching orgasm.

"You are amazing," Ulric gasped as Evie's hands gripped his shoulders.

She looked up at him, their hips moving as one, their bodies pressed together, their climax building slowly. Evie's thighs trembled, her body, full of endorphins, was no longer her own. She could only see Ulric, everything else had disappeared. Then Ulric picked up the pace, gradually thrusting faster, as their orgasms neared. The delay made their bodies so sensitive, it was almost unbearable. Ulric kept the momentum going, his fingers gripping the bed clothes on either side of Evie's shoulders. Evie cried out in pleasure as he lost control, erupting inside her.

With his hips shuddering uncontrollably, Ulric slowed down, his phallus throbbing inside of her. He slid his arms under Evie, and a moan escaped him as he rolled, keeping her close with their bodies still connected. She laid on top of him. Both of them panting and covered in sweat. Ulric held her tightly, his chest moving rapidly as he regained his composure.

He tenderly kissed her and murmured, "I love you."

Evie gazed deeply into his eyes and smiled softly. "I love you with all my body and soul."

Ulric grinned, his features flushed. He planted a passionate kiss on her. His arms never wanted to let her go.

"Now that's how I will wake you every morning," he promised.

Evie laid her head on his chest and smiled. "Better than coffee."

Ulric's chest rumbled with a chuckle. "Nay clue what coffee is, lass, but I'm taking that as a compliment."

She grinned and kissed his chest as she peered up at him. "It is."

FORTY NINE

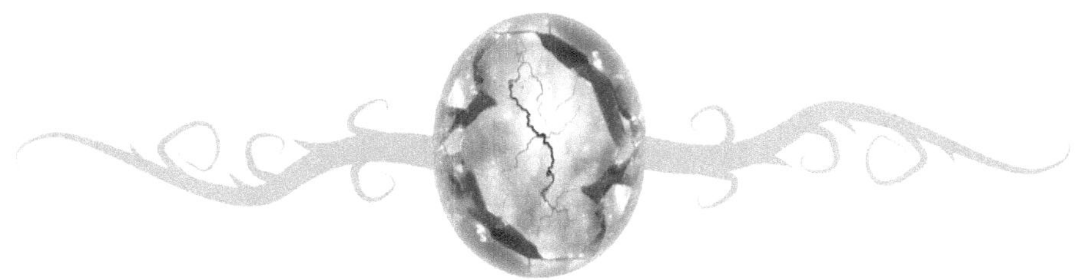

The three regarded the diagram of the city on the wooden table in the witch's cluttered study. Handrea eyed the two and chuckled softly. It had been hard not to hear what they had been up to just before dawn. She winked at Ulric when he glanced at her questioningly then shook his head, redirecting his gaze to the plan.

She chuckled, turning her focus back to the task at hand and stated, "My friend has spies watching the twit and he has taken over a house just off the main square."

Evie glanced at her. "What about the residents?"

"Any that could escape did. But now he has locked the city tight. Almost everyone that could not flee has gone into hiding."

"What of the ones who caused the distraction so I could rescue Evie?"

Handrea looked up at Ulric. "In hiding. Some scattered when the twit's men gave chase. But my friend is making sure all are ready when you face him."

Ulric slowly made an affirmative gesture; his expert eyes concentrated on the plan. "Then we face him here." His large finger rested on the area of the main square. "Handrea, can your friend ensure we have help?"

"Aye," responded the witch, "She will make sure they are there. But..."

Ulric raised an eyebrow. "But, what?"

"She thinks more men are coming."

Evie swallowed. "More?"

The witch looked at her. "Aye, lass. In the fight to help you escape, she told me some of the twit's men mentioned reinforcements."

Ulric cursed. Evie gazed at the plan, then back at her companions. "Then let's hope our backup arrives in time."

Ulric slowly made an affirmative gesture; his expert eyes concentrated on the map. "We will force him out into the open. The square is large enough for us to see what's coming. Handrea, you teleport us down this side alley. We can assess, then challenge him."

Evie glanced at him, and agreed with his plan. "He'll be pissed that I was freed. I'm certain he'll just want to fight."

Ulric glanced at her, expressing his amusement with a headshake. "You have some strange sayings, lass." He redirected his attention back to the map, contemplating scenarios, and then back at Evie. "We'll enter through this point. How did you put it? Guns blazing?"

Evie laughed. "Yes, that's how I put it."

Handrea chuckled while observing both of them. "Ya both make one formidable couple."

Ulric gave her a stern look. "Just make sure your friend brings those reinforcements."

The two emerged from a portal in a side alley. Ulric glanced at Evie, then pointed ahead. "The main square is this way. His residence is to the north of it."

They hurried to the end of the alley and peered out at the impressive, cobbled square. Affluent buildings surrounded it. There was a tavern, an armourer, a couple of shops and the rest were houses. All adorned with vibrant window boxes and hanging baskets. At the heart of it all, stood an impressive dragon statue, over six feet in height. The dragon sat on its haunches with its wings folded behind it, its neck arched upwards and its jaw wide, roaring at the sky.

Evie pulled her eyes away from the statue when Ulric pointed to the far end of the area. Four men were guarding a residential building, looking bored. That had to be where Bazertari was staying. Evie instantly knew the warlock's reasoning behind selecting it, it stood out as one of the most refined structures in the square.

She glanced at Ulric. "Looks like there are only four."

He responded, his eyes on their target, "Aye, but there could be more within and don't forget about what Handrea warned us about."

Evie expressed her frustration, "I know. It makes sense for Bazertari to ensure all the men that are still loyal to him end up here. If he takes this city, he will have a stronghold in the north."

"Aye, and we can't have that." Ulric peered at her and grinned, showing the gap between his teeth. "So, guns blazing?"

Evie kissed him on the cheek and answered, "Why not?"

The two stepped out from the side alley and strolled towards the building, drawing their swords. One guard turned their way and was astonished at seeing them.

The shorter of the four awkwardly drew his sword. "H— Halt!"

Ulric glared at them, holding his broadsword firmly. "Tell Bazertari we have some unfinished business."

One guard ran inside, the others pulled their blades free, joining their companion as he stepped away from the building. Evie eyed them as they strode towards her and Ulric.

Suddenly, the men lunged at them. Ulric was fast, and one was down within moments. He turned to the next man and the two then split off. Evie faced the small man who was first to spot them. He was quick on his feet and dodged her parries with ease. It appeared that he lacked experience in battling sorceresses, for he only concentrated on her sword. While he was distracted, Evie released a powerful electric surge from her other hand. The man shot across the ground, his body smouldering. She glanced to see if Ulric needed any help as he brought the other down.

She faced the house and yelled, "BAZERTARI!"

After a few moments, Bazertari's men came out of the building, the man who had alerted them close behind. Bazertari stepped out last, walked past his men and stopped. When the warlock saw Evie, he shouted, "*Bitch!*"

She sneered at him. "Time to pay."

He laughed and shot a plasma bolt in her direction. She dodged it, and hurled her own at him. He deflected it away and sent another. Evie moved to dodge the attack, but was not quick enough. The blazing orb singed her shoulder and knocked her to the ground. Evie cursed, sheathing her sword. She glanced over to see Ulric fighting the guards that had come out of the building with the warlock. She turned back to her objective.

The evil man's eyes were on her. He snarled, "So you won't join me?"

She tilted her head as she got back to her feet, both hands free to fight magic with magic. "No. Think I prefer you dead."

He laughed. "We will see."

Bazertari hurled a bolt of lightning at her. Evie deflected it. The energy struck the statue of the dragon in the middle of the square, shattering it. Evie quickly counteracted with a plasma ball. It lost its trajectory and hit the warlock's arm. Bazertari swore, glancing at his singed jerkin sleeve. He pulled a face of distaste and launched a powerful shockwave at Evie, sending her flying across the square. She crashed into a wall and slid down, landing in the bushes in front of the building. Winded, she sat up and cursed. She crawled out from the plants and stood, quickly brushing down her clothes. Evie turned and faced the warlock. Her eyes widened as she saw the warlock aim an orb at Ulric, who was completely focused on his fight with the five guards.

She cried out, "*Ulric!*"

He turned towards her in time to see the warlock preparing to shoot plasma at him. The Sword shifted to the side.

At the same moment, Evie unleashed a powerful shockwave against the warlock that catapulted him across the square. The plasma bolt shooting from his hand was thrown off target, hitting one of his own men.

Evie heard Ulric curse and she turned to see blood pouring from his arm. It seemed when he was distracted by her call, one man had seized the moment. But the Sword was unphased and continued to attack the remaining men. Evie quickly sent a plasma bolt at one of his attackers, sending them to the ground. Ulric gave her a quick nod in appreciation.

Her attention was pulled away when she heard Bazertari snarl, "Bitch."

Before she could form more plasma, another shock wave hit her, and she smashed against the same wall she had hit before. She hit it hard and fell into the bushes, dazed. She cursed, shaking her head trying to clear her vision. The warlock was stalking towards her. Evie took a deep breath and struggled to her feet, her back in agony. Thorns ripped at her clothes. She sent a plasma bolt back at him, but he deflected it. His features were full of rage as he sent a ball of plasma back at her. Evie ducked as it hit the wall behind her, sizzling. As she looked up, he was sending another and Evie brought up her hands, making a force field and the ball dissipating across it. She gritted her teeth as several more hit the shield, forcing her back towards the bushes she had just climbed out of. Evie took a deep breath and with all her might, catapulted the shield towards Bazertari. He counteracted with his own; the force sending them both in opposite directions, Evie crashed into the wall again.

Evie cursed, getting to her feet. "I hate that fucking wall."

She climbed out of the bushes again, several cuts covering her body and looked across the square to see the warlock getting to his feet, brushing down his clothes. She stepped forward and felt her bloody fingers tingle as more plasma grew in her hands. Just as she was about to send another bolt, an arrow drove deep into her shoulder. Evie cried out in pain as she was spun round from the force of the impact. She tried to see where it had come from. When another arrow whizzed past her ear and she looked upward to see an archer on the roof.

The warlock drew her attention when he said, "He is ordered not to kill you."

Her eyes narrowed on the warlock as he strode towards her. Her fingers glowed with plasma. His sly features smirked with amusement.

Bazertari tutted as he stopped a few feet away from her. "Now, now. His next aim is your lover and he has orders to *kill* him."

Evie stilled and looked across to see Ulric bring down the last man he was facing, oblivious to what could happen next. He turned towards her his eyes flicked from her wounded shoulder and then behind her. She followed his gaze back towards the archer, knowing he had seen where the next arrow was aimed. Then Evie heard running footsteps and a hoard of men came into view. Evie cursed. This was the warlock's reinforcements.

The group of at least forty men swarmed into the square, surrounding the warlock and blocking the exits. Bazertari smirked. "Surrender or die."

Evie limped towards Ulric, her body deflated in defeat. The Sword eyeing the arrow in her shoulder, and battered body. "Lass?"

She shrugged, looking across at the men. There were too many for them to face. Looking down at her hand, she felt the magic stuttering in her fingers. Evie turned her gaze back at Ulric.

Is this it? Will we be unable to save Moonstar from Bazertari's grip?

Her magic was faltering and she would need all she had to recite the spell. She swallowed looking back at Bazertari. She could not let him win, even with these odds. With a firm grip, she snapped off the arrow lodged in her shoulder. Crying out in pain.

Evie looked back at Ulric. "It has been an honour to fight by your side."

His gaze at her was full of affection, his grip tightened on the hilt of his bloody sword. "You sure lass?"

She snorted, "No."

Ulric glared at the men before them and mumbled, "I do like the odds."

Evie chuckled and turned her attention back to the warlock. Who stood between his men smirking in victory. She felt what remained of her magic buzzing through her as plasma formed in her hand. The ball stuttered for a moment, but she took a deep breath and it held firm. She squared her shoulders, ready to face the uneven odds.

The group of men before them became distracted and the two heard swords clashing at the back. Then there was the sound of running footsteps at the far side of the square. Men and women wielding swords, sticks, pitchforks, and even frying pans came into view.

Evie let out a relieved laugh and turned back to Bazertari, the plasma in her hand growing. "Think your time is up."

The warlock sneered and looked towards the archer on the roof. Evie followed his gaze to see the man dead, slumped over the wall, an arrow in his chest. She turned back and sent the plasma at the warlock and then a shock wave, sending him and his men backwards into the thinning crowd, as the others turned to their new attackers.

Ulric let out a war cry and ran at the scattering men. Evie kept her eyes firmly on Bazertari. One of his men ran towards her, but Evie was already sending an electrical charge at him. The large man cried out in pain as his body burned. Evie did not even pay him any notice, her gaze fully on the warlock, who sneered at her, both his hands crackling with red particles. He then shot one ball after the other at her. Evie deflected one and quickly formed a shield so the others dissipated before they could hit her.

Evie's shield failed as the warlock continued to bombard her with plasma. She quickly rolled to the side as a bolt of electricity shot over her shoulders, singing her hair. She gritted her teeth as she rolled onto her wounded shoulder. As she righted herself, Evie sent an electrical charge back at the warlock but missed. He sneered and using magic, lifted the dead body of one of his men and catapulted it towards her. Evie rolled out of the way and sent a plasma bolt back. Hitting the warlock's hip. He cursed in pain and glared at her.

Evie staggered to her feet, her body exhausted. She took a deep breath, she had to stay strong. Her eyes flicked towards fighting between the city folk and the warlock's men, Ulric in the middle of it all. The enemy was thinning. If any man tried to attack her, Evie deflected them. But most were too distracted to pay her any attention. She just had to do her part and hold on. With her attention back on the warlock, Evie continued to bombard him with magic. Most he deflected, but some of her plasma found its mark. Evie bit back the pain in her body, and continued to fight magic against magic.

Evie took a deep breath, she had to bring Bazertari down soon, otherwise she would not have the strength to recite the spell. Feeling the magic surge through her, she sent a shock wave at the warlock. Bazertari flew backwards, hitting the side of the house nearby.

Evie snarled, "See how you like it!"

Bazertari shook his head, staggering to his feet. With the warlock dazed, Evie sent several glowing blue orbs at him, all finding their mark.

Bazertari screamed in pain as half his body burned. Evie sneered at him. She walked towards the evil man as lightning burst from her fingers. The warlock whimpered as he experienced more pain.

She growled, "That's for Slan." She stepped closer and sent another. "That's for Garth." She hurled one for every name she called, "For Corun. Iesha. The royal family. For everyone you fucking hurt or killed!" She paused before releasing the next, then snarled, "And that's for putting a *fucking* parasite in me!"

Bazertari writhed on the ground in agony, the acrid smell of burning flesh filled the air.

One of the warlock's men ran towards her. Evie braced herself for an attack, but he stopped short as something hit him full in the back. Evie looked past him to see Ulric already turning to fight the next man who came at him. The attacker fell to the floor with a dagger embedded in his back. Evie turned away as she heard Bazertari whimpering in pain.

Evie stopped a few feet from him. "And this is for Moonstar."

She recited the spell that Landor had taught her all those years before. The stone on her bracelet grew brighter, and then a blinding beam of blue light shot out of it, sending Evie flying backwards. Evie quickly looked up from where she had fallen.

The light engulfed the warlock, and Bazertari cried out in terror. It pulsated as he tried to use his powers to break free. But as each moment passed, his attempts lessened. Bazertari turned towards Evie as his power, gained from evil spirits, was pulled into the ground. Black tendrils seeped from him, tethering the warlock to the spot. He screamed out in pain and the coils quivered in response, draining him of the source that had sustained him. His features withered with rapid ageing, his lean body became crooked and twisted as the dark energy continued to leak back into the earth. The black wisps throbbed faster, pulling him down into the ground. The warlock screamed in tremendous agony, then his body collapsed in on itself. There was a sudden flash of light that quickly vanished, along with the remains of Bazertari.

Silence fell over the square. The last of Bazertari's men had been killed by Ulric's blade. Evie briefly glanced at the sky above and smiled before losing consciousness.

Evie groaned as a gentle hand tenderly brushed against her cheek. She slowly opened her eyes and directed her attention to Ulric looking down at her.

He smiled. "You did it."

She massaged the nape of her neck, tasting blood in her mouth. "*We* did it."

He stared at her and kissed her intensely. He helped her to her feet, and she looked round the square as she held his arms to steady herself. Bodies were scattered everywhere, and a shattered statue stood at the centre. People were cautiously coming out of hiding, driven by curiosity. The ones who had been fighting were tending to the wounded.

She asked, "Any others?"

Ulric shook his head. "As soon as Bazertari was gone, they ran. The folks here gave chase, so they will not last long."

Evie leaned against him, overwhelmed by a sense of light-headedness.

He regarded her with concern. "Are you alright?"

She nodded, regretting the movement when her head throbbed. "Yes, I just need a drink."

Ulric laughed, holding Evie tightly to him. "Well, there is a tavern just across from us." He glanced down at her shoulder. "And I need to get that out."

Evie glanced down at the shaft of the arrow that was still in her shoulder. "If you could pull it free, I'll heal it, but I need a drink first."

Ulric chuckled and supported her as they strolled across the square. "You are a true Sword if you want a drink after a victory."

Evie glanced upwards towards him. "Think we both deserve one after the past few days."

He squeezed her shoulder. "Aye, lass. That we do."

FIFTY

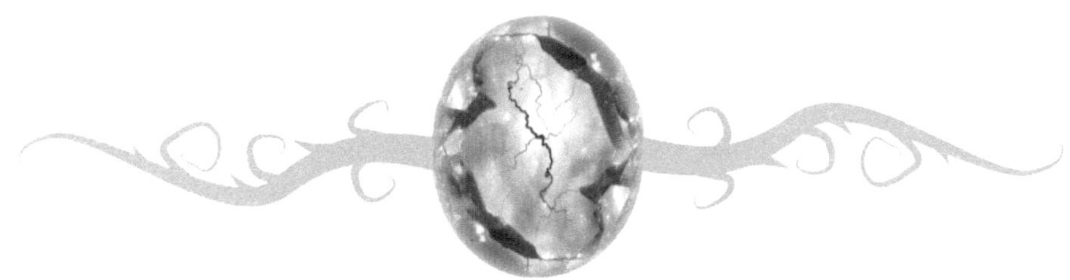

Garth took his time to open his eyes, sensing pain all over. His head was pounding and his throat was sore. He attempted to rise, but a hand gently touched his shoulder.

"Nay lad, ya need to rest."

Garth attempted to swallow, but his throat had the sensation of being filled with sand.

He croaked, "W—water."

The battered man sensed a hand slide behind his head, aiding him in raising it slightly, then water touched his cracked lips as the person gently provided him with a little. Garth tried to concentrate on the person offering him the drink, but his vision would not focus.

He asked, "W—where am I?" as the person removed the water from his lips.

"Safe, lad. Ya're safe."

Garth attempted to sit up again, but his body refused. He briefly closed his eyes. Every part of him was in agony. He took a deep breath; pain burned through his chest from the healing ribs. It amazed him he was even alive. When Ulric helped him out of the tower, he was convinced that he would not see another dawn. He had been in such misery, his heart was so weak, he expected Rosh to take him.

Garth croaked, "Where are Ulric and Evie?"

"Fighting the twit." Garth frowned as the person added, bitterness in their voice, "Bazertari."

Garth's eyes snapped back open, and he tried to get up. "I have to help them."

The person gently pushed him back down. "Nay lad, ya can't even stand."

He focused on his helper, his vision clearing enough to see her wrinkled features. His attention was fixed on her eyes, seeing a kindness that he was not accustomed to seeing.

"They need—" He took a sharp breath as pain shot through his body.

The woman sighed, "Ya nearly died, lad. On the goddess, I'm still not sure how ya survived. Now rest."

Garth gave a slow, confirming gesture. She was right; he was no use to them.

He shut his eyes and whispered, "Just for a little while."

When Garth came round later, he tried to get into a seated position. Pain still seared through his body, so only managed to prop himself up on an elbow. He glanced around, curious about his whereabouts. To his right, an old woman dozed in a chair next to him. He looked downward and noticed he was lying on a large wooden table. Garth strained to see more of the room in the low candlelight. He was in some sort of cave. With a frown, he looked back at the woman. He wondered where he was exactly. He endeavoured to sit upright again, but a gasp escaped his lips as it hurt too much.

The old woman stirred. She stared at him and got to her feet, stepping over to him. She lifted a mug of water and placed it to his lips. "Here."

Garth sipped at it slowly, still propped up on his elbow, gazing up at her. As she took the mug away, he asked, "Who are you?"

She smiled warmly. "Handrea. Ya are safe here. When Ulric brought ya, ya were in a terrible way." She observed him, regarding his features. "The swelling is going down now, but it will take ya a while to heal fully." She chuckled. "Ulric mentioned ya were a stubborn fecker, and he was correct."

Garth snorted in amusement and asked, "Where are they?"

"Ya asked me that in the night. They fought that twit."

Garth frowned. "Fought?"

She answered, "Aye. And they killed the twit."

The battered Sword smiled at the reference. "I must go to them."

Handrea shook her head. "Not today, lad. Ya won't get far, and I want to keep an eye on ya a little longer."

Garth tried to sit up to prove a point, and grimaced as pain shot through his ribs. He glanced at Handrea as he slowly laid back down. She was right. He would not get far.

He sighed, "Alright, I'll rest a little longer. Are they both alright, is Evie—"

She responded softly, "She's alright. She was more concerned for ya."

He smiled, a look of relief on his features as he slowly propped himself back up on his elbow. "Glad all is well."

Handrea held onto his hand and sighed, "This bond ya have with Evie is strong."

"Aye. We were lovers in another world, before this one got fecked up. Yet—" He directed his gaze upwards.

"Yet, as much as ya care for her, ya can't be that Garth." He lowered his head towards her and nodded, sorrow reflecting in his eyes. Handrea continued, "Lad, what we have here is, well, an unbalance with nature. Ya and Evie had a destiny. But even though yar connection was strong, it was always meant to be apart. Yar destiny for her love was to die protecting her. For Evie, she was never to stay here." She paused, analysing him with tenderness, "Someone manipulated yar destiny in this time. When ya killed the traveller, nature became unbalanced, yar destiny unfulfilled. Slan righted it slightly by bringing Evie here. Ya then sensed the connection. Her presence helped get ya back on the right path. But destiny still stood. And as much as it pains me to say it, ya will never be together."

Garth sighed, glancing away from the witches' eyes, "Aye, I feel it. Evie seemed to hope I would be the Garth she once knew. Those memories she showed me; that Garth was like a stranger to me. But—," he sighed deeply, "I can't stop caring for her. Not like a lover—"

"I understand, lad. And she will always care for ya. But here in this land her heart is now with Ulric's. That's her destined path in *this* Moonstar."

Garth nodded, looking at the old woman. "I saw their love, and I felt it. And . . . I'm happy for them."

Handrea smiled. "Yar're going to have to make a tough choice, but ya know ya have to walk away."

"I do. And I will."

Handrea stroked his cheek. "Ya may have strayed from yar path Garth, but ya're back on it now." She looked at his features. "Get some rest. If I bandage ya tightly in the morn, you should be fine to join them."

He signalled his approval, taking her hand. "Thank you Handrea. Thank you for explaining it to me. To know what our destiny will be now."

"Ya already knew, lad. Ya could see it, and so could Evie. I was just confirming it for ya."

Garth slowly nodded; sorrow evident in his eyes.

Handrea gently touched his cheek. "But I see love in yar future. Ya will be with someone, and yar offspring will do great things." He arched an eyebrow. The witch added, "But ya have a multitude of responsibilities to fulfil before then. Keep yar promise to Evie."

"To make amends?"

"Aye. There are many out there that will feel yar blade and then Moonstar will be free, and ya will gain the forgiveness of the land."

Garth smiled softly, sensing exhaustion slowly overpowering him. He leant back, closing his eyes. He just needed to rest a little longer.

FIFTY ONE

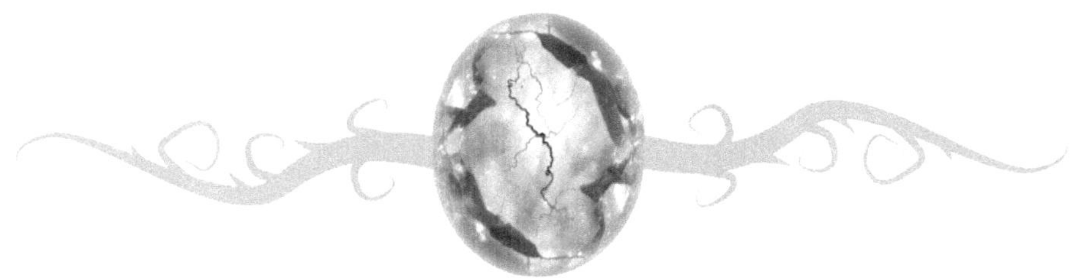

In the aftermath of Bazertari's demise, Evie and Ulric were in complete agreement that notifying the King was imperative. That morning, Evie teleported back to the palace, leaving Ulric to assume command of the city. He planned to track down all of the mercenaries that had gone on the run with the help of the fighters from the day before, as well as finding anyone who was left of the city guard that had not already come forward to help.

As Evie finished sharing her story of how she and Ulric had defeated Bazertari with the help of the folks in the city, King Tarian observed her with interest.

"So the warlock is dead?"

She responded from where she stood before his thick oak desk, "Yes."

His Majesty looked down at his paperwork. "Good." He threw a glance in her direction. "You mentioned nay more of that traitor. Did you encounter him again?"

Evie bit down on her lower lip. Upon mentioning Garth's presence at the tower, the King's response gave her the impression that revealing every detail would have been unwise. She had left out all that she could, but it seemed she would have to tell him more.

"Your Highness, I believe Garth is no longer the enemy. He could, in fact, be an ally. I know he has already tracked down and killed many of Bazertari's followers."

King Tarian's eyes narrowed, "Him? An *ally?* Nay. We will try him for treason. Garth Ashforge is an enemy to the land, and he will be punished accordingly."

Evie glanced away from his cold eyes. "Of course."

She lifted her eyes back to the King, wondering if she could argue Garth's case more, but could see by the King's stern features it would all fall on deaf ears.

The King paused, taking a long breath, and regarded Evie. He turned his gaze towards his paperwork, deep in thought for a moment, and then said, "Before you return to the city. I have some, I hope, good news."

She stared at him. "And that is?"

"With yours and Ulric's efforts in freeing this land, you for the second time, I wish to propose something for you both." He paused and rose to his feet. He walked around his desk to position himself in front of her and held her hand. "We can never repay your deeds for Moonstar and for my family. I hope you will consider the role of royal advisor, and I am hoping you will convince Ulric to take the position of general in the royal guard."

Evie fixed her eyes on the King. Almost lost for words, "I—I don't—"

He patted her hand. "Think about it. Nothing will be official until I am crowned. But I hold in high regard both your council, and believe this kingdom requires trustworthy souls."

She responded, "Thank you. We will consider it carefully."

He smiled and stated, "I will let you return to the City of Light. Inform Ulric that I will send some of the palace guard to help him reestablish authority in the city, and regain some normality. Also, I request that both of you attend my coronation. Of course after this we will also remember Slan."

She nodded. "Yes, of course." Evie paused adding, "He will be missed."

The King stated, "Aye, he will. And again, thank you for saving this land."

Evie acknowledged with a nod as a portal materialised behind her, and she walked through it.

Evie stepped out of the portal in the bedroom that Ulric and she were sharing at the inn in the City of Light. She was going to have to explain to Garth that he would need to stay hidden until she could clear his name. She half wished that she had lied and said Garth had died at the tower.

Evie knew she could not put it off forever, so she breathed deeply and left the room. As she descended into the main part of the inn, she wondered how Ulric was doing in finding the remnants of the city guard.

When Bazertari had taken the city by force, he had killed most of the guards and some innocent bystanders. The guards who were not on duty had gone into hiding. Luckily, the warlock did not have the city under siege for long. Which had been an advantage when they came to her and Ulric's aid in the square. Ulric informed the returning guards he was actively working towards reestablishing authority to restore some normality in the city, and to locate any fugitive individuals that they had not already killed or arrested. He knew that most of Bazertari's men would have abandoned the city that night. But he was also certain some would have stayed behind, and wanted to ensure the guard had enough resources.

Evie surveyed the inn, finding Garth sitting in the corner, his face still covered in bruises. She smiled as she sat opposite him.

He glanced up from the food he was eating. "How did it go?"

Evie regarded him. "Not too bad. Except . . ."

He looked at her intently. "What?"

She leant forward, taking his hand in his. "I'm sorry. I tried to convince him, but he was adamant."

Garth glanced down, swallowing. "Oh." He turned his gaze upwards again. "So, will you take me in?"

Evie disagreed by shaking her head. "I cannot stop the bounty, well, not for a while. But I will not hand you over and

Ulric won't either. I'm sorry Garth, I had hoped you wouldn't have to be a fugitive."

He smirked. "Don't be sorry. I deserve it."

She regarded the younger man's sad features. "I think when the King sees your actions, he will understand."

"That may take a while." He sighed, "Then again, I cannot rest till I know they are all dead."

Evie gazed at him, nodding. "But first you need to rest. I got you a room here. Rest and heal. Handrea said you are still not well enough to travel. I can place a protection spell over you, so you could hide here for a while."

He smiled softly, studying her, his hand taking hers. "Thank you."

"I will never stop caring for you."

Garth nodded, glancing down, then turned his gaze up towards her. "Handrea explained a lot to me while I was recovering. What we have, it's—"

Evie cut him off. "It's destined to be apart, I know. I may love Ulric now, but you will always have a place in my heart. You aren't my Garth but I—"

"I know." He peered at her affectionately, his eyes full of sadness and love. He inhaled and glanced past her, pulling his hand away. Evie turned to see Ulric.

Evie stood and kissed the older Sword. He seemed exhausted and came over to sit with both of them.

He informed them, "I think this city will be back on its feet within a day or two." Ulric gazed at Evie. "How did it go?"

She glanced over at Garth. "Good and bad. The King is sending some of his palace guard to help. Also, we are being honoured for saving the land, but . . ."

Ulric cast a brief glance at both of them, observing the sadness in Garth's features. "But?"

Garth glanced up. "I have a bounty on my head."

Ulric sighed, "Sorry lad. I thought he would have felt different."

"So did I," responded Garth.

Evie sighed, leaning against Ulric when he embraced her. "I spoke with him at length, but His Highness wouldn't waver."

Garth smirked. "It's what I deserve."

Ulric disagreed, "Nay lad, you don't. Not after the deeds you have done in penance."

Garth responded, "Maybe I need to do more, and I will not rest until I have. This land is how it is because of me, so it should be me who finds all of them and kills them. Till then, I will never rest."

Evie eyed him, stifling a yawn. It had been a long day. "But rest is needed for now."

Garth's gaze shifted to Ulric for a moment.

The older Sword kissed Evie on the lips and said, "It's been a tiring day. Go up and get some rest. I'll follow you shortly. I would like to have a chat with Garth for a while."

She fixed her eyes on him, briefly looking at Garth. She whispered in his ear, "Don't be too hard on him."

Ulric gazed at her and smiled. "I won't."

Evie looked across at Garth. "Promise me you will get some sleep." The young Sword indicated agreement. Evie smiled and said as she stood, "Good night."

Evie left, returning to the room. She perched herself on the bed and sighed. In her gut, she had a strong belief that that would be her last encounter with Garth for a while. He did not say it, but she noticed the expression in his eyes. He would not stay. She just hoped he took care of himself. He was badly beaten and needed to heal. Evie hoped Ulric got him to see some sense, but knew the outcome would still be the same and he would be gone by the morning. Evie cursed, having hoped the King would have been more lenient. Then again, maybe she could persuade him to change his mind. It was worth a try.

Ulric took a big gulp of the ale he had just ordered. Despite weeks without any, one would not harm him after their ordeal. He directed his attention to Garth, who sat opposite him. The young man's features were still bruised, but the swelling had gone down and he was back on his feet. The young lad fiddled with the handle of his tankard, the ale untouched.

Ulric asked, already knowing the answer from the expression on his face when he was talking with Evie. "What's wrong lad?"

The younger Sword inhaled deeply as he directed his eyes towards him. "I need to go. Leave the city."

Ulric regarded him. "Look, I can talk to his Royal Highness. Get him to see. If I can forgive you, then a King can."

Garth's lips turned up slightly. "To be honest, it was only your forgiveness I wanted." He eyed Ulric. "I would never have thought we could have done this after everything."

"Look lad, I still feel bitter." Ulric sighed, "But you have shown me how you want to redeem yourself and, well, Evie won't forgive me if I don't forgive you."

"You really love her, don't you?"

Ulric replied, glancing up to where Evie had gone to bed, "Aye I do. Never thought I'd ever love anyone again. But—"

Garth finished for him, "But she's an amazing person."

Ulric nodded, focusing on Garth's hand as he fiddled with the tankard handle. "Look lad, I'm fully aware that you and her have this destiny and all."

"But she chose you, Ulric, and I am delighted for you both. Even though she shared her memories, I will never be *that* Garth. I have done too much, changed too much, to be the person she wants me to be." He made eye contact with Ulric. "I care for her, and always will. But like a sister, or a close friend. It can be nothing more."

Ulric replied, "Evie has informed me of the same."

Garth sampled his ale. As he put the tankard back down, he said, "Listen. Those men that were under my command are still out there, along with any remaining followers. It's my duty to find every single one."

Ulric regarded him. "I could help."

"Nay, you need to be with Evie. Also, I believe His Majesty may offer you a post at the palace. Think he needs a decent general at his side and you would be perfect."

Ulric responded, "Well, it remains to be seen if he offers it. It would seem strange remaining in one place, but I believe I'm getting too old to travel as a Sword."

Garth snorted with amusement. "Well, true. You are old."

Ulric laughed, then became sombre. "So, when will you leave?"

Garth let out a vast sigh, "Tonight."

Ulric frowned. "But Evie?"

Garth's hazel eyes were full of sadness. "I can't say goodbye to her. Can you tell her I'm sorry?"

"Sorry for what?"

"Everything."

Ulric placed a hand over the young man's. "It's the past. We all make mistakes."

"True, but I fecked up so many lives." Garth glanced down and sighed, taking a large gulp of his ale. He glanced in Ulric's direction. "Goodbye, old man. Maybe I will see you around in a few years."

Ulric went to protest, but Garth pulled up his hood, and walked out of the inn, still favouring a slight limp from his injuries. The old Sword let out a weary breath, gazing at where Garth had slipped out into the night. He wondered whether he would ever see him again. He hoped, despite the fact that he had once wished him dead, that he would. The past few days he had seen the Garth he remembered; a young boy with big dreams, taking on a responsibility that was not his destiny. He exhaled slowly, drained his ale, and made his way to his and Evie's room.

Evie exhaled heavily when Ulric broke the news that Garth had left, even though part of her was not surprised. She laid her head against Ulric's bare chest and asked, "Do you think we will cross paths with him?"

He shrugged as his fingers traced gentle circles on her bare shoulder. "In my opinion, I believe we will. He has a heavy weight on those young shoulders, and until he feels he's redeemed himself; he will never rest."

She briefly glanced in his direction. "What about the bounty on his head?"

"I don't know. The King doesn't understand like we do. But in time, I feel he will get pardoned, maybe even avoid time in the dungeon."

Evie replied, "I know there'll be a day when he'll walk as a free man."

Evie perched herself on her elbows, regarding him with affection. Once Ulric had entered the room, she had shared with him the news of King's offer and Ulric, after only a moment of thought, agreed to the appointment. He mentioned that Garth had thought they would offer him such a position.

Ulric gave her a gentle peck on the forehead. "So, as the advisor to the King, you think you will convince him to change his mind."

She pursed her lips, eying him. "I have my ways."

Ulric chuckled and kissed her passionately. "Well, those ways won't work on me."

She gasped and playfully hit him. She raised an eyebrow. "I beg to differ."

Evie sat up and straddled him, her groin against his. She moved her hips, making his body betray him.

Ulric closed his eyes and grunted. "You wicked woman."

Evie laughed, and the two made love all night.

FIFTY TWO

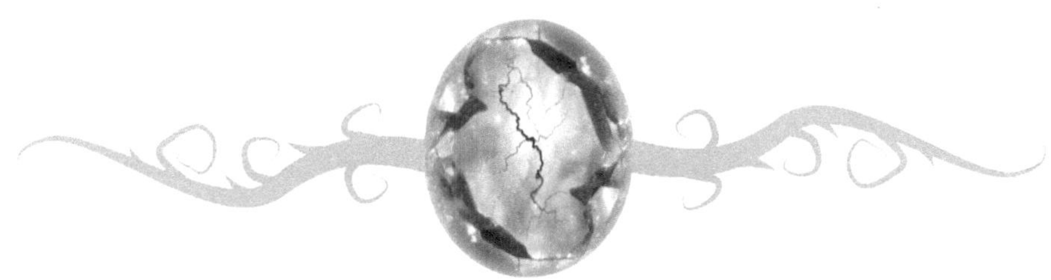

The royal chamber was filled with the murmur of noblemen, high-ranking officers, and renowned citizens from throughout the kingdom. Positioned on the dais, in the ornate silver throne, was the soon to be crowned King, wearing an elegant blue dress uniform. To his left, on similar, but slightly smaller thrones, were the soon to be Queen along with their eldest son. Both of them were also dressed in their finery.

Everyone stopped chatting when the procession entered the impressive room. The crown was at the front, resting on a red cushion, held by a young curate. The palace priest in his fine, dark blue robe, who would perform the ceremony, walked behind him. Four palace guards in shining armour trailed behind the two.

All gasped in awe as the crown passed. The jewels twinkled in the sunlight that shone down from the high windows inside the grand hall.

Evie peered at the procession as it moved towards them. She had to suppress a giggle as Ulric squirmed in his dress uniform. She whispered, "Stay still."

He took a brief look at her and murmured, "But it's too tight."

She eyed him. The King was seated on the throne to the left of them with his advisors on either side. She leant towards Ulric, her head facing the procession before them, but her eyes were on a couple of high-ranking officers looking their way with disdain.

Evie whispered from the side of her mouth, "Everyone is looking at you."

Ulric regarded the sizable crowd before them. He wished the King had not insisted they both stand next to the dais in full view.

He muttered, trying not to move his lips, "The neck's scratchy."

Evie sighed, and behind her back, her hand glowed. "Is that better?"

The material irritating his neck eased. "Aye."

He winked at her, his gaze on her corseted, deep green gown that accentuated her figure.

Evie arched her eyebrow and scolded, "Behave."

Ulric suppressed his amazement, and looked ahead once more.

The procession halted before the King. The priest stepped forward and stood on the steps of the dais.

He faced the crowd and bellowed. "We are gathered here today to crown his Royal Highness, Tarian Cloudbane, to become the new ruler of our beautiful land of Moonstar."

Everyone nodded their heads as the rotund man turned, taking hold of the crown and stepped towards the middle-aged man who was seated on the throne. The priest stood before him, holding the crown aloft.

The priest glanced at Evie and Ulric, and the other people in high-ranking positions who stood on either side of the thrones. "Please give witness."

They all turned to face the King and watched as the priest lowered the bejewelled silver crown. Once it rested on Tarian's head, the priest stepped back and bowed, far more deeper than was needed.

He said, as he stood up straight, "May the gods bless his Royal Highness, *King* Tarian."

Each person in the room echoed the same words, Ulric and Evie among them.

King Tarian regarded the crowd and stated, his voice firm and in the deliberate tone of a King, "I am honoured to be taking this crown and all the responsibilities it bestows." He glanced towards Ulric and Evie. "As my first act, I announce recognition to two brave souls who brought light back to our land. I bestow Ulric with the position of General of the Royal Guard and all the duties it will bestow."

Ulric inclined his head and stepped forward. He knelt on one knee before the thrones. The King stood, and placed a pin of a silver sword on Ulric's lapel.

As he pinned it into place, King Tarian whispered, "Don't worry, these dress uniforms aren't needed too often."

Ulric briefly glanced at him and muttered, "I will get used to it, Your Highness."

Tarian smiled. "If you discover a method to stop them from itching so much, let me know."

Ulric nodded.

The King turned his gaze towards the crowd and exclaimed, "Rise Ulric as General of the Royal Guard."

The Sword stood, and faced the applauding crowd. He then stepped back next to Evie.

He whispered, tilting head towards her, "Now it's your turn."

The King addressed the audience again. "Some will see her as a legend in our tales; but for us now, she is the savour of our land. I honour Evie with the position of Royal Advisor and Sorceress."

She stepped forward. With her gown's hem in her grasp, she kneeled before the King, imitating Ulric's motions. The King stepped forward and placed a pin on the ruffled shoulder of her dress. The pin was of a silver star.

As he attached it into position, the King whispered. "I am grateful again for you saving us."

She briefly glanced in his direction and smiled.

The King stepped back, and he stated, "Rise Evie, Royal Advisor."

She repeated Ulric's actions and turned to face the spectators, and as they clapped, she went to stand next to Ulric.

Then the King addressed the room.

Ulric's hand crept across to Evie, lacing his fingers into hers. He whispered, "I want to get that dress off the *Royal Advisor* later."

Evie flushed and glanced at him. "Shhhh."

He eyed her and grinned. "As soon as we have done our duty with this event, I will have my way with you."

Evie stared at him intently, longing to kiss him there and then. They both understood the need to lead by example.

She pressed her lip between her teeth and breathed, "Can't wait."

Once the King had finished his speech, the doors to the royal chamber opened, and all followed the King and Queen out to the grand ballroom. Inside was a band playing and servants serving drinks and food.

Ulric pulled on his uniform's collar again and Evie slapped his hand away from his neck. "Stop fiddling with it."

He glanced in her direction and cursed, "It still itches."

She giggled, taking a couple of drinks off the tray as a servant passed and gave one to Ulric. "Drink this and relax."

He took a sip and gazed at her. "You seem to relish in this."

Evie gestured to her appearance with her free hand. "A chance to wear a pretty dress, and to have the most handsome man on my arm? Of course, I am."

Ulric beamed. His eyes travelled up the rich, forest green gown she was dressed in. "Lass, it's me who is honoured. You are breathtaking."

He leaned towards her, and kissed her gently. They parted when someone cleared their throat. The two turned to see the King.

Both bowed their heads, and he smiled. "I know you both want to leave here as soon as you can, and Ulric, I don't blame you. These dress uniforms are not designed for comfort."

Ulric responded, "Aye, they are not."

The King smiled and continued, "Just a little longer. Evie, I wish one dance, and then she is all yours, Ulric."

Ulric grinned. King Tarian held out his hand to Evie, and she took it, passing her drink to Ulric, then the two walked to the dance area. The band stopped playing, waiting for the King and Evie to take their place. The Queen stood alongside her with their eldest son, then the other dignitaries fell into position. Once all was ready, the band played.

The King spoke to Evie as they danced, holding each other's hands, skipping down the floor, the others following. "So I have heard rumours of an assassin taking out many of Garth's former men and followers of the warlock."

Evie glanced at him. "Well, whoever it is seems to be helping us."

The King regarded her, then they parted for the dance move. As they came back together, he added, "Aye. I think you may know who it is."

Evie gazed at the King's features as the dance required them to sidestep along the row of dancers. "Why do you think that?"

They spun, and the King pulled her close as they dipped under the arms of their fellow dancers. "I am aware you saw Garth after Bazertari had been killed, but you decided not to inform me where he was," the King accused Evie. "I will let this one lie. But now that you are my advisor, I suggest you tread carefully." Evie locked on his eyes, but he smiled softly. The King added, "I would have made the same choice. But as monarch, I must think of the laws."

The dance ended. The King regarded her and said, "If you cross paths with the assassin, send him my thanks." He then turned, leaving Evie alone.

Evie watched the King approach his wife. It seemed his hands were tied, but there was also some hope. They would soon pardon Garth, as his actions were being noted.

A hand slid across her waist, and Ulric whispered in her ear. "Now you are entirely mine."

Evie smiled and turned to him, gazing up into his blue eyes. "For as long as you'll have me."

He embraced her, and as he caressed her cheek, he breathed, "First, I want you out of that dress."

Evie giggled and let Ulric take her hand, leading her out of the ballroom and to her new life with the man she loved, and the land that was her home.

EPILOGUE

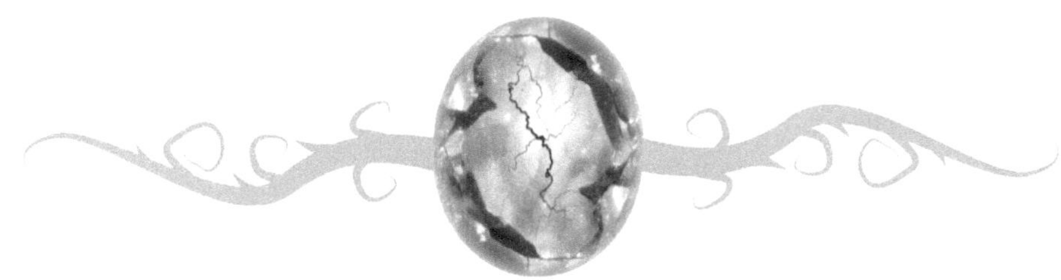

Ulric regarded the stone steps. "Are you sure it's down here?"

Both Evie and Handrea looked at him, the witch replying, "Aye, lad. I'm never wrong about tracking things like this."

He nodded his head slowly. "Alright, but it smells like a werewolf's arse down there."

Evis giggled and pulled a face. "Yes, it does, but we have to destroy it."

It had been months since they had defeated Bazertari, but they knew the creature that had produced the parasites that infected both Evie and Garth was still alive. Since she had removed the parasite from Evie, Handrea had been searching, knowing the creature had to be found. Then a few days earlier, she had teleported to the palace at Great Oak, informing Evie she had found it.

That was how they came to be back in the dungeon of Bazertari's abandoned tower. The three slowly descended into the depths. Evie created a glowing blue orb to light their way.

A tunnel was at the base of the steps and the stench grew. Ulric gagged. "On Rosh, what the feck is down here?"

Handrea gazed back at him. "A devil worm, and if I'm correct, a queen."

Evie asked, as they continued to walk, "And you have a spell to destroy it?"

The witch eyed her. "Well, not destroy."

Evie stopped mid-step. "I thought that was why we were here."

"Well," responded the witch, "to destroy it would take far more power than either of us have."

Evie looked at her. "Sooo, what are we going to do?"

"Send it back."

Ulric asked, "Back where?"

Handrea looked up at him. "To the dark realm. It does not belong here, and to regain balance, we must send it back to where it belongs."

Evie slowly nodded in agreement as she looked ahead down the dimly lit tunnel. "Okay, let's get this done."

They continued in silence. The three slowed when they saw an opening ahead. Once close enough, Evie sent a second glowing globe into the dark area and it illuminated an enormous cavern. There in the centre was a grotesque blob of a creature. The three stopped at the entrance and looked down into the area below. There were carcases of animals and humans laid all around the creature. As they watched, the creature stirred and craned its neck to face them, its small mouth dripping with saliva.

"It seems I have to thank you," stated the creature.

The three frowned and Evie questioned, "Thank us?"

It struggled to move its immense weight to turn towards them. Then its beady eyes focused on them. "You killed my tormentor."

The three looked at each other and Handrea whispered, "It's a victim too."

Evie stepped closer. Ulric tensed, drawing his blade. "Careful, Evie."

She glanced back at him and did not go any further. Then she regarded the creature. "How long have you been Bazertari's prisoner?"

It wheezed. "I have nay knowledge of time. But he tormented me and my children. His servant took them."

Evie looked back at her companions. "Servant?"

The creature chuckled and its fat body rippled as its head looked down towards the surrounding bodies. Evie made the globe grow brighter and saw the remains of a crooked man that seemed familiar, but she was not sure why.

The creature continued, "He became complacent, and he will never take my children again."

Evie glanced back at Handrea as she stated firmly, "We are here to return you to your home."

The creature turned back towards them and asked, "How?"

The witch responded, "I have a spell."

The worm stared at them, tilting its head to one side. "Then do it."

Handrea and Evie both stood before the creature, and as Handrea chanted the spell, green and blue tendrils of magic seeped from Evie and the witch. The tendrils slivered towards the creature, encasing it. Soon the entire worm glowed with a blue-green light.

The ground shook, and black tendrils seeped up from the ground, taking hold of the creature. It cried out as it was pulled downwards. The carcasses moved aside like water as the creature was enveloped by them and was pulled further down.

Evie joined Handrea in chanting the spell, the ground began shaking more as they both spoke louder, the magic flowing strong and steady from them. There was a flash, and the magic engulfed the entire cavern. Then the light faded. All that remained were the bodies, the devil worm had vanished.

Ulric looked at the space where the worm had been imprisoned. "So it's gone?"

Handrea nodded, looking drained. "Aye, it's back in the dark realm where it belongs."

Evie looked back at the Sword. "Let's get out of here and seal this place up."

Handrea agreed. "And I'm destroying that statue of the twit."

The three laughed as they made their way out of the cavern, knowing they were to live their lives in a Moonstar full of hope once more.

AJ Ashton

THE END

EVIE WILL RETURN

DO YOU WANT TO FIND OUT WHO ULRIC'S GREEN EYED SWORD WAS?

THE TARRENFALL CHRONICLES

Once guardians of the innocent, the Tarrenfall bloodline fell to ruin, leaving Lara, a forbidden hybrid of lycan and vampire, to protect her younger brother in a world that sees her as an abomination. From hunted exile to legendary Sword, Lara carves her path through betrayal, love, and survival, determined to forge a future where she and Derwyn can belong.

But destiny has other plans.

As decades pass, Lara faces contracts that threaten her soul, reunions that reopen old wounds, and enemies born from secrets buried deep in her past. From leaving her homeland behind to forging a new life in Barberium and Lost Island, she finally returns to Moonstar, where the truth of her lineage, the cost of immortality, and the fire of a love that never died await her.

Spanning generations and realms, The Tarrenfall Chronicles is a sweeping saga of sacrifice, resilience, and the unbreakable will of a hybrid Sword who refuses to be forgotten.

About the Author

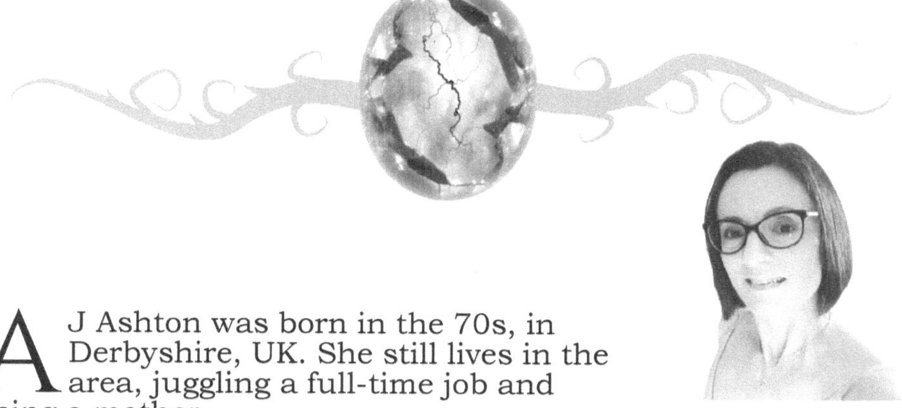

AJ Ashton was born in the 70s, in Derbyshire, UK. She still lives in the area, juggling a full-time job and being a mother.

From the age of seven, after seeing a rather famous sci-fi film, for the first time. Her creativeness to write was born. Inspired by a strong princess being rescued by a notorious smuggler. She wrote sci-fi, but her passion was soon drawn to fantasy. Where the world of Zentos was born.

Quest of the Broken Stone is her fourth novel in the Zentos series. It will give you more insight into her fantasy world, with more mystical creatures, magic, and swords. With a sprinkle of romance.

For more information about the world of Zentos, visit her website for maps and a bestiary, which will be continually updated. You can also sign up for A J Ashton's monthly newsletter.

www.ajashton.com